"I can't wri[...]
as I sh[...]
for [...]
there would be little else
in this account but Charlotte."

In the early summer of 1792, young David Treloar left his native England for Paris—and landed in the middle of one of history's most intense dramas, the infamous Reign of Terror. There he fell in love with quiet, darkly beautiful Charlotte Lamotte, and together they set out to escape the growing conflagration....

FAREWELL THE TRANQUIL MIND is more than a love story. It is a thrilling panorama of the French Revolution, filled with men who made history—flamboyant Danton, cunning Marat, gentle Louis XVI, fanatical Tom Paine. It is a tale of flight, of almost unbearable suspense. It is a touching tribute to the ordinary men and women who faced the Terror with steadfast courage.

But most of all, this is the deeply moving story of David and Charlotte, who discovered amid the tumult of revolution a love that would outlast kings, governments, and armies—if fate allowed them to live.

FAREWELL THE TRANQUIL MIND
was originally published by Werner Laurie, Ltd.

Are there paperbound books you want but cannot find in your retail stores?

Farewell
The Tranquil Mind

R. F. DELDERFIELD

PUBLISHED BY POCKET BOOKS NEW YORK

FAREWELL THE TRANQUIL MIND

Werner Laurie edition published October, 1950

POCKET BOOK edition published May, 1973

This POCKET BOOK edition includes every word
contained in the original, higher-priced edition. It is printed
from brand-new plates made from completely reset, clear, easy-to-read
type. POCKET BOOK editions are published by POCKET BOOKS, a division
of Simon & Schuster, Inc., 630 Fifth Avenue, New York, N.Y. 10020.
Trademarks registered in the United States and other countries.

L

For my oldest Friend
E. V. WHITWORTH
in appreciation of his
advice and help over
a quarter-century.

R. F. D.
Exmouth, October, 1949.

O now, for ever,
Farewell the tranquil mind! farewell content,
Farewell the pluméd troop, and the big wars,
That make ambition virtue!

OTHELLO, *The Moor of Venice.*
Act III, Scene 3.

Author's Note

A brief explanatory note is necessary in this record if
only to explain an occasional modernity of phrase which
might puzzle the purist in such matters. The fact is that
only about one-third of David Treloar's story has been
reproduced in anything like his own words, and even this
proportion has been almost entirely rewritten. I took this
liberty reluctantly but editorial despotism was essential,
for even the revised version of David's original statement
was not set down by his own hand but by that of his
grandson, Abel Treloar, of Westdown and Littlecot in
East Devon.

I do not know whether Abel Treloar collaborated with
his grandfather in the revision. He might well have done
for David did not die until the late eighteen-forties. David
Treloar's original record, i.e. the one he compiled for the
authorities whilst lodged in Exeter Castle Jail awaiting
the Assizes, was seemingly not written in anything like
the style employed by the present-day novelist. David
probably learned to write some years after he learned to
read and it is doubtful whether he had ever written anything longer than a letter until he began the chronicle of
his adventures during his imprisonment. Moreover, it
should be remembered that David's reading and writing
exercises were based in the main on the Old Testament,
eighteenth-century news sheets and Tom Paine's *Rights of
Man,* and it is therefore not unreasonable to suppose that
his style was very far removed from that of a professional
diarist or journalist.

His grandson's revision, although clearly written, was
less than half the length of the present book and there
were several gaps in the narrative. The most serious
omissions dealt with David's actions both immediately before his flight to France in the spring of 1792 and imme-

diately after his arrest off Ushant some twenty months later. David was also reluctant to put on record more than the barest outline of the murder his wife committed in Paris shortly before their escape from the maison de santé, although he did not seem to mind describing his own cold-blooded (but to my mind necessary) crime on the road to Chartres.

To remedy these and other minor discrepancies I had to rely on my old friend Frank Treloar, who, until his death just before the outbreak of the Second World War, returned each summer to spend a holiday in Devon.

Frank was a lovable character, naively proud of his smuggling ancestors. I suspect that his reverence for the shadier members of the East Devon Treloars was considerably greater than that he entertained for the hero of his book. It was Frank, of course, who first introduced me to the Devon Treloars, the family having left East Devon and returned to Cornwall thirty years before I settled in the west. He always considered David a bit of a prig, and he told me he had often heard his Great-Uncle Abel describe David's French wife as the most grasping old matriarch this side of the Channel. Charlotte doesn't sound miserly to me, but maybe she became so in her old age, for the Treloars, like other small farmers in this area, must have had a great deal of trouble with the authorities during the Enclosure Acts period of the early nineteenth century.

I must bring this preamble to an abrupt close lest it tends to develop into a Treloar saga.

I need only add, in closing, that the bulk of this narrative is based upon hearsay: stories such as this exist in most old-established West Country families, and I have heard Devon yarn-spinners tell far more improbable stories than that of David's flight across Revolutionary France, or his clever French wife's brazen blackmail of the Naval Commissioners at Plymouth.

R.F.D.
St. Cyr,
Exmouth, 1950.

Exeter Castle.
January 3, 1794.

When I first arrived here in mid-October last year I faced a dilemma rare even to prisoners without resources, for even the poorest felon can call on an associate or two to testify in his favour. In my situation I cannot even do that, for any friend willing to come forward would probably do my case more harm than good.

My situation is a very odd one. I am charged with being a renegade French spy and an emissary of the Convention, still, it appears, happily engaged decapitating the guilty and the innocent in Paris. I have repeatedly denied the charge, of course, but I cannot call evidence to establish my innocence without admitting my true identity, and to do that would virtually convict me of even more serious charges concerning which there has been a warrant out for me these two years.

When an innocent man sheds his identity for the purpose of avoiding trouble he often forgets that he may land himself in worse trouble than that he seeks to avoid, and that is what has occurred in my case. As André Briand I am a French Terrorist, a familiar of Deputy Couthon, Butcher of Lyons. As plain Davy Treloar I am a runagate smuggler who is supposed to have shot Exciseman Vetch through the belly at Westdown on a night two years ago.

I pondered a great deal on the relative advantages and disadvantages of these two identities. As the one I shall be sent to rot in the hulks as a particularly malign prisoner of war; as the other I shall probably hang or, at best, be transported for life.

The war will have to end one day. That is why I stoutly maintained my French nationality, but yesterday Jenner, the most communicative of my jailers, informed me they are trying to locate East Devon witnesses for the trial and

1

if they succeed in doing that and I am finally unmasked in the dock as David Treloar, late of Westdown, Littleham, I shan't have much time left to justify myself.

That is why I sent for the castle commander and discussed with him the advantages of a statement recording the simple truth. He expressed himself warmly in favour of such a measure, only he called it a confession. He says that I have ample time to write one, for jail fever in Dorchester has led to the cancellation of the Spring Assizes and I look like being here for another four months, but he felt he would like to discuss the matter with the deputy sheriff before making a final decision and promised to come and see me again tomorrow.

Since then I have had no other visitors but the yellow-eyed gull with the tarry patch on its underbelly. The gull often alights on the slate ledge of my window and gobbles the crusts I lay out for it, and I look forward to hearing its flutter, for I like to imagine that the patch of tar he wears was picked up on the beach at Budley Haven hardly a minute's flight from Westdown.

Because I feel certain that I shall never see that red plateau again I find some consolation in looking at something that can go there at will and swoop on the worms turned up by the plough in the fields adjoining our land. I don't suppose that our fields have been worked since the night I left them, almost two years ago. Jenner said he thought they were still under the sequestration order issued a day or two after the raid and the killing of Exciseman Vetch on the manure-heap outside the kitchen door, but the Linnet boys, who were our neighbors, have probably poached an acre or two of the Goyle Meadow, which adjoins their farm, and so saved the entire holding from slipping back to the gorse and bracken that covered it when my father first came into Devon from his native Cornwall, bringing my mother eight months gone with me.

If I stand on my stool, and level my elbows on to my slate window sill, I can hold myself in position just long enough to get a glimpse of the edge of the Aylesbeare

Common, over which the white road winds down to the coast and, ultimately, to Westdown.

Often, in my mind's eye, I can see beyond the crest and through the pine clusters to Woodbury and the blue-grey Channel beyond.

I don't have to imagine the smell of the sea, for when the wind blows from the south-west, as it does on two days out of three, it stings my nostrils as it never did when I walked the plateau as a boy, or munched my bread and beef on the cliff top during a brief respite from my single-handed labours in the fields.

I hang there, bruising my elbows for the best part of a minute, and then my biceps complain and my shoulders ache, so that I have to let go, bound off the stool to the flagged floor and I sit on my straw mattress nursing my strength for another peep.

I have been well-treated since they brought me here from Plymouth, having a large cell to myself and the friendship of most of the castle jailers. Why should they be other than friendly when they are my own countrymen, and fellow Devonians? I was always more Devon than Cornish, despite a Cornish father and a Breton mother, and I always felt at home here, far more so than any of the others. I sometimes wondered why this should be. Perhaps the relief with which my mother dragged her swollen body into the Westdown kitchen after their flight from Cornwall has some bearing on the matter.

To revert to the purpose of this story. The deputy sheriff came to see me a short while ago and urged me, in my own interests and those of the country I am supposed to have betrayed, to make a full confession before the Assize comes to Exeter again. He said such a document might enable me to dodge the gallows after all and get off with transportation, but I can't decide whether this alternative is as merciful as he promises, the only man I knew to return home from Botany Bay was old Tom Phillips, a member of the Coffyn's crew, and Tom declared that the West Country lads who were topped at Heavitree gallows after each Assize were the lucky ones. He said it was better to choke in five minutes than starve

in ten years, or to be torn to ribbons by the cat at the
marines' tripod in the clearing.

When you hear things like that it makes you wonder
why all Englishmen regard the recent happenings in
France with horror and disgust. I saw plenty of brutality
in Paris, and even more on the way through the war-rav-
aged west, but men are no more cruel and thoughtless
there than they are here or anywhere else, and I fail to
see why a public execution is more welcome to the victim
at the Heavitree gibbet than on the scaffold in Place de la
Revolution, or in the ravines of La Vendée.

Wherever one goes one encounters stupid, ignorant
brutes living side by side with warm-hearted, gentle crea-
tures like old Rouzet, whom they guillotined. Perhaps I am
prejudiced in favour of the French because I fell in love
with a French girl, but I don't think so, it is merely that
two years in France broadened a mind cramped by twen-
ty-odd years on a hundred-acre farm. These fellows here,
who speak with the same Devon burr as myself, have
never been further than Plymouth and have to accept everything told them third or fourth hand about our Revolution as factual truth, resting on the out-of-date *Times*
bulletins, or the prejudiced testimonies of emigrés. It is
true, of course, that the Revolution is now controlled by
a set of ruthless fanatics, but I keep thinking of the
prophecy of one of the Brissotin deputies I met who declared that he and his friends had been torn down while
the people lost their senses and that the Jacobins would
go to the scaffold when the people regained them.

I met some very fine men during my stay in France—
kind men like poor old Rouzet, imaginative men like
André, and men with faith that nothing could shake like
Tom Paine, now in jail like myself according to *The
Times,* and, of course, I met Charlotte, who killed a man
because he would have killed me.

Indeed it seems ironic that Charlotte and I should have
gone to such pains to get away from France in order to
exchange the lot of fugitives there for closely guarded
prisoners here. I assume that Charlotte is still a prisoner,
although she isn't in any immediate danger such I am.

I wonder constantly what can have happened to her. We've been separated the better part of three months now and I have only received that one message from her, a mere note urging me to keep hoping and to trust to her to get us out. I was glad to know that she was well, but I didn't take her message very seriously, for she can hardly speak a word of English and I cannot imagine what she could do to convince the naval authorities that I am not a clumsy spy planted upon them by Johnny Frenchman in Paris.

If this was the sum of trouble I have found myself in since the pair of us were forcibly picked up by the British frigate off Ushant it would be quite enough to justify me directing my thoughts to the next world, but there is the second charge which rests on a somewhat firmer foundation, namely that of being a Treloar, of the Westdown Treloars, and of killing Exciseman Vetch in the farmyard on the night of June 23rd, 1792.

● ● ● ● ●

Since writing the above I have had an interview with the deputy sheriff, who tells me that the Assize clerk and others seem disposed to favour the idea of a written statement and he brought the aldermen's clerk to see me. Being a lawyer he knows more about these matters than either of us.

The clerk, who seems to be more of a parson than lawyer, said that a written statement would carry no more legal weight than a verbal confession made from the dock, but if I wrote a fair hand it might find a wider audience and, in any case, it would probably relieve me of a crushing burden of guilt and thus help to prepare me for the inevitable. He had known men, he said, who walked almost gaily to the gallows cart once they had committed their crimes to paper, and he thought the same might apply in my case, providing I told nothing but the strict truth about my own infamies and those of my rascally masters in Paris, where, he was informed, people were now making maps and purses out of the flayed skins of young aristocrats, and playing ghoulish games of football with the heads of their king and his courtiers.

This said, he ordered Jenner to bring me a large table, a bundle of pens and a mountain of coarse paper, and bade me commence my statement without delay, for he much doubted whether I had sufficient time to make a full inventory of my bloody career in the mad capital over the water.

I doubt whether my confession will satisfy him when it is completed, for in all crimes recorded, save two, I shall appear a bystander, and a shocked one at that, but I will try to observe his injunction about the truth, but put down all that I remember of the circumstances that led me to deserve the rôle of the most distinguished felon in Exeter Castle.

Chapter One

CALAMITY overwhelmed my family in a single night in the early summer of 1792.

The deaths of my father, mother and three brothers, and the ruin of our farm, were due, at least indirectly, to myself, for had my parents' dispute over me been less violent I think that Saul, my father, would have taken his partner's advice and cancelled the shipment. Having regard to my father's character, however, I realize now that what happened was more or less inevitable.

For the better part of twenty years my father had enjoyed more luck than a man of his headstrong temperament deserved; perhaps the final disaster was merely a lesson in the law of compensation.

My father came to Westdown, in East Devon, in the winter of '72, after the break-up of the Trevannion gang on the Cornish coast. Although only twenty-five years of age he was known by sight and reputation to every exciseman west of Plymouth and a change of scene was imperative. He lost most of his relatives and business associates in the customs operations of that year. A few were hanged, for the Trevannions were a murderous lot, but the majority were transported and he never heard of any of them again. He and his French bride, then in her first pregnancy, crossed the Tamar with all their possessions on their backs and came over Dartmoor and down the Exe Valley looking for a small-holding. They didn't find anything to their liking until they reached Littleham, a hamlet midway between the fishing village of Exmouth and the declining wool port of Budley Haven at the mouth of the pebble-choked Otter.

Here they were offered Westdown, a derelict farm of something under a hundred acres, and my father, who must have salvaged something from the Trevannion débâcle, bought a long lease from Saxeby, Squire Duke's agent. I was born at Westdown about a month after they had settled in and started to repair the old building and clear the land which had been badly neglected, partly owing to the inroads of the Press Gang among the labouring population, but more so, because of a sequence of bad seasons and the consequent agricultural depression.

We could have been very happy at Westdown. It was a beautifully situated farm and its red soil was very good in most places. The buildings stood on the crest of a gentle slope, about half a mile from the sea and the same distance from Littleham in the valley behind. To the east our land extended as far as a deep, briar-grown stream bed (called a "goyle" in these parts) which carried all the springs and rivulets of the watershed to the sea, dropping some twenty feet over a low cliff to the beach at an outfall we called "Waterchute."

On the west our border merged with the Linnets' farm, the only one between us and Exmouth, and the soil of the slope, and the red plateau that topped it, was some of the richest hereabouts.

Between the sea and the farm were two broad meadows and an orchard and behind the two-storied cob house was a large vegetable patch and a wilderness of outbuildings stretching almost as far as the goyle.

It was a sheltered spot and something of a sun-trap, for on each side we were bounded by headlands that broke the force of the winter gales. We kept a small herd of cows, plenty of geese and poultry, a few pigs and more ponies than we needed for farming.

I came to love the place as I grew up. The old house was snug and solid and the air on the plateau sweet and invigorating whatever the season. The yield of the land under the plough was a fair one, but without my brothers' help I could never break as much as I wished and had to abandon several potentially good meadows to pasture. I did well enough, however, and had I been left alone I might have made Westdown the best holding on the estate.

I suppose my father and mother must have started

their violent quarrels about his principal occupation from the time they settled in Devon. Saul, my father, had been reared in the trade and could never regard farming as anything more than a convenient cloak for the running and distribution of contraband. My mother, the daughter of a Norman tenant farmer, was aware of this when she married him, for they had met and courted during my father's weekly cross-Channel trips when he was hardly more than a boy. Her family was closely connected with the export side of the trade and her brother was at that time dragging a shot in the Brest galleys for his share in a raid on the Cherbourg customs house.

She saw nothing wrong in smuggling and even applauded it when it was safe and profitable, but I don't think my father ever understood that she regarded contraband running as a prank or, at best, a spare-time occupation to help tide over a bad harvest. She never confused it with the real business of life, the cultivation of land and the care of beasts.

With my father it was very different. During the twenty years he was at Westdown he came by considerable profits but he never put aside more than an odd guinea or two. The greater part of his income was devoted to buying half-shares in galleys, speculating big sums on Virginian tobacco run in by the Savannah crews and, more often than not, watching his vessels rammed and sunk by patrol cutters, or his hogshead located and hauled up by the revenue officers who were always combing the shallows of the cove for our market buoys.

Saul didn't talk much and I never had an opportunity of discovering his reasons for preferring uncomfortable nights at sea, and the constantly increasing risks of his profession, to regular hours of sleep and a modest living on the farm, for he might have had that and more if he had spent the profits of an occasional enterprise on Westdown and reclaimed some of the cliff-edge land that had gone back to gorse and thistle. Perhaps the pull of his Cornish seagoing folk was as potent as that of my mother's land-hungry peasant ancestors. Their dispute continued through the whole of their married life and in some ways it helped to make my childhood and boyhood wretched.

When I was fourteen my father proposed that I should accompany him to France in order to make arrangements for a cognac run and I remember how excited I was over the prospect of the voyage. The proposal, however, was bitterly contested by my mother and in the end Saul gave in and took Noah, my brother, who, from then on, trained as my father's lieutenant and never did any more work about the farm. There were two othei boys, Ham, who trailed after Noah like a cockei spaniel, and Bat, who was only fifteen when he died. Both Ham and Bat joined father's crew when they were still children and my mother let them go without protest; she could run the farm successfully with me and our hired man and she wasn't interested in any of us as individuals, only as sources of labour at Westdown.

That was the arrangement at the time of the disaster, my father and three brothers working by night, myself and mother occupied with the farm from dawn to dark. After that first disappointment, natural enough to a boy, I didn't resent my isolation from the others but came to accept it and gradually assumed stewardship of the farm under the capable direction of my mother.

I might have continued like this all my life if Saxeby, the agent, hadn't indulged a whimsical fancy to teach me to read and write, or my father, enraged at the loss of a cargo, hadn't organized the raid on a customs house where a confiscated cargo had been stored.

As far as I know I am the only Treloar who learned to read. Saxeby was a secret Whig, and a devotee of Tom Paine, whom he had known in Norfolk as a boy. He kept his opinions to himself in East Devon for Mr. Duke, his employer, would have discharged him on the spot if he had suspected that his own agent sympathized with the current disturbances in France. Saxeby was a gentle. benevolent old man, with a huge round head and a slavish addiction to snuff. His waistcoats were always stained and his eyes were usually red-rimmed as though he had gone a week without sleep. I was the only member of our family who came into contact with him and as a boy I used to ride over to his neat, red-brick house at Tidwell Rise once a month, carrying the rent. I don't remember how our friendship began, but I know that when I was fourteen I started calling on him regularly three times a week and that during a bad winter, when my father and brothers were landbound and helped me on the farm. I had more time to myself and applied myself to his patiently given lessons.

My first exercise was a passage from the Bible, David's lament over Saul and Jonathan, commencing, "Saul and Jonathan were beautiful in their lives . . ." and ending with that chapter. I chose this passage myself, after he had read it aloud to me, because I liked the sound of the words. They gave me the same sort of sensation as the sight of the first periwinkles in the Littleham lanes, or the sound of the waves sucking at shingle down in the cove. After I'd learned to spell out that passage I became greedy for more Scripture, but Saxeby said he didn't want to make a thieving parson out of me and I had better read something that would prove of some use to a farmer, and handed me a treatise he himself had written on sheep-rearing.

I made good progress after that and had the run of his library, although he would never let me take a book away I went through Foxe's *Book of Martyrs,* Defoe's *Robinson Crusoe* and *Journal of the Plague,* part of Raleigh's *History of the World,* Shakespear's tragedies, any amount of sporting journals and ultimately, when I was nineteen, his pocket-soiled edition of Paine's *Rights of Man,* which was just published and which the Government was trying hard to suppress. I can't pretend that I enjoyed this book as much as Defoe's or even the Old Testament, but parts of it interested me, largely because Saxeby made a hero out of Paine and it made the book more real to me. Saxeby said it was the most important book ever written, more important by far than the Bible, which would keep people like me slaving for the privileged for the rest of my life because Holy Writ sustained the legend that a Creator had ordained laws of social inequalities.

I must have absorbed more of Paine than I imagined, even though nearly everything I read at that time was badly digested, because about this time Noah brought me some French papers that had been used for packing tea, and I shall never forget the impression made on me by a copy of *Le Vieux Cordelier,* one of the hundreds of inflammatory journals published during the early days of the Revolution, when complete freedom of the Press had been established by the constitutional Government. I didn't have much trouble learning to read French as well, perhaps even better, than I read English, because mother had taught all of us to speak French fluently and, although my brothers soon forgot theirs and lapsed into the soft local dialect, I never used any other language in conversation with my mother. I read this paper right through and then told Saxeby about it; he couldn't read French and had me read it aloud to him, which I did after he had made sure that the window was closed and the curtains were drawn. When I had finished he said:

"Fox is right, it's the biggest thing that's ever happened. If I were a younger man, I'd be in the thick of it, like Tom Paine. I've heard he's been invited to Paris. Do you think you could get any more of these papers?"

I said I'd ask Noah and I did, but we only got one more, a smaller publication issued by one of the more fanatical writers called Jean Paul Marat. Marat seemed to me to be bordering on lunacy. He kept calling for more and more blood, and sackloads of heads. In the paper we read he offered to organize a nation-wide hunt for counter-revolutionaries and undertook to assassinate all of them. His estimated death-roll was something around three hundred and fifty thousand men, women and children.

Saxeby didn't like Marat or Marat's paper. He said that people like Tom Paine and Lafayette, the French nobleman who was leading the Revolution at that time, would have serious trouble with fellows like this before long and would have to close down their newspapers if they wanted to control the course of events in France. He said that the trouble with revolutions was that Marats

came to the top like scum and became so extreme that
they soon disgusted the intelligent people and undid all
the good the progressive party had achieved. Saxeby
wasn't in favour of a republic but a limited monarchy, on
the English pattern, only much more liberal in its attitude towards the dispossessed.

We talked a good deal along these lines during that
last winter and I became very interested in the old fellow's views. I think he came to regard me as a sort of
protégé because once he said: "There'll be a revolution
here before very long. I shan't be here to see it but you
will and I count on having made my contribution by
teaching you how to find out things by yourself."

I don't want to pretend that I took politics very seriously at this time. My study of them, such as it was, was
hardly more than an offshoot of my interest in books,
itself a welcome relaxation from the grinding manual labour of the farm. I understood very little of British politics, in spite of Saxeby's insistence that I should read
the Parliamentary debates from month-old copies of *The
Times* he was able to borrow from Squire Duke. Party
strife in London didn't worry us very much in Devon.
Most of the Tory landlords were benevolent autocrats
and our livelihoods, as smallholders and fishermen, depended to a far greater extent on the weather than anything decided in London.

It was soon after my twentieth birthday that an event
occurred along the coast that had a direct bearing on the
future course of my life. My father and his Budley partner, Sam Coffyn, were surprised by a cutter off Dawlish
and had to abandon their cargo and swim for it. They got
away in the darkness, but the shipment, consisting of
forty-four casks of cognac and seven chests of Indian tea,
was a serious loss, and as soon as they found out where
it had been stored, in the customs depot at Teignmouth,
they determined to emulate the Poole smugglers in similar
circumstances and attack the depot with a view to getting
it back.

My father had a good deal of influence with some of
the more enterprising characters along the coast and en-

listed their help by the promise of a percentage of profits. Mustering nearly thirty strong, they descended on the customs house two nights after the confiscation, broke open the door and made off with their own goods and several bales of contraband silk they found in the store.

Unfortunately, Dorkin, the local exciseman, had more courage than sense. He challenged them as they were crossing the sandpits opposite Dawlish and got a bullet through his neck for his pains. Nobody ever found out who fired the shot, but the murder jolted the Plymouth authorities into reprisals and for several weeks our district was teeming with preventive officers, dragoons and naval patrols. The latter coasted between Beer and Start Point every night, making the most modest run a very risky enterprise.

Throughout the spring of that year my father and brothers hung about the house quarrelling with one another. Inaction bored them and they were useless on the farm. I wasn't indoors much but I felt the tension growing and I knew that if they were prevented much longer from making a run there would be an explosion of one sort or another.

It came the night one of their French agents slipped through the blockade and crept up the goyle with a message from the Argots, my father's principal agents on the other side of the Channel. The Frenchman said that contraband was accumulating in the French depots and would have to be disposed of. The Argots intended to run in three galleys the following Monday, blockade and patrols notwithstanding. They had fast boats and reckoned to outsail any opposition if they were spotted. If my father's group wouldn't accept the cargo it would have to go into one of the Sussex ports.

Saul called a conference. Sam Coffyn and his boys, their cousins the Cheetahs, and one or two other local men assembled in our kitchen and my father outlined a plan. He proposed a decoy run into Teignmouth in their fastest boat, a yawl owned by Coffyn, aimed at drawing off the cutters and concentrating the dragoons on the far side of the estuary whilst the galleys discharged cargo

in our cove and left it in the goyle for piecemeal distribution. He had used decoys before and they usually
worked. In spite of integrity and dogged perseverance,
the average exciseman was seldom a match for the veteran smuggler on the south coast.

Coffyn gave his reluctant consent, but his boys, badly
scared over the Dawlish murder, raised objections. They
were supported by the Cheetahs, who declared that the
tide would not give them sufficient time to ferry the
amount of stuff three galleys would bring in. They were
ready to take a chance on one cargo but not three.

My father raged and swore at them but made little
headway. For all his success he had never been popular
with the Devonians, who liked his profits but were chary
of sharing his risks. Before Saul's arrival at Littleham,
local smuggling had been a spasmodic, easy-going practice, averaging less than a cargo a month. It was father
who turned it into a highly paid and skilful operation,
with a line of batsmen to fend off dragoons and sometimes as many as a hundred carriers to haul the stuff inland to distributing points.

I wasn't surprised at the Coffyns' and Cheetahs' aversion to this latest enterprise. They recognized in it an
element of risk foreign even to Saul. Always more bold
and enterprising than most local men, he had never been
foolhardy in his operations but made a practice of cal-
culating risks against profits and arriving at a delicately
balanced decision. He was less of an adventurer than a
practised gambler, willing to take chances as long as there
were circumstances slightly in favour of the man with
the initiative. That was why he always found men willing to work for him. But on this occasion circumstances
were not in his favour. Somewhere between Beer and
Torbay were five naval cutters and six troops of dragoons, in addition to a full establishment of excisemen.
To run a cargo in the face of this opposition was, notwithstanding the decoy, an extremely hazardous operation, and Ben Cheetah, a truculent fellow, said bluntly
that it was sticking one's neck in a noose and he would
have none of it. He emphasized his decision by getting

up and stumping out, followed by his brother and the two Coffyn boys.

Old Sam stuck by my father and so did Noah and the other two boys. The Frenchman, who had hardly understood a word of the discussion, asked for instructions, and my father told him to run the entire cargo in on the full tide and mount swivel guns on each of the galleys.

I saw my mother look up when he said this, but she made no protest until Coffyn and the others had gone and the decoy plan had been worked out in detail.

Noah said: "We'll need every man we can get to unload those galleys before the tide turn. Who's going with Sam in the decoy? He can't manage the *Swallowhawk* by himself."

"Young Bat can go," said my father. "He's as handy with a tiller as any o' they rabbits."

Bat's eyes sparkled. He was just fifteen and adored my father Saul was never lavish with his praise and I could see that the lad was immensely flattered.

My mother had something to say, however. She got up and looked Saul straight in the face.

"You'll not have Bat on a run like that, Saul. He can wait until he's grown as big and as foolish as you!"

"He won't come to no harm, not with Sam," said Noah. who invariably sided with his father.

"He's big enough to make a hole in any Georgie between Solent and Start Point," growled my father, and getting up, went over to the Dutch dresser, pulled open a drawer and took out a long boarding pistol which he tossed over to Bat, saying: "Let's see you shoot the candle out Bat."

The boy grinned and reached for a powder horn from the shelf just above his head, but my mother got it first, flicked open the catch and poured the contents into a can of beer that stood on the table.

It might have been the contempt expressed in the action that infuriated my father, or more probably the strain and worry of all those weeks of inaction since the Dawlish affair, or perhaps he was still inwardly raging at the mutiny of the Coffyns and Cheetahs and only needed this final piece of defiance to kindle his rage. Whatever it was, it made him act as I had never seen him act in the past. He grabbed a heavy sea boot from beside his chair and flung it with all his strength at my mother's head. It struck her on the jawline, just before the left ear, and she reeled against the edge of the table, grabbing at Bat's head to avoid falling into the fire.

I know Saul regretted his action the moment the boot had left his hand. He and Annette had been leading a cat-and-dog life ever since they came to Westdown, but Saul respected her and I don't believe he had ever struck her before. I was on the far side of the kitchen when it happened and the moment I had recovered from my surprise I moved to get between them and, if necessary, pitch my father into the yard. He was a powerful man and an expert wrestler in the Cornish style, but I was six foot two and broader than him about the shoulders, so I had no doubt about mastering him, and Noah, too, if he had tried to intervene.

My mother was before me, however, and grabbed a broad-bladed potato knife from the table, throwing herself at Saul, who was still sitting, and aiming a vicious blow at his face. Noah flung himself in front of father and Ham grabbed at mother's other arm, but the blow descended and the blade missed my father's cheek by less than an inch, ripping through the lobe of his ear and grating against the heavy metal earring he always wore. His blood spurted all over Noah's breeches.

After that I can't remember what happened beyond a general scrimmage, but I know it took three of us to disarm my mother and lock her up in the buttery, where she continued to scream threats at father and the rest of us in French.

The shock of the incident sobered my father. After we'd patched up his ear and tidied up a little, he called Bat over and took his pistol away, tossing it back into the drawer.

"Go over to Knowle and ask Mark Toller's boy if he'll sail as Sam's tillerman," he told Noah. "Bat won't be going on Monday."

I saw Bat's face fall but he had enough sense not to argue. We'd had enough trouble for one evening.

After that we sat about a bit without saying much until my mother quietened down and stopped kicking the buttery door. Finally, my father got to his feet and jerked his head at the boys.

"We'll go on up," he ordered. "You stay down here an' let her out when she's quietened, Dave."

As soon as they were safely upstairs I went and unlocked the door and let mother into the kitchen. She was very pale and her black hair had broken loose from its clasp and hung down each side of her face, but she was quiet enough and went over to the inglenook to sit down. I fetched two mugs from the pantry and poured out two shots of cognac from a bottle of the best father always kept back for himself. She sipped the brandy for a moment. Then she said:

"I'll tell you where the money is, Dave."

"What money?" I asked.

"The money I've put by. You'll soon be alone here the way they're acting. I always knew it would happen, but he had so much luck over the years that I stopped thinking about it. It's too late to save Bat now."

I said: "Bat isn't going. Father thought better of it, he was just piqued over the Coffyns and the Cheetahs defying him. He'll get back all right."

"I hope they do get him," said my mother, and meant it. "They'll all be topped or transported by next year. You're the only one that matters now. You'll have the farm, your own farm. There won't be any need to go dodging about out there in the dark."

She got up and stood on tiptoe in front of the fireplace. There was a large roasting hook slightly to one side and she pulled at it. A brick came out with the hook and inside the cavity was a fat moleskin bag that jingled when she swung it on to the table. I watched her uncord it, tip it up and pour a stream of guineas on to the table. I'd never seen so much money together before. There must have been all of four hundred there. I was too astonished to do anything but gape.

"It's taken me the better part of twenty years," she said, after locking the staircase door and shooting the greased bolt. All our doors had heavy locks and bolts and part of Bat's duty was to keep them well oiled. "I always sold cattle for a little more than I gave him and sometimes I got better prices in Exeter for the barley. I sold some of the timber on Beacon Hill without him knowing and sometimes, when he'd had a good run, he'd throw me a guinea or two, and that went in. He doesn't know about any of it. Squire Duke's boys are gambling in London and he'll sell this place for less than its worth. Don't pay him a penny more than three hundred and use the rest for stock. There's always more money in stock, especially over here, where you get full grazing rights."

"If anything ever happened to the others," I told her, I'd stay on here with you. I don't want the money now, I wouldn't know where to put it. You keep it."

She tied the mouth of the bag again and I noticed how nimble her fingers were and how lovingly she stroked the bulging sides of the little sack, as though it were a kitten.

"I'll put it back," she said. "I only wanted you to know where it was. It's just as well you should, your father and I might have killed one another tonight."

"What made you do it?" I asked her. "You've had disagreements before without using a knife."

She replaced the brick and finished off her brandy. I noticed that her jaw was lopsided where the swelling centered round a violet bruise.

"I've never been able to make him see what was important and what was not. Money isn't worth a bushel of straw, not when you use it the way he does. Where's his profit over the years? At the bottom of the sea mostly, or rotting in excise cellars up and down the coast. I was never against his way of making a living if he'd been able to put his profits to better use, but you can't run contraband without other people climbing on your back and most of those people don't take your risks. It's different with land. All you put into it you get back, either in your belly or your strong box. Think of that four hundred! I got that out of scrapings. What might we have had here with five men in the family!"

I understood her then for the first time. She had no moral scruples about my father's way of life, not even when it amounted to murder. What disgusted her with the trade was its lack of real profits, all the bribes and pensions and bonuses that drained away capital accrued, the inevitable element of gambling entailed in buying a cargo and finding customers on this side, the long chain of risks between acquisition and disposition. With a farm there were comparable hazards, bad harvests, storm and flood, cattle disease, but these were natural risks, uninvited, unpredictable and out of human control, not courted as Saul courted the bullets of dragoons or, worse still, the jettisoning of goods that cost him English guineas.

I put some arnica on her jaw and went up to bed. I lay awake for some time listening to the creaks and scuffles of the old house and to Ham's whining snore, but she didn't come up and go into father's room. He wasn't snoring and I guessed that he was lying awake, too.

Chapter Two

ON the day the shipment was due, I was out stake-cutting and manure-carting long before any of the others were astir. When I came in for my midday meal only my mother was there, Saul and the boys having gone down to the cove to make preparations for the night's work. I asked my mother about Bat and she said he was sulking, Mark Toller's seventeen-year-old son having been given the job of assisting Sam Coffyn in the decoy. When I pressed her to tell me whether Bat was taking any sort of hand in the run she muttered something about his being given charge of the ponies, but she obviously didn't want to discuss the thing further and seemed unusually morose. Later I talked to one of my father's regular carriers and gathered from him that the party was short of labour. Whilst I was still eating, a boy came up from the village with a message from the Puddicombes, declining my father's request for a loan of their ploughing horses at the outrageously high figure of half a guinea for the night's work. Saul must have been near desperate to put such a price on a couple of draught horses.

Soon after noon my mother went off marketing to Exmouth, taking the trap. I returned to the fields and didn't see anyone until supper time. Just before sunset, as I crossed the plateau overlooking the bay, I saw Sam Coffyn's yawl *Swallowhawk* tacking away to the south-west, heading for Dawlish, and guessed it already had a couple of spyglasses trained on it from the balcony of the customs house at Exmouth.

I got back to the farm and found Noah and Ham in the kitchen cleaning and loading pistols. Just after I finished supper young Bat came in with my father, carrying fishing tackle they had cleared from the boat. They dumped the tackle in a corner and ate their supper without saying a word. I thought my father looked unusually agitated. The muscles of his jaw kept twitching and twice when he tried to light his pipe the spills went out.

Soon it began to get dark and Noah, who had put away his pistols, crossed over to light the oil lamp. My father suddenly growled out:

"Leave it alone and sit in the dark!"

The silence in the room was oppressive and presently my mother, who seemed more on edge than father, got up and went into the buttery where I heard her busying herself with some task. I said, for something to say:

"What time is high tide?"

"Shade after midnight," said my father. They were the last words I ever heard him speak.

We watched the clock round for nearly an hour and then Bat got up and went out to the stables. The three ponies were there, already saddled. Ham took a cutlass from a rack near the dresser and buckled it on, winking at me as he jerked the belt tight. Ham was my favourite. I never saw him out of humour; he was always more of a boy than young Bat and never had a thought in his head beyond cider and women. He was much more easy-going than the others and would have made a good farm-hand if they'd left him to me.

Bat called from the yard. "I've got 'em, Dad, bring the shiner!"

My father unhooked the horn lantern, shuttered it and went out, Noah and Ham following. I heard them clump across the flags in their heavy boots but the led ponies didn't make a sound. Bat must have muffled their hooves with sacking. My mother came out of the buttery and helped herself to a swig of brandy. I heard the neck of the bottle rattle against the rim of the mug and the sound told me she was trembling. Outside it was dark now so I closed the door, which Ham had left open, and settled myself in my father's chair. It wasn't long before I felt drowsy, for I was tired with forking manure all day, and, although it was a sultry night, my mother had made up the fire before she went back in the buttery. In ten minutes I was sound asleep.

The report of a single shot jerked me awake and I stood in the dark straining my ears. There wasn't anything very unusual about hearing a shot in the middle of the night in our district, it might have been one of the villagers rabbiting on the edge of the common, or one of Mr. Duke's keepers beating poachers out of the plantations on the other side of the valley, but I felt certain that this was a pistol shot and hadn't come from a fowling piece. I blew on a faggot and looked at the clock, which said a minute or two to half-past twelve. Presently, hearing nothing more, I relaxed and called my mother. She didn't answer and then I began to feel anxious. I shouted again, this time at the top of my voice, and, getting no reply, I ran upstairs and looked into her room. It was empty, the bed hadn't been disturbed. I knew then that she must have stolen out whilst I was asleep and gone down to the cove. I didn't even wait to arm myself but slipped on my boots and ran through the yard and across the orchard towards the path that curled over two fields down to Watershute and the beach. There was no moon and hardly a glimmer of stars, but I knew every clump of thistles and every dip in the ground, so the darkness didn't lessen my speed. In less than a minute I was through the orchard and racing across open fields.

I must have covered about half the distance to the cliff steps when a fusilade of shots rang out and I was close enough to see the ring of flashes from the beach. They seemed to come from somewhere near highwater mark and there must have been a dozen at least. I stopped then, and moved forward cautiously, not wanting to fall foul of a dragoon picquet. There was sure to be one at the head of the steps.

A minute or two after the volley somebody shouted and there was a good deal of splashing, then another spatter of musketry and finally a vivid flash and a deeper detonation from about a hundred yards offshore. I knew something more than a skirmish was going on below and that one of the swivels on the French galleys had come into action. Lying there in the gorse on the cliff edge I began to sweat with fear. I didn't see how

any of them were going to break through a beach cordon
of that size and the swivel gun meant that a cutter had
moved in to block a retreat out to sea.

I wished then that I had thought to bring a musket.
One marksman firing from the fields might have given the
excisemen and dragoons the idea that they were being
ambushed from behind and made them draw off from
the beach. Five minutes' respite would have enabled my
father and brothers to have reached the shelter of the
goyle, where nobody could have followed them, and they
could have slipped inland and made off over the Landslip towards Budley. Having no firearm I did the best
thing I could think of, crawling inland for a distance of
fifty yards or so and setting up a halloo, urging a long list
of imaginary comrades to attack the dragoons at Watershute and drive them down on the beach.

My feeble stratagem must have been partially successful,
for several men began to blunder through the undergrowth
towards me. I ran eastward, still shouting, and dived into
the goyle about three hundred yards from its outfall.

It was pitch dark down there in the tall ferns and it
took me some time to find the path. When I did I followed it along the stream bed, scratching my face unmer-
cifully on the briars and sometimes plunging shin deep
into the red mud that bordered the shallow water-course.
When I got to the outfall, where the stream dropped per-
pendicularly to the beach, I ran straight into my mother,
who was crouching in a foot of muddy water, straining
her eyes into the darkness below.

She whipped round on me, her voice hoarse with rage.

"Get back," she hissed, "get back to the farm and hide
your clothes. I don't want you taken as well. Haven't I
done enough for one night?"

I was going to ask her what had happened but at that
moment pandemonium broke out below, shots, shouts,
the vicious, metallic scream of the swivel gun and the
deeper, more businesslike roar of a six-pounder on the
cutter. For all the concern I felt for my father and brothers, fighting it out against impossible odds in the shallows, I began to wish myself well out of the business, and

it occurred to me to drag my mother back along the path and into the farm under cover of the goyle. I reckoned that I could make the journey in less than half an hour, long before excisemen called at the farm and began to search and ask questions.

This plan had only half-formed in my mind when it was checked by a sharp sound, midway between a bark and a cough, coming from the beach immediately below us. I knew instantly that it was Ham imitating a fox, which he did very realistically. I leaned over and called, as loudly as I dared: "Dave here; is that you, Ham?" I could imagine Ham grinning in the darkness. I don't know why he thought of signalling to our perch but I imagine they must have left someone on duty there who had long since scuttled away inland.

Ham said: "There's a ladder under the white rock."

I cursed myself for being such a fool as to forget Watershute ladder. There was a routine patrol point for the excisemen at the head of Watershute steps and whenever that way down to the beach was likely to be watched the smugglers always came up by the goyle, particularly when they were handling portable shipments that didn't require ponies.

I found the ladder in two seconds and tossed it down, hooking my end into a pair of iron stakes driven into the sandstone for the purpose. Ham came up very slowly and I thought he was badly wounded until his head and shoulders were silhouetted against the sky; then I saw he was carrying someone. It was young Bat, half-dead and bleeding freely from nose and mouth.

He laid the boy beside the stream and turned to say something. I think it must have been "Father and Noah are dead . . ." but he never finished the sentence because a volley, directed up at us from less than thirty yards' range, whipped through the undergrowth all round us and a confused shouting broke out immediately below. Ham's laboured ascent must have attracted the attention of the dragoons on the beach and they were now milling round the foot of the ladder.

I picked up Bat, who was unconscious, and my mother

shouted in my ear and, turning her back to the sea, plunged on ahead. The last thing I remember of that desperate ten minutes at the outfall is the rasp of Ham's hanger and, hardly a second later, a hellish uproar as he leapt down into the group of men on the beach.

My mother went ahead of me all the way up the goyle and, in spite of the darkness and obstructions, moved at a pace that I had difficulty in maintaining. Bat was a well-grown boy and weighed as much as most men. By the time I got to the gully, where the goyle climbs into the open alongside our Dutch barn, I was near the point of exhaustion.

The yard was deserted and we got into the kitchen all right. I laid Bat on the table and bolted all the doors while mother washed the blood from the boy's face and went over him for wounds. He had a pistol bullet through the fleshy part of his right arm but that was nothing compared to the crack on his head. Somebody must have got in a lucky blow with a bludgeon and we saw at a glance that there wasn't much hope for him. His skull had been fractured and his breathing could have been heard in the yard.

Mother sponged him and tried to force some brandy down his throat and all the time she was making soothing little noises as though he was a baby disturbed in his cot. She hadn't lost her head, however, for she called to me over her shoulder: "Get the money and make for the Landslip!"

It was then I realized my own position. In a matter of minutes the Georgie would be hammering at the door. Saul and Noah would have been recognized and once the battle on the beach was over our farm would be the next objective. I hadn't touched any contraband but nobody was going to believe that. I was covered with mud and my face was bleeding in half a dozen places from scratches. Even if I stripped and concealed my clothes it would prove hard to convince the dragoons I had spent the night in bed. My mother's appearance, however, was equally telltale.

"They'll take you, too," I told her. "It's seven years for succouring wounded."

She turned away from Bat and looked straight at me. Even then I thought how young and attractive she seemed for a woman who had worked all her life on a farm and borne four children before she was twenty-three. The briars had ripped her dress open at the shoulder and the skin shone through white and cool-looking against the jagged edges of homespun fustian. Her black hair glowed in the lamplight and her brown eyes met mine without a hint of flinching.

"They won't touch me," she said. "I sent them down there!"

I gaped at her, utterly unable to absorb the statement. She went on hurriedly: "There's no time to explain why— I only want you to know I didn't intend this, I thought they'd get away by sea and that once over the Channel they'd have had to stay there and leave you to your farm. I meant the patrol to fall on them before they began discharging cargo, but that fool Vetch, he never gets there in time, that's why he never catches anyone. Get the money and go over to the Landslip; I'll find a boat and send word to you in less than twenty-four hours."

I stood there staring at her. I don't think I felt any violent aversion for her, not even with young Bat dying on the table, and father and Noah washing about in the shallows down in the cove, or silly old Ham hewn to pieces at the outfall; I was just stupefied by the lengths to which her passion for the farm had driven her. I don't think that even I was important to her as a man but simply as a means of maintaining and developing the farm, of using the money she had scraped together over the last twenty years for this purpose. She was not sorry for what she had done, only sorry that her scheme had gone awry and that her family had been almost wiped out because of a chance naval cutter and tardiness on the part of the principal customs officer at Exmouth. Her idea had been to free Westdown, and incidentally myself, from the menace that had overshadowed it for twenty years.

Once Saul and the boys had gone and were prevented, by prescriptive warrant, from returning, she meant me to cut myself adrift from the trade and use her money to build Westdown into one of the most important farms in the area. I could have done that and she knew it, that's why she had shown me the money a few days before. She must have been meditating something like this for a long time and her attempt to save Bat from being involved had been the single human weakness in her inhuman plan. I was so astounded by the cold-blooded deliberation of it all that I couldn't even protest, but just stood there staring at her.

Two things happened then. Bat let out his last breath and, almost simultaneously, somebody started pounding on the yard door. There was no mistaking the significance of my brother's long-drawn gasp. My mother only glanced at him and then, before even the knocking could be repeated, crossed the room, pulled away the brick, swung out the moleskin bag and crammed it into my coat pocket.

Outside men were crowding into our yard and a voice that I thought I recognized as Mr. Vetch's called on us to open the door.

I suppose I might have stayed on and tried to proclaim my innocence if my mother hadn't made her admission to me, but now there seemed no sense in remaining, for my mother's act in informing on her husband placed me in an impossible position. If I hadn't been down to the goyle, if I really had spent the night in bed and the state of my clothes supported the claim, I daresay my mother's evidence would have been accepted by the authorities and I should have been absolved from any part in the run; but, even so, I should have gone in fear of my life once it had got about that the attack on the galleys had been the outcome of an informer. I would have been the only person to benefit from my father's death and the faintest suspicion that I had anything to do with it would have been enough to to earn me a knife in my ribs the next time I crossed the plateau on my way home for supper. I don't know whether my mother thought this far, maybe

she had a plan to divert suspicion, but as things had
fallen out I should have been lucky to have escaped the
gallows for my share in getting Bat up the goyle. There
was no one else who could have carried him from the
beach to the farm.

I knew it would be useless trying to persuade my
mother to run for it. For one thing she wouldn't be likely
to abandon the farm for which she had been capable of
sacrificing the lives of her husband and three of her sons,
for another there was no point in her fleeing from authorities with whom she had entered into alliance. I knew how
I could get out of the building without being seen and I
wasn't going to be caught and run the risk of a trial or
jail fever waiting for the Exeter Assizes if I could help
it, so I took off my boots and ran up the stairs whilst my
mother was calling out to Vetch to give a chance to un-
bolt the door.

I climbed out of attic window and on to the stone
gutter than ran under the tiles. It was still pitch dark
and the fools in the yard hadn't thought of lighting
torches so I was able to cross to the roof of the small
barn, which adjoined the north side of the farm, and
clear the thickset hedge that enclosed the vegetable patch.
It was a jump of about fifteen feet, but I landed on
turned soil and didn't hurt myself. A minute later and I
was over the sty wall and into the goyle again without so
much as advertising my flight.

I didn't go down the goyle again for fear of running
into dragoons, but cut straight across it to the Landslip, a
series of broad terraces, overgrown with gorse, sloping
down to the beach on the Budley side of the cove. I
knew a large badger's earth here where I could lie hidden
for a week if necessary and I went on down to it on my
hands and knees in case the dragoons had left a patrol
on the cliff path.

Just before I turned into the earth I looked back and
saw a dull red glow in the sky. I also fancied I heard a
single shot and then a faint burst of firing which made
me think they were still hunting fugitives from the beach.
The glow in the sky probably meant that the revenue

men were setting fire to our ricks to help them in the comb-out of the farm buildings. They weren't over-scrupulous when their blood was up.

I gathered an armful of bracken, enough for a bed and to cover me over in the unlikely event of Georgies entering the Landslip. Over towards Otter Head the dawn showed in a single silver streak, but the beach below me was still in darkness and the scene of the battle cut off by the smooth bulk of Shag Rock. I lay back in the fern and went over the day, which had begun for me so normally and ended so disastrously. I can't say I much regretted my father and Noah, but I was miserable when I thought of young Bat, whose life, it seemed to me, had more depressed by the fate of poor old Ham, who had been tossed away for less than nothing, and I was even more depressed by the fate of poor old Ham, who had died as unselfishly as he had lived. But for him, mother and I would never have got back to the farm.

Thinking it all over made me bitterly resentful of my mother's perfidy, for somehow I felt partly responsible for it. The more I pondered her action the more unclean I felt, until I had to thrust it out of my mind and force myself to think of more cheerful things, of my father coming in from a run on Christmas Eve when we were all boys and tossing us a few trinkets picked up from colleagues on the Cherbourg peninsula, of Noah and Ham asleep in the same bed with their arms thrown around one another, and of my mother, dressed in her poor best, haggling with dealers over the price of barley in Ottery market, little unimportant incidents which had seemed mere routine at the time, but now, in retrospect, were already assuming a warm glow of peace and jolly companionship. Surrendering myself to these memories, I fell asleep just as the first light of morning began to filter through the fronds of the bracken screen.

It must have been past midday when I woke up, for the overhead sun was beating directly into the hollow and I had the gnawing hunger that comes from sleeping in the open. I sat up and peered over the rim of earth, and the first thing I saw was a French galley, beached on my side of the Point. About fifty yards off, anchored in less than a fathom, was a naval cutter, with two or three tars moving leisurely about her deck. I wondered what had happened to the other galleys and whether they had managed to escape. The beached craft looked as if it had been badly knocked about. There was a gaping rent in the starboard gunwhale and another shot had splintered the little deckhouse. Higher up the beach I saw two or three dragoons, presumably the guard, cooking something on a driftwood fire, but otherwise land and seascape were empty.

I crawled out of the earth and through the tall bracken to a spur of rock where I could cover about ten yards of the cliff path. Just above the escarpment I could see a stationary smudge of smoke and guessed that our rick had not yet burned itself out. Getting hungrier and thirstier all the time, I watched the path for more than an hour, but nobody came by. I suppose no one wanted to be challenged by the patrols and questioned about the raid.

I was still debating how I could reach one of the cliff fields to appease my hunger on a turnip and perhaps get a drink and a wash in one of the streams that fed Watershute, when I saw Thirza Venn, the ten-year-old granddaughter of Jake Venn, our carter. Thirza came from a smuggling family—her father having been transported years ago—and I knew that it would be safe to reveal myself to her. She was out looking for plovers' eggs and already had a few in her apron. I whistled to her and she came over, having the good sense to move casually in my direction. When she was a few yards off I said:

"Don't come any nearer, Thirza, leave your eggs and go back and tell granpa you've seen Dave on the Landslip. Ask him to bring me some cider and bread and cheese."

She put the eggs down on a rock and went off without a word. I snaked out and grabbed them, bolting all five before making my way back to the earth and covering myself up to wait for Jake.

Thirza couldn't have wasted much time, for Jake came

clambering down the cliff side in less than an hour. He slipped into the earth and we got down out of sight. I didn't say anything until I had wolfed half the bread and cheese he brought me and had drained his leather cider jack. I never remember a meal that tasted half as good as that one.

"They'm looking for 'ee, Master David," said Jake, "but you'm safe enough yer. You'm might smart ter zit down on top of 'em like you be."

"You'd better get my mother out here tonight," I told him. "Tell her to meet me on the edge of. . . ."

I broke off, for I saw Jake starting at me with a particularly stupid expression.

"Lor. dorn 'ee knor?" he ventured.

"Know what?"

"Er's dade, Master Dave."

"Dead?"

"Her was burned up, or shot mebbe bevore the vire got a holt. 'Er got Maister Vetch tho', got un dru the belly wi' both barrels. I zeed un laid out in byre, bleeding like a pig, but it took 'un all 'is time to die; 'ee wad'n gone 'til long arder sunnup!"

Jake wasn't as bright as his granddaughter and I had to get him to tell me his story slowly. Intoxicated with the prospect of pouring out sensational news, he kept branching off into a mass of irrelevant detail. He'd heard all about the raid before dawn, but he didn't bargain for finding the farm in ruins when he tramped up from Littleham to the stable about six o'clock. By that time everything except the byre had been destroyed and Mr. Vetch was laid out on the wet straw with a three-inch hole in his stomach. He must have been one of the most surprised men in Devon when my mother let fly at him through the kitchen window, a few minutes after I had scrambled out via the roof. Her shot must have been the one I heard shortly before I reached the shelter of the Landslip. After Vetch had been accounted for a regular siege set in and she kept up such a hot fire from various parts of the house that the excisemen concluded that a party of fugitives from the beach had taken refuge there and they sent into Exmouth for reinforcements. In the meantime, however, Vetch's deputy set fire to one of the barns hoping to smoke out the opposition. The fire spread so rapidly that the attackers had great difficulty in saving the cattle, which they made every effort to do, for, under the current laws, our stock was due to be impounded for prize money. I didn't puzzle overmuch on my mother's second act of treachery. Since I had become involved her entire plan had been rendered impotent and I think the knowledge that she had been directly responsible for the disaster made her savage to be revenged on somebody. Vetch was the obvious victim, pounding away at a door he had every reason to suppose was friendly, and she must have poked the barrel of my father's fowling piece through the kitchen window and fire at him point blank. The fire burned itself out by breakfast time and they found the remains of my mother in the buttery. She was still clutching the buckled remnant of the gun and close by were two of Noah's pistols.

I suppose it was illogical on my part but I felt a good deal better about the whole business when Jake had finished his story. Somehow her single-handed defence of the farm wiped out my mother's treachery and placed her alongside Saul once more. I think even Noah would have forgiven her if he could have known that she had fought off nearly a score of Georgies for two hours, killing one and badly wounding two others. Something else occurred to me when I thought it over. I think she had intended to put up a fight the moment I was out of the house and had never had the slightest intention of opening the door to Vetch. It was her way of atoning for an impulsive piece of folly that had cost her so dear and it was as much in character as Ham's crazy act in turning back at the outfall and jumping with drawn cutlass to certain death. I was sickened by the stupidity of it all but somehow proud of the desperate courage they had all shown.

Jake told me a little more about the fight on the beach. My father and Noah had made the galley after the first sign of an attack, but they prevented the French from casting off without Ham and Bat. Both had been cut down when the cutter came in from the south-west and boarded. The other two galleys had made off without a fight One way and another excisemen's the attack had cost the Georgies dear, five fatal casualties and another three wounded, one dangerously. It was a high price to pay for one cargo and the lives of three men, a boy and a woman.

I debated with Jake the prospect of slipping along the coast to Beer or Lyme, and finding a vessel to take me overseas. He said the entire countryside was thick with Georgies and yeomanry had been called out at Exeter. I couldn't stay in the badger's earth indefinitely, but there was something to be said for Jake's view that the dragoons wouldn't look for me so close to home. I thought about it for a spell and then decided I had better trust myself to Saxeby. Theoretically he was on the side of the Georgies, but I knew he would help me if he could and do it with a clear conscience, because he would know that I had only become involved in circumstances. Jake said he would take a message to Saxeby but thought it better to arrange an assignation for the following day, as the agent had better not be seen prowling about the Landslip by night. He would try and get him out first thing in the morning.

With that Jake left me and I settled down to spend a second night in the earth. I didn't sleep as well as before because all night long the men from the cutter were patching up the galley, preparatory to towing it into Teignmouth Harbour. Their hammering and sawing kept everything on the Landslip awake and fidgety.

Saxeby was a wise old bird. About seven o'clock the next morning I caught sight of him wandering vaguely about the upper slopes of the Landslip carrying a large butterfly net and a satchel. He didn't make straight for the central ledge, where he must have known I was lying, but zig-zagged about the broken ground and finally fetched up within a few yards of the earth and sat down to mop his brow.

I stayed where I was until I saw the cutter and its prize pass behind Shag Rock; then I crawled out and whistled him. He got up, replacing his floppy hat, and ambled over to the earth.

"Well, young man," he began, when he had settled himself and lit up his pipe, "what makes you think I can get you out of this?"

I confessed that I was desperate and had only sent for him because I had no other alternative. I daresay some of the villagers might have helped me get out of the district but I knew all my friends in the locality would be watched.

"Suppose you do manage to break out," he said, "where do you think you can go?"

I said that I had been lying here thinking about America; I'd heard that the ex-colonists were giving grants of land in Georgia and Virginia and were reputed to be particularly hospitable to men on the run from their late enemy, King George.

"Aye," he agreed, "I daresay you'd do well enough if you ever got there."

"What's to stop me, once I'm on board ship?" I asked.

He grunted, the way I remember him exclaiming when I made a particularly glaring error at my spelling lessons.

"Your father would have known better than that," he said. "Every outward-bound merchant brig gets a shot across its bows somewhere between here and the Azores. There are special frigate patrols with instructions to weed every crew for naval recruits. Even the East Indiamen put into Port Royal and Jamestown with skeleton crews of greybeards and children working the yards. You'd never get anything fast enough to outsail a frigate and those bosuns don't leave a cockroach undisturbed when they've once got aboard."

I admit I had overlooked the Press Gang, which was as active at sea as on land. Conditions in the Navy were so bad that no man in his senses enlisted of his own free will. On the other hand, at any sea-coast town I was likely to reach, I should still have to run the gauntlet of the naval patrols and I said as much.

Saxeby puffed away for a minute in silence. Finally he said:

"Your father and brothers averaged two cross-Channel runs a month, didn't they? Most of the time they never so much as sighted a frigate. If you run for France you can cross in the dark. The man I'm sending you to hasn't lost a cargo for years; his name's Muttford and you'll have to look for him in Bideford."

That was the first time I had an inkling that old Saxeby was an agent for the trade. It made a number of things clear to me, the mildness of my father's attitude to my being taught to read, for instance, and the occasions when I had ridden over to Tidwell House only to find my tutor was out of the county. I opened my mouth to exclaim but the old rascal cut me off with a gesture of impatience.

"Never mind that now, Dave, you're in more trouble than I'm ever likely to be. The point is, even starting from France you'll run the same risks of being pressed if you ship west. You can't make Savannah or Boston in a night nor yet fifty nights. Every sail on the horizon might mean the next ten years on a King's ship. You'd do better to give yourself up and stand trial."

I began to see what Saxeby was hinting at. "Do you mean you advise me to settle in France?" I asked him.

He looked at me, grinning, his pale blue eyes disappearing under a shoal of wrinkles.

"And why not?" he said. "You took a deal of interest in 'The Friend of the People,' did ye not?"

He leaned back in the bracken and thrust his short legs deeper into the hollow.

"Ah, Davey boy," he said, "if I were twenty, ten years younger, what wouldn't we see over the water with old Tom Paine and a king who has to do what he's told?"

I remember thinking Saxeby's view of the Revolution was eccentric at the time, a mere whimsicality that went with his Quakerish conviction that the young should be taught to read and write, but although I now saw him as landlord's agent, smuggler, would-be republican and drawing-room revolutionary, Saxeby wasn't so odd as I had imagined. There were thousands of Saxebys in Britain after the fall of the Bastille became known, and their study of abstract literary works caused them to regard the French Revolution as the first rumble of world revolution; they saw in the overthrow of the most despotic court in Europe an earnest of the people's will to destroy caste and privilege from Lisbon to Muscovy, and do it bloodlessly, or almost so, within a single generation.

The errors of these well-intentioned men were those of every group of intellectual reformers. They had an exalted notion of human nature and they read so rapidly and so indiscriminately that they never had time to digest their information. Events were always catching up with them and leaving them a phase out of date. Not one of them, except perhaps Saxeby's hero Tom Paine, was a man of action. Faced with the clamour of a London mob they would have succumbed to the inevitable as the theorists of the Gironde went under in Paris, but they have never realized this, not even since the Terror was well established, attributing the failure of the French moderates to sheer ineptitude and not to what it really was, the futility of the attempt of a group of enthusiastic theorists to dam a torrent with words.

I knew nothing of this at the time; to me everything Saxeby said about France, or any other subject outside of farming, was as much a fact as the printed words in the books he lent me, but I used to think of him a lot later on, when I was in Paris, and wonder how he would adapt his republican theories to his warm-heartedness and naturally humane disposition. He didn't know then— and how could he?—jogging from farm to farm along quiet Devon lanes, that when a system breaks down it isn't the man with a reasonable alternative that gets first hearing but the man with the brassiest lungs. The Saxebys of this world sound convincing in organized debates but they can never talk the language of the mob, and when a government is overthrown the mob take charge until the movement loses its initial impetus. By that time the Saxebys are all dead.

Squatting there in the badger's earth he drew for me a picture of France that had its image in the heart and brain of every liberal-minded man on both sides of the Channel. It was a very pleasing picture, a picture of plenty, of government by reason, of universal justice for the humblest in the land, but it was only a dream, there weren't any man-hunts in it, not even of the guilty, much less of the innocent and confused.

I suppose my principal reason for deciding, then and there, to go to France was simply because it was the safest journey. There was a good deal of commonsense in Saxeby's warnings about the Atlantic run, and, even if I had decided to attempt it, it would have meant a much longer wait in a British port, whereas anyone with a few guineas in his pocket could make the French coast at any time he chose. Apart from this, Saxeby's talk of France stirred my imagination. I had never been outside the borders of East Devon, and Exeter was the largest city I had ever visited. I was just twenty, and as curious about the outside world as most young men and, perhaps, because of my haphazard reading, more curious than the average countrybred boy. I didn't want to settle abroad permanently and even then entertained a vague hope of returning if and when I could clear myself with the authorities. There was enough of my mother in my nature to love Westdown and its untidy acres and a man can't put more than ten years' work into a patch of land without ploughing part of himself into the soil. Pondering on this, I remembered my mother's money and showed Saxeby the bag. He didn't seem very much surprised.

"I knew she was hoarding," he told me. "She came to me more than once pleading poverty and I got Duke to remit a quarter's rent when there was any excuse for it. You'll need that money, David; it's a good thing she saved it for you."

It was then that I had a notion that I can't explain to myself, even at this distance. I couldn't determine to take that gold out of the country.

I knew that a man landing in a foreign country could make things very easy for himself with four hundred in gold under his belt. Four hundred guineas is a tidy sum of money in any part of the world, and in revolutionary France, where the currency had broken down and everyone hated accepting the Government-issued assignats, it would have kept me in comfort indefinitely, but it seemed to me that the money was only mine so long as I invested it in land and I had no intention farming on the Continent. If I had gone to Virginia it might have been different. There I could have bought myself a plantation and doubtless enough Negroes to man it, but in France I knew that I should only spend the money in driblets until it was all gone and I should have felt that I was betraying my mother every time I passed a gold piece. Only myself, and possibly Saxeby, could assess the amount of thought and effort that had gone into the accumulation of that sum and, although he told me that I was a young fool when I tried to explain my squeamishness, I think the old fellow understood and agree with me. He had the same grudging respect for Annette as my father had had and in the end he stuffed the bag into his satchel and said he'd answer for it if I ever came back to Westdown. He insisted, however, that I took twenty-five guineas and a handful of silver, out of which I would have to pay Captain Muttford five for my passage to Honfleur, at the mouth of the Seine.

He gave me directions then on how to reach Bideford and whom to contact when I got there. I don't know what means he had of communicating with a colleague more than sixty miles away, but it had all been arranged within a few hours of Jake telling him I was hiding out on the Landslip. He told me to make a wide detour round Aylesbeare Common and hug the left bank of the Exe until I was well beyond Tiverton, then strike north-west for South Molton and reach Bideford over the edge of Exmoor.

We shook hands then and he wished me luck. He was moved at our parting, but like most warm-hearted men he hated to show emotion and the effort of controlling himself made him sound gruff. I watched him toil up the escarpment and when he got to the cliff path he waved his absurd butterfly net without looking round and moved off through the gorse towards Tidwell. I never thought to see him again, and the prospect depressed me for he was the best friend I ever had.

That night I crawled eastward along the Landslip as far as the Beacon and struck inland at Ottermouth, following the river as far as Ottery St. Mary and putting more than twenty miles between me and the few square miles of the world I knew.

By the third night I had reached Bideford and established contact with Muttford, a spare, taciturn man who operated from the Scillys and North Cornish ports and dealt mostly in smuggled currency. He appeared to expect me and his eyes glowed when I paid him two of the guineas in advance, but that was the only interest he showed in me. I lay on board his vessel all day, keeping out of sight and feeling desperately hot in his cubbyhole of a cabin. An hour after sunset we ran for the Lizard and Muttford said I could show myself on deck. When I came up a young moon was rising and Hartland Point was a blurred mass to starboard. It was my last glimpse of Devon for a long time to come.

Eighteen hours later we were running up the coast of France and towards the wide mouth of the Seine. I took stock of myself. I had just over twenty guineas, the clothes I had forked manure in, with the burrs of the Landslip still sticking to the breeches, a small pocket pistol and powder horn I had purchased from one of Muttford's crew, and an intense curiosity to see the city that permitted the publication of such outspoken journals as *L'Ami du Peuple*.

Possibly the only advantage I had over my hero Crusoe, when he cast upon his island, was a sufficient knowledge of the language to enable me to pass anywhere as a Frenchman from the Norman coast.

Chapter Three

MUTTFORD ran me as far as Rouen, and entered the harbourage in broad daylight, putting me ashore with no more secrecy than if I had been a *bona fide* ambassador.

Accustomed to my father's furtive journeying, I was amazed at the apparent lack of interest among the port authorities in a vessel quite obviously engaged in the trade, but Muttford, who had a glorious contempt for the French. soon enlightened me.

"They're so damned glad to lay their dirty paws on British guineas that the *douaniers* are almost in partnership with us," he explained. "Any merchant in Lower Normandy would give a sackful of their worthless assignats for a single Jimmy-o'-goblin!" He stared, speculatively, at the balance of the fare I handed him, thrust it into his breeches pocket and frowned, drawing his thick brows together. "Got any more o' these?" he asked bluntly.

I told him I had about twenty, besides a pile of loose silver, and his manner changed towards me immediately.

"Wouldn't care to invest in cognac? I'll let you in on a third share and raise you to equals on the return trip if you can get more Jimmies!" he offered.

I told him no, I had had more than enough of the trade for the time being, and he took my refusal calmly, as though he had half-expected it. Possibly Saxeby had informed him of the circumstances under which I had left Devon. "The trade's not what it was. There's anarchy on this side and too many Georgies on the other. Wasn't always like this. Over here it used to be simple—we only had to buy the same man once. Ever since the Revolution we find new *douaniers* every trip and they all make you dip. It'll cost more than it's worth if they don't settle down soon."

We went into a little café on the quay, where several Frenchmen greeted Muttford with a cordiality he did not trouble to return. I could see that something was bothering him. Presently he looked me straight in the eyes.

"Where are you heading for, young Treloar?" he finally asked.

"Paris," I said, trying to convey the impression that I resented cross-examination.

He laughed suddenly, and pushed a glass of green liquor in my direction. It had a cloying taste but scalded the gullet after it had gone down.

"I knew your father," he admitted, "he did me a good turn off Penzance some years back. Fired on a cutter that was trying to board me. We got off all right by ramming him between us. Never had a chance to repay him. Here . . ." and he thrust two of the guineas I had paid him across the table. "Can't feed off each other," he grunted, almost shamefacedly.

I took the money and thanked him. He was a hard skipper, as tough as my father had been, but like all men of his profession he was a slave to his own code of conduct. I wondered what he would have said if he had known the truth about my mother.

"Know anyone in Paris?" he went on. And then, without waiting for an answer. "Of course you don't. You're green, aren't you? Shouldn't have thought it o' Saul Treloar's boy, but mebbe he kept you ashore. Here . . ." a slip of paper followed the guineas across the wet table, "you don't go to Paris to take the waters these days, you may need me again. Try here first and then work through this list. You'll run across me in one rathole or another. Learn that by heart and then destroy it. If you trust to luck you won't have your guineas long. Full o' thieves like every other town over here! You can trust some o' the Landjacks but they're all rogues in the towns!"

He got up abruptly and held out his hand. I had the impression that he had embarrassed himself with so much talk and so much consideration for a mere landsman.

By the time I had memorized his addresses Muttford had drained his glass and stamped out into the bright sunlight. Through the open door I saw him exchange an authoritative word with a squat, grubby little seaman on the quay and then turn and stride away over a litter of cordage and nets towards the tall warehouses that lined the waterfront.

The thickset seaman Muttford had addressed hesitated a moment and then ambled into the café and approached me.

"Paris?" he said, speaking in French. "I'll take you by barge for a silver crown. You'll find it more comfortable than coach travel without papers."

I nodded and made a move, but he stood firmly in my way extending a filthy hand. I gave him the coin and he bit it before putting it carefully away in a little chamois bag that hung round his neck on a length of fine chain.

An hour later I was squatting in the open deckhouse of his long, sleek barge, cooking his dinner and my own, goose eggs, onions and a piece of liver, washed down with sour *vin ordinaire*. His boy was at the tiller, and Friant, the skipper, having himself a cook willing to pay for his passage, sprawled on the hatchcover and seemed disposed to talk.

It was Friant, the genial bargee, who introduced to me the state of affairs in France. A man of poor appearance and unpleasant personal habits, he none the less proved astonishingly well-informed upon all matters of current interest His was a realistic view, gained from actual experience and daily contact with the stream of passengers passing up and down the Seine between Paris and Rouen. Primarily a carrier for a firm of masons, with premises near the Quai Dauphine, he earned a good deal of money on the sly, carrying passengers like myself who were without proper passports and liable to enormous inconvenience and possible arrest at the barriers if they travelled by road. The disorganized *gendarmerie,* who had wielded considerable power in the days of the old régime, were not disposed to worry overmuch about the river traffic and were even more open to bribery than in former days when papers, providing one had money, were virtually unnecessary. These were the days immediately before the formation of the Committee of Public Safety and freedom of movement was still possible for the class of traveller who was obviously not an *émigré* or a proscribed priest. Friant said that a man was safe from molestation if he had coarsened hands, for the agents of the Jacobins (who were still in a minority in the National Assembly, but had enthusiasts in every town in the provinces) always judged a man's status on the evidence of his hands. Roughened palms meant you were one of the people; a white, smooth skin laid you open to truculent interrogation, particularly since the previous April, when France had declared war on the German League which, under the Duke of Brunswick, was daily threatening to cross the Rhine and restore Louis XVI to the throne and was supported by a horde of dispossessed aristocrats who had fled the country during the storms of the last three years.

There were many Frenchmen like Friant, who applauded the accomplished fact of the Revolution, the throwing down of class barriers and the breaking of the stranglehold that aristocratic privilege and tax immunity had exercised over private enterprise, but were, none the less, troubled by the rising power of the Jacobins. Friant belonged to the prosperous working class, and aspired to becoming one of the minor bourgeoisie. For this type of man the Revolution had proved an unlooked-for opportunity towards advancement. Friant himself had been a deckhand on the Seine mixed cargo boats at the time of the fall of the Bastille. Now, thanks to the quick profits to be made out of the disturbed times, he owned his own barge and the possession of property had greatly modified his political outlook. To his mind the Revolution had gone far enough. Any further developments might be dangerous to all but the riffraff of the *faubourgs,* from which element the Jacobins drew their strength. By controlling the Paris mob they virtually controlled the Assembly and through that body the departments. The bargee was frank enough about his cooling ardour for change and the overthrow of the Church and State in its original form.

"Yesterday I had holes in my breeches," he confessed, "today I have a new pair! I should be a fool to risk them in striving for two pairs while there are still two years' wear in these."

Having thus expressed himself he grinned, picked his nose with an air of pleasant abstraction and fell to scratching himself, slowly but systematically. When he seemed more comfortable I asked him his views on royalty; was he in favour of a republic and the permanent banishment of the Bourbons?

He said he was a constitutionalist like Lafayette, who was even now in the field against the Prussians and the *émigrés* instead of strutting about haranguing a crowd of screaming fishwives, or preening himself, for all to admire on the galleries of the Paris Assembly like the semi-extreme deputies of the south, whom he referred to, collectively, as the "Brissotins" after their leader, Brissot, or "Girondins" after the department of the Gironde from which many of their more talkative members came. Whilst awaiting his turn to discharge cargo at the Paris quays Friant had taken time off to visit the National Assembly and had come away contemptuous of all he saw and heard.

"They call themselves men of the people," he grunted, "and spew out whole mouthfuls of high-sounding phrases about liberty and the will of the common man. There isn't one of them that would soil his hands with a bag of cement, or be seen in the street without a cravat. They bob up and down like the monkeys in the Havre menagerie, calling one another 'citizen' and 'brother-in-liberty'! Even the scum of the sections are better than they are, bloodthirsty devils mostly, but at least they know what they want and are prepared to risk the skin off of their hides getting it!"

He spat with an accuracy born of long practice, and polished his blade on his new breeches preparatory to sampling my grill. "I saw the Jacobin mob over at the Tuileries not long since," he went on. "They burst in the doors to try and get poor old King Capet to remove his veto. Capet's conscience troubles him, aye, and his wife does, too, I wouldn't wonder. He won't sign a decree they've scribbled for him to proscribe all priests who won't take the civil oath and another to form a camp of twenty thousand to guard Paris. Everyone thought there was going to be murder when they cornered the king and his family in the Palace, but the old fellow's got some sense left; he put on a red cap of liberty and took a swig out of a bottle they offered him. There wasn't any blood-letting for all their song and dance about it. The mob went home again then, like brats who've enjoyed a day in the country, and Capet still hasn't signed the decrees, nor will, I reckon, as long as Lafayette's in and out of Paris and holds on to the National Guard."

"What influence has Marat on affairs?" I asked him, thinking of old Saxeby and his headshakings over *L'Ami du Peuple*.

"Ah—there's a man to be reckoned with," replied Friant. "Rotting they say he is, rotting with scabs and sores picked up in the sewers when they were hunting him in the old days. They don't hunt him now. He sits like Louis-le-Grand and receives his visitors in a bathtub. It stop his itch, you see, and he does all his writings there, but he's too sick to take much part in anything else. The Jacobins leave that to Danton and young sparks like Desmoulins, who can get a mob moving across Pont Neuf in less than a minute, they tell me. That's what comes of being able to say you were first on the ramparts of the Bastille, though I saw the taking of the place and there weren't all that many in range of the cannon."

It was a very different revolution from the one I had pondered about in Devon, when Saxeby and I had sifted through the newspapers Noah had brought in for me. All my reading, such as it was, was out of date. Events had moved forward day by day, almost hour by hour, in the frenzied atmosphere of the first city in Europe to declare that men were born equal and to attempt to build a new society on the dictum. Marat, whose ravings had seemed almost comic at Westdown, was comic no longer, but a real power in the land, and, according to Friant, the moderates who framed the constitution and persuaded

Louis to accept it were everywhere in the decline, even in the provinces.

I had thought of the young republicans, the Brissotins or Girondists Friant dismissed so contemptuously, as eager young statesmen, ready to die for the constitution, but Friant warned me that the much vaunted constitution wasn't worth the blood of a scratched pimple and that most of the deputies were screaming for a republic and would get one, no doubt, before the summer was over.

"The party in favour of a limited monarchy on the English pattern is practically extinct," he told me. "Some of them have been won over by the Gironde and others have already bolted, or are serving up yonder with Lafayette. There are only two sorts of politicians left in Paris, talkers, like young Vergiaud and his set, who can't agree about anything except how clever they sound exchanging bits out of books over Minister Roland's pretty young wife, and the mob orators, like that fellow Danton, who bellows like a bull but enjoys standing up to anyone and never works but to plan. These parties are in alliance for the time being, sweeping up the pieces of the limited monarchy men and the constitutionalists like Lafayette, but as soon as they control the Assembly there'll be the devil to pay. The dreaming republicans may have the departments behind them, but what good is a ballot box when it's all that stands between your backside and the pikes of St. Antoine and St. Marceau? Men like Danton and the little ferret Robespierre will sweep the Gironde out of the way overnight when they've used them to gain control of all Paris. I wouldn't give paper money for Brissot and Vergiaud and Roland when Danton tells the alley scum to march. They'll snatch Capet and his wife, too, if I'm not mistaken. They'll be lucky to get out of this with heads on their shoulders."

All the time he talked Friant crammed food into his mouth and finished his meal by wiping the plate clean with fragments of stale bread that he crushed in his short, blunt fingers.

"That was good, sonny," he told me, when the last scrap of grease had been sponged away and he had commenced to worry his filthy beard with a minute portion of comb. "Listen here, if you haven't business in Paris why don't you stick with me? I'll pay you three francs a day and full board. It's a good life on a barge; it's got all the freedom of the sea without any of its inconveniences, eh?"

For a moment or two I was half-inclined to accept his offer. I hadn't any clear idea of what I was going to do when I got to Paris. I knew that my money would last me some time if I was careful and I was determined to wander about the city and see for myself some of the things Friant had discussed. I hadn't abandoned the idea of getting to the Virginias and farming my own land, and had a notion to travel south and look for a ship in a Mediterranean port, when I had a better chance of enlisting as a Frenchman and clearing the frigate blockade, but Friant's conversation had quickened a curiosity already whetted by Saxeby and the newspapers, and finally I decided against staying with the talkative bargee and sailing down the river again once we had discharged cargo in the metropolis.

Friant never stayed in Paris longer than he could help. He had a wife in Rouen and, being a man whose philosophy it was to sit on the fence, he preferred to watch events from a safe distance. He pressed me two or three times during the remainder of the voyage, for he seemed to like my cooking and was doubtless flattered by my interest in his flow of conversation, but when I had declined a third time he shrugged his shoulders and went about his business. I could see that he was convinced I had a secret object in visiting the capital and perhaps regretted having talked to me so freely. The time wasn't far distant when views such as his would have been enough to bring him to the scaffold.

I don't recall as much of the barge voyage as I remember of Friant's first conversation. I know that we had a stiff breeze behind us most of the way, and the current being sluggish we made good progress under the square sail. The river wound this way and that between rounded hills of even height until it emerged into a broad, flat valley, where the landscape reminded me very much of Devonshire.

Friant slept a good deal of the time and left the navigation to his one-man crew, and once or twice, when I tried to get him to talk again, he refused to be drawn beyond the utterance of non-commital monosyllables.

He brightened up when, as we drifted within sight of the city's crowded spires, I gave him a gratuitous crown piece.

"If you're looking for a lodge you can't do better than put up at the Havre de Batteliers in rue de Gascoigne, near to where we discharge," he advised. "The wine's cheap and good and the company's as honest as one can expect hereabouts."

I thanked him and promised to bear the address in mind. On that we parted and I stepped ashore on a smallish quay, just below a bridge I later came to know as the Pont Neuf. Choosing at random one of the crowded streets that ran down to the river bank, I climbed the long hill into the heart of the Cordelier district, a network of thoroughfares full of little shops and tall, dilapidated houses.

The streets were so narrow that the strong afternoon sunlight only penetrated to one side of them, the other remaining in deep shadow.

I was amazed at the vastness of the city. I had never been to London, which they tell me is much larger than Paris, but I reflected as I walked, that Exeter, up to that time my sole standard of comparison, could have been swallowed up over and over again in the section of the city that I covered that first afternoon.

I don't know why but at that moment, a few minutes after I had quitted the barge, a powerful exhilaration swept over me, making my step light and buoyant, and stirring in me a strong desire to sing. For the first time since I had been working in the fields on the afternoon before my father's final run, I was able to banish the past, ignore the future and savour only the present. I took no heed of where my steps led me but walked on, turning left or right at each crossing as inclination directed me, and I was soon lost, contentedly so, in the maze of courts, alleys, street and markets of the oldest city in Europe.

Chapter Four

I SHALL never forget those first few hours in Paris. Never before, or since, have I felt so free and elated. I was in rags, without much money, a countrybred youth in a strange, foreign city, an exile from my own land with a modest price on my head and, as far as I knew, without a relative in the world, yet I felt like a king setting out on a tour of his domains. Looking back, after nearly two years, I can still partially recapture the mood of that hour, and absorb once again the vivid sights, sounds and smells of that summer afternoon in the Paris of '92.

I knew then, instinctively and intuitively, the source of that storm of energy that had gathered itself during centuries of sloth and burst upon France just three years previously, to tumble the Bourbons from a pinnacle they had occupied since the days of Louis the Great. Notwithstanding the indeterminate stench that rose from the sultry streets, I sensed the current of vitality that eddied about those narrow streets like a south-easterly breeze soughing across the high plateau of Westdown. There was something in the step and the bearing of every individual I passed that proclaimed the Revolution. Perhaps I noticed it the more because I had lived all my life in the feudal atmosphere of a Devon village where, despite obvious points of contact that existed between squire and tenant, tenant and labourer, smallholder and shopkeeper, the stamp of patronage and condescension is discernible to the casual onlooker and this will always estrange human beings and sour their relationships. Class privilege, for so long a hundredfold more absolute than its counterpart on our side of the Channel, seemed to have been swept completely away, leaving an impression of easy fellowship that was none the less exhilarating for being clownish and faintly artificial. The man with hardly a shirt to

his back greeted the well dressed without a glimmer of
conscious inferiority and addressed him as citizen at the
top of his voice. I saw a young, neatly dressed woman,
who might have been the wife of a prosperous merchant,
step from a smart cabriolet and haggle light-heartedly
with a trio of filthy crones at vegetable stall in one of the
dozen markets I traversed. I saw an officer of the National Guard, smart and soldierly in plumed hat, tight-
waisted tunic and tricolour sash, embrace a young girl
in a gown so rent and tattered that one of her breasts
was bare, and greet her as though she was a bride from
whom he had been separated through a dozen campaigns.
I saw a battalion of volunteers march past in ragged,
cheerful formation, carrying arms that ranged from reg-
ulation musket and bayonet to homemade pike and butcher's cleaver laced to a ten-foot shutter-pole. Not a man
among them was dressed like his comrade. Some had the
clothes they had worn when they slipped out from their
employer's counters to enlist, others wore white military
gaiters and grenadiers' busbies. They had two things in
common—enormous tricolour cockades and an ebullience
that promised to carry them right up to the enemy's cannon, notwithstanding their fantastically improvised armoury.

The air was full of shouts and laughter and strident
voices raised in argument; every here and there I came
upon a blacksmith, his forge glowing and his hammer
shaping, not shoes but foot-long pikeheads, which he
flung down to be seized while still hot by lads engaged
in fitting them to staves.

The street orators Friant had told me about were
everywhere, some haranguing from first-storey windows,
others holding forth to small, animated audiences on the
footpaths, and all, without exception, doing the work of
a dozen recruiting sergeants with a passion that reminded
me of my mother extolling the importance of land.

Nor were their efforts mere exercise in rhetoric. In the
forecourt of an inn, the name of which had been osten-
tatiously altered from Louis Quinze to Le Prussien Mort,
was an improvised recruiting centre, presided over by

noncommissioned officers of the National Guard, who were enrolling recruits, some of them younger than poor Bat, at the rate of more than one a minute. All the recruit was required to do was to make his mark on an enlistment form, publicly swear an oath of fealty to the Constitution, collect his franc and his docket for arms and uniform issue, if such were available, and march off to the depot named by the sergeant in charge. There were scenes of hilarious enthusiasm round the booth, the crowd thrusting forward old men in their dotage and, in one instance, an infant in arms, whose mother had crowned it with the Phrygian cap of liberty.

My curiosity to witness these extraordinary enrolments almost brought me into collision with the crowd, for as I stood by, a number of elderly people, the majority of them women, began to propel me towards the table. When I pretended not to understand them, two of the women began to abuse me, calling me coward, counter-revolutionary and a number of other things, some of them very obscene. I was saved from being physically propelled into the volunteer force by a quick-witted bystander, whose patriotism might have been suspect, but whose intelligence was far nimbler than mine, for he strolled up to me and, under cover of the volley of abuse shouted in my direction, muttered: "Limp away, you idiot, you're a cripple!"

I turned, and did as directed, dragging my left leg and hanging my head, as though overcome by shame at being prevented by grave physical defect from marching towards the Prussians alongside my able-bodied comrades.

Far from being shamefaced at what should then have seemed an unjustifiable attack on a disabled man, the drabs who had first drawn attention to me shouted with laughter and burrowed into the crowd to look for other reluctant protagonists of liberty.

Even this incident, which ruffled me somewhat at the time, did little to spoil my mood of rich enjoyment. Toward evening, when the heat of the baking streets was tempered by a soft breeze blowing up river, I found the gardens of the Luxembourg, which were open to the pub-

lic, despite the fact that the palace itself was being used
as a prison for suspects and National Guards lounged on
the steps and terrace.

I sat down on the grass and took off my shoes. It was
much quieter here and a golden light bathed the walls of
the elegant building, making it look a little like an illus-
tration of a fairy palace I had seen in Saxeby's edition
of Bohemian fairy-tales. Here, the scent of trampled grass
and clover carried me back to the lanes and coppices of
Devon and for the first time since I had crept from the
Landslip I felt a sharp pang of home-sickness.

At twilight the scene softened. Gone were the eager recruits and the street orators, the bustle and heightened
colour of the streets and squares; instead, a couple of
lovers caressed one another in the long grass a dozen
yards away, and other couples, young and old, strolled
quietly about the paths, arms about one another's waists
or arm in arm. Old men sat reading newspapers and I
wondered if any of the sheets they scanned were Marat's
frantic appeals for heads. If so, they seemed disinclined
to obey his summons yet awhile, but presently nodded
off, to the distant music of children's laughter under the
trees higher up the slope, or the murmur of the guards
impatiently awaiting their relief on the terrace.

I was almost asleep myself when I observed a man
standing immediately before the upturned soles of my
feet, looking down at me with a slightly cynical smile. A
long grass stem protruded from his lips.

He was tall and spare, with an unusually small head
and sharp-cut, regular features. His eyes were grey and
thoughtful, his complexion pale and in vivid contrast to
his oiled, shoulder-length hair, which was blue-black, as
dark as my mother's had been. He was painstaking to a
point of foppery about his attire, a full-skirted coat, blue
with silver facings, plum-coloured breeches, fine silk
stockings ending in neat buckled shoes, and a frothy
cravat descending over his frilled cambric shirt to a low-
cut yellow satin waistcoat, decked with an intricate network of pink flowers.

His expression had in it intelligence and kindness, but

a hint of mockery lay in the firmly compressed lips, and I noticed that his hands, half-covered by lace ruffles matching his cravat, were finely shapes, with long, slender fingers and carefully tended nails. I remember thinking: If he were judged on his hands he would soon find himself among the suspect *émigrés!* We looked at one another for fully a minute. Then he said:

"Where are your crutches, Englishman?"

I recognized him then as the man in the crowd who had given me such opportune advice, but he must have changed his clothes in the interval or I should have recalled him more readily. It flashed across my mind that he was about to arrest me as a suspect alien, but any idea I might have entertained of flight was precluded by the fact that I was still in my stockinged feet. Realizing this, I decided to try bluff.

Deliberately emphasizing my mother's Norman accent, I said: "I'm from Honfleur, citizen, and I believe I owe you thanks."

His mouth twitched. It might have been a smile or a nervous habit.

"No, citizen"—there was, I recognized, a note of deliberate irony in his use of the word—"you're from England, recently, and you owe me no thanks. I had a purpose for doing what I did over yonder."

I felt convinced now that he was a Government agent and my mind was busy with excuses to explain my presence in Paris. He must have read my thoughts as clearly as if I had spoken them aloud, for he suddenly laughed, dropped his quizzical manner, and sat down beside me, taking care to arrange the folds of his coat to avoid creasing.

"You can relax, Englishman," he said lightly, "I'm not a party man. I wish to God I were, maybe then I'd get something more substantial than mild amusement from all this," and he waved his elegant hand, implying that "all this" could only refer to the Revolution.

I took confidence then, for his manner was very agreeable and he had an unusually pleasant voice. I told him I had arrived in Paris that morning and said something, though not too much, of the circumstances that had brought me there, concluding by asking him how he had so readily identified me as an Englishman, particularly before he heard me speak.

"If I had heard you speak I might have doubted my suspicions," he told me. "You are safe enough from identification so long as you wag a Norman tongue, but you must change your clothes and particularly your shoes. We can't make shoes like that in France." He glanced at his own shapely foot. "We make footwear for elegance or hard wear. We never try to merge the purposes. No court shoemaker in France could turn a shoe for the road and no local shoemaker could make anything better than a *sabot*. Why did you choose Paris?"

The manner in which the remarks were addressed were a clue of the character of the man. André Lamotte always liked to disguise his curiosity and had developed the technique of masking questions by languid small-talk. It took me some time to accustom myself to his way of talking but when I did I found it quite easy to pay no great attention to anything he said until he was nearing the end of an observation. His irony was only assumed. He was intensely interested in his neighbours and enjoyed speculating upon the most trifling details of their lives.

I said: "If I answer that will you oblige me by telling me why you helped me get away from the recruiting booth?"

"I'll tell you first, just to set your mind at rest," he said gaily, "for you still suspect me of being a police spy. Imagine! A party man in these clothes! My dear fellow, they'd cost him a thousand votes an hour!"

I had seen sufficient of Paris to know that he jested in earnest; indeed, I could not imagine how he dared to parade himself in such extravagant attire, but that again was one of Lamotte's eccentricities, a game of double bluff he played with himself and with Paris, his theory being that no man actually possessing aristocratic connections would be such a fool as to proclaim the fact by wearing silks and satins and was, therefore, much safer in fine clothes than in rags, which could never adequately conceal an air of breeding or even a preference for personal cleanliness.

"I couldn't allow you to think that I helped you out of sympathy for your plight," he continued. "My real purpose was much less praiseworthy. You see, I made a bad miscalculation in supposing that the mass emotions of the sections are at the mercy of even such a feeble fellow as myself. I've seen it work before but it didn't work this time."

I said I was unable to follow him and he laughed again. It was the most infectious laugh I have ever heard.

" 'Pon my soul, it's really extraordinarily simple, citizen. See here—the fishwives, who will not go within a hundred leagues of a cannon themselves, are the most strident in their demand for blood sacrifices. They work upon themselves, and upon each other, until the mere suggestion that a man has objections to getting himself blown to pieces appears to them arrant cowardice, unworthy of a sovereign people proclaiming the first free state in the history of the world. It is then pointed out to them that they are somewhat in error, namely that they are reviling a man not for his lack of spirit but for a physical defect, and immediately their mood swings, or should have swung, to the other extreme, to one of maudlin sympathy for a poor wretch obliged to watch others do what he himself longed to do, that is, to march about in the mud until his profitless wanderings are cut short by violent death. That, citizen, as I feel sure you are aware, is the fate of all soldiers under the rank of general! Where are you sleeping tonight?"

I told him that the only address I had was that of the lodging house maintained for Seine bargees. He made a wry face.

"My dear fellow—citizen—if you go there you will arise tomorrow as full of fleas as Paris is of orators. You had far better come home with me. Papa and the girls will coddle you, as they do every loquacious bird of passage that Marcelle's fine friends send to the house. I am always advising Papa to take down his perfumier's and wigmaker's sign, and why not, since perfumes and wigs are unfashionable, and set up as an innkeeper. There's good profit in beds now that Paris has become the shrine of the deluded."

He got to his feet and helped me to mine, carefully brushing away a few blades of grass that clung to his close-fitting breeches. Not knowing what else to do, or where else to go, I followed him and we passed through the open gates of the gardens and down the gentle hill towards the river. André talking glibly of one thing and another as he minced along as fast as his high-heeled shoes would allow.

I could hardly have found a better guide. As we threaded our way through the maze of narrow streets he pointed, left and right, to anything that he thought might interest me.

"Danton lives there. A lion of a fellow who'll go far if his larynx holds out. That's Desmoulins' house. He's honeymooning at present but his friend Danton doesn't give him one night in three with his adoring young bride, poor child. Imagine honeymooning with a man who is dragged out to sound the tocsin every few hours? He must sleep like a hog after such orgies of bell-pulling. Marat lives just around the corner, up there beyond the railings. He was in your country once and spent most of his time in the debtors' ward at Bristol, I believe, or somewhere in the west. Why didn't you keep him there and spare us his Jeremiads? We have a surfeit of them over here and could do with one less, but perhaps Burke arranged his deportation in the hope that he would encourage bloodshed and keep us occupied killing one another."

So he rambled on and I had neither time nor inclination to say a word in reply, nor did he wish me to, for he was evidently enjoying himself, and we came at last to a street of respectable looking houses called rue l'Ecole de Médecine and, having traversed this, turned into a pretty little square called Cour de Turenne, containing about a dozen shops and houses enclosing three sides of a grass-grown rectangle, with a single large elm spreading its foliage in the centre.

Several people greeted my escort as we crossed the court, but none of them looked twice at me. By the summer of 1792 the Parisian had grown accustomed to seeing strangers in his neighbourhood and in any case it was now almost dark and most of the shopkeepers in the Cour de Turenne had long since raised their shutters and retired into the rear of their premises for supper.

We passed under a painted sign illustrating a tall earthenware pitcher full of long-stemmed flowers, lupins or delphiniums they appeared in the half-light, and under the pitcher, in bold, yellow letters, was the legend: *Rouzet—Parfumeur, Perruquier.*

We went through a sort of *salon,* set with plush chairs, a row of tin bowls and lines of shelves loaded with pots and jars, into a low-roofed corridor that gave access to the stairs. From above came the sound of voices and, as we commenced to mount, someone in one of the rooms above began to scrape out a tune on a violin, and the voices, one of them a young woman's, began to sing an air that I did not recall having heard before but which gave me the strongest impression of familiarity, so strong indeed that I felt tempted to hum the refrain.

André, who was immediately in front of me, chuckled as he reached the landing, where we paused outside the door.

"That's Marcelle at it again," he remarked. "We hear the air at least a dozen times a day. She's turning our home into a barracks!"

"Is it an old tune?" I asked him, thinking I might have heard it at market-day fairs in Devon, though the words were French and unmistakably martial in sentiment.

André laughed. "No, it's very new," he said, "about a month or so old, I'd say. It's the song of the Revolution, and came to Paris from Strasbourg, though the Marseilles federals popularized it when they adopted it for their marching song." He hummed a few bars. "It has something, one can't deny that."

Standing together in the darkness we heard the song through and the burst of applause that followed it. That was my first experience of the "Marseillaise," which was to carry French battalions a long way in the next two years. Its peculiar ability to stir martial feelings in the most unresponsive heart struck me at the time and I have often reflected that I was probably among the first half-dozen Englishmen to hear it through. When the clapping had died away André opened the door and we walked into the circle of light where he was greeted by a dozen voices.

The room, which was immediately above the *salon,* was large and agreeably furnished, but it looked smaller than it was because it was so crowded.

There were large bow windows overlooking the court and the broad window seats were occupied by a group of young men, all well dressed, though none so extravagantly as André, and all vaguely resembling one another, as though they were members of a single family. These were some of Marcelle's fine friends referred to by André, and I later ascertained that most of them were Provincial Deputies of the Legislative Assembly. One of them, a handsome young fellow called Biron, was Marcelle's fiancé.

Over by the empty fireplace was the violinist, a pretty girl of about seventeen, with dark curls and features so like André's that one could readily identify them as brother and sister. She wore a simple white gown and lace fichu, with a red rose pinned to the breast and red sash about her small waist. She was flushed by the applause, her grey eyes were sparkling and her ripe mouth trembling on the edge of laughter. She looked dainty and artless standing there with her bow and violin poised and I could well understand the enthusiastic applause I had heard on the landing. This was Marcelle Lamotte, André's young sister and Papa Rouzet's niece by marriage.

Rouzet himself, a rotund and rubicund little man, sat between me and the window, beaming pontifically on the assembled company and obviously enjoying himself immensely. Bland good nature shone in his polished cheeks and everything about him gave me the impression of roundness, from his shining bald pate down to his bulging calves, which appeared to be straining at the little moth-

er-of-pearl buttons that terminated his black breeches. He
wore no coat or waistcoat and patches of perspiration
had discoloured his white shirt under the armpits, for
Papa Rouzet had so much flesh that he sweated freely
in warm weather, even when sitting still, but although of
considerable girth he was not flabby and his skin was as
clear and healthy as the girl's.

I had only time to absorb this much of Marcelle and
her uncle before André introduced me with the mock
gravity of a master of ceremonies. Immediately he mentioned the fact that I was from England the young men
on the window-seat, who had greeted me civilly but without more than a formal show of interest, crowded round
me firing questions one after another without waiting for
a single answer. What sort of progress was Fox making
in his championship of the Revolution? Was England
likely to remain neutral in the war against France? Was
there any truth in the rumour that the manufacturers in
the north were having serious trouble with their factory
workers? When was that great champion of liberty,
M'sieur Paine, coming over again to take a seat in the
French Assembly that had been won for him in Calais?
And a hundred other questions, half of which I did not
hear, much less find myself in a position to answer.

André retired from the mêlée and stood back against
the wall, smiling his crooked smile, and I guessed he was
enjoying my embarrassment, but at last his sister intervened and shooed the young politicians back to their
corner, shouting: "Give the man time to breathe free
French air before you plague him for information. Can't
you see he's a fugitive from the Oligarchy?"

Marcelle and her friends always referred to the ruling
class of Britain as "the Oligarchy" and as I never remembered having heard the word spoken before (although
I might have encountered it in Saxeby's copies of *The
Times*) I was ultimately driven to look it up in André's
English-French dictionary. At the time, however, I was
more intrigued by Marcelle's powers of observation,
which seemed to match those of her brother, and con-

cluded that she, too, had been able to make accurate deductions from the pitiful state of my clothes.

Papa Rouzet clapped his hands. "Take him to the kitchen, André, and give him something to eat," he wheezed, "Charlotte's out there, clearing the supper things. These young wolves have emptied the larder, but Charlotte will find him something, she's never at a loss. Be off with you now, the young man's famished. Gentlemen! Let the concert continue!"

I had eaten nothing since leaving Friant's barge, having been far too absorbed in my tour to give a thought to food, but now that I was reminded of it I was extremely hungry and was glad to get out of the range of all those questions and into the kitchen, a large room built on to the house as a sort of annexe, the real kitchen having been set aside as a workroom in which Rouzet and the girls mixed and prepared their perfumes.

The entire house smelled like a rose garden, for all day the coppers on the ground floor were alight and the dozens of herbs and compounds Rouzet employed in his preparations were lying around in open jars, sending out a sickly but not unpleasant odour, midway between that of crushed rose petals and resin. I got used to the smell in a day or two and soon failed to notice it at all, but during that first evening it was all-pervading and I could never smell a rose or enter a pinewood afterwards without seeing that eager circle of faces in Rouzet's upper room the night André piloted me home from the Luxembourg.

As we passed into the kitchen André said: "Charlotte's our Martha. She never has time to sit at the feet of Jesus, or even any of the Chosen, she's too occupied filling their bellies and ironing their shirts. I often wonder what would happen to us all if Charlotte should sip the cup of liberty. A frightening thought, we should degenerate into *sans-culottes* overnight, or die of the gripe caused by Marcelle's cooking." He stepped aside and revealed a young woman about two or three years older than Marcelle.

"Here's Charlotte, at the washtub, of course, but

where else should she be? Another customer, Charlotte, from England this time. Papa says feed him. I'll take the opportunity to change my clothes; one can't expect provincial deputies to appreciate the cut of a coat like this," and he went out, leaving me alone with the young woman at the tub.

Among the few personal possessions they left me when they took away my valise the day I arrived here is a framed oval miniature of Charlotte, drawn by André, probably a few months before I came to the house in Cour de Turenne. I have it by me now. It shows her as a woman with features as strongly marked as André, but without Marcelle's pink and white prettiness and none of her cousin's sparkle. Her eyes are large and soft brown, the same colour, perhaps a shade lighter, as her hair which, when I saw her that first evening, had broken loose from the broad white bandeau she wore when at work in the kitchen and had tumbled down to her shoulders. She had André's mouth, small and slightly compressed, but her nose, unlike his, was slightly *retroussé,* and at odds with her smooth, broad forehead. André has caught her expression, one of slightly frowning intensity, as though constantly occupied with solving the complicated domestic problems of a highly disorganized household. She had little colour but the fine, pleasing skin texture that characterized the family. She was not very talkative—in contrast to André, Marcelle, and even Rouzet, she seemed hardly to speak at all—but this was due rather to a sense of responsibility than to shyness. She was not a woman men would look at twice in the street, as they invariably did at Marcelle, but she had the advantage that goes with all women of reserved character, a restfulness that made her improve on acquaintance, even as Marcelle's volatile personality soon palled if one didn't happen to share her extravagant enthusiasms. I thought then as I think now, that André's initial description of Charlotte as a Martha was an apt one, she got on with the business of living whilst everyone around her was preoccupied with talk and theory. If there had been one or two women like Charlotte in the Girondist faction, and they had been persuaded to exercise as much influence over the deputies as did Manon Roland, or precocious children like Marcelle, then the party might have resisted the onslaught of the Jacobins the following summer and lived to consolidate their beloved republic, instead of being hunted down like rats and dying with more heroism than historical significance.

As it was, Charlotte was not interested in the Revolution. She had no time for theorizing on anything more grandiose than the next meal, attending to the laundry or, whenever the demand of housewife permitted, the holding together of the remnants of her uncle's once prosperous business, upon which all of them except André, who had inherited a small income, depended.

It was strange that Rouzet interested himself in politics for the Revolution had all but ruined him. An Alsatian, from a small town near the frontier, he had come to Paris as a young man and worked hard as a journeyman hairdresser in the rue St. Honoré, subsequently branching out on his own and setting up as a perfumier and wigmaker on the proceeds of his late wife's dowry.

In the last years of the old régime, when the extravagant fashions set by the young queen had made fortunes for men in Rouzet's profession, he had been engaged in building up a thriving little business, but when an expensive *coiffeur* was liable to advertise tacit opposition to the sovereign will of the people, and the leaders of the Revolution publicly declaimed against the use of perfume as effeminate and walked the streets with hair cut short and tied in a queue (like a chain of galley-slaves en route for Brest, as Rouzet described the new mode), he had gradually given up the struggle and reverted to his original trade of barber and face masseur. Charlotte, and Marcelle, too, when sufficiently goaded by Charlotte, still made an attempt to maintain the perfume trade and repaired, though never assembled, the wigs of the few customers who clung to the old fashions and refused to be intimidated by the gibes of the Cordelier *gamins*.

The presence of André, Charlotte and Marcelle at No. 12 Cour de Turenne was due, in some measure, to Papa

Rouzet's impulsive good nature. André and Marcelle were the children of his wife's brother, formerly a doctor in Arras, who had died when the children were very young. Rouzet's wife had invited them to Paris, where it was intended that André should study at the School of Medicine, barely five minutes' walk from the shop. The youth had been entered at the school the year the Revolution broke out, but the disturbed times had seriously upset the curriculum and now he hardly ever went to a lecture, although, at the time I met him, there was some talk of his concentrating on surgery and practising it in the army.

Charlotte was the only child of Rouzet's brother, who was still living in Lille. She came to Paris to keep house for her uncle when his wife died some eighteen months previous to my coming to Paris. Her own mother had died a year or two before and her father had married a woman younger than his daughter, so that she came gladly and Rouzet soon found her indispensable about house and shop.

Thus Papa Rouzet, himself childless, had acquired a son and two daughters through family bereavements, and he loved them dearly, and had plenty of affection left over for any friends they cared to bring into the house. Marcelle had met her lover when he came into the shop for a shave one day and once their relationship was established Deputy Biron encouraged his friends and colleagues to patronize the jolly barber, a circumstance which might have improved business had not the gay young provincials, encouraged by Marcelle and by Rouzet's own openhandedness, used No. 12 more as a club than a hairdressing *salon* and disposed of any profits their custom accrued by their regular performances as trenchermen at Rouzet's table. In the circumstances, all that Papa Rouzet extracted from his Girondist patronage was good company and day-to-day reports of discussions and resolutions in the Hall of Assembly, where his customers talked all day and came home prepared to talk all night, providing they were fed and laundered by Charlotte, flattered and cosseted by Marcelle, and faintly encouraged by Rouzet himself.

Charlotte, by this time fully accustomed to the demands of strangers in her pantry, gave me an excellent meal of bread, wine and cold chicken and told me there would be a bed for me in one of the stockrooms if I didn't mind making the best of a straw palliase and a single blanket. Beyond telling me that, and clearing the table when I had finished, she ignored me altogether and soon returned to her washtub.

André returned, in more sober clothes, and asked me if I would care to rejoin the company, but I pleaded extreme fatigue and begged him to show me to my stockroom, which he did, waiting to see me comfortable and giving me the brief summary of the Rouzet establishment which I have set down above. When I was rolled in my blanket he blew out the candle and wished me good night, promising to rouse me in the morning and act as my guide in a tour of districts on the other side of the Seine.

I lay breathing in that strong, sickly odour and listening to the faint strains of music that still came from the room over the shop, where the concert continued until long after midnight. From where I lay, on a rustling palliasse laid across two empty crates, I could see, through the small barred window, the stars over Paris and hear the hum of wheeled traffic and the clatter of hooves as light carriages and *fiacres* passed up and down the rue l'Ecole de Médecine. Paris never goes to bed until the small hours and even then the interval between the passage of the last pedestrian and the rattle of early morning *sabots* is hardly noticeable.

I felt comfortably drowsy and contented as I waited for the sleep that is always long coming to an overtired man. I wonder now if I should have slept at all that night had I an inkling of all that would result from my chance introduction to No. 12 Cour de Turenne?

Chapter Five

I LOOK back on these first week at Papa Rouzet's as among the most pleasant and stimulating of my life.

In spite of Rouzet's protests, which were ultimately overborne more by Charlotte's practical decree than my own importunities, I persuaded him to accept a modest sum in payment for my board and lodging, after which I felt free to accept his hospitality during the period of my wanderings about the city.

They were all kind to me in their different ways. Rouzet, still a tradesman despite his recent addiction to politics, offered to teach me the art of hairdressing, massage and even chiropody. Marcelle, once she realized she had found a ready audience, chattered to me about the events of the day whenever her lover's absence at the Assembly left her free to commune with a fugitive from the Oligarchy, and Charlotte, who, although she spoke very little, regarded me as a welcome source of augmenting the family's uncertain income, which justified her spending rather more time in ministering to my personal comforts than to those of her cousin's admirers. These young sparks were readily persuaded that their spate of talk more than paid Rouzet for the quantities of food and drink they consumed.

There never was such a house for talk. Accustomed as I had been to the long, morose silences of the Westdown kitchen, I was at first half-stupefied by the incessant declarations and rodomontades that accompanied every exchange of ideas round the supper table.

I was soon accepted by family and visitor alike. The Girondists, or Brissotins as they were usually called, were all personable fellows and not exclusively concerned with politics, although this subject formed the basis of most of their discussions. They were great readers and regular

theatre-goers, and some of them were themselves engaged
in writing tragedies and epic poems. They talked of Vol-
taire and Rousseau as though these celebrities were next-
door neighbours, and through their conversation I gained
a sketchy knowledge of current French writings other
than the heady nonsense contained in the pamphlets and
newspapers of the day. One and all they referred to me
as "M'sieur Dah-veed," and treated me with the sympathetic courtesy that they felt was due to a victim of a
terrible despotism over the water, sometimes making me
feel that I had recently escaped from the bagnios of the
Grand Turk, where I had been subjected to nameless
tortures.

Nobody could live at No. 12 Cour de Turenne for more
than a week without absorbing a wide, if uncorrelated,
idea of the personalities and political topics of the day,
together with a hundred speculations upon the probable
course of the Revolution. In this way I became familiar,
almost without knowing it, with the principal figures
then holding the stage in the Assembly and their various
idiosyncrasies, vices, political backgrounds and immediate
prospects.

The Jacobins—men of the Mountain they were called
on account of the elevated seats they held on the left tier
of the Assembly—were usually represented to me as ruthless scoundrels, intent upon using their popularity with
the mob, whose language the moderate deputies did not
speak, in order to enrich themselves at the expense of
the pilfered middle-classes. Danton, a typical example of
this faction, was said to have accepted vast bribes from
the monarchists and to have dissipated the money at the
gaming-table. Marat, the ferocious journalist, was beneath
the Girondists' contempt, and Robespierre was at that
period little known; I only heard his name mentioned
once or twice in discussion. Considering the eminence to
which this man rose in the next two years (I am informed
that he now virtually controls France) he must have
played a very clever game during the last days of the
Legislative Assembly. Desmoulins, a fiery young journalist who declaimed from the shadow of Danton's for-

midable bulk, was far more feared by the provincial republicans, for he possessed a facile pen and undoubted oratorical talent. Lafayette, I gathered, after leading the Revolution against the original champions of limited reform, was rapidly losing his influence, as were all the men who had supported the new constitution which aimed at retaining Louis on the throne and perpetuating the monarchy.

It seemed to me, as I listened to the interminable debate in Rouzet's parlour, that there were three distinct parties jockeying for absolute power and that the party of the Gironde, by far the most numerous and best informed, was by no means the most likely to succeed, for they possessed no influence at all with the Paris mobs, admittedly under the spell of Danton's extremists. Even to me, a stranger and foreigner, it appeared that the men who controlled Paris were the virtual dictators of France and that the future of the Revolution, if it was saved from the attack from the east, was in their hands, and theirs alone.

The third party, that of the constitutionists, had commenced its decline some time before I reached Paris. The position of moderate reformers had been considerably weakened by the attempted flight of the royal family the previous summer, and although Louis had since signed the constitution, and the occasion had been marked by celebrations that many interpreted as the final phase of the Revolution, the imminence of foreign invasion and, on July 30th of that year, the issue of the Duke of Brunswick's absurd manifesto threatening death to all Frenchmen acting on the defensive, produced a wave of desperate patriotism in the capital that swept away all hope of a compromise on the English constitutional pattern. Louis was living in the Tuileries, but he was guarded night and day, while at the Salles de Manège, where the deputies met, the fate of the monarchy was being decided by a majority of unrepentant republicans.

Throughout the eventful summer of that year the deputies of the Gironde and the demagogues of the faubourgs were in uneasy alliance against the few outspoken stal-

warts who still desired the rallying point of a throne, but
nobody imagined that the alliance would endure once the
King had been dethroned and the new constitution
scrapped to make way for a republic. It was for this
event that the men of the Mountain were preparing, and
it came, in the attack on the Tuileries, rather sooner than
the Girondists expected or intended.

It was André Lamotte, the dandified cynic who had
introduced me into the household, who was my constant
companion during these exciting days. I grew very fond
of him during those strolls about Paris on which he was
almost invariably my guide. He was a highly intelligent
young man, with little of the high-flown idealism that
characterized Marcelle's fiancé, Biron, or any of the other
provincials whom she introduced into the house. He had
received an expensive education and had supplemented it
by disciplined reading, so that the classical metaphors of
the Girondists, and the more homely expletives of the
Jacobins, seemed to him equally fatuous in the situation
in which France found herself, with Brunswick and the
émigrés massing on the frontier and nothing but a few
old fashioned fortresses and a spate of enthusiastic doc-
trine between Paris and Prussian bayonets. André had a
cold, clear logic that made Girondist rhetoric sound like
the prattle of enthusiastic schoolboys, and Marcelle's
friends soon ceased to address their remarks to him, dis-
missing him disdainfully as a base and cynical materialist.
He might have thrown in his lot with the extremists in
our neighbourhood, for he had a grudging admiration for
the giant Danton, whom he considered an uncouth ge-
nius, but André was a humanist and for all his contempt
of talk he preferred it to the orgy of blood-letting that
everybody anticipated once the mob-orators gained undisputed control. He had the weakness and ineffectuality
of all honest scholars, an easy tolerance that prevented
him from coming down on one side or the other and in
the Paris of '92 almost all men of his type were doomed.
André himself was not unaware of this. He once said to
me: "There is no place in revolution for tolerance. The
need is for action, any action, whether based on human

rights or not. It is better to make wrong decisions than
no decisions at all."

Almost all the deputies that I met at Rouzet's were
very agreeable fellows and half a dozen or so were unmistakably talented. Louvet, a dramatist of small stature
and great personal charm, was the only one who tolerated
André's fence-squatting, and the nearest the group ever
came to finding a leader was in the dominant personality
of Barbaroux, a man of striking appearance, handsome but
rapidly running to fat. Barbaroux was an intelligent libertine and something of a braggart. He came from Marseilles and was hugely enjoying himself in Paris, where
he could make speeches all day and mattress conquests
all night. There was another deputy, Buzot, whom Marcelle declared to be head over heels in love with Manon
Roland, the wife of a grave, elderly Minister of the Interior. Buzot also was handsome and talkative, with rather
more practical energy than the others, as he proved later
when this fine coop of barnyard roosters were scattered
in hiding. Manon Roland I never met but I heard a good
deal about her. She kept a *salon* for the Girondists at the
Ministry and, according to Marcelle, reciprocated Buzot's
passion and had already informed her husband that she
could give him nothing more than the chaste affections
of a daughter for a virtuous father! There was always a
hint of feminine malice in Marcelle's voice and manner
when she spoke of Madam Roland, and I suspected that
she regarded the older woman as a rival in the hearts of
the men who paid court to both of them. She was undoubtedly in love with Deputy Biron but this did not prevent her from flirting outrageously with witty Louvet and
handsome Barbaroux. She was only seventeen and the
elegantly phrased flattery of the provincials would have
turned wiser heads than hers.

It was from one of these deputies, Louvet I think, that
I learned the latest news regarding Saxeby's hero, Tom
Paine. Paine had been elected a deputy by the Pas-de-
Calais department and although he could not speak a
word of French had been invited to come to Paris and
take his seat in the Assembly. His literary outpourings,

particularly Saxeby's favourite book, *The Rights of Man,* had made him immensely popular in France and someone had gone over to London to collect him and bring him to a country where his far-reaching theories on egalitarian government could be put into practice. I looked forward eagerly to meeting this man whose political treatises had been indirectly responsible for my finding myself in Paris.

The weather was fine and, at times, oppressively hot, just the temperature for working on the passions of the sections, and as André and I went about Paris, sometimes by cab but more often on foot, we saw unmistakable signs of an approaching insurrection. We spent a day in the Assembly, Louvet procuring the necessary passes, and heard fiery speeches by several prominent deputies and one heated duel between Vergiaud, the speaker of the Girondist faction, and Couthon, a malevolent cripple, who conveyed himself to and from the sessions in a remarkable contraption midway between a bathchair and a self-propelled Roman chariot. Couthon, André explained, was as vicious as Marat. Both men were handicapped by grave physical disabilities which made them particularly savage in their dealing with active, able-bodied opponents. Couthon traded on his infirmity and placed men like Vergiaud at a disadvantage, particularly when making a sneering reference to the presence of young politicians in Paris at a time when their more conscientious comrades were thronging to the frontiers in defense of liberty.

On this day I also saw Danton for the first time and, in spite of my disapproval of his violent attitude, I was hypnotized by his audacious oratory. He was a lion of a man, with broad, pockmarked features, a ready wit and a voice that would have carried across the Exe Estuary. Desmoulins was there, too, extraordinarily handsome with his mane of jet-black hair and fine, sparkling eyes, now glowing with fanaticism, now as soft and gentle as Marcelle's. The general impression I got, however, at the Assembly was that of entering a tower of Babel. The president's bell jingled incessantly but it hardly affected a lull in the hurricane of debate. Proposition and counter-proposition, amendment and counter-amendment were bandied backwards and forwards across the galleries, while deputies were constantly leaping up and accusing one another of every crime from veniality to venery. The hall echoed with impassioned speeches, halting speeches, gusts of laughter and shouted interjections, all directed to I know not what end, and I very much doubt if the majority of deputies could have related the proceedings in the hall to the ends they were pursuing.

As we left André remarked, with a smile: "What a people for liberty. It's just a plaything for them. In England you'd get more true liberty under Nero!"

That was just before copies of Brunswick's manifesto began to appear on the streets. Until then there had undoubtedly been an atmosphere of strain and uncertainty in the city but, for the most part, ordinary men and women had gone about their workaday lives and left politics to the relatively few enthusiasts. I remember being surprised, during my walks with André, at the tolerant jocularity of the average Parisian, who appeared to be participating in some sort of gay charade, rather than conducting a revolution. During those first few days I witnessed no single instance of mob persecution. The only prisoners I saw were a batch of malefactors en route for Toulon or Brest, witness to the fact that the ordinary processes of law had not broken down, although I did hear from André that only the most vicious brigands could expect this severity from the recently purged tribunals. Most of the judges had too much sympathy with the underdog to impose the savage sentences of the old régime.

The army of the Princes, and their allies the *émigrés,* left Coblentz on July 31 and moved leisurely across the frontier during the first days of August. News of the advance caused little panic in Paris, for the populace had great faith in the volunteer levies and told one another that the invasion would shortly end in disaster for the Prussians. It was Brunswick's manifesto that sounded the first note of dismay and brought about the cleavage of opinion that led directly to the destruction of the monarchy and, a month later, to the massacre of the suspects crammed into the prisons at the Abbaye, La Force, the Temple and a number of converted public buildings.

The manifesto was certainly a frightening document. Couched in the most imperious language, as though the French nation was an assembly of cowardly serfs enjoying a brief interval of licentious freedom, it called upon man, woman and child to welcome the invaders with open arms on pain of instant death and confiscation of property. There could be no mistaking the intentions of the *émigrés* once they had re-established themselves and their foreign allies in Paris. Bloody reprisals were indicated and the sternest application of the law proscribed for all who would not make instant submission.

Brunswick's declaration was more than a piece of unimaginative folly, it was the greatest stimulus that could have been given to the Revolution. It strengthened the republicans in their determination to go forward and it won over to their side most of the waverers who now saw that a victory for the *émigrés* would mean the loss of every privilege won during the last three years. It proved an enormous filip to the Jacobin extremists and correspondingly weakened the moderates. Incidentally it proved, ultimately, to be the king's death warrant and the elimination of what remained of the constitutional party.

Within a few hours of its publication the atmosphere of the city changed and indications of that change were immediate. Priests known to have evaded the oath but so far protected by the king's obstinate refusal to decree their outlawry were rounded up, packed into open carts and driven to the prisons. I saw one vehicle surrounded by an hysterical mob and a massacre was only prevented by the heroic efforts of the escort of National Guards. At one point along the rue de Quatre Vents the escort of another coach was overwhelmed and three suspects, one of them a woman, were dragged into the street and butchered, their heads being paraded on poles up and down the district until a troop of mounted grenadiers hunted the murderers into the alleys and captured their grisly trophies. The journalists of the Mountain worked night and day and a torrent of pamphlets poured into the streets, all claiming pre-knowledge of counter-revolutionary plots aimed at freeing Louis from the Tuileries, recalling the volunteers and opening the gates to the Prussians. Further plots were said to be hatching in the crowded prisons and the queen was reported to be in constant touch with her brother, the Austrian Emperor, who was preparing an army of a hundred thousand to join Brunswick's hordes in the investment of the frontier fortresses.

Mutual distrust and suspicion replaced the bonhomie of the faubourgs. Gone were the flamboyant exchanges of greeting, citizen to citizen; men conversed in undertones and looked malevolently at anyone wearing Sunday clothes or driving his own equipage. I began to get nervous of being seen alongside André's sky-blue coat. After we had been challenged in the Cour de Commerce, I persuaded him to go home and change back into fustian.

Every day the streets became less inviting and I began to spend my mornings in Papa Rouzet's *salon,* helping his boy Joseph to prepare the lather pots, and listening to the conversation which was all devoted to the war and the manifesto.

Joseph was a wretched little waif who owed his position as apprentice solely to Rouzet's careless good nature, for the boy was deaf and dumb and his filthy rags were no advertisement to the establishment. Joseph was not unlike a fox in appearance. His face was long and narrow and his eyes, set close together, peered from a forest of wiry hair which had even less acquaintance with the tools of his trade than his ears and scraggy little neck had with soap and water.

Charlotte, who was also kind to the boy, went to the trouble of cutting down some of Rouzet's cast-off clothing and altering it to fit Joseph, but the lad preferred his rags and soon disposed of the makeshift suit in the fish market where he was reputed to live. Despite his affliction, he was a bright, cheerful little scamp and devoted to Rouzet, to whom he was very useful as an errand boy. He seemed to take to me, also, which is more than can be said for Vizet, the journeyman.

Vizet was Rouzet's only employee apart from Joseph and members of the family, and, like the boy, he was a denizen of the labyrinth of courts and alleys on the north side of the rue des Cordeliers. He was a sullen, furtive young man and, according to André, had political ambitions and was likely to abandon his work at any moment and take up a full-time post at the Commune headquarters. I didn't take much notice of him at the time but both he and Joseph have a place in this story later on.

Charlotte shared my distrust of the journeyman and had more than once asked her uncle to discharge him, but, for one reason or another, Rouzet retained his services and I am certain that he carried back to his slum a full and doubtless richly embroidered account of all the political claptrap he overheard in the shop.

I was pottering about the shop one morning in early August when André beckoned me into the perfumery, where Charlotte and Marcelle were occupied at the large vat. André took from his pocket two documents, each folded in three and overprinted in bold script. I picked up one of the papers and glanced at it.

It was a contract for temporary enrolment in the Cordelier battalion of the National Guard. One document bore his name and the other my own. When I asked for an explanation he laughed.

"Things are hotting up, David. It's time we took some measures to protect ourselves. It isn't safe to walk as far as the Pont Neuf unless one's breeches are in tatters. Maybe we'll have leisure to regard events more sedately in the uniform of the sovereign people."

He always talked like that and I had soon become accustomed to it, but Marcelle could always be relied upon to rise to this particular bait and he knew it and teased her accordingly.

"There are plenty of gaps in the volunteer battalions.

You could get all the powder smudges you want on the frontier with the rest of the boys," she told him tartly.

I saw Charlotte raise her eyes but she said nothing and addressed herself vigorously to stirring the vat.

André sidled round to Marcelle and encircled her tiny waist with a show of mock affection.

"You wouldn't have your only brother blown to pieces by the Prussians, would you, Marcelle?"

She put down her mixing pole and faced him squarely. Marcelle, like the majority of politically inclined young women, had an underdeveloped sense of humour.

"Plenty of others are doing it, why not you?" she asked. "I should have thought able-bodied young men would have something better to do than stroll about the streets sight-seeing from morning to night."

"Oh, I wouldn't hold that against us," joked André, "there's more to be learned in the street than in the parrot-house up yonder! They could recruit a whole army of ardent young soldiers up there, and all of them falling over each other to pour out their blood for liberty!"

This dig at Deputy Biron made Marcelle flush with rage.

"René's work is in the Assembly," she screamed, "that's what he was sent here for! How dare you suggest that he uses his seat to stay out of the fighting! If you had a spark of his patriotism you would have been on the walls of Verdun long since instead of strutting about in your fine clothes, sneering at everything people like René are trying to do for us!"

This was too much for André, who shouted with laughter, and I believe Marcelle might have swung her dripping pole at him had not Charlotte intervened in her usual quiet way.

"Can't you see he's only teasing, Marcelle? Run off and join the National Guard, André; join a menagerie if you wish, but leave us to our work."

I was eager for Charlotte's opinion, however, for it was sure to be an unbiased one. I was aware that she had none of Marcelle's enthusiasm for the Revolution and she had never given me the impression that she shared André's jocular cynicism. All the time I had been with the family I had never heard her express an opinion on any matter outside the spheres of *salon* and kitchen.

"Suppose you were a young man, Charlotte," I asked her, "what would you do?"

"If I were a man I'd go about my business, m'sieur," she replied bluntly.

She had always addressed me formally and had never used my Christian name like the others, but somehow on this occasion her reply made me feel uncomfortable, as though it was a broad hint to take myself out of their house.

It was left to André to interpret her correctly.

"Charlotte's the only sane person in Paris," he said, and for once there was no mockery in his tone. "Tell him what else you think, Lotte. Tell him you think we ought to be governed by women."

Charlotte lowered her gaze and looked slightly embarrassed.

"He isn't interested in my views," she said.

"Indeed I am, Charlotte," I told her, and even Marcelle forgot her indignation and looked curiously at her cousin.

Charlotte picked up her pole and began stirring the compound with wide, deliberate sweeps.

"I used to think that," she said slowly. "I thought it a long time, until I saw the march on Versailles, that is, but I don't think it any longer, the women are worse than the men. Nothing can save us now, nothing except flight, and how many of us could do that? He might"— she perked her head in my direction—"but he won't because he's like everyone else, always looking for something new, without a thought for the things that really matter."

I can't explain why, but the strange fatalism in her tone made me shiver, as though the heat had suddenly gone from the afternoon and the little room, heavy with the fumes of the compound and bathed in the golden

glow of the sun that poured through the skylight, had
been suddenly and inexplicably plunged into the deepest
shadow. As she spoke I had an intense conviction that
death would strike this house the way it had struck at
my family three months before, and I believe that Marcelle experienced a similar premonition, for she stared
at Charlotte for a moment like a frightened child, her
knuckles gleaming white on the pole she was holding.

The sensation passed, dissolved by André's ringing
laugh, and Charlotte, as though ashamed of her outburst,
turned back to the vat and began to apply herself whole-
heartedly to her work once again.

André and I went upstairs and spent an hour or two
over the newspapers. I wanted to discuss Charlotte's
prophecy with him but he did not seem disposed to talk
about it and fell instead the listing his arguments in
favour of our accepting three francs a day and a kerb-
stone view of events in the ranks of the National Guard.
His arguments made good sense. Sooner or later every
young man in Paris would be expected to wear uniform
and in the civic guard we could at least be certain of
sleeping in our own beds two nights out of three. Enlistment terms were generous; it was a volunteer force,
but, unlike the field levies, carried the advantage of a
short-term contract. It was possible to sign on for periods
of three months at a time and extend or terminate one's
engagement at will.

After supper we went down to the Hotel de Ville and
handed in our contracts, and the following morning presented ourselves at the depot and drew tunics, a musket
and bayonet apiece, and large, cockaded shakos. There
were no breeches and we had to find our own shoes.
My hat was a size too large so I lined it with two copies
of *Père Duchesne,* one of the more violent of the journals
on sale at the street corners. We drank a bottle of Burgundy and went home to show ourselves to Papa Rouzet
and the girls.

Any uniform was better than no uniform to Marcelle,
who forgot all about the quarrel and received us as

though we had returned from a victorious campaign. Rouzet, who only needed the merest excuse to celebrate, sent out for a case of Moselle and set Charlotte preparing a supper party which began as soon as young Joseph had put the shutters up and left the premises.

We all spent a jolly evening in the room over the shop. Deputy Biron and his friend Louvet came in about sundown, and Marcelle sang her repertoire of popular airs. Even the silent Charlotte thawed a little under the influence of Rouzet's wine and it must have been getting on for one in the morning when Marcelle, giggling and moving a little unsteadily, escorted Biron to the *salon* door and André and I took ourselves off to bed.

I had drunk rather more wine than I was accustomed to and as soon as I lay down on my palliasse I began to hiccough. The atmosphere of the little room was stifling, in spite of the fact that I had flung the window wide open. Immediately below, Marcelle and Biron were still bidding each other good night, and seemed disinclined to make an end of it. Biron's deep tone and Marcelle's rippling laugh came up to me at regular intervals between their embraces.

At any other time I might have chuckled to myself and rolled over to sleep, but tonight their simple love-making irritated me. My head began to throb and my mouth felt parched and leathery. I had to make an effort to prevent myself shouting something uncivil from the window.

At last they parted and I heard the deputy stride off through the empty streets and Marcelle shoot the bolts of the front door and come slowly upstairs to the room she shared with Charlotte at the rear of the premises.

It was quiet now but the room was stifling hot. Presently I gave up trying to sleep and, getting out of bed, I crossed to the window. I cursed the little grille which prevented me from leaning out, but here, with face against the bars, it was at least a little cooler. I groped for my pipe, the clay I had brought with me from Devon, and, getting out my pouch, began to fill the bowl.

At that moment the first boom of the tocsin rolled across the court smiting my ear like a thunderclap and making my heart leap. Before it had been rolling a half-minute a second bell joined in, then a third, then half a dozen, until the night rocked with noise and the insistent summons clamoured from every steeple in Paris.

Chapter Six

It was not until André came, half-dressed, into my room that I remembered I had contracted to be something more than a passive spectator of insurrection.

On receiving our uniform issue the previous day we had been instructed, in the event of a general emergency, to report to our battalion headquarters situated somewhere behind the School of Medicine, but as neither André nor myself had yet had occasion to go there we stood little chance of finding it in the dark, particularly as the turmoil of the streets was increasing every minute.

André was in the best of spirits. He buttoned his tunic, crammed on his shako and shouted to me to hurry before we were cut off by the crowds streaming towards the Pont Neuf. I asked him if he knew what was happening and he said he believed that the tocsin heralded a Jacobin attack on the Tuileries.

"They'll have their precious republic before sunset!" he prophesied.

It was just beginning to get light and as I pulled on my breeches I glanced through the window and across the court to where the rue L'Ecole de Médicin crossed the narrow entrance of the cul-de-sac in which Rouzet's house stood. In the half-light the narrow street seemed to be moving like a spring torrent. Armed men, most of them clad only in shirt and breeches, were jostling by, intermingled with stragglers of the mounted *gendarmerie,* groups of our own battalion of National Guards and a hotch-potch of half-dressed sightseers, the majority of them women and children.

The uproar was deafening. To the persistent clamour of the bells, which increased in volume every minute as though the ringers were spurred by mounting fury, was added the rattle of ten thousand *sabots* on the cobbles,

and the shouts of a wildly excited multitude pressing
down towards the Pont Neuf and Pont Royale, where the
outpourings of St. Antoine and St. Marceau, the two districts principally concerned in the outbreak, converged in
a human flood in the area around the Tuileries.

We managed to get out of the house without encountering Rouzet or the girls, for which I was thankful, for
Marcelle at any rate would have insisted on accompanying us and she would have proved an impossible embarrassment in such a *mêlée*.

As we were swept along on the tide of revolutionary
fervour we gleaned a few details of the rising, which had
apparently been planned by Danton, with the tacit support of the Girondists and a majority of the Assembly.

Nearer the bridgehead some of the leaders, previously
selected by Danton and the Paris Commune, began to
marshal the semi-hysterical mob into some sort of battle
order. Some of the Marseilles and Brest Federals marched
up and I saw that they were better armed than the rabble
and had three pieces of cannon in their column. Two
men seemed to be in charge of the assault and one of
them, a plump-faced, powerfully built young fellow in a
general's uniform, was mounted on a huge white horse
which he controlled admirably. André pointed him out to
me as Santerre, formerly a brewer of rue de Reuilly, who
had early won popularity with the mob by sending horses
to participate in the attack on the Bastille three years
previously and had more than compensated for his absence on the rampart by regaling the victors with free
liquor when they brought him the fortress keys. Subsequently he had further enhanced his reputation as a republican by distributing 150,000 francs' worth of stew
to the starving rabble during the hard winter of '91. His
reward was the honour of leading the attack on the
Tuileries. Later on I got to know him and found him a
vain and rather stupid man, whose sudden popularity
had completely turned his head. The other, Santerre's principal lieutenant, a gigantic Alsatian called Westermann,
was a very different type of man. Utterly fearless, he
combined the ideal qualities of an ideal mob leader with

those of an experienced soldier. His energy on that memorable August 10th, as he went about mustering that crowd into controllable units, was phenomenal, and an hour or so later, on the fringe of the Place de Carrousel, immediately adjoining the main buildings of the Tuileries, I observed him still exercising his talents as organizer of an assault column.

Once I had recovered from the initial excitement I was confused and uncertain. I was by no means as anxious to fight as most of the men around me, but I did not see how fighting could be avoided. Our precipitate rush from the house, and our presence in the midst of such a martial-minded mob, made a show of belligerence imperative. Then, and not for the only time during the next few hours, I had cause to regret my stupidity in allowing André to talk me into enlistment. It is one thing to risk your skin in defence of your home and family; it is quite another to face volleys of musketry in a battle to which you have been attracted by curiosity.

However, there was no drawing back now, for here we were, both carrying muskets and cartridge boxes, mixed up in the flotsam of our own battalion and the civic guard of St. Marceau, and men like the huge Westermann were already pushing us into line on the flank of the Marseilles Federals, who had marched all the way up the dusty summer roads from the south for just such a scrimmage as this.

The royal family and the constitutionalists must have had warning of the outbreak for someone had posted cannon on the Pont Neuf with the object of preventing a junction between the St. Marceau rabble and that of St. Antoine just across the river. The cannon, however, were never fired and we swarmed unopposed over the bridge into the Place de Carrousel, where our column lost its identity in the large gathering of half-armed insurrectionists from St. Antoine and other districts.

By this time it was about seven o'clock in the morning and the clear blue sky promised another fine, windless day. I remember remarking to André that it was likely to be our last, but he only laughed, excitedly, and

I saw that he was genuinely enjoying himself. He was a restless young man and I think he welcomed this opportunity for action after weeks of time-killing since the closing down of the School of Medicine.

Part of the mob detached itself from the vast concourse to invade the Hotel de Ville and I suppose this must have been part of the plan to terrorize those of the Legislature who discouraged bloodshed and armed insurrection in the presence of the king.

The rest of us milled about in the Carrousel for the better part of an hour and then André, who had been talking to some of Westermann's henchmen, came back and told me that some of the deputies had persuaded the king and his family to vacate the royal apartments and take shelter in the Assembly, and that Mandat, commander of the Swiss Guards and of the three to four hundred loyalists still surrounding the king, had been foolish enough to quit his place among the troops and comply with a deputation's request to present himself at the Hotel de Ville. During the time we had been mustering in the Carrousel and the rue St. Honoré he had been butchered by the mob and the Tuileries defence force was now without its commander.

Shortly after André had delivered this piece of news, it was announced that the king had actually left the palace and it then looked as if our pikes would recross the river unbloodied after all. I suggested to André that we had better make our way out of the press and slip off home, but he was for staying to see what would happen if the Swiss refused to lay down their arms. I didn't care to risk desertion by myself so I stayed on, cursing him for his stupid curiosity and upbraiding myself for cowardice. I did not know for certain how I would behave when the cannon balls started flying but I had a very good idea that I would be terrified and have no scruples about revealing as much.

Presently the Marseilles Federals began to move forward and we entered the forecourts of the palace by the way of the Porte Royale. Here, however, was an end to our progress, for the redcoated Swiss had retreated to the main building and were lining the windows, all of which bristled with muskets pointed in our direction.

I had an insight then into the mass emotions of a mob. Up to that minute everyone around me had been shouting for action and urging their section leaders to hurl them upon the hated monarchists. Everybody brandished a weapon of some kind, a pike, a butcher's knife laced to a pole, a scythe mounted on a staff, with here and there a musket and bayonet from the arsenal pilfered on our side of the river soon after the first note of the tocsin. There were swords, poniards and clubs studded with nails and the emblems of this heterogeneous array were equally unconventional. One man carried a standard made of a pig's heart and part of the animal's entrails, which were nailed to a shutter pole. Another waved a staff supporting a pair of breeches with the seat torn out, signifying, I suppose, the defiance of the alley-dwellers.

There were at least fifty placards with labels reading "Vive la Republic" and "A bas M. et Mde. Veto," or similar slogans. Prominent among the most vociferous of the attacking force was a woman, her belt crammed with pistols and her right hand clutching a sabre. She stormed and raged about the terrace like a drunken fury, directing a stream of gutter invective at the stolid Swiss, who doubtless did not understand a word of it. This was a prominent St. Antoine harridan called Theroigne, who was more of a joke than an inspiration to the mob. I saw her later in the day, entertaining a party of her admirers by systematically mutilating a dead royalist on the main staircase of the palace.

They were the filthiest people I ever rubbed shoulders with and they carried into the streets the stink of tanneries, fish-quays and the verminous hovels in which most of them lived. I saw faces in that crowd that reminded me of the illustrations in Saxeby's edition of Dante's *Inferno,* pockmarked, tortured faces, faces without noses, faces on which the oppression of centuries was written, and the smell that accompanied this mob, a stench of sour sweat, bad breath and I know not what other offensive compound, was the most sickening of my experience,

making the summer reek of Westdown pig-sties sweet in
the memory.

All these people were chock full of martial ardour up
to the moment we had penetrated to within point-blank
range of the Swiss muskets, and then the foremost wave
came to a straggling halt about sixty yards from the windows and someone called loudly for the Federals' cannon, which were being manouevred into position at
various points covering the chateau.

I kept up with André more out of shame at disclosing
my real feelings than out of any anxiety to distinguish
myself in the assault.

The brewer Santerre kept out of range but the audacious Westermann went forward to parley and shouted up
at the Swiss in his guttural Alsatian. Some of the south-
ern Federals approached the windows higher up the forecourt and addressed the defenders in their soft Provençal
accents.

The Swiss opposite Westermann threw out some car-
tridges as a token of their willingness to agree to a truce
and this action was received by the insurgents with shouts
of delight not unmixed, I conjectured, with relief, for it
now looked as though the palace would be occupied without bloodshed. André and I edged a little nearer to hear
what Westermann was saying.

Then it happened. Some idiot of an artilleryman loosed
off a field-piece from the direction of the Porte Royale
and a ball, aimed far too high, crashed through the slates
of the roof. The next moment the Swiss had opened fire
and more than a hundred men in the front rank of the
rabble went down under a hail of well-directed musketry.
In less than two minutes the forecourt was cleared and the
survivors of the volley went tumbling back across the
Carrousel and into the street and alleys giving on the rue
St. Honoré.

I have never moved so quickly in my life. By what appeared to me a miracle, neither André nor I was hit and
we rushed towards the Porte Royale as fast as any of
the patriots. The instantaneous change of front must have

tickled André's odd sense of humour for even as he ran
he roared with laughter.

I glanced over my shoulder as we emerged on to the
Carrousel and saw the redcoats sallying out of the chateau to clear the gardens. They need hardly have bothered. A few of the black-browed Marseillaise stood firm
and were cut down in a few seconds, but for the next
half-hour the Swiss had it all their own way and Westermann was hard put to, to rally enough men for a coun-
ter-attack. André and I edged into the ranks he was assembling behind the Federals, but I took good care to
place myself well in the rear. I think André would have
pushed into the vanguard if he had been by himself, but
probably out of consideration to me he made no protest
when I attached myself to a fresh body of National
Guards which had come up too late to participate in the
first assault column.

I wondered then if anyone apart from the Swiss were
defending the chateau, for from where we stood it looked
as though the entire National Guard had come out on the
side of the people.

Some of the men who joined us now had actually
formed part of the Tuileries defence force earlier that
day and told us that Louis had held a pitiful review about
five in the morning when he visited all the barriers and
had been met with shout of *"Vive le Nation"* instead of
"Vive la Roi." When I heard this I didn't blame him
quitting the chateau, particularly as he had his wife and
children with him, but André was contemptuous of his
behavior.

"With a bodyguard like those Swiss he could have overturned the Revolution in an hour if he had shown some
spirit," he declared. "Why should they die for him now?
He is as feeble as he was last time."

He referred to a previous occasion when the riverside
mob had first invaded the palace and had retired without
bloodshed after the king had placed the red cap of liberty
on his head. It was well known that Louis, hating violence and determined to be loyal to the new constitution,
was prepared to go to almost any lengths to avoid civil

war. We learned later that the queen had opposed the royal family's evacuation of the Tuileries on the latter occasion and had declared to Roederer, the Syndic who advised it, that she would sooner be nailed to the walls than abandon the Tuileries to the mob. She had the spirit of any three men about her.

It was more than an hour after the first repulse before Westermann felt sufficiently confident of his rabble to return to the attack and lead his column over the shattered palisade towards the inner court, where the Swiss had now mounted cannon loaded with grape.

If we had had to storm the court unaided there is no doubt in my mind that the first discharge would have swept the head of the column away and Westermann with it, for the Alsatian marched several yards in front of the foremost Federals and again called upon the Swiss to surrender.

At that moment firing broke out from the south and rapidly increased in volume as a second column of insurgents, urged on by Santerre on his prancing steed, rushed through a gap between the Tuileries and the gallery of the Louvre and poured into the courts on our immediate left.

Taken in the flank by a murderous enfilading fire, the Swiss began to withdraw, but they kept their discipline and maintained such a hot fire from the windows, chimney stacks and low, ornamental walls of the gardens that our column made little headway until we joined up with the party attacking from the direction of the river.

There was another lull then and the word went round that the king had sent a message from the Assembly ordering the Swiss to cease fire. The wretched Hervilly, who commanded the defence, was thus placed in a terrible position. He knew that if he obeyed the order and commanded his men to lay down their arms, the attackers, maddened by losses and smarting under the shame of their precipitate retreat, would probably butcher the Swiss to a man.

I never found out exactly what occurred. I only know that firing soon broke out again and that a short time after the parley the mob broke down the main door and surged up the staircase, where the battle quickly resolved itself into a massacre.

Disorganized by their contradictory orders, the Swiss put up little or no defence after we were once inside the building. Every cornered redcoat was hacked to pieces and the attackers went whooping along the galleries and corridors, rooting out terrified palace servants and treating them all with the same barbarity. Cooks, valets and gardeners went down before the first savage rush.

The moment there was no one left to butcher an orgy of looting commenced. Tapestries were ripped down, statues and ornaments smashed and overturned, furniture slashed, beds ripped open and thrown from the windows and every corner of the huge chateau was soon filled to suffocation point with a shouting, screaming, hysterical mob.

The Federals, who had done most of fighting, tried to restore some sort of order, but their efforts were not even partially successful once the cellars had been forced and wine had been distributed to all who could shoulder their way through the press jamming the back staircases.

Revolted by such an insane display of violence and cruelty and badly shaken by the ordeal of the attack, I would gladly have made my way back to the Carrousel and gone home across the river, but in the confusion of the first few minutes on the staircase I had lost sight of André and I did not care to leave the chateau without him.

I had had neither food nor drink since the previous evening and the heat and stench generated by the crowds were intolerable. I felt I would have given the remainder of my guineas for a pint of water and ranged about the bloody corridors looking for a tap or a tank where I could quench my torturing thirst. I was crossing the spacious gallery above the main staircase on the first storey when I heard my name shouted. I fought my way through the crowd towards an intersecting corridor where the sound seemed to originate and soon found myself in what I imagined had been a bedroom for one of the lesser nobility. It was small and simply furnished but situated too near the front of the building to have been used as a servant's apartment.

Standing with his back to the open closet, in which a wounded white-faced Swiss was crouching, was André, resolutely defending the soldier against a group of ruffians intent on dispatching him with their pikes. The Swiss had been shot in the neck and his blood, now clotted by the powder shaken from his disordered peruke, had run down over his white waistcoat and drenched his gaiters. He was unarmed and his musket and bayonet lay at the feet of a half-naked man brandishing a cleaver.

I took in the situation at a glance and levelled my musket, which had not been discharged during the attack, at the semicircle of butchers threatening André. A gleam of hope shone in the redcoat's powder-bleared eyes, and André, from a posture of defence, immediately assumed an air of brisk authority.

"Thank you, citizen," he called to me. "This man is a prisoner of the second battalion of the National Guard and I am answerable for his life and custody!"

One of the pikemen growled out something about there being no quarter, but André pushed him on one side and helped the Swiss to his feet. The man reeled against the wardrobe, clutching feebly at André's cartridge belt.

"Out of the way you," barked André to the man with the cleaver, "or I shall be obliged to ask my comrade to increase the sovereign people's casualty roll!"

The group shuffled about indecisively, temporarily awed by André's masterful manner and my musket. André moved forward, supporting the soldier with his free arm, and I stepped across the room to cover his retreat. There were enough men present to have killed all three of us, but nobody wanted my ball in his stomach and in the general hesitation we got into the corridor and out on to the gallery.

André was sublime. Pushing his way through the revellers with the self-assurance of the Mayor of Paris, he directed me to take the half-fainting Swiss over my shoulder and shouted:

"Make way there, this prisoner is for the Hotel de Ville by special orders of Deputy Biron from the department of Gers!"

The crowd made way for him, as a crowd will that lacks leadership and directive cohesion. One of the Brest Federals on the stairs greatly assisted our exit by shouting that the Assembly had ordered all prisoners still living to be conveyed to the prison in the Petit Marché, where they were to be held for interrogation by the deputies.

The Brest man followed us into the forecourt, where huge bonfires added to the scorching heat of the noon sun. Drunken men and women were dancing and singing among the wounded and slain who lay everywhere, especially under the windows of the main gallery, where we had received the first point-blank volley. The scene in the open was scarcely less hellish than that in the corridors.

The young Federal glanced from side to side, his sun-burned face twitching with scorn.

"To think I blistered my feet all the way from Quimper for this," he muttered. "These people in Paris aren't fit to be given charge of a dunghill!"

He told us, as we made our way over the palisade and into the rue St. Honoré, that he was one of fifty volunteers recruited by the local committee to march in defence of the constitution against Brunswick's Prussians. Although only twenty-five he was a veteran revolutionary and had enlisted in all good faith, but since arriving in the capital had begun to entertain doubts. Today's business had resolved him. He would never have left his father's farm in Brittany if he had anticipated having to contribute to such a shambles.

"This is only the beginning," said André grimly. "All the best men are on the frontiers. Only the windbags and thieves have been left behind, but that is the usual course of revolutions; you should read more history, citizen."

The Brest man said he could not read but added that he did not need books to tell him that this sort of behaviour would soon disgust every nation in Europe and bring the Revolution into universal odium. He told us bluntly that today's events had determined him to go home. He found us a hired cabriolet and helped us to lay the unconscious Swiss on the leather cushions.

"What are you going to do with him?" he asked André.

"God knows," replied André lightly, "we'll discuss that as we go along. Rue l'Ecole de Médecine, driver!"

The coachman edged his horse through the eddying crowds towards the Pont Royale. I looked out of the window and caught a final glimpse of the Federal looking mournfully after us, a picture of bitterness and disillusion He was typical of provincial opinion at that stage of the events. All over France young men had welcomed the Revolution with open arms and thronged into the volunteer battalions marching on the capital. Once there they had become disgusted, almost overnight, with the wild excesses of the Paris mob, with whom they could find no point of contact, and whose open brigandage soon shattered their dream of building an ideal state on the ruins of feudalism. A few of them became accustomed to scenes of butchery, but the majority soon drifted into the ranks of the republican armies.

I wondered whether our particular man would keep his word and return to his father's farm in Brittany.

When we were clear of the crowded streets and were rattling over the cobbles towards the left bank of the Seine André began to peel off the Swiss soldier's bloodstained tunic and gaiters. With my help he stripped the poor fellow of his small clothes and rolled his discarded uniform into a bundle which he thrust under the seat. We were obliged to tumble the man to and fro in the process of undressing him and our rough handling caused his wound to reopen. André staunched the flow and made a rough but effective bandage out of his neckcloth. The wound was not mortal and it looked to me as if rest and medical attention would soon restore the fellow to normal health. I could not help noticing the deft way in which André tended him and decided that my friend's interrupted studies at the School of Medicine had not been entirely wasted.

I was sympathetic with the poor wretch who lolled between us but I felt sure that he might prove a source of considerable trouble if we took him home to Rouzet's and I said as much.

André looked at me bleakly. "What else can we do with him?" he demanded.

I shrugged my shoulders. After all, I was only a lodger at Number 12 and I knew that Rouzet's warm heart would not permit him to hand the prisoner over to the authorities, at least until he had recovered from his wounds.

I was right about that but I hadn't bargained for the stir we caused when the cab deposited us at the narrow entrance of the court. We carried the Swiss sedan fashion and a crowd, anxious for the latest news, surrounded us as we crossed the green.

André, as usual, had a plausible explanation.

"A comrade from Savoy," he explained briefly, in response to a dozen eager questions. "The tyrants shot him in the neck as he went forward to parley!"

There was a murmur of sympathy and I resisted a strong desire to chuckle, the story was so typical of André and his impulse to give everything a theatrical twist.

We had some difficulty in keeping the sympathetic crowd out of the house, and carried the Swiss upstairs into my room, where André bathed the wound and with his forceps quickly extracted the ball, which had travelled downwards towards the shoulder-blade. The man winced once or twice but seemed easier after we had forced some brandy down his throat. He lay there on my makeshift bed, breathing noisily.

Charlotte came up from the perfumery, where she had spent a normal day at the tubs.

"You'd better carry him into my room," she said, "it's much quieter at the back."

That was like Charlotte, no questions and no fuss, just charity and plain common sense. It wasn't until Marcelle came in that the trouble began and then we had plenty of it, all through the evening and far into the night.

Marcelle had been down to the Assembly in search of news of her lover. She came back with eyes shining and told us that the deputies were already passing decrees abolishing the monarchy and the constitution and that the royal family were now State prisoners and preparations were being made to house them in the Temple Prison.

"Why don't you assassinate them and have done with it," observed André tartly. "The Dauphin wouldn't take much killing and surely he's earned it; they tell me he's got all the vices of his mother. Very promising in a seven-year-old!"

Marcelle snapped: "If you still believe in the constitution why have you and David been supporting Santerre and the people all day?"

André looked at her pityingly. "If you and your precious deputy had seen how the people conducted themselves in the Tuileries you might have some doubts as to whether this thing is going to be resolved by speeches about Brutus and Cato," he told her.

"Pooh, you can't wonder at the Jacobins getting a little out of hand," she urged, "they lost fourteen hundred in the forecourts and their blood was up."

"I know," grunted André, "I was there; was Biron?"

"The Swiss deserved all they got," retorted Marcelle, hotly, but refusing to be drawn on the subject of her lover's alleged gun-shyness. "They shot down our people during a truce—that man you've got upstairs is proof of their villainy, isn't it?"

André chuckled. "That man upstairs is himself a Swiss," he announced and, taking a large apple from a bowl on the sideboard, bit out a huge chunk, swung his long legs from the table and regarded her mockingly, enjoying the sensation he had caused.

Marcelle was horrified and even old Rouzet was badly scared. Only Charlotte's expression remained immobile as she went about the business of laying the supper table.

Marcelle spoke at last. "You've brought a Swiss into the house?" she exclaimed.

"I'm a would-be surgeon, I must have a little practical experience," grinned André.

Papa Rouzet said: "The people are in an excitable mood, André, there might be a little trouble. . . ."

"I thought of that," replied André, "why else do you think I got rid of his uniform? Everyone in the court thinks he's a patriot and even Marcelle seems to have heard how the poor fellow was shot in defiance of all rules of war!"

"Just the same, he'll have to leave here as soon as he's well," mumbled Rouzet.

"He'll leave here tonight," said Marcelle. "Just wait until René hears about this. What are you trying to make of us? Counter-revolutionaries?"

"You'd better fetch the deputy," said André calmly, "we shall need him to get us a passport. That Swiss will be fit to take the road south in less than a week!"

"Do you think Biron would be a party to smuggling a royalist out of the country?" shouted Marcelle.

"Oh, I don't know," said André jocularly, "he'd probably prefer that to bringing his bride-to-be and her family into collision with the sovereign people. He won't want the patriots interrupting any of his wonderful speeches from the tribune!"

Marcelle glared at her brother with something like hatred in her eyes and, seeing the futility of trying to change his attitude of cynical realism, she turned, despairingly, to Rouzet and Charlotte.

"You can't let him do this," she appealed. "You can't let him drag René and the rest of us down to be spat at by everybody in the neighbourhood."

"Odd how a revolution changes the social code," commented André, still feigning preoccupation with his apple. "Since when has common humanity become so odious in the neighbourhood?"

"But he's a mercenary," shouted Marcelle, almost beside herself with rage, "he was brought here and trained and paid to keep the monarchy's shackles on Frenchmen!"

Charlotte cut across the argument, checking André's mocking reply with simple, feminine logic.

"He's a human being," she said, "and he can stay here as long as he's helpless!"

And that was the end of it so far as Rouzet *ménage* was concerned. Marcelle remained unconvinced and inwardly boiled at this blatant betrayal of her creed, but she had enough sense to enter into the conspiracy and it was left to her to persuade Biron, who did not need a great deal of persuading, to provide papers for the Swiss. He remained with us about a week and ultimately left Paris as a watchmaker and made for his canton near Thun. He was a stolid, matter-of-fact fellow, and I don't think he ever fully appreciated the debt that he owed that household, or André in particular. I tried to converse with him when he was convalescing, but neither Rouzet, Charlotte nor myself made any headway for he spoke a bastard Bavarian dialect which even André, who spoke a little German, could not understand. We did ascertain that his name was Bauermann, and that he was a tradesman's son who had preferred soldiering to long hours at the counter. He must have been born under a lucky star for nearly all his comrades had been slaughtered on August 10th, the majority in the chateau and others as they tried to fight their way out of the gardens in the rue de l'Echelle. A few gained a temporary asylum with the Assembly but these were almost all massacred when the Jacobins purged the prisons during the first week of September. The main effect his stay had on our household was to widen the rift between Marcelle and André. The latter refused to take his sister's republicanism seriously and his attitude towards her remained jocose and mildly deprecating, as though she were a child who bored adults with an excess of enthusiasm. I could understand her being infuriated by his attitude for he could be maddeningly irritating when he liked and often was to all of us except Charlotte, whom he invariably treated with grave respect.

I wasn't very happy myself during the next few weeks. The shock of the savage spectacle I had witnessed at the Tuileries set me wondering whether or not I would do better to be on the move again. My detached alien's attitude towards the Revolution had undergone a sudden change in the forecourts of the chateau, and now that bad news was coming in from the frontiers, where the Prussians and *émigrés* were making considerable headway against the raw volunteer levies, the mood of August 10th prevailed everywhere, even in the Assembly. Pressure of events had almost extinguished the moderate party and mob rule, canalized by the Jacobins, seemed likely to lead to all manner of excesses against the middle classes before the summer was out.

After we had got the Swiss safely out of the way, André and I reported for duty as National Guards almost every day and we had plenty of opportunity of observing the growing panic of the capital as first Lafayette abandoned the cause and made his unsuccessful dash for America, then the frontier fortress of Longwy fell, and finally Verdun was invested. Dumouriez, Luckner and other generals aware of the inexperience of their battalions, manoeuvred and exhorted and drilled in a race against time, but it was not their frantic efforts that finally turned the tide in favour of the republic but rather the lethargy of the allied high command.

The man to emerge head and shoulders above everyone else in this crisis was the giant revolutionary Danton, whose courage never faltered but who seemed rather to gain strength and inspiration from each fresh reverse. As Minister of Justice he became the idol of Paris and his speeches were largely instrumental in rousing the people from a state of bewildered apathy that might have sapped their will to resist the tide of invasion from the north-west.

Listening to him, as he thundered from the tribune on the one or two occasions I was doing duty in the Assembly, was an inspiration.

He would stand there, jaw thrust forward, chest flung out, like a figure out of some heroic legend of the past, sparing with Gallic gesture but lavish with Gallic wit, his oratory plunging quickly from classic majesty into frank obscenity. There were no interruptions when Danton mounted the tribune and when he stepped down, after one of his thunderous demands for courage and audacity, the roar of applause accorded him would rock the chamber and resound far out over the anxious streets and alleys of the capital, until it touched the hearts of the shoeless rabble of volunteers locked with Brunswick in the autumnal slush of the Ardennes, and sent the mercenaries of the princelings stumbling back from the mill at Valmy, saving the infant republic from murder in the cradle.

Other men, other orators were not lacking at those memorable sessions, but there were none like Danton, the shabby lawyer from Arcis-sur-Aube.

I remained in Paris after the horrid butchery of September largely because of the magnetism of this one man and the fascination of watching him, as it were, poised at the tiller of the Revolution, steering this way and that in a whirlpool of fear, malice, place-seeking and downright human wickedness. That kept me from moving on, and so perhaps did Charlotte, who never had any illusions about what would happen when the people's wrath should change its course and rush downhill, sweeping away everything, good and bad, that stood in its way.

Chapter Seven

SINCE that far-off day when Saxeby stood over me and heard me spell out my first, independent reading exercise from the book of Kings I have read many books, mostly romances and chap-books, both French and English. Nearly every romance deals, in greater or lesser degree, with the business of love, but it seems to me that story-tellers cannot represent love as being anything other than a stormy, passionate emotion. It would seem that the love of Rebecca and Isaac strikes them as improbable. None of them ever try to present it as a warm current that flows on almost unnoticed for months, perhaps years, until the man and the woman are suddenly brought to realize that each is the most important part of the universe to the other.

This is the sort of love that Charlotte Lamotte and I found in each other, something of slow, unconscious growth that never stopped growing, even when we were hundreds of miles apart.

I can't write about our love as I should like to for if I could there would be little else in this account but Charlotte.

The figures of the men I met and rubbed shoulders with, men who, as Danton prophesied of himself, have even in this short interval left their names on the Pantheon of History, would have no more place in the story than chance pedestrians, passed almost unnoticed in the street. Writing about Charlotte, and trying to describe to strangers what she was like, and what we meant to one another then and since, is like trying to describe my deepest feelings for the few square miles around West-down. I could point to a clump of foxgloves, standing like guardsmen at ease among the green bracken stems of Hayes Wood, or to the steel-bright gleam of dew on a fresh-turned furrow in the Landslip Meadow, but these things are not Westdown but only a flash of the handful of jewels Nature scatters each day as a farmer's year unfolds.

In the same way I could point to some of the hundreds of tiny characteristics of Charlotte, to her slow, restrained smile, to the habit she had of drawing her brows together in a broad "V" whenever she pondered a trifling problem of workaday life about the house, to her utter steadfastness towards those she loved. But this would still be an utterly inadequate picture of the quiet, untroubled young woman who looked after our daily wants in the days before tragedy and desolation dulled the sparkle and stifled the effervescent gaiety of the house in the Cour de Turenne.

My love for Charlotte, like André's deep, fraternal respect for her, was passive and unrecognized by both of us for a long time. Charlotte was like many a good, rewarding thing in life, taken for granted until such time as the violent shock of external events threw her character into a high relief which seemed to make a background of terror and human misery much less significant. Then I saw it for the precious thing it unmistakably was, something that, for me at all events, reduced the scenes around us to the proportions of a dance on a marionette's stage. After that nothing that happened was able to shock, frighten or even depress me to the degree that I had been moved by the scenes witnessed inside the Tuileries. My brain and my memory absorbed the images presented by the turmoil of the ever-quickening drama of death played out in Paris, but the events lacked the power to move me except in relation to her, and to our future together.

It was as though, up to the moment we realized we loved one another, I had been only half-alive, that I had dreamed my boyhood and youth away in Devon and had even witnessed the wiping out of my family in a single night, in the mood of a bystander watching a procession in which he is not expected to take part. If this sounds unfeeling I cannot help it, for it is the plain truth.

On the first day of September news of the investment

of Verdun was published in the streets and its effect upon
the populace was salutary. To the already feverish
public mind was now added the stress of immediate defeat at the hands of the Prussians, and all the horror
and degradation of a foreign occupation. Men looked back
into the recent past and recalled with terror the parts,
big and small, they had played in the overthrow of the
monarchy, the expulsion of the nobles and the disestab-
lishment of organized religion.

The Revolution was less than four years old and the
common man was still near enough to feudalism to recall
the sanguinary penalties meted out to recalcitrant peasants. They recollected systematic hunting down and execution of casual poachers, mutilations for the slightest
infringement of the game laws, the monstrous inequalities of taxation which kept the peasant in a hovel and
the townsman in a slum, and they knew that there was
not one of them who had not openly rejoiced at the turn
of events that made them masters and the nobles despised exiles.

Nor were these fears of a restoration confined to the
lower classes. The Revolution had, for the first time in
the history of the nation, thrown open avenues of advancement to the middle classes, previously held back
by the place-hunters of the privileged. Out on the great
plain west of Paris men who had inherited the conditions
of mediaeval serfs were now tilling their own land,
wrenched from a corrupt Church or a *seigneur* who
spent two-thirds of his year fawning and intriguing at
Versailles. In Paris, and in all the great towns of the
departments, younger sons who would have lived their
lives as half-starved clerks and copyists were now making their way as advocates and independent merchants.
In the fourteen armies of the republic, volunteers who
would have been fortunate to aspire to a sergeant's cane
under the old régime were leading divisions in the field.

In a thousand Government offices up and down France
men were showing that a bureaucracy is only cumber-
some and inefficient so long as the men who staff it are
prevented from exercising imagination at their desks. All

these Frenchmen, and the bulk of their womenfolk, dreaded a return of a régime that showed by its manifestos that it had learned or forgiven nothing and, if it regained power, would clamp down even heavier shackles upon the will and energy of an imaginative people. The knowledge made them desperate and the measure of their desperation was the ammunition of the men who led them, men for whom, almost without exception, there could be no turning back.

The Jacobins reacted swiftly. No bad news was kept from the people. Every bulletin from the reeling armies at the frontiers was published in full and new volunteer battalions were flung into the gaps caused by the panic and desertion of their predecessors. The manufacture of arms and material was speeded up, women and children working through the intense summer heat in the chain of powder factories established in private cellars throughout the city. Having done everything possible to bolster up morale in the armies, the men of the Mountain turned to the danger from within—the supposed conspiracy of the royalists in the capital, many of whom were said to be plotting an insurrection in the crowded city jails.

There were many, and André was among them, who scoffed at the idea of such a rising and declared that the story was merely an excuse on the part of the extremists to destroy personal enemies and former political opponents under cover of the general panic, but it is just possible that some sort of conspiracy might have been hatched among a minority of the prisoners, all of whom were in the closest possible contact with one another owing to the inadequacy of cell-space and the veniality of many of the jailers.

If this is so then most of the guilty escaped, for the September massacres were among the most ill-planned haphazard acts of the Revolution. The majority of the victims were harmless old priests, terrified women and luckless young men unfortunate enough to attract suspicion during the brief interrogation that followed the inspection of the prison registers. This was all any of the victims had of a trial and a few quick-witted men seized the opportunity to justify themselves and obtain their immediate release.

Some ridiculous mistakes were made by the two hundred or so murderers hired by the Paris Commune. At one prison nearly a hundred common thieves, awaiting transfer to the galleys, were massacred as aristocrats. At another some prostitutes under detention were slaughtered side by side with the wives and daughters of fugitive noblemen.

The first I heard about the massacre was during midday meal on Sunday afternoon. I had been on duty at an arsenal all the morning and come in tired and thirsty soon after noon. Marcelle and André were out and Charlotte shared my cold luncheon, which we ate in customary silence. We were both too shy to converse unless a third person was present. We had almost finished our meal when we heard someone enter hurriedly through the *salon* door and stumble upstairs.

A moment later Papa Rouzet burst into the room like a thunderclap and stopped just inside the threshold, one hand clasping the door frame for support. I had never previously seen him out of countenance, but now his expression shocked me, for he looked as though he had run headlong into an apparition on the stairs.

His usually rubicund cheeks were grey and his mild blue eyes, always prominent, seemed to be starting from his head. He was trembling violently from head to foot and was greatly distressed from want of breath. His cotton shirt clung to him with perspiration and little streams of sweat had run down from under his peruke and beaded in the folds of his numerous chins.

Charlotte was the first to recover from the surprise caused by his entry. She jumped up, assisted him to a chair at the head of the table, and poured him a glass of brandy without asking a single question. He swallowed the liquor in a single gulp but it did not have much effect on him for he began drumming the table with his pudgy fingers and exclaiming, "My God! Oh, my God!" over and over again.

Charlotte took his hand and began petting him as though he were a terrified child.

"What is it, Papa? What's happened to you?"

He began then to stutter out his story, but so disjointedly that I was hard put to make sense of it at a single hearing.

He had been over the river to make arrangements for the delivery of soap and had called on a soap-boiler with whom he dealt in the rue St. Marguerite. He had finished his business about noon and was skirting the Abbaye Prison, in the direction of the church of St. Germain-des-Prés, when he saw a string of carriages approaching him, surrounded by a crowd of people who seemed to be conducting themselves in a most threatening manner towards the escort of National Guards which marched in loose formation on either side of the procession.

As the foremost carriage approached him it was brought to a halt by the surging mass of people converging on it from all sides. Papa Rouzet, who always believed in making himself scarce whenever violence threatened, tried to dodge through the alleys towards the Petit Marché but was prevented from doing so by the density of the crowd. Instead he was jammed willy-nilly against the harness poles of the leading coach and from this uncomfortable position was compelled to witness everything that took place.

Two or three of crowd clambered on to the driving box and threw the coachman to the ground, while the carriage escort, seeing themselves hopelessly outnumbered, formed into a group and jostled their way to a safe distance, where they stood with grounded arms and watched the mob tear open the carriage doors and pull the occupants, a party of surpliced priests, on to the *pavé*. The same thing happened to the passengers in the other carriages. Groups of men converged on the vehicles, shouldered guards and coachmen out of the way, and dragged the priests into the open.

In less than a minute most of the wretched prisoners had been hacked to death in front of Rouzet's horrified eyes. One or two of them made a show of resistance and one priest, ejected from the first coach, beat about him manfully with a heavy cane, but he only prolonged his sufferings and had his arm lopped off by a frenzied youth wielding a sabre. His blood spurted all over Rouzet, who became almost hysterical when he came to this part of the story and fell forward on the table groaning and burying his face in his hands.

Apparently only one priest was saved and he by the courageous action of another bystander, a working man who rushed under the raised scythe of one of the murderers and screamed out that this particular man was a good friend of the people and not to be confused with traitors and royalists. Rouzet saw a crowd collect round this man and hustle him towards the forecourt of the Abbaye. The remainder were cut down and murdered to the last man.

When at last he had freed himself from the exultant mob, Rouzet ran all the way home as fast as his short legs could carry him.

Charlotte administered another stiff glass of brandy and the old fellow began to calm a little, although he continued to call upon his Maker to witness the barbarity of the human race and his own craven cowardice in making no effort to oppose the butchery. For my own part I was thankful that he had kept his mouth closed, but I shared with him his admiration for the man who had spoken up for one of the priests and thereby undoubtedly saved his life. I found out later that night that the sole survivor of this massacre, a mere prelude for the butchery that continued all over Paris during the next four days and nights, was the Abbé Sicard, a man universally respected and loved by the poor of his section and a priest whose manifest sympathies with the people had not prevented him from refusing to swear an oath of fealty to the new order at the expense of all that he held sacred. The name of his heroic saviour was Moton, a watchmaker.

After half an hour or so the brandy began to have its effect upon Rouzet and the horror of the scene he had been forced to witness began to recede a little. He asked us where André and Marcelle were and confessed himself tortured with fears of their being exposed to the danger of the streets. In the next breath he spoke of getting Marcelle to contact Biron and have the deputies take instant retaliation on the murderers.

Neither Charlotte nor I knew where André was to be found, though we had an idea that Marcelle and her lover were spending the day in the country. Rouzet wheezed out a protest aimed at the young men of the Assembly: "What a time to be gathering blackberries in the country! This city is going mad, mad! Where will it end? That's what I should like to know, where will it end? Trade will be ruined before they have all finished with their devil's talk!"

Even the terror inspired in him by his recent experience could not blind Papa Rouzet to the commercial disadvantages of insurrection. He was a tradesman first and last and, for him, blood in the gutters could only mean less money in the till.

I got out my half-uniform and musket and told Charlotte I would go over to the Abbaye and see what was happening. I told her to tell André where I was if he happened to come in and to ask him to join me at the prison. I felt at the time that the more sober units of the civic guard might be useful in assisting the authorities to restore order. I had seen what an unrestrained mob could do at the Tuileries.

Charlotte warned me not to leave the house and I should have taken her advice. She was always right on these occasions and her instincts were worth a peck of male logic, but I went out nevertheless, after advising Rouzet to bolt the *salon* door and put the shutters up; he and Charlotte could watch for André and Marcelle at the window and direct them to go round to the back gate and wait for admittance into the yard.

Outside the streets seemed quiet enough and I had a good walk around noting that the majority of the theatres were still open and that groups of people were sunning themselves at the café tables, as though nothing out of the ordinary was afoot in the vicinity of the prisons.

I visited the Conciergerie first and found everything quiet and drowsy in the early evening sunlight. Then I turned west and went through the Cordelier district towards the St. Germain section and the Abbaye. I saw one or two groups of men marching about, but there was nothing unusual about that, as recruiting and drilling in the streets went on day and night at that time. I did remark, however, upon the brooding atmosphere of the city, as though at any moment the quiet might be shattered by the rumble of artillery caissons or the angry clamour of the tocsin, but this may have been a result of Rouzet's story, which had set my nerves on edge.

When I turned into the rue St. Marguerite, close to the scene of the attack on the carriages, I saw a sullen crowd of idlers hanging about exchanging rumours with one another. A respectable looking man in a beaver hat stopped me and said: "Have you heard about the risings in the prisons, citizen? Is it true that the royalists have massacred their jailers at the Conciergerie?"

I told him that I had just come from the Conciergerie and that everything was quiet and orderly over there.

He seemed relieved, but added: "There's been the devil to pay in the Abbaye. Citizen Maillard has just gone in with one of the deputies. Some of the Commune officials are already there; they'll give those damned traitors something to think about!"

His conversation was typical of the mood among ordinary citizens that evening. Terrified by the news of Verdun, and the advance of the Prussians, he had proved an easy prey to the spate of ridiculous rumours that the leaders of the Commune were putting about. He was certainly not one of the denizens of the St. Antoine alleys, I could gather that much from his attire and his speech, but he took care when addressing a man in the uniform of the National Guard to refer to everyone inside a prison as "a damned traitor." During the months that followed the Parisian learned to be artful about this sort of thing. It was always as well to give the impression that one was a wholehearted patriot for any error in this respect might lead to prescription and arrest on the chance report of a common informer. This man's attitude would have been unremarkable after the king's execution but it was not yet the general rule in street conversations. These had been free and easy enough when I had arrived in Paris.

I went up to the Abbaye forecourts, looking about for a sign of André but not seeing anyone I knew, or any other member of my battalion.

About an hour before dusk, when I was thinking of returning home, a postern of the Abbaye wall was flung open and an officer of the National Guard came out, anxiously scanning the crowd. He caught my eye and beckoned to me. I moved over to him reluctantly and he caught my arm and pulled me into the courtyard, slamming the postern behind him.

"Which section do you belong to?" he asked me.

I told him to the Cordelier battalion.

"Where are your comrades?" he asked sharply.

I explained that I had come up to the Abbaye unofficially on hearing of disturbances in the area.

"If I had fifty like you I might be able to do something," he muttered. "How do I know these people are acting on orders? There won't be a prisoner alive by morning!"

He looked about him distractedly. A dull, confused sound issued from the barred windows of the main building, the slamming of doors, shouts, cries and the continuous clatter of *sabots* on stone corridors.

I have seldom seen a man more worried and indecisive. He chewed his moustache and kept glancing nervously up and down the yard, as though at his wits' end what to do next.

"They burst in here waving a bit of paper with the Ministry of War's stamp on it," he went on, talking more to himself than to me, "turn the prison upside down and drag all the prisoners before their trumpery tribunal on capital charges! How do I know their authorization papers aren't forged? What does the commandant expect me to do about it?"

He had been going on in this strain for a minute or two, more, I suspect, because he was glad of someone to complain to than with any hope that I could be of assistance to him, when suddenly the air was rent with a single, piercing scream. It seemed to come from the direction of the inner courtyard, on the far side of the main block of buildings, and it went through my brain like a red-hot needle. The officer's nerve snapped. He whipped round on me and shouted: "Get inside and see what you can do, I'm going to the deputies for reinforcements!"

He set off at a run towards the postern and within a few seconds had disappeared, leaving me alone in the court with the echo of that scream ringing in my ears.

I obeyed his order blindly and, looking to the priming of my musket, crossed the open space and went in through the central arch of the prison. It was nearly dark now and the hall was dimly lit by a few pitch-pine torches, thrust into the brackets of the walls. The light evening breeze sweetened the dank odour of the prison and made the torches gutter, throwing distorted shadows on the rough surfaces of the walls and ceiling. It was like entering the portals of Hades.

Once inside the building the indeterminate sounds I had heard from the open became more distinct and individual. From the series of little corridors branching off the low-ceilinged chamber in which I stood came the constant clanging of heavy doors, and the echoing shouts of jailers calling one to another from various parts of the building. I did not care to explore the corridors so I stumbled on towards the far end of the hall, holding my musket at the ready and telling myself I was a fool not to have retreated into the streets with the officer or, better still, to have remained at home as Charlotte advised. It was, however, the memory of that scream which stirred my conscience, and kept me from bolting, and I crept gingerly across the foyer and into the bottleneck at the junction of two corridors, emerging presently at the top of a short flight of steps giving access to a sort of guard-room, much better lit than the entrance hall and crowded with men. I can recall every detail of the extraordinary scene that then presented itself.

On my immediate right was a trestle table littered with papers, bottles and long-stemmed pines. Behind it sat three men, two of them young and neatly dressed in some sort of semi-official uniform and the third elderly and in filthy rags. One of these judges was a tall young man with a sallow complexion and large, expressive eyes. He was dressed entirely in black, and before him was a thick ledger which I assumed to be the prison register. He was examining the book intently and ignoring his two companions, who were engaged in desultory argument.

Round the walls, on three sides of the room, were benches on which a number of men, a dozen or so at least, were sprawled, some of them fast asleep, and one or two in the final stages of intoxication. Their mouths were wide open and they snored like hogs, the snorts providing a discordant bass to the high-pitched buzz of general conversation. Muskets were stacked in various parts of the room and on each side of the little iron door, directly facing the arch by which I had entered, stood a sentinel with drawn sabre.

It was the aspect of the sentinels that first claimed my attention. Their clothes were confirmed to shirt and breeches, but both wore the cockaded slouch shako of the Sainte Antoine National Guard. Their shirts, hands and forearms were covered with blood.

After the half-light of the corridors the glare of the guardroom dazzled me, and it was a moment or two before I could see any signs of prisoners. Then I observed a middle-aged man held fast by two jailers on a bench in the corner and another man, who looked like a priest, standing in front of the young man with the register and attempting to argue with him. Nobody took the slightest notice of my entry and I was permitted to stand just inside the archway, gazing down at this strange tribunal.

The little priest in front of the table was waving a paper and shouting something about it being a recommendation from the Croize-Rouge section, but the young man with the sallow complexion did not appear to be listening to him for he stifled a yawn and waved his hand, which was apparently a signal to the two men on the door. Immediately they stepped forward and dragged the priest, still shouting, towards the door. As he struggled

he threw something on the table and I saw that it was a
rosary. It clattered down amongst the pipes and shattered
one of the bowls. Then the low iron door swung outwards
and a hellish uproar penetrated the room from the prison
garden immediately outside. I caught a glimpse of faces
and torches and the glint of weapons, and then the door
clanged again and the hubbub subsided a little. The man
in black signalled to the guards in the corner to bring
forward the next victim.

This man, far from shrinking from the ordeal, seemed
eager to comply with the summons, for he bounded in
front of the table and began to address the principal
judge in a high-pitched confident tone.

"I am accused of editing a royalist journal, accused
of recruiting royalist troops in the provinces; it is nonsense, nonsense!" he shouted.

"Prove it!" demanded the ragged judge. "Were you not
in the Tuileries shooting down the people on August 10th?"

"I was there under orders of my commanding officer,"
declared the prisoner. "Up to that day I was admittedly a
royalist but afterwards I refused to combat the Revolution
and threw up my commission. As soon as Louis vacated
the chateau I gave orders to cease fire. I could prove. . . ."

At this stage the tribunal was rudely interrupted. The
concierge ran into the room from another door on the left
of the judges and, addressing the young man in black,
declared that one of the prisoners was in the act of escaping up the chimney. At the same time a volley of shots
sounded from the corridor through which the concierge
had come. The sallow judge looked at him dully and
stifled another yawn.

"Light a fire under him," he ordered laconically, and
was turning back to the register when the spirited prisoner
facing him cried out:

"Gentlemen, I insist that you give me a proper hearing; I've never needed one more!"

This sally amused the judges and several other men
in the room who roared with laughter. The inordinate
volume of the laughter in relation to the joke, if a joke
was intended, made me think that it was not only the

prisoners who were suffering from hysteria. However he intended his remark to be taken, it was a fortunate one for the prisoner and probably saved his life. The flustered concierge disappeared and the principal judge looked up.

"Is there anyone here who can corroborate the prisoner's claim?" he asked.

One of the sentinels stepped forward.

"He's right, Citizen Maillard," he chimed in. "I saw him when we broke through at the Long Gallery and heard him order his section to cease fire!"

That clinched the matter and Maillard, the judge, abruptly removed his hat, an action immediately imitated by the other judges.

"Prisoner acquitted," he announced. "See that he has an escort to his home! Next!"

I suddenly saw my chance to get out of this dreadful place and crossed the room to take up position beside the officer. Still nobody commented upon my presence and the two sentinels flung open the iron door and all four of us passed into the garden, the guards taking care to precede the prisoner and announce the decision of the court to the crowd assembled outside. Before I was through the door, deafening shouts of *"Vive la nation!"* were set up and we were almost swept off our feet by a horde of the most villainous looking ruffians I have ever encountered.

Their enthusiastic embraces, of which I came in for a generous share, prevented me from seeing the court immediately, but when I did see it the impact of the spectacle made my senses reel. The enclosure, originally a flower garden, was a shambles that might well have shocked Beelzebub himself. Half-naked patriots, all of them smeared with blood, capered about the trampled flowerbeds waving cleavers, dungforks, pikes and half a hundred other improvised weapons. On one side of the court, stacked against the breast-high wall, was a pile of mangled corpses, half-covered with bloodstained rags. Cavorting on the summit of this hideous mound was a grey-haired woman, her tattered blouse open to the waist revealing a pair of skinny, repellent breasts, and beside her, perched on the wall, was an idiot boy with grotesquely twisted limbs, who flourished a girl's head impaled on a long length of iron railing.

I only had time to glance at this awful spectacle before I was half smothered by the frantic embrace of a half-naked ruffian with a patch over one eye and the longest, filthiest beard that ever disgraced a face. This wretch was more persistent than his comrades and every time I thrust him from me in disgust he returned to fling his brawny arms round my neck and roar *"Vive la nation!"* within an inch of my ear.

It occupied us the better part of five minutes to fight our way to the gate leading into the street for our group became the centre of a crazy demonstration of joy, presumably patriotic exultation over a sinner reclaimed into the ranks of liberty. The brutish ferocity of these people was only equalled by the apparent relief and fervour with which they greeted a reprieve. To this day I still think that most of them were either raving mad or hopelessly intoxicated. They pressed round us shaking the prisoner's hands and exhibiting every manifestation of joy, as though they were his relatives who had been anxiously awaiting news of a loved one's acquittal and not an assembly of wild beasts ready to hack a man to pieces if the verdict went against him.

At last we got into the street and one of the guards summoned a cab, of which there was a rank presumably detailed by the Commune to stand by for the purpose of conveying acquitted prisoners to their homes.

Our fortunate fellow, dazed by the uproar and his miraculous escape, allowed himself to be pushed inside and the two guards and I swiftly followed him. As the hackney moved forward, however, I saw my enthusiastic friend with the patch over his eye leap on to the step and shout something to the coachman. Apparently he could not bear to be parted from me so soon.

I don't remember very much of the drive as I was feeling violently sick, but I recall the refusal of the two sentinels to accept a gift of money from the prisoner when we at length deposited him at his home in the rue Crois-des-

Petits-Champs. We accepted a glass of brandy, however, of which I stood in desperate need. When the coachman turned his vehicle to go back I mumbled something about being late for duty at the Cordelier Club and, without waiting for an answer, dived into the nearest alley and ran off at top speed, not caring which direction I took in my eagerness to get away.

I had not gone far, however, before I heard running footsteps close behind me. I stopped and pressed myself into an angle of the wall. My heart was beating violently and I still wrestled with an overwhelming desire to vomit. Then a voice I recognized shouted my name and I stepped out of the deep shadow and came face to face with André. He had stripped beard and patch from his face and stood there in his rags, clasping my hands and calling my name over and over again.

I think it was the immense relief of seeing him in those circumstances that caused me to break into wild, uncontrollable laughter. André didn't laugh, he knew that I was only giving way to hysteria, and he waited quietly until I had sufficiently recovered myself to speak. I didn't suppose for an instant that his presence at the Abbaye, in that ridiculous disguise, meant that he had joined in the slaughter of those wretched people. I knew instinctively that there was an explanation that harmonized with his freakish outlook on life, and I was right, for by this time I knew André reasonably well. My guess was that this new prank of his was simply another aspect of that streak in his character that demanded public attention. It accounted for his foppery at a period when fine clothes were the label of the counter-revolutionary and it explained his methodical pricking of the bubbles of self-esteem blown out by Deputy Biron and his associates. Tonight it had driven him to witness scenes that must have revolted a man of his sensibilities.

He would not have admitted as much, even to himself, and was ready with an explanatory half-truth. He told me that he had heard of the impending massacres earlier in the day and had determined, in partnership with one or two of his former Medical School colleagues, to do his utmost to snatch a life or two from the bludgeons and pikes of the Commune's assassins. It was a hazard characteristic of a man who would have jumped, fully dressed, into the Seine to rescue a cat.

I never found out what he actually achieved by aping the most bloodsthirsty of that gang of cut-throats in the Abbaye gardens, but I learned afterwards that several persons were indeed spirited out of the prison before they had been summoned to the guardroom. One of these medical students—André himself perhaps—intervened to save the life of the sixteen-year-old daughter of the Duchess of Tourzel, the Dauphin's governess. I like to think of André and one or two other bold spirits risking their lives in that charnal house while the rest of Paris kept their doors closed and didn't condemn the massacres until they were all over.

We walked home together through the silent streets. The moon had risen and the air was balmy and I wondered how many Parisians, sound asleep in their beds at that hour, were aware of the frightful scenes that were being enacted at La Force, the Abbaye, the Conciergerie and elsewhere. Danton knew but did nothing. He claimed afterwards that he was powerless to intervene but that wasn't true. He was the one man in Paris that week who could have checked the slaughter. Some of the patrician Girondists knew but for one reason or another, perhaps a secret hope that the extremists would weaken themselves in the Assembly by such excesses, they preferred to register no protest until it was all over. Marat, the thunder and lightning journalist, knew, had possibly planned the coup and recruited the murderers. Men like Rouzet and the elderly man in the beaver hat I encountered knew but they feared for their own skins, and how could I blame them when I myself had actually witnessed the butchery and was even now thanking my stars that I had escaped with nothing more than an indelible impression of horror on my memory? Nothing, literally nothing, would have persuaded me to return to the Abbaye that night; I would have as soon blown out my brains with the loaded musket that swung from my shoulder.

Yet André went back, not only that night but every night until the savagery was brought to a standstill for lack of victims. If there had been a thousand men like André in Paris that summer we should never have heard of ice-hearted egotists like Robespierre, or wretches like the infamous Carrier and Joseph Le Bon who, so they tell me, are now slaughtering thousands helpless men and women in Paris and the provinces. The Revolution would have passed into history as an event of great and enduring significance. It would have been ranked as one of mankind's finest achievements instead of the confused era of bloodshed and party strife that journalists and politicians are labelling it today. There never are enough men like André in any national upheaval, they are always eliminated by the cruel and the greedy, and sometimes by the ignorant and passionate who may be cruel and greedy without knowing it.

Whenever I think of André I always apply to him a remark he made respecting Lafayette, a man whom he consistently admired. When we heard that Lafayette had abandoned the struggle for moderation and been taken prisoner by the Austrians whilst attempting flight, André said: "There is always a Lafayette, David, and the same fate invariably overtakes him; he gets gobbled up in the second year of the Revolution!"

André wouldn't come any farther than the back gate of No. 12 with me, but commanded me to hold my tongue about having met him in the Abbaye. When I protested that Papa Rouzet and Charlotte would be most anxious on his behalf, he said jocularly: "Tell them I'm on duty over at Vincennes. I'll turn up again and I promise I won't bloody the parlour carpet!"

With that he turned away and directed his steps towards the river. I guessed that he was going down to the Conciergerie and I admired him enormously, but without wanting to walk by his side.

There was a light in Charlotte's room above the kitchen so I threw up a handful of gravel and presently her grave face appeared for an instant at the window. A moment later she unbarred the back door and let me into the mixingroom. I was never more glad to see anybody in my life.

Chapter Eight

By noon on Monday news of the massacres was all over Paris and a sort of shamefaced fear hung over the city like an autumn fog.

I broke my promise to André and told Charlotte where he had been that night. She wasn't much surprised, knowing his true character a good deal better than any of us, but we agreed to say nothing to Rouzet or Marcelle for fear that either of them should attempt to find him and expose him to the danger of recognition. He might have justified himself satisfactorily but Charlotte and I had a conviction that this might be even more dangerous, for we felt certain that the day would come when men would go to any lengths to disavow their share in the September massacres. We told Rouzet that he was in charge of a recruiting centre at Vincennes and would be absent from the house for several days.

Rouzet shook off the horror of the scene he had witnessed a good deal more easily than I was able to wipe from my memory that fleeting glance of the mound of corpses in the Abbaye garden. I have since noted that the man who gives way to a shock at the time he experiences it usually regains a carefree frame of mind more rapidly than a person like myself who fights to repress his natural emotions. In less than twenty-four hours Rouzet was going blithely about his business, humming as he shaved his customers and cracking his customary spate of feeble jokes about pimples and pockcraters on the lather-crusted faces of his patrons. I was less fortunate. Later on I was to witness so many similar scenes in Paris that my fibres toughened and I could witness an execution without a qualm, but nowadays I suffer more from my recollections of the horrors than I did from witnessing the events themselves, and I can never be sure of lying down to sleep

without the prospect of waking in the grip of a night-
mare.

After Charlotte had let me in she made me some broth
and carried it up to my room where we talked through the
remainder of the night. It was only the second time we
had exchanged anything but small talk and I think it
wasn't long before we became aware of our affection for
one another.

I had to tell somebody what I had witnessed at the Abbaye and I told her, then and there, whilst she sat on the
end of my couch watching me sip the basin dry. I said
the events of the night had determined me to leave Paris
and attempt the journey to Virginia, no matter what risks
I ran from the frigates' press-gangs. I was sick of the ugly
scenes and stench of a city where, it seemed to me, the
mass of ordinary, decent citizens were rushing downhill
with the impetus of the Gadarene swine. I don't think
my decision surprised her. She must have sensed long
since that I was a bred-in-the-bone countryman who could
never settle permanently in the stuffy confines of a town,
and that night I told her of my brief but recurring bouts
of homesickness for Devon, of the smell of the sea on the
plateau, and the leafy solitudes of Hayes Wood in high
summer, where the bracken grew waist high and the foxgloves reared themselves out of pools of sunlight. I told
her something of the satisfaction a man feels when he
strides, with sweeping scythe, among his own wheat stalks
and of the pleasant ache that steals over every muscle of
his body when winter dusk is falling and the cattle are
being herded down the lanes towards the byre.

I had never been able to talk about these things to
André, much as I had grown to love and admire him, but
I found her the most sympathetic listener in the world.
She smiled when I confessed that smells and sounds and
sensations that I had taken as much for granted as the
changing seasons had returned to me in the form of rich
and vivid experiences since I had crept out of the badger's
earth on the Landslip and headed north for Captain Muttford's five-guinea passage. The pungent smell of a bonfire
on a vegetable patch behind the court made me long for

the smell of my own burning weeds in Ten Acre and Short Paddock. I yearned to grip the smooth handles of the plough again, to see the red Devon earth cleave under the share, to hear the shrill wail of the gulls hovering just above my head as they fought over the worms in the furrows. She listened with close attention. It was odd that Charlotte should have understood these longings so well. I don't suppose she had even spent more than a day or two in the country and the area around her original home, in north-east France, was devoted more to industry and agriculture. Yet somehow I felt sure that she had the instincts of a countrywoman and I had the impression that she would applaud my decision to strike out for a grant of land in the republic across the Atlantic. But I was not prepared for the unresponsiveness of her tone and the bleakness of her expression when I told her that I meant to put my decision into immediate effect and confessed how glad I would be to leave streets and houses behind and find somewhere I could breathe fresh air once again.

"Paris wasn't always like you found it," she said at length. "Once we had jolly times here, Papa, André and little Marcelle when she was just a child. It all seems a long time ago now, but things were different then I can tell you. Everyone in this court was neighbourly and no one who was ever sick, or going through hard times, went short of food to eat or logs to burn."

I thought of the stories I had heard about the miseries of all but the rich and powerfully connected under the monarchy, but Charlotte went on:

"They'll tell you we were groaning under a despotism and how they took all our money in taxes and spent it on banquets and fêtes out at Versailles; they'll say we had famines every winter and thousands of people here hadn't a roof to their heads or a shirt to their backs. Well, that's true enough, but it's also true now; the Revolution hasn't changed that sort of thing and never will. It's a part of life everywhere and you won't get rid of it by throwing everyone who owns anything into prison just because they don't agree with you. I've heard so much talk in this house and what does it amount to when you render it down? Every word uttered here isn't worth a single turnip from one of your fields. You can't eat proclamations and decrees and constitutions. The things that grow are all that matter to most of us!"

It reminded me of my mother to hear her talk like that. André would have told her that even a nation of peasants needs a social organization to govern it, and Marcelle, of course, would have called Charlotte's simple philosophy the creed of a serf, but at that time it made good sense to me, nothwithstanding Saxeby's cautiously imparted Whig politics and Tom Paine's warm gospel of reasonableness. I had been in Paris less than two months and I had already had enough liberty to tide me over the rest of my life. All I wanted now was to find some land I could farm without excisemen setting torch to my premises or the sovereign people slaughtering helpless old men in front of my eyes. This was before I actually talked to Paine. I was only twenty and I had a good deal to learn. The wants and needs of common folk seem modest enough if you think them over and jot them down on a piece of paper, but they aren't as simple to attain or, once attained, to keep and develop. Maybe they will become so one day, but not in my lifetime, or in my children's either. Even Charlotte, who always looks everything squarely in the face, had this lesson to learn as she sat on the end of my bed and poured scorn on the clumsy, well-meaning efforts of men like Biron and all the other fine fellows who came tumbling up from the south to build a grand new world.

We must have been talking for the better part of an hour, but I didn't notice the time, it was so restful and pleasant to sit with a person like Charlotte after all I had experienced since supper. She was about the best medicine I could have had and by the time Rouzet was astir, and I heard him taking down the shutters, I felt much better and ready for a good sleep.

I kicked off my boots and began to rearrange the bed. Charlotte was looking tired also and I advised her to go to her room and lie down after she'd given Papa his coffee. She said she would, but remained standing by the open door and I couldn't undress in front of her so I removed my tunic and stock and stretched myself out.

Suddenly she said: "David!"

I was half-asleep by that time but the urgency of her tone made me sit up again. She was still standing near the door and I noticed that her cheeks and neck were flushed. It was the first time I ever saw Charlotte blush, and the high colour made her look younger and prettier than I would have believed possible.

"I want you to promise me something. I haven't any right to ask it, none of us have, but I'm going to ask you nevertheless."

I said wondering: "What is it, Charlotte?"

"Don't make up your mind to go simply because of last night. Stay a while longer—stay until New Year."

"Why?"

She looked disconcerted and fumbled with the door latch.

"Things may get better," she went on lamely. "Maybe last night's happenings will make the deputies take some action to keep order. . . ." She broke off and added: "I find this difficult to say, David."

I don't know why but when she said that I felt a great tenderness for her. Up to that moment I had always seen Charlotte as a person able to maintain complete command of herself but now she was trembling and miserably ill at ease. Her acute embarrassment made her seem weak and helpless.

I climbed off the bed and crossed the room, taking her by the hand, which was cold as a stone. She sat down on the end of the bed again, blushing more than ever. I had an idea that she and Rouzet had been having words over the family's budget and jumped to the idiotic conclusion that she wanted to ask me to pay more rent but found it difficult to put into words.

"You'd better tell me what you've got in mind, Charlotte," I pressed her. "You've been kind to me, all of you here, and I'd do anything I could to help. Is it money?"

I said it clumsily but I meant well. I had about ten guineas left but if Rouzet's family were badly in need of money I had a vague idea that there were methods of getting some from Saxeby, if it would only mean going to Honfleur and finding Captain Muttford. I guessed that he was making at least two runs a week and would have been ready enough to bring me a sum on commission.

I'd made a bad mistake, however, for Charlotte blazed up immediately and this time she was flushed with anger.

"Good God," she exclaimed, "is that all you know about me? To suppose I should come to you begging? Are you blind as well as stupid, you English? Can't you see what's going to happen to us all before long?"

I must have looked foolish and wretched and I began to stutter out some sort of apology, but I'd hardly said a word when her anger evaporated and she smiled, all her embarrassment and hesitancy disappearing in a flash.

"Poor David," she murmured, "you haven't nearly enough subtlety for a Frenchwoman. A Frenchman would have understood long ago!"

"Understood what?" I growled.

At that she laughed openly. "I wonder what Marcelle would do with you? One walk in the dusk with her and we should have you taking ship to America in the morning."

I didn't see what Marcelle had got to do with it and said so. When I had asked her to sit down and tell me what was worrying her I was convinced that Rouzet had been overspending, or that some member of the family was in serious trouble of one sort or another, but now it seemed to me that she wasn't worried at all but amusing herself at my expense. I hadn't one jot of previous experience with women and a man like me doesn't know these things instinctively. All my life I had been accustomed to plain speaking and Charlotte's sudden lack of it made me a little sullen.

I said to her: "If you want anything from me why don't you speak out plainly. You people are the only friends I've ever had apart from Saxeby and if I can help you I will, so long as I know what you want, but I can't be of service to you so long as you won't speak out!"

She suddenly took both my hands in hers and pulled

me round facing her. Her eyes were shining and even my
ill-humour couldn't prevent me from thinking how pretty
she looked in her spotless fichu and plain muslin dress.

She said: "Even Marcelle would be shocked at what
I'm going to say, David, but Marcelle's a born coquette
and would never hold up her head again if she got a
serious rebuff. I'm not like her, I wish I was but I'm not
and that's why I don't mind you knowing that I can't bear
to think of you going away from us. It's really very simple.
I'm in love with you, David."

It was said quietly and without the slightest calculation
for effect. I stared at her incredulously, unable to believe
I had heard her correctly. Up to that moment I had
admired her innumerable qualities, her common sense,
efficiency, cooking, but mainly the way she took the whole
family under her wing and let them prattle their heads off
whilst she went quietly about the business of running the
home. In my heart there was already a warmth for her
in excess of that which I felt for André and I believe also
that, from time to time, I had often thought her handsome
and desirable as a woman and had noted her serene sort
of beauty in such contrast to Marcelle's pink and white
prettiness. For all that I had never, in my wildest speculations, supposed that I was anything more to her than
an inoffensive lodger in the house, a mere hanger-on of
the sparkling André, who paid for his board regularly and
slept, contentedly enough, on two crates and a straw palliasse in a stockroom. Perhaps I had been too busy absorbing my new experiences and watching the changing
pattern of the Revolution in the streets. Perhaps, in ordinary times, I might have noticed her looking at me in
her pensive way, or performing a hundred and one little
services for me over and above her routine duties as hos-
tess. I daresay many another man might have noticed
these things but I didn't, not until this moment, when her
simple declaration filled me with a measure of joy and
well-being that is impossible to put on paper. I knew then
that I loved Charlotte as simply and sincerely as she
wanted to be loved and that I could never, under any circumstances, leave the city without her, or leave knowing

that she, or the three people she watched over so stead-fastly, were in trouble or distress. I knew also all she had been trying to say to me for the last ten minutes and why a look of alarm had shown in her eyes the moment I told her I had made up my mind to go.

I didn't reply to her directly, there was no need, I simply took her in my arms and kissed her eyes and mouth and hair, speaking her name over and over again and wondering what I had done to deserve such a privilege. All the sombre events of the past few weeks, from the night I had struggled up the goyle with young Bat in my arms, to the silent walk through the streets beside André with the horrors of the Abbaye garden fresh in my mind, had no power to dull the sparkle of that moment and we remained in each other's arms as the sun climbed over the jumble of chimneypots of the rue l'Ecole de Médecine and filtered through the branches of the elm tree outside my window.

We heard Papa Rouzet come up from the *salon* and plod along the corridor towards the kitchen shouting *"Lottë! Lottë!"* in expectation of his early morning litre of coffee. Outside in the court other shutters rattled and tradesmen's carts began to trundle down towards the quays. Rouzet called again, more loudly this time, and Charlotte slipped from my embrace, smiling.

"Do we tell Papa now, Charlotte?" I asked.

She shook her head. "Not yet, David, wait until André comes home and there isn't so much to think about."

I could hardly bear to let her go, even for an hour. There was so much to talk about now and to plan. A dozen half-formed schemes raced through my bewildered brain: our marriage, a farm in the provinces, money from Saxeby, consultation with Rouzet and André about leaving Paris and settling elsewhere until better times. But Rouzet, surprised at not finding Charlotte at work in the kitchen by the time he had unlocked the shop, and probably supposing that her absence had something to do with last night's disturbances, was now hammering at the door. Charlotte slipped from the room and called to him from the stairhead. I heard him come down and they went into

the kitchen together, Rouzet grumbling, Charlotte soothing.

I undressed and lay down on the mattress, meaning to
relive the bliss of the last hour in the way young people
in love have done since the beginning of time, but a day
and a night without rest proved too much for me and I
was soon sound asleep, remaining so until Charlotte gently
awakened me and whispered, between kisses, that my
supper was waiting.

Chapter Nine

WE didn't say anything to the other members of the household at any time. All that week the disorders continued until, on the Thursday, there was an uproar about it in a private session of the Convention. Although the Commune was able to justify itself the members thought it judicious to call off its assassins and destroy all the available evidence. Even now reports of what actually took place at the Abbaye, Conciergerie, La Force, and elsewhere are, I believe, obscure and contradictory. One version puts the total number of victims as high as ten thousand but this is a ridiculous figure; probably fifteen hundred is nearer the mark.*

I daresay Charlotte and I would have told Rouzet we were in love and asked his permission to marry if we had been given an opportunity of discussing the matter with him alone, but the opportunity was never forthcoming, for Marcelle's friends started coming to the house again on the Monday evening and from then on the parlour was crowded with deputies and their hangers-on. Those of the Brissotins who were not frequent guests of the Rolands used our premises as a sort of social headquarters and Biron did quite a lot of his writing there. None of us ever got to bed until the small hours and Charlotte and I were lucky if we snatched ten minutes' privacy together in my room or in the kitchen.

André looked in on Tuesday night but was gone again within an hour. He told me he was over at the Temple and I thought he was showing signs of great strain. His eyes were red from lack of sleep but he still displayed

---

* In the light of subsequent research, David's guess is a fairly accurate one. The total announced by contemporary royalist historians is considered to have been exaggerated.

plenty of that nervous energy which he possessed in such abundance. He wore his National Guard uniform when he entered the house. I suppose he had changed out of his bloodstained rags at the lodging of one of his friends. He winked at me over a glass of Rouzet's burgundy but he didn't say anything in front of the others, although Biron and Louvet were discussing the massacres at the time and condemning the Jacobins out of hand.

I have since heard the Provincial deputies criticized for their supposed part in this horrible business and the fact that nearly all these deputies were themselves hunted down the following year has been pointed out as a just retribution upon them. This is plain nonsense. I knew Biron, Louvet, Buzot, Barbaroux and many of the others very well and not one of them would have countenanced such acts, or failed to make every effort to stop them had they been forewarned. The fact is that the massacres were over before they passed from the sphere of street-corner rumour into that of undisputed fact. If the Brissotins were at fault at all it was because they kept their noses too close to the classics, and the elegant speeches they were constantly preparing, to realize what was going on around them. Even so, I doubt very much if they were sufficiently powerful at that time to have brought the leading Jacobins to justice, for that was what public reprobation would have entailed. They had a numerical majority in the Convention but that didn't count for much for their cultured voices were always lost in Danton's leonine roar and Marat's shrill ravings. The real power of the Revolution was vested in the Paris Commune, not in the Assembly of elected representatives. As time went on the Convention came to mean less and less and Danton's Committee of Public Safety more and more, until it was sufficiently powerful to bring down every man who inclined towards mercy and compromise.

If I have so far given the impression that the Revolution was nothing but a series of demonstrations by an armed and vicious mob, I have done less than justice to a great people. The two instances of barbarity I actually witnessed in the summer of '92 were perpetrated under the shadow of foreign invasion. The attack on the Tuileries, although staged by the lowest and most ignorant section of the people of Paris, was a rough and ready military operation up to the minute the mob gained entry, and, as I have pointed out, the Federal Volunteers, who bore the brunt of the fighting, did their best to mitigate the barbarous treatment meted out to the survivors of the garrison.

The final overthrow of the monarchy, and the scrapping of the once-popular Constitution of '91, would never have occurred had foreign princes, alarmed for their own thrones and encouraged, to a certain extent by the queen, allowed the new Government of France a breathing space in which tempers might well have cooled and Louis been given a chance to consolidate his brief popularity as a constitutional sovereign. This was rendered impossible by the arrogant threats of the *émigrés* and their champion, the Duke of Brunswick. The latter's proclamation, more than any other factor, was responsible for the wave of panic that inspired the September massacres.

All this is now history and I only re-state it because, to my mind, the peoples of Europe, and more particularly those of Great Britain, are being gravely misled by statesmen and journalists, most of whom have never set foot in France, much less witnessed the Revolution at close range as I did. The impression that the overthrow of the old régime was accompanied by violent repressions and indiscriminate slaughter was current in England even before I set foot in Paris. I remember being vaguely surprised by the general air of good humour and absence of violence during the first few days I walked the streets. Up to that time, there had been comparatively little bloodshed and even the royal family's attempted flight, which badly frightened the Paris population, had occasioned little more than demonstrations. Once the king had put his signature to the constitution most people thought the Revolution was over, and so it might have proved if the new France had been left to settle its own affairs. As it was things went from bad to worse and for the greater part of the time that I spent in Paris subsequent to the September massacres the city was in the grip of men who were either dominated by the scum of the city, centralized in the authority of the Commune, or tossed this way and that by individual fanatics, like Danton and later still, Maximilien Robespierre, a dry, humourless little lawyer animated by ruthless egotism.

The guillotine has become symbolic of the French Revolution. To read accounts in current English journals and newspapers one would suppose that "the national razor" (as Barère, one of the Jacobins, dubbed the instrument) has been working day and night, from the fall of the Bastille in July, 1789, to the present day. The guillotine was not erected in Paris until April, '92, a month or so before I arrived, and the first public execution I witnessed was that of the king, in the following January. After that Executioner Sanson was more heavily engaged, and is still busy if the newspapers are to be trusted, but the real Terror did not commence until all the Moderates were out of the way and the field was clear for scoundrels like Couthon, Billaud-Varennes, Barère, Lebas, Carrier and, of course, their figurehead, Robespierre, who is not the bloodthirsty beast he is supposed to be, but a sober, fussy little man, whose inhumanity springs from a fixed belief that he is the predestined high priest of the new god Reason.

Two important events occurred in mid-September. The tide of invasion was checked and turned back at the Battle of Valmy in the Ardennes, and Tom Paine arrived in Paris to take his seat in the Convention, to which he had been elected by the Pas-de-Calais department. I predict that the first of these events will have a strong influence on the future of Europe; the second had a relatively important effect upon me.*

The unexpected defeat of the Prussians by General Kellerman eased the tension in the capital and set the patriots capering with joy. Bonfires were lighted in the

---

* Another intelligent observation. The victory of the French at Valmy shaped the course of European history for the next twenty years.

streets and victory salutes boomed monotonously from the parks and arsenals. Deputies embraced one another at the foot of the tribune and strangers saluted one another in the streets. On the very day of the announcement of victory Tom Paine, outlawed by his native country, arrived in Paris and took lodgings at White's Hotel, in the rue de Petit Pères, an establishment frequently by the few English-speaking residents of Paris most of whom were Americans.

I was very eager to set eyes on Paine and keenly anticipated the pleasure of hearing him speak. Old Saxeby, from whom I had learned almost everything I knew of the public affairs of my own country, regarded him as a saint and hero and his book *The Rights of Man* had made a great impression upon me although, at first reading, I don't think I understood more than a third of its contents.

As soon as I heard of his arrival I went over to White's and hung about outside, watching the ebb and flow of distinguished people who flocked to make the acquaintance of this famous Englishman.

Paine couldn't speak a word of French and several of his friends, men like Brissot and Condorcet, whom he had met during his previous visit to France; acted as interpreters. There were so many people passing in and out of the foyer on that occasion that I realized it would be impossible to make myself known without an introduction, yet I guessed that Paine himself would probably be pleased to hear news of an old acquaintance like Saxeby and might even enjoy an opportunity to dispense with the tedious services of an interpreter. Accordingly I sought out Marcelle and asked her to get me an interview with Deputy Pétion, then the Girondist Mayor of Paris and a known sponsor of Paine.

Marcelle, always eager to display the extent of her influence with people of importance, readily complied and forty-eight hours later I was being shown into Pétion's lobby at the Hotel de Ville, where I took my place among a string of petitioners seeking audience with the mayor.

I had a long wait but the time passed quickly for the

petitioners and their suits proved a source of considerable amusement and interest.

On my left was a garrulous old man with a wooden leg who declared that he had sacrificed his limb at the taking of the Bastille and was now seeking a compensatory pension. He talked to me scornfully of the part played in that great event by now-celebrated people like Camille Desmoulins, who had gathered all the credit to themselves by the simple expedient of talking and writing ceaselessly of their own valour, whereas heroes like himself, who had swung an axe at the drawbridge chains had been left to hobble about the streets and scrape the garbage boxes for sustenance.

"To hear some of the prattle in the cafés," he grumbled, "one would suppose that half Paris was concerned in the business. How many were there all told? A hundred maybe, a hundred and fifty at the most, with ten thousand others bawling for the commandant's head just out of long musket range! I tell you, citizen, it makes an old soldier vomit! Even Capet would have seen that I got something to lay by for my old age if I'd come by this stump on one of his battlefields. Glory was all I got out of it, glory and a pot of bad beer from Santerre the brewer, who managed to earn himself a general's epaulettes by setting fire to a few dung-carts and making a smokescreen that spoiled our marksmanship!"

He went on grousing and thumping the leather kneepad of his stump until his turn came and he was ushered into the mayor's office. I don't know whether he ever got his pension but I doubt it, for Paris was full of legless and armless men who were supposed to have left their limbs in the Bastille ditch. If even half their stories were true there would have been no need to sever the drawbridge chains, the people could have stormed up to the grille on a rampart composed of the fallen.

On my right was a very different peitioner, a young girl whose brother was now in the prison St. Pélagie awaiting trial as an accomplice of the traitor Lafayette. According to the girl her brother had been selected to carry Lafayette's unsuccessful appeal for a counter-revolution to an outlying corps, whose commander happened to be an earnest Jacobin. Her brother, she declared, had been arrested and sent to Paris on the strength of this man's denunciation, despite the fact that by delivering the manifesto he was only carrying out the orders of his superior officer in the field. She was here with a petition on her brother's behalf, signed by over a hundred residents of their section. I hope she succeeded in getting Pétion to authorize the young soldier's release for if he was still in prison when the Brissotins fell from power his execution would have been a certainty.

I talked to one or two other people in the anteroom, an old woman with a grievance against men of the Sainte Antoine National Guard, who had helped themselves to her fruit in the Palais Royal and gone off without paying, even with paper money. There was a Creole from Martinique awaiting the mayor's signature on his credentials for a trading mission to Portugal, and an eccentrically dressed old Basque who claimed to have invented a new sort of captive balloon which would, if adopted and turned out in numbers, enable detailed observation of enemy behind the lines on all the republican fronts. I didn't have to wait very long in that lobby to discover why men like Pétion were always overtaken by the rush of events. They were the natural prey of every crank and complainant in the country and it made me think there is a great deal to be said against the system of granting free access to the great by the humblest in the land. This is laudable in theory but it means that the real business of government will soon be submerged in a welter of pettifogging private concerns.

At last I was admitted into Pétion's office and found him readily receptive to my request. He was a pleasant, intelligent man, handsome, like nearly all the Brissotins, but inclined to overdress and affect a mincing elegance. He spoke good English with a slight lisp and asked me how I came to be in Paris and what I thought of the Revolution. I told him I was a fugitive—that part of my story was always acceptable to all classes of republicans—but I was non-commital in my political outlook. I was already learning the art of fence-squatting and saying nothing in long speeches and I became very adroit at it as time went on. Maybe that is how I managed to stay alive.

Pétion wrote me an introduction to Paine and promised to mention my presence to him that evening. He kept his promise, which I thought quite remarkable in view of the demands made upon him that day, and I went home to persuade Charlotte to leave Marcelle to cook supper for her friends and to spend the evening walking with me in the Tuileries Gardens, which had been considerably tidied up since the business of August 10th.

We spent a pleasant two hours in there and I made her laugh describing the people I had met in Pétion's anteroom. Even a city convulsed with revolution can be a pleasant background for young people in love. We saw many couples there, walking with arms round one another's waists or lying full-length on the grass plots between the shrubberies, interested in nothing but each other and behaving as though they didn't care an old pair of shoes whether the Convention was dominated by the Jacobins or the Emperor of Cathay. Charlotte and I talked about getting married and settling down on a farm as though the future was as rosy for us as it promised for the children of the Golden Age.

Looking back it is difficult to reconcile the promenaders of those warm September evenings in the Tuileries and Luxembourg gardens with the frenzied assemblies of patriots soon to gather in the Place de la Révolution and roar *"Vive la nation!"* every time the axe clanked down. Yet these people were the same, today enjoying the evening sunlight in the gardens, tomorrow lining the pavements and windows of the rue St. Honoré and witnessing, without pity, the evening processions to the scaffold.

During the first days of the Terror I used to watch the faces of the crowd when I was on duty in the Place, or along the route between Pont Neuf and rue Royale. Sometimes I saw evidence of honest exultation but more often a stony indifference or that satisfied smugness that occasionally shows in the features of a man who thanks his stars that he is a witness and not an actor in a street drama. Pity I never saw, not because the average Parisian is incapable of feeling for the men and women in the tumbrils, but because pity for the condemned is treason against the people and no man could be sure of the men standing next to him in the crowd. I learned a good deal about human nature on those occasions but I also learned a simple lesson in the art of government and the lesson was this: However noble the end, nothing can justify terror as a means, for terror crushes the spirit and in its shadow no man will speak the truth, not even to himself. He learns to lie with his eyes as well as his tongue.

I have good reason to know how degrading this form of self-deception can become, for more than twenty months I practised it myself.

The next day I called at White's Hotel and sent the janitor up to Paine's suite with Pétion's letter. He was only gone about five minutes and when he came downstairs he was closely followed by a tall, broadshouldered man, aged about fifty-five. I saw at a glance that the middle-aged man was Paine; he had an expression of benevolence and integrity that I had never seen in the features of another.

He was well above normal height and carried himself with a slight stoop. His dress was neat and well tailored but without a trace of dandyism or ostentation. He walked with the light step of a much younger man and wore his hair queued, with lightly powdered side-curls, that made him look vaguely old-fashioned in a city where this style of hairdressing was years out of date.

His features were unusual without being distinguished by the authoritative good looks of his old leader George Washington. He had a very large nose that only just escaped ugliness and his chin was firm and obstinate without being aggressive. I later saw several portraits of Paine but none of them did full justice to the philosopher's singularly brilliant eyes, which were large, piercing and full of alert intelligence. When he spoke Paine always looked at his audience squarely but one was never conscious of the embarrassment that so often accompanies a frank stare.

He never raised his voice and his manners were as mild and forbearing as those of a humble village parson so that, once his eyes were fixed on you, it was impossible to doubt the sincerity of anything he said. I don't think Paine could have told a successful lie, or ever did, throughout the whole of his life.

He advanced into the foyer and looked about him, interrogatively. When the janitor pointed me out his face lit up with a generous, welcoming smile and he crossed to where I stood, extending his hand and seizing mine in an exceptionally powerful grip.

"Mr. Treloar—Saxeby's postman?—My dear young fellow, I can't say how pleased I am to see you!"

I wasn't prepared for such cordiality and must have betrayed my surprise for he threw a reassuring arm about my shoulders and ushered me up the short flight of stairs to the first floor, where he occupied two pleasant rooms, now strewn with baggage, books and newspapers. The larger room had a little balcony looking out on the rue Petit Pères and it was here that he seated me in a comfortable armchair while the porter brought in some excellent coffee which Paine himself served. He showed me the courtesy he might have accorded President Washington or the British Ambassador.

"Come now," he began, as soon as we were settled, "how did you get here, how long are you staying, how was that scamp Saxeby when you last saw him and what do you think of affairs in Paris? Bless my soul, you'd hardly believe what a pleasure it is to ask questions in English and know that they will be answered in a tongue I can understand. I shall never learn French now, I'm too old. Foreign languages must be learned in the nursery or not at all and when Joel isn't about me I'm hard put to find the way to the toilette!"

The "Joel" he referred to, was Joel Barlow, whom I afterwards met, in common with several other of Paine's American friends. They were a jolly, hospitable set of people and proved extremely loyal to Paine when he later came into collision with the Convention. "Clio" Rickman, Paine's London publisher, had not then arrived from

London, where the authorities were hunting him with a
writ for issuing seditious libel. He ultimately turned up
without a penny-piece, or a scrap of baggage, but chock
full of schoolboy glee at having successfully dodged both
law officers and port authorities. Paine himself had had a
lucky escape from being arrested at Dover, an order for
his arrest having arrived in the town an hour after his
vessel had sailed for France.

In less than five minutes I felt perfectly at ease with
this great man. He had that trick of establishing confidence so rare in a man who has elevated himself by his
own efforts and brainpower. There was never a shred of
condescension or patronage about Tom Paine and his
everyday conversation was as plain-speaking and reasonable as his written precepts. He was big warm, eager,
lovable and as gentle as the collie dog that used to follow
me about my fields at Westdown.

There followed one of the most pleasant morning I
have ever spent. I told him, without reservations, of all
that had happened to me during the last few months and
he chuckled when I described how Saxeby had taught me
my letters on a passage from the Book of Kings but had
sternly replaced the Bible with *The Rights of Man* as soon
as he felt confident that I could spell out a passage without constant reference to the lexicon.

He was particularly interested in my account of the
storming of the Tuileries but his gentle expression grew
very sombre when I described the occurrences at the Abbaye Prison on the night of September 2nd. He asked a
thousand questions, some of which I could answer but
the majority I could not. When I had finished my account
he got up abruptly and foraged among a pile of French
journals that lay on top of his valise, returning with a
current copy of Marat's ever-popular paper, *L'Ami du
Peuple.* There were the usual diatribes against traitors
and counter-revolutionaries but Paine ignored these and
pointed to one article, signed by Marat and printed in
the boldest possible type. It was titled: *"J' Accuse Capet"*
and the text was surmounted by a crude wood-cut of the
guillotine.

"Be so good as to translate that for me?" he asked.

I did so, rapidly, for Marat always expressed himself in the most unmistakable language, with none of the high-flown classical hyperbole of the pamphleteers like Desmoulins.

The article was a violent attack, not only upon the king, who was described as a monster eager to subject Paris to a reign of terror under the Prussians, but upon several of the Girondin deputies, namely Valazé, Pétion, Vergiaud, Barbaroux and the witty dramatist Louvet, whose recent speeches against the Jacobins, and against Robespierre in particular, were described by Marat as masterpieces of vile, counter-revolutionary slander. Marat called Louvet a cringing jackal and Barbaroux a dictatorial libertine, but Robespierre was described as being "the high soul of virtuous republicanism." The article concluded with a strident demand to bring Louis to the bar of the Assembly for trial on a capital charge.

When I had finished, Paine said: "Having read these journals and presumably met some of these people this summer, Mr. Treloar, what is your honest opinion of our prospects of being able to rescue the Revolution from misanthropes like this fellow Marat?"

I spoke out then and was surprised to find how his personality gave me confidence and helped me to express myself lucidly. Over at Rouzet's I had done little talking but I had listened to a great deal and I surprised myself by the accuracy of my knowledge on the day-to-day political scene.

"Nearly all the Girondins I have met are honest, decent fellows," I told him, "with the good of the country and the interests of the mass of its people at heart, but hardly any of them are men of action capable of standing up to leaders like Danton, or even Marat. They don't speak the language of the gutter and they are constantly intimidated by the Paris mob. The Convention no longer rules France, sir, that is the prerogative of the Commune and the Jacobin Club. The Brissotins certainly represent the departments but the departments might be foreign countries for all the contribution they are allowed to make to the reorganization of France."

Paine scratched his huge nose, a habit of his when he was concentrating.

"What remedy would you suggest?" he asked flatly.

"I would enrol a section of the National Guard to do permanent duty in the Convention and keep the mobs away from the deputies," I declared.

Paine shook his side-curls. "How can that suffice when you cannot rely on the loyalty of the National Guard?" he countered.

He had only been in Paris a few days but I could see that he had wasted no time in assessing the situation.

"Suppose the seat of government was temporarily removed from Paris?" he added.

It was a brilliant idea and I wondered whether any of Marcelle's friends had considered it. At a safe distance from the capital the moderate deputies, who had a clear majority, might conceivably be able to legislate without the constant threat of mob coercion, but Paine raised the principal objection to his own solution.

"It would mean that we laid ourselves open to the accusation of federalism," he went on. "It might even mean civil war, but as I see it the republic must have breathing-space. If it doesn't it will slide into anarchy."

He closed his brilliant eyes and leaned back, his chin tilted towards the ceiling.

"We hoped so much from this revolution," he said. "It was to herald the dawn of freedom for the whole of Western Europe, much as America's triumph will establish a new sphere of freedom on the other side of the world. What a tragedy it will be if the forces of kings and of privilege take heart at witnessing the birth of a new tyranny here, if they can turn to the millions now toiling in their masters' fields, or moving away from their filched commons to seek a wretched living in the mills of the merchant adventurers, and say: 'Here is a people who reached out for the freedoms you demand, but what happened to them? They merely exchanged the whips of the high-born for the scourges of gutter bullies. Reflect, paupers! Is a struggle in which defeat means the gallows or transportation worth the lifting of a finger?' For that is what they *will* say, Mr. Treloar; moreover, that is what they will have every right to say!"

"You can point in turn to America, Mr. Paine," I interposed. "There, at least, your gospel has succeeded!"

"Ah, America," said Paine sadly, "but that is no parallel. America is new territory, unencumbered by the traditions of a thousand-year-old feudalism. It is a land where the brave and the steadfast can carve for themselves free acres out of God's wilderness and, having wiped the sweat from their eyes, can shout: 'This is mine and my children's! I made it, I own it!' And there is none to march in with hired soldiers and take it from them!"

"There was such a one, less then twenty years ago," I argued.

"There was," he agreed, "but Mr. Guelph's uniformed serfs were obliged to sail three thousand miles to point their muskets and march through forests as wide as France to grapple with an enemy they seldom saw, much less laid hands upon. You can fight tyrants under those conditions, Mr. Treloar, but here, in Europe, you fight among yourselves on the best method of opposing your enemies."

"Do you then despair?" I asked, for his talk half inclined me to go home and persuade Charlotte to pack her valise and set out with me that night for Virginia.

His face lit up with a great, beaming smile. It was like nothing so much as the sun rolling unexpectedly from a screen of clouds, spreading warmth and hope on a winter countryside.

"Despair, Mr. Treloar?" he cried. "Before God I never despair! Man is a courageous and highly adaptable animal. The conditions he lives under are brought about largely by his own passions, but as soon as enough men find those conditions intolerable they change them, as the people of Paris acted in concert when they advanced against the Bastille. It has always been so. These people will find a way out, just as we across the Channel will find our own solution sooner or later. My only concern is to try and persuade them to do it without imitating their oppressors and meeting tyranny, not with repression and terror, which belong to the armoury of kings, but with reason and high purpose. What will it avail them if they slaughter Louis? They will make him the martyr that we made Charles Stuart, and Louis's son, or his brother, or his second cousin will return here with trumpets and bonfires and the Revolution will be a page in the history books of the future."

"What, then, do you suggest they do with their king?" I asked.

"Banish him," said Paine shortly. "Ship him off to America where he can observe free people at close quarters. Bless my soul, if that happened we should have Louis seeking a seat in the French Assembly in no time. Can't you envisage it? 'Louis Capet, deputy representing Versailles'!"

It was Brissotin talk with a difference, the difference being that reason had been substituted for rhetoric. It occurred to me that if Tom Paine could only learn to speak fluently in a language the Convention could understand, if he could rally the failing deputies of the Plain and weld them in an active, aggressive unit, owing allegiance to nothing but their own faith and idealism, there was some hope of his dream of a European Republic. He tried, in the months that followed, to do all this and he withstood all the vicious attacks of the Mountain, who even made the absurd accusation that he was an English Government spy, but his voice was not heard and at last he sat on the benches alone, a lonely, eccentric Englishman, with all his friends killed or scattered and nothing between him and the guillotine but his friendship with Washington and his own matchless courage.

I left him that morning without underestimating his abilities, or the extent of his influence. What I did underestimate was his shocking handicap in being totally unable to address Frenchmen in their own inspiring tongue. To a great extent it was that drawback that cost Paine his dream, most of his friends their lives, France an agony it might easily have been spared, and England and the rest of Europe an irresistible lead towards enlightened government.

Chapter Ten

MARCELLE and René Biron were married in the early autumn. It was a purely civil ceremony, performed by the Mayor of St. Marceau, and to my mind more like a casual visit to the hustings than a wedding ceremony, but that was how they wanted it, with no trimmings and no priest, a simple contract symbolic of the new freedoms, political and domestic.

Charlotte, André and myself attended as witnesses, and Rouzet presided over a sumptuous breakfast in the assembly room of one of his business associates, who kept a café in the rue l'Ecole de Médecine. Most of Biron's intimates attended and there was a good deal of roystering and practical jokes, but already a good deal of the spontaneity had gone from the younger Brissotins. The group was being subjected to daily attacks by the Mountain and all the deputies were feeling the strain. I think one or two of them, Valazé and Vergiaud for instance, realized even then that they were fighting for their lives and they were none of them men of Danton's stature who could jest in the face of annihilation. It took a good deal of Rouzet's wine to keep the party going after Biron and his young wife had left for Rambouillet, where they were spending a day or two with one of Biron's friends.

Charlotte and I were spared the necessity of making a declaration concerning ourselves. Marcelle, who possessed a highly developed feminine instinct in these matters, soon guessed Charlotte's secret and gaily circulated the news round the family circle and beyond. I think it helped to improve the relationship between the two girls for up to then Marcelle, with all the cruelty of the very young, had been inclined to patronize Charlotte as a predestined spinster and to flaunt her own precocious charms (together with the young gallants they attracted to the house) in

the face of her shy and sober cousin. Now that Charlotte
had found a man of her own, Marcelle's attitude towards
her softened. She was a good-hearted little thing and
what faults she had were those of youth and her inexperience in matters other than coquetry. Charlotte undoubtedly loved her for all her tiresomeness and thoughtless
intolerance. She made Biron a good wife during the brief
time I saw them together and in normal times she would
have settled down very conventionally the moment he had
given her the child for which she longed. I hope with all
my heart that she found the ecstasy she expected in her
René's arms. They hadn't very long before terror and
separation shattered their idyll.

Rouzet took very kindly to me as a prospective son-in-
law and even proposed taking me into partnership, a
matter he discussed, to my intense annoyance, in front of
the rat-faced assistant, Vizet, who smirked and grimaced
like a malevolent baboon. I was very non-committal about
his offer, unable to see myself shuffling about his *salon*
with a shaving-mug for the rest of my life, but not caring
to hurt the old fellow's feelings and admit, then and there,
that Charlotte and I were determined to farm, if need be,
in America. Somehow during that autumn and winter there
was no real opportunity to assemble the family and discuss
the future. Something was always happening to one or
another of us, and outside, in the sections, the Jacobins
nursed their strength for the final eruption that was to
bring them to power.

I spent a good deal of my time with Paine or, at any
rate, working on Paine's behalf. Shortly after our first
meeting he sent a message to me though Pétion and Biron
to meet him by appointment in the anteroom of the Assembly committee lobby, where he was working twelve
hours a day on the new constitution. The committee of
nine engaged in this mammoth task were strange col-
laborators, ranging from self-confessed moderates like
Pétion, Brissot, Vergiaud. Condorcet and Paine himself,
to demagogues like Danton and shifty, any-way-for-a-dram
deputies like Barère and the Abbé Sieyes. The committee
might have taken itself less seriously had it realized that

within less than eighteen months scarcely a man among the group would have a head on his shoulders.

Paine came striding out of the lobby to greet me as soon as I had sent an usher in with my pass. Long hours of poring over manuscripts (for somehow he found an hour or two or devote to his new book, *The Age of Reason*, in addition to the mountains of paper work foisted on him by the Convention) had left him drawn and listless. He greeted me cordially enough and put his arm around my shoulders, telling me he had employment for me if I cared to supplement my guardsman's wages by extracting passages from Jacobin newspapers relating to the impending trial of the king, and translating them into English for his benefit. He particularly wanted extracts from the more violent journals such as Marat's, and Hébert's scurrilous *Père Duchesne*.

I agreed to undertake the work for nothing. It interested me and I was in no great need of money, having more than sufficient for my board and lodging without depleting my small capital of guineas. I knew that Paine himself had little enough money and had arrived from England almost penniless. His American friends helped him with small loans which he afterwards repaid in full from a mysterious hoard he got together immediately prior to his arrest and confinement in the Luxembourg. He accepted my offer gratefully and we exchanged a little polite conversation, but he did not enlarge upon his views expressed to me at White's Hotel, only making a single comment regarding the state of affairs in Paris. When I asked him to assess Louis's chances of surviving a trial he said bluntly: "I shall fight for banishment. I shall go on fighting whatever happens!" With that he went back to the committee room and I returned home with an armful of journals.

I had no time to scan them during the next few days, however, for on my return to No. 12 I found a message from André awaiting me, asking me to go immediately to the Temple.

It was now late autumn and my walk was through a Paris chill and drab. The splendid green mantle of sum-

mer had dropped from the streets and squares and the
trees in the Tuileries gardens were bare and dripping
under a never-ending drizzle. The gutters of the main
streets, never very salubrious in the heyday of the monarchy, were now choked with rotting garbage and discarded
newspapers. Seemingly, it was no longer anyone's business
to sweep the highways and unchoke the drains that fed
the sewers. The men of the Commune were far too busy
planning seizure of power to compel their workmen, whom
they numbered among their doughtiest pikemen, to perform such menial offices, and pools of black slime gathered
at all street-crossings where there were no gradients to
carry the filth into the river.

Vandalism had increased at an alarming rate since the
final overthrow of the monarchy on August 10th. As I
passed through the Place Vendôme I saw workmen level-
ling the site around the shattered plinth of the statue of
Louis XIV. The statue had been removed and melted
down and would probably soon be replaced by one of the
new gods or goddesses, like the huge monument "Liberty"
in the Place de Révolution. On his way to the Temple
Prison three months previously Louis was halted in Place
Vendôme to witness the overthrow of the statue of his
famous ancestor. One of the deputies escorting him remarked: "You see what we do to kings, Capet?" The
mild Louis is said to have replied, with unusual irony:
"It is fortunate when you only reap vengeance on in-
animate objects, my friend!"

During the previous three years there had been a good
deal of this senseless destruction of public monuments,
but it was only now that the frenzy of demonstrating a
complete break with the past had been officially sanc-
tioned. Even the calendar had had to be changed and we
were now living in the Year One and endeavouring to get
used to the new names for each month and the ten-day
week.

In the densely populated area between the Tuileries and
the Temple du Commerce many of the public buildings
had been damaged in one or other of the street insur-
rections and their walls and shutters still showed the

scars of artillery. A little farther east, where hundreds
of workmen were engaged in the leisurely razing of the
Bastille, the huddle of houses that had once confronted
the mighty towers were now almost hidden in jagged
heaps of masonry, flung down pell-mell by patriots during the first orgy of demolition. It was impossible to
pick one's way down the rue St. Antoine without getting
splashed to the knees, but the steady drizzle had one
advantage, it reduced the stench rising from the labyrinth
of hovels on either side, and after the heat of the summer
this, at all events, afforded great relief to the pedestrian.

I got into the Temple without much trouble, for, in
addition to André's pass, I could display my uniform,
complete by this time. The blue tunic was a passport into
any building where the National Guard did picquet duty.

The Temple, which had been selected as the house of
detention for the royal family, was formerly the headquarters of the Knights Templar and was surrounded by
the once pleasing garden of the Grand Prior. It was at first
considered that the Luxembourg Palace would be more
suitable for a royal prison but this had been vetoed by
the Jacobins because the Luxembourg was supposed to
contain many underground passages by which Louis
might have escaped.

Accordingly a section of the Temple, consisting of the
huge, gloomy tower, was set aside for the Capets, but as
it was uninhabitable they were temporarily housed in the
little tower close by which had been the residence of the
archivist of the Order.

Meanwhile, workmen made many structural alterations
to the main tower, dividing the large rooms into four,
barring the windows, fitting an unnecessarily large number
of iron doors and grilles, and finally isolating the tower
and a small section of the garden by the erection of a high
brick wall. In the rain the place now looked particularly
forbidding and gloomy.

At the time I visited the Temple, Louis had already
appeared before the Convention for his preliminary hearing and had, on his return, been separated from his family.
He now occupied a first-floor apartment, and the queen

and her children, together with Madame Elizabeth, the king's sister, were housed on the third storey.

The prisoners were guarded by a select body of Commune troops under the command of a ruffian called Rosenthal, who, with his two lieutenants, Riseby and Rocher, and the turnkey, Simon (afterwards famous for his wardship of the wretched Dauphin), did all they could to make the ordeal of the captives as irksome as possible. The prisoners, at that time, had been left with a single servant, a loyal fellow called Clery, who acted as handyman and *valet-de-chambre* to them all.

I finally located André in a temporary structure, built under the lee of the wall dividing palace and tower. This wooden chalet, I soon discovered, was his permanent headquarters.

The hut had been fitted up as a surgery. It had a long, solid-looking bench in the centre and a series of racks and cupboards screwed to the blank walls. All the shelves were loaded with jars and bottles and in one of the cupboards, which had swung open, was an assortment of unplaned wooden legs which I recognized as such by the leather straps and buckles appended to them.

André, wearing an ankle-length leather apron over his undress uniform, was engaged with a patient, from whose bloody hand he was skilfully removing a crushed fingernail. The patient, evidently a jailer, was either a stoic or had been generously dosed with rum, of which the hut reeked, for he neither winced nor groaned but stolidly smoked his pipe until André had bandaged the wound and told him to go.

He turned to me with a grin as the fellow stumbled off into the yard.

"That's what becomes of overcrowding prisons, David. One of the prisoners over in the east block slammed the door on our old friend Filotteur, and as there are so many men in the cell they can't discover the culprit!"

He washed his hands in a leather horse-bucket and took off his huge apron which he hung on a nail beside the wooden legs.

"Are you the official surgeon here?" I asked him, for

it seemed evident that he held some sort of appointment in the prison and was no longer a simple member of the garrison.

"Since more than a week ago," he replied, lighting up a pipe and taking a seat on the end of his operating bench. "The concierge's wife fell down a flight of steps and broke her arm. I was able to set it on the spot and ever since then I collect six francs a day and have my own elegant quarters!"

He waved his pipe in the direction of a trestle bed below the cupboards.

"You'd be surprised at the variety of my practice in a place like this," he went on. "There are close on a thousand potential patients in the palace, suffering from everything from dysentery and common jail-fever to cracked pates and the Italian sickness. I treat 'em all, jailers and prisoners alike, and I flatter myself that I'm appreciably reducing the mortality, though to what end I haven't yet discovered, for soon enough there will only be one way out of here and my efforts will be mainly directed towards ensuring that the executioners don't want for work."

"Are there many executions?"

"They average two a day but that total will be increased very considerably once the tribunal gets used to its new responsibilities. There's been trouble already over the number of acquittals. Citizen Hébert, they tell me, is furious!"

André spoke with his customary irony, half-intended to amuse and to screen his real thoughts, but I thought I detected something new in his tone, a hint of desperation or perhaps mere disgust engendered by his squalid and depressing surroundings.

He went on speaking with studied flippancy.

"Did you know that I had been elevated to the highest level of my profession? It's true, David, I'm king's physician. Think of it, at six francs a day and paid out of the Commune Treasury! I was called in to examine Louis yesterday. His digestion is giving him trouble, a common enough complaint in this hotel, particularly if you can't get permission to have your meals sent in from outside.

He used to have everything sent in and still would, I
don't doubt, but the concierge here is terrified that Capet
will persuade a loyalist chef to bake a brace of files and
a rope ladder into a rabbit pie, or send in enough poison
to save Sanson a job and do the patriots out of the spectacle they've been promised. The queen's here as well but
they've been separated now by express order of the Commune. By the way, ask Biron what he and the other
popinjays do with themselves in the Convention, will
you? They surely find it hard to fill in the time now that
the Commune is doing the governing for them. I heard
your friend Tom Paine has taken his seat. How does he
find the womb of liberty? Pregnant with new constitutions
or approaching the sterility of middle-age?"

I wasn't in a mood to listen to too much of this badi-
nage, so I cut him short with a direct question.

"Why did you send for me, André?"

He parried the question, giving me a distinct impression
that he was withholding something.

"Wouldn't you care to see Louis? It isn't often that a
mere runagate like you gets an opportunity to contemplate
fallen grandeur."

He could be very irritating when he was in this sort of
mood, but I knew him well enough by that time to realize
that if I were to get from him the real reason for my summons to the prison he would have to be humoured. Something was troubling him and I saw that he had not yet
made up his mind to share his problem. He was a man
who sacrificed self-esteem every time he asked for help,
even from a person like myself, whom he knew he could
trust.

I said: "All right, André, let's take a look at the king!"

"Take my bag and be my assistant," he said, heaving
himself up and adjusting his cravat in front of the polished
canteen that served him for a mirror. I took his surgeon's
case and we went out into the thin rain, crossing the
isolated piece of garden and entering the tower by the
main door, which was heavily guarded.

"This is a great privilege for you, David," he said, as
the turnkey unlocked the first of the grilles. "Rosenthal

and his patriots guard Capet as if he was a man-eating tiger. But perhaps he was, or is, or would be if the Prussians broke through. I'm prepared to take their word for it, though I must admit he seems to have more of the appearance of a trapped mouse!"

We passed through two more steel wickets and at one of them André stopped and exchanged a joke with the turnkey. Finally we reached the king's apartment, where the guard let us in without question, for André had been a constant visitor for the past few days. The sergeant left the door ajar, however, and I advanced no farther than the threshold of the gloomy little chamber in which Louis was sitting at a flimsy table under the half-shuttered window trying to make the best of the miserably inadequate light.

There was no fireplace in the apartment but a charcoal stove was giving out heat and fumes, and its escape pipe, which ran up the wall and through the window, further reduced the amount of light and air that might have struggled in from the sunless garden.

I had never seen Louis before and forgot André and his problems in my intense curiosity. The king was a plump, undistinguished little man with an air of anxious amiability. In happier circumstances, he would have passed anywhere for the host of a prosperous inn, or the bachelor uncle of a large, cheerful bourgeois family. His pale, fat face was puckered with concentration on the piles of books and papers that were stacked around him, and his blue eyes were red-rimmed with the pungent fumes of the stove. He was neatly dressed in a maroon silk coat with gilt buttons, a white sleeve-waistcoat and black breeches. His hair, worn short, was tied back and lightly powdered.

Sitting beside him, scratching away at a brisk pace with a large quill, was his principal advocate, Malesherbes, a distinguished old man in his late seventies, who had voluntarily undertaken the onerous task of defending the king. Malesherbes took no notice of André's entry, but the king got up and smiled as André made him a short, formal bow. I heard Louis say "Better this morning" and pat his paunch, and they went into the bedroom together, leaving

me close to the door, taking stock of the furniture and the
mass of manuscript in front of the advocate. A glance at
the table told me that Malesherbes intended to make a
bold fight at the trial, but I wondered then whether the
deputies would give him the opportunity of reading half
the defence to a court already determined on verdict and
sentence.

André didn't stay with the king more than a few
moments and when they came out of the bedroom they
parted with another grave bow. I saw the sergeant of the
guard, who never let me out of his sight, glance at André
in astonishment when he bobbed. He was evidently not
accustomed to a display of etiquette in front of the prisoner
and this did not surprise me, for the walls of all the
corridors we traversed on the way to the royal cell were
scrawled with ferocious slogans, directed against Louis
and his wife, and some of them had been crudely illustrated
by drawings of the gallows and guillotine.

I came out of the royal apartment with mixed feelings.
I was surprised at the inconsistency of the Commune,
which housed the king in comparative comfort, yet surrounded him by a set of such inconsiderate ruffians, and
I quite failed to understand why such a mild little man
had been represented to the people as a bloodthirsty tyrant.
The spate of Jacobin abuse appearing in the journals
might well have applied to certain of the Bourbons, but I
am certain that once having met Louis none could suspect
him of encompassing the death of a gnat. I was surprised
also by the elaborate precautions they had taken to
guard the prisoner, who, I felt sure, had long since
abandoned any idea of escape, particularly while his wife
and children could be used as hostages.

I had supposed that on quitting the king's apartment
André would conduct me out of the tower, but instead of
re-passing the grilles he led me up one of the spiral staircases to another floor and then through another iron door
into a long, draughty corridor, lit by a single narrow
window at the far end.

About halfway along he touched my arm and motioned
me to look to my left, where a nonchalant sentry was

leaning against the wall beside a half-open door. The sentry, who recognized the prison surgeon, took his pipe from his mouth and grinned.

"Not so cosy as the Trianon, eh, citizen?" he said, addressing André, who immediately spat and replied:

"Bitch and whelps should discover how the people have to live!" He nudged me, and gave me one of his swift winks.

I glanced through the door into the queen's apartment. It was larger but by no means as well equipped as her husband's. The room had been divided by a makeshift curtain, which cut off most of the light and plunged that section of the room nearest the door into miserable gloom, only partly dissipated by a single rushlight burning in a saucer.

From inside the dingy room came the babble of children's voices and the sound seemed unnatural in such a forbidding place. There were two or three unmade beds and a mattress stretched on the floor, which was covered with the same type of coarse matting that Rouzet used in his *salon*.

The queen was sitting on one of the beds, her back propped against the wall, and two children, a handsome, pallid boy of seven, and a pretty little girl a year or two older, were playing some sort of instructional game with her. From what I could see in the brief glance I took, it appeared to be a game designed for the teaching of geography. The Dauphin was holding up coloured sections of a map and trying to fit them in their correct place on a frame held by his sister. André told me later that the game had been invented by Louis as a means of passing the time.

Behind the screen I could see the feet and high *coiffeure* of Madame Elizabeth, who must have been engaged in laundering, for some of the women's small clothes were drying on a line stretched in front of the stove.

The children, absorbed in their game, seemed happy enough, and while I watched the Dauphin gave a shrill peal of laughter which brought a tired smile into the face of the queen.

I had heard that Marie Antoinette was a beautiful woman and she might well have been before her troubles began to show in her face. Now, although some traces of good looks remained, her face was haggard and her eyes had a permanent squint, as though she had the greatest difficulty in seeing across the room. There was a vivid spot of rouge on the cheek turned to me, but it only accentuated the unhealthy pallor of her complexion and made the cosmetic look like the make-up of a circus performer. I knew her age to be round about thirty, but she looked at least forty-five, for although her figure was still that of a young and attractive woman her thick hair was generously streaked with white, and her lips, which she kept firmly compressed, were almost bloodless.

The sight of her sitting there in that dismal setting, trying to distract her children from the miseries that beset them all, was indescribably pitiful, and I suddenly flushed as I realized that André, and my own curiosity, had made me a Peeping Tom. As we moved on and began to descend the steps to the guardroom, I hated André for his ability to mask a pity I knew he must feel under a clownish performance of ultra-patriotism.

Immediately we were in the open and heading for the gate in the wall that separated palace and tower, I asked him point-blank to explain himself. He hesitated a moment and then took my arm and pulled me across the garden to the street gate.

"Let's get out of this tomb and have some coffee," he said. "I know a good place near here."

We went into a café in a mean little street off the rue de Saint Laurent. There were very few customers in the place and the proprietor greeted André civilly and served us some excellent black coffee, which we had to drink unsweetened. Sugar was almost unobtainable in Paris owing to revolts in the French West Indian possessions.

André seemed disinclined to open the conversation, so I said: "I can understand you taking the chance you did at the Abbaye in September but what is your object in keeping up the masquerade? You aren't a Jacobin and you don't have to stay in a place like the Temple. If you intend to renew your contract with the civic guard you could very well do occasional duties as I do. Why don't you stop playing the fool and come home?"

"I meant to have shown you the reason, David," he said speaking slowly and deliberately. "She wasn't a stone's throw from where we stood, but I couldn't be sure you wouldn't pull one of your stern, Calvinistic faces. She disapproves of what I'm doing, of course, but her opinion doesn't count for she's safe in jail. Your warning might be different, you would have called in the family and given her fresh ammunition. It's tiresome to plan and to argue at one and the same time."

"Have you got involved with a woman?" I asked incredulously. He grinned self-consciously. Ever since I had known him he had mocked at the man who allowed his relationships with a woman to influence his decisions. Biron's willing enslavement was a favourite subject for his banter, and although he admired Charlotte, he always adopted the patronizing tone of the carefree bachelor when he referred to our engagement. Now, it appeared, André himself was in the toils and I found myself wondering what the girl was like and wishing that I could see her.

André cut into my speculations.

"I'm turning her loose, David," he told me. "That's why I sent for you."

I gaped at him. His statement did a good deal towards clarifying the situation. It explained his long absences from home, his acceptance of the odious post of surgeon at the Temple, and his studied attempts to give the impression of ultra-Jacobinism, such as his comment to the sentry outside the queen's apartment. He was deliberately setting out to gain the confidence of the Commune's garrison at the Temple, presumably with the object of using his trusted position to arrange the escape of a prisoner. I had noted the temper of the guards in the precincts of the prison and it seemed to me that André was embarking on what promised to be a very dangerous adventure. One slip and he would find himself in even closer company with his mistress.

"I'm prepared to admit that I'm behaving like a starry-eyed fool," he went on. "I took a chance or two at the Abbaye in September, but love is a rather more exacting taskmaster than pity, David. Maybe you'll have a chance to find that out before all this is over."

I wondered what I would do if Charlotte was in the same situation as André's girl. Something had changed him during the past few weeks for he spoke of love without a trace of his customary irony. I might have been tempted to refer to his former attitude but something in his expression stopped me. He looked as if he was very unhappy.

"Who it is?" I asked.

"You wouldn't know her," he replied, absently tracing a pattern in the coffee drips on the table. "Her name's Lucille Souham and she comes from Le Mans. She was a milliner in the suite of the Princesse de Lamballe before they got separated when the king was brought to the Temple. The little idiot has more loyalty than common sense. She stuck by her employer when the rest of them made off in the crowd. She doesn't know how lucky she is to be alive. If they had let her accompany de Lamballe to La Force, as she begged to do, we should have had her head as well as her patron's waved under the Austrian's windows."

"I'd heard they did that," I admitted. "Did you see it?"

Suddenly he swept the glass he was twirling from the table and splintered it against the buttress of the alcove in which we were sitting.

"Sweet Christ, what do they hope to gain by these butcheries?" he cried out. "Already the country stinks from pole to pole! I used to believe in the ordinary man of Paris, David; I thought he had more courage, more enterprise and a stronger sense of humour than any city-dweller in the world. What's happened to him since August? Is it courageous to massacre terrified women because they happen to wear brocade? Is it enterprising to make a revolution and hand over the fruits of office to the illiterate scum of the sections? Did American colonists have to do that sort of thing when they switched their system of government? Can't the wretched little Capet be laughed off the throne instead of—"

I leaned over and struck him hard on the mouth. He broke off, partly in pain and partly in astonishment. I didn't like striking him in that fashion but there were other people in the café and his voice had suddenly risen from a petulant mutter to a bellow of protest. His lips, crushed against his rather prominent teeth, began to bleed and he wiped it with the back of his hand. I got up, threw down the score, and walked out, motioning him to follow.

As soon as we got into the street I realized that I was a good deal more upset by the incident than he, for he chuckled and said: "You know, David, for an Englishman you've got an alert head on your shoulders. I'd completely forgotten that the Jew's Legion used that café. I deserved all I got."

The "Jew" was the ruffianly Rosenthal. His squad was always referred to as "The Legion" and any one of them would have sold his father to the Commune for a pipe of tobacco.

André massaged his mouth ruefully and as I made no reply he added: "Why didn't you tell me that you had a punch like one of your professional box fighters? By God, I'd as soon kneel behind a bad-tempered mule!"

We had got as far as the Temple precincts, where we stopped. I turned on him, suddenly.

"Come back home, André," I placed. "You owe it to Marcelle and Charlotte!"

He shrugged his narrow shoulders. "Marcelle and Biron have got their own troubles right ahead, and Charlotte, she's got you, hasn't she? I don't owe either one of them a sou!"

"Well, Papa Rouzet then, he's been as good as a father to you."

André smiled and leaned with his back against the palisade.

"Rouzet's had his life, or the better part of it," he said. "The poor fellow doesn't understand what's happened to him these last few years and one day he'll wake up, maybe a month or so too late. I tried to get him and the girls out of Paris months before you arrived. I could see then that they'd started something here the best of them could never control. You just watch and wait. Biron, Danton, all of them, they'll eat one another up and I'd wager a hundred louis that the Bourbons will be back at Versailles before you and Charlotte have a grown child." He continued more seriously. "I've done a lot of thinking lately, and no doubt you'll scratch your head when I tell you I believe more in the revolution in your country than I do in ours. You think you haven't got one over there but you have, and it's the only sort of revolution that works; a passion for everyday justice married to a love of law and order! You're slow to act, you chuckleheads across the Channel, but the best of you think and read, and then go on biding your time and touching your cap when the squire trots past. You're building up a new class over there, people who own industries and whose sons won't be able to make them show a profit if they don't take their labourers into their confidence. Those Guelphs, and the landowners they lean on, are already outmoded and on the high road to the debtors' ward. Soon enough these new people will move into their fine houses and into the government and, as most of them are traders, with one eye on their balance sheet and the other on a comfortable seat in paradise, they'll vote for reform. They'll make you a revolution all right and when they do it won't be done by waving pikes but credit slips."

"That's all very well, André," I told him, "but I can't go back there, and I don't intend to stay here much longer. If you do succeed in getting this girl, Lucille, out of jail where do you propose taking her?"

"Perhaps that depends on you," he said bluntly. "How much English money have you got?"

I was a little taken aback by this but I told him, a matter of about ten guineas.

"Could you get more?" he asked.

I said I thought I could. If I could contact Muttford at Honfleur it seemed probable that he could get some money from Saxeby. It might take time but I knew Saxeby would help if he could.

"Then get it now," urged André. "Get a hundred guineas over. Lend me fifty and I'll repay you a month after we get there!"

"Get where?" I asked, irritably. I wasn't in the mood to ponder his riddles.

"America!" he answered, and before I could say another word he had turned on his heel and passed through the wicket into the Temple garden.

I stood looking after him, feeling more pleased with life than at any period since Charlotte and I first embraced the night I returned from the Abbaye.

Chapter Eleven

THAT was the beginning of our little plan, and I went straight home to discuss it with Charlotte. We guessed that André had some scheme for effecting Lucille's escape from the Temple, but although he came home twice a week and we discussed all other aspects of our proposed flight he didn't say a word regarding this vitally important factor.

We deliberated a good deal on the prospects of inviting Marcelle but finally decided against it for the leading Brissotins, including her husband, were still acting as though they were blind to the dangers confronting their party. Most of them were now clamouring for the condemnation of the king, and although a great number subsequently voted for imprisonment rather than death, they quite failed to realize that their alliance with the Jacobins on this issue could only end in their extinction as a party. They had some sort of fixed idea, subsequently epitomized in Danton's famous phrase, that the trial of Louis would unite France against the foreign kings, but they overlooked the fact that the execution of the king would destroy the last vestige of sympathy for the Revolution abroad, already as good as cast away by the September massacres. The Jacobins were only tolerating the party of the Plain until they felt sufficiently strong to assume complete control in the Convention. They had another six months to wait.

Marcelle and Biron were quite outspoken in their opinion that the king's death was necessary to the safety of the republic. I agreed with Charlotte that, in view of this uncompromising attitude, any mention of André's intention to connive at the escape of a Commune prisoner, however humble and unimportant she might be, would be regarded by them as an act of treachery. I wouldn't have been surprised if Marcelle, intoxicated as she was with the patriotic clap-trap dinned into her day after day by the men of her husband's party, had considered it her duty to inform against us. This seems fantastic, I know, but republicanism burned in Marcelle like a high fever and common sense or family feeling had long since been swamped by her enthusiasm for the new order.

Rouzet, of course, was different, but we didn't tell him either, not because we didn't trust him but because he trusted everybody who came into his *salon* and might have gossiped about our plan to customers or the journeyman, Vizet.

The first part of the scheme went very smoothly. I wrote a letter to Saxeby telling him that I had met Paine and was in great need of money. I didn't say why and I didn't sign the letter, but asked him to entrust Muttford with a hundred of my mother's guineas and pay the smuggler half the usual ten per cent transit fee in advance.

I felt sure I could trust the gloomy sea captain and I wasn't wrong, for André, who had acquaintances in most walks of life, found a postilion to deliver a covering letter to Muttford personally and I got a reply from him within the week agreeing to convey my letter to Saxeby and wait for a commission. The money arrived three weeks later and with it was an unsigned note in Saxeby's crabbed handwriting which read:

"I am touched that you have met Uncle Tom. Kindly pay my respects to him and inform him that the news I received from Paris in September made me anxious for his health. I think of you a great deal, nephew. The harvest at Westdown has been disappointing this year."

That was all, but it was enough to start another surge of homesickness in me. I didn't see Muttford, the money coming to me through the same postilion, who charged me a further ten guineas for running the capital risk of being caught transferring money and messages from a port. At that time, January, 1793, France and England were on the brink of war and this explained Saxeby's excessive caution. I put the remaining eighty-five guineas with my ten and we thus had more than enough to pay for a comfortable crossing to Philadelphia, the refuge we selected after a discussion with André in my stockroom.

In the meantime, Charlotte packed a large valise and wrote a letter to Rouzet explaining where we had gone and urging the old man to sell up and follow us.

She found it difficult to behave in this furtive way but André was insistent upon Rouzet being kept in complete ignorance. As every person leaving Paris was subjected to a strict scrutiny at the barriers, and we might easily have been mistaken for *émigrés* and potential allies of the Prussians, I think he was right. Our only anxiety was to get started before England declared war on the republic, which was sure to mean a naval blockade of all the Biscay ports.

We had determined to travel as a party of American merchants and their French wives. André spoke excellent English and I was confident that I could fool the majority of people with my West Country drawl. It was agreed that I should do most of the talking.

We planned to leave in the last week of January. I was in favour of going before because it looked as though the fate of the king would be finally decided by that time, but I did not care to press for more spreed as André had the most difficult part of the business—the freeing of Lucille— to carry through alone. I let him choose the date and he selected January 23, categorically refusing my offer to assist him in any way I could.

"That's my concern and mine only," he told me. "It doesn't become a joint venture until I bring her in here on the night of the twenty-second."

Charlotte was very worried about this part of the business and continually plied me with questions about the routine and personnel of the Temple garrison. I had more faith than she in André's ingenuity and in his considerable powers of bluff. She could never see him as anything but a good-natured dilettante, but she loved him as a brother and, being a woman, understood far better than I the extent of the risks he was prepared to take on behalf of the girl Lucille Souham. I might as well admit that it would have pleased me if he had abandoned that part of the project altogether and left her to talk her own way out of jail. She wasn't a very important hostage and I didn't think she was in any great danger at the moment.

I went over to the Temple again especially to see her about a fortnight before we were due to leave. This time André took me on his rounds through that section of the old palace used as a general house of detention. The prisoners were crowded but otherwise were treated well enough, having to endure few of the rigours imposed upon the royal family across the garden. Those under arrest mixed freely with one another and most of them accepted their detention philosophically. Only a few of the known royalists were locked in the cells. The others expected to be released when the excitement occasioned by the royal trial had abated.

We found Lucille Souham sitting in the enclosed court, which was used as a general exercise yard, I was rather disappointed in her. Somehow I had expected to find her looking more like a traditional lady in distress, or at any rate possessing physical attractions that might account for André's interest in her. The girl I saw sitting on a stump of the balustrade was a very ordinary little thing, dark, small-boned, rather sallow and flat-chested; as far as I could judge, in the few moments we spent with her, she wasn't particularly intelligent. That she was head over heels in love with André, however, I hadn't the slightest doubt, for as we approached she looked up at him as though he was something midway between Adonis and Hercules. He treated her playfully, as one might treat a pet spaniel; indeed, she reminded me somewhat of my little spaniel bitch, Mary, who used to leap off the inglenook seat whenever I came in from the fields, and lollop across the kitchen floor for her pat. I couldn't imagine a man like André being attracted by such a mousey little individual and I began to suspect then that he wasn't telling me the whole truth of the matter.

We couldn't single her out in any way, of course, and

André behaved towards her as though she was just another patient, pretending to examine the pink tongue she shot out at his command and feeling her pulse with a professional air of abstraction. I stood beside him watching, hardly knowing whether to be amused or sympathetic. It was rather pitiable to watch her reactions to his visit, for it was obvious that she had been watching and waiting since early morning for this two-minute contact and I sensed that she was savouring every second of it and would hoard them for the remainder of the day. He said, with rough jocularity:

"Nothing the matter with you, child. Keep out in the open as much as you can. Did you eat all the figs I sent in?"

"Most of them," she told him. "I gave some to Marie."

"Who's Marie?" he asked, gruffly.

"You know Marie, the washerwoman."

"Ah, yes," said André, as though he was not particularly interested, and then, swiftly, "How are they treating you?"

"Oh, I can't really complain," she said vaguely. "It would be all right if I knew. . . ."

She trailed off and her tiny mouth quivered like a child's.

"Keep hoping," he muttered, and then, raising his voice for all to hear, "I'll speak to the concierge about the food."

He moved on to examine an old man with an ulcerous calf. All the prisoners treated André with deference and one or two of them gave him oral messages to deliver to anxious relatives outside the walls. He didn't stay long with anyone and soon took my arm and directed me through the guarded wicket into the garden. He didn't ask my opinion of the girl and I'm glad he didn't because I shouldn't have known what to say. He only said, as we returned to his squalid hut: "All those poor devils think they'll be out the moment Capet sneezes into the sack, but they won't, David. There'll hardly be one of them alive this day six months!"

I wasn't going to argue with André, so far he had been right on every issue, but I went on wondering what had attracted him in Lucille. I had to wait a long time for the right answer.

Louis's fate was put to the vote four or five times in the New Year. On several occasions there was uproar in the Convention, deputies standing up and shouting at one another, some demanding recounts, others fighting for an appeal to the people, a majority growling fiercely at every delay in bringing Capet under the knife. Through it all sat Tom Paine, unable to understand a word of the debates, but rising gravely every time he was asked to vote and repeating, with the vilest accent, the only French phrase he knew—"I vote for the detention of Louis until the end of the war and after that perpetual banishment."

It was absurd and might have been laughable, had the issue been less grave, to hear this great-hearted revolutionary solemnly mispronounce this simple phrase in the midst of that bedlam of debate and dissension. His steadfastness in voting for the merciful alternative was admirable but it cost him most of his waning influence in the councils of the republic and the Jacobins soon began to spread the story that the decree of outlawry, pronounced against him by the British Government, was a mere cloak for his activities as a spy.

At last, at three in the morning on Sunday, January 20th, the final vote was taken and three hundred and eighty-seven of the seven hundred and twenty-one deputies voted for death within twenty-four hours. The narrow majority sufficed and Louis was taken back to his tower to see his family for the last time. Three days' respite was refused but they granted his request for a confessor.

André came in to see us about midday that Sunday and after a meal motioned me upstairs. As soon as Charlotte had joined us he said:

"You'll have to attend the execution, David!"

I protested vigorously, having no wish whatever to see Louis die, but André had his reasons for asking.

"You're still a member of the National Guard and every man jack of each section is to parade in the streets tomorrow," he reminded me.

"They won't miss one," I argued.

"They will indeed," he replied quietly. "Every section leader has orders from the Commune to make a nominal return of his men on duty. All those failing to muster are to be listed as men disavowing the execution. If your name goes down on the Cordelier list you'll be under suspicion and that might well ruin everything. Louis is as good as gone anyway; we can't stake our future on a piece of sentimentalism!"

He was right, of course, and I had to admit it, but I wished more than ever that we had decamped the previous week.

"Will you be there?" I asked him.

"Part of the escort," he replied; and then, winking, "if you get near enough, David, warm your hands at my glow of patriotism!"

Charlotte said nothing but I saw that her lips were set very firmly.

"Is everything else ready?" I queried.

"Even to passages," he reassured us. "I've booked four on the American barque *Savannah*. It sails from La Rochelle on February 4th." And then he cracked one of his customary jokes. "Are you a good sailor, Charlotte? I'm told seasickness is harder to bear than lovesickness!"

We went downstairs and had to listen to Biron holding forth on the wisdom of the Convention's decision. Marcelle listened to him with shining eyes although on that occasion I don't think she was much concerned with judicial murder. Her pretty figure was swelling and she was probably lost in an ecstatic daydream that was to have its climax round about June.

We listened to Biron for an hour or so after André had returned to his post and when we felt we had heard enough we put on our outdoor clothes and went for a walk in the Luxembourg gardens.

We didn't talk very much, it was a dull, cheerless day and I was depressed by the prospect of tomorrow's spectacle. Once or twice I tried to picture for Charlotte our prospects in America, and the house we would build as soon as I had obtained a grant of land, but it all seemed so far away and so much of a pipedream that I couldn't even convince myself. The only thing that seemed real that afternoon was the light touch of her arm, laid along mine; everything else was as drear and depressing as the winter landscape. It was a very different prospect from that of the gardens in the previous summer on the golden evening when I had watched lovers stroll past the lounging guards on the terrace. We found a felled tree trunk in one of the leafless copses and sat on it, holding hands and each trying to look a good deal less doleful than we felt.

Presently she said: "It was stupid of Marcelle to get herself with child."

I asked why and then I realized what had prompted the remark. Charlotte was feeling conscience-stricken at leaving her cousin, the more so now that within a few months Marcelle would be helpless. The thought made me very petulant. I told myself that what happened to Marcelle and her child was not my affair nor Charlotte's either. We had all we could do to look after ourselves. First we had to get caught up with André's troubles and now Charlotte was worrying herself about a married woman who hadn't enough sense to leave politics to her pompous husband.

"Let Biron talk them out of any trouble they get themselves into," I advised.

Charlotte must have recognized gruffness in my tone for she made no reply. Relenting, I kissed her, but her lips were unresponsive and her eyes looked more troubled than ever. Presently we got up and walked across the dead leaves back to the rue St. Michel. When we got into the court it was dusk and Rouzet's lamp was burning in the parlour window. We let ourselves in through the *salon* and went upstairs. On the landing I took hold of Charlotte's shoulders and pulled her round facing me. Her cheek was ice-cold and she was trembling.

"What is it, Charlotte?" I demanded.

"I'm afraid," she said, "afraid for all of us."

Across the landing someone began to play Rouzet's spinet and then Marcelle's voice came to us, muffled by the heavy door curtain. She was singing her favourite "Marseillaise."

Chapter Twelve

THE Cordelier battalion of the National Guard mustered under arms about six o'clock the next morning.

It was pitch dark and the raw cold struck through the thick underclothing I had donned. I soon discovered that André's information regarding the muster roll was no rumour. There was a roll call and each file had its names taken by individual section commanders. There were very few absentees.

I think what they were about to do appalled even the most hardened scoundrels of St. Marceau. There is something terrifyingly final about executing a king, particularly when most of the neighbouring states are already in arms against you, but although the prospect had a very sobering effect upon the rank and file that morning, I realized even then that the Commune, and those of the deputies overawed by the Commune, had shrewdly estimated the temper of the mob and forced them to perform an office from which there could be no turning back, not even for the humblest pike-trailer in the ranks. Once he had been a party to regicide he was committed to the Revolution for life. If the invasion armies triumphed, and the Prussians and *émigrés* succeeded in taking Paris, few could expect mercy. The killing of Louis was therefore more an act of defiance than an act of policy and I am bound to say that, viewed all round, it was a successful one from the point of view of the Jacobins.

Our section had been assigned that part of the route to the scaffold where the rue Royale debouched into the Place Louis Quinze, now styled Place de la Révolution. The colour-sergeant told me that eighty thousand troops were on parade and as the column marched down to the Pont Neuf I could well believe it, for fresh battalions joined

the main stream at every crossing and some of them
brought artillery, with the gunners carrying lighted matches.

It was the strangest march imaginable. Nobody joked
or exchanged more than a word or two with his neighbour.
The only sounds to be heard were the steady shuffle of
feet and the rattle of sidearms, with here and there a
soggy tattoo on a damp drumskin, or the hoarse command of an officer at the head or the rear of the column.

Every shop was heavily shuttered, as though the pro-
prietors expected street warfare to break out at any
moment. Naked pine torches provided what light there
was until the reluctant sun struggled over the wet roofs
between our line of march and the sharp bend of the
Seine. Over towards the Temple and the Vincennes road
bluish mists still shrouded the silent streets.

We broke step to cross the Pont Neuf and the sudden
cessation of the rhythmic tramp seemed to loosen tongues
and lessen the general tension. Everybody began talking
at once but the buzz of conversation soon subsided and
we tramped on in silence. A file in front began singing
and several companies took up the song, but the chorus
lacked the usual spontaneity and soon died away, despite
the efforts of the drummers to keep it going. In this way,
each man a nervous prey to his own gloomy thoughts, we
defiled into the rue St. Honoré and turned left along the
densely packed thoroughfare towards the rue Royale.

I noticed that there was hardly any wheeled traffic to be
seen and not a single civilian was aboard. The pavements
were lined with a double row of National Guards, standing shoulder to shoulder facing the route along which
Louis would come. At every crossing was a knot of gendarmes, most of them mounted.

We took up a position about fifty yards from the broad
junction of the rue Royale and the Place de la Révolution,
opposite some men of the St. Antoine muster who were
smoking long pipes and freely passing the brandy flask to
keep out the biting cold. It was then about nine in the
morning and we still had about an hour to wait.

It was the longest hour in my memory. For a while I
tried to fix my mind on the details of our escape, wonder-

ing whether I should stand a two months' voyage on the
Atlantic with as much fortitude as a forty-eight hour trip
across the Channel; then I asked myself for the hundredth
time how André proposed to spirit his little milliner out
of the Temple and into No. 12 Cour de Turenne without
attracting the attention of our neighbours, or how Charlotte would face the cold, overland journey to La Rochelle
and what sort of reception the republicans would give us
in Philadelphia if we ever got there. I tried to keep my
mind on these things, but it was useless, for always it returned to the insistent significance of the scene before me,
to the long lines of expectant guardsmen, the façade of
blind-eyed shutters on each side of the road, the burning
cannon-ball of a sun, floating across a snow-laden sky,
like one of my father's copper marker-buoys in the grey
waters of the cove.

These things, and the heavy, unaccountable silence of
the streets, fully absorbed my faculties and I soon abandoned the attempt to ponder anything more personal.

Presently the man beside me, a wizened, undersized
volunteer about fifty, plucked the sleeve of my tunic and
I saw that he was offering me a swig of cognac.

I accepted gratefully, and the man began to talk gen-
eralities, discussing the weather and the news from the
frontiers but carefully avoiding any mention of the thing
that must have dominated his thoughts.

I made a number of noncommittal replies but had difficulty in restraining my intense curiosity to know what he
really thought about the business on hand. In doing so I
realized that almost every remark exchanged in that mighty
assembly must have been as banal as this man's remarks to
me, for each was overawed by the rest and not a man
among us would care to face the consequence of an ill-
chosen expression of opinion.

My mind went back to an account of King Charles's
execution that I had read in one of Saxeby's books and I
wondered if the Parliamentary levies massed in front of
Whitehall scaffold nearly a hundred and fifty years previously had been tongue-tied by the same instincts of self-
preservation.

It became colder and colder and all feeling went out of my feet. Across the road some of the St. Antoine guardsmen were now slightly tipsy and one of them shuffled a little dance but was sternly checked by an officer wearing the municipal scarf.

At last, just as the church clocks were striking ten, the attention of the ranks on my side of the road was drawn to a vague stir higher up the incline. Looking in that direction, I saw two or three officers scurrying about the junction of the rue Royale and rue St. Honoré.

The man beside me put his flask away and gripped his musket so firmly that his knuckles shone white.

"He's coming," he said, as we both caught the sound of measured hoofbeats and the accompanying jingle of harness and an axle-squeak.

Complete silence settled over the pavements. There was not even a cough or a shuffle. The sun, triumphing for a few seconds over the thick banks of grey clouds, twinkled along a curving row of bayonet tips that stretched up the hill as far as the cordon of cabriolets blocking the end of the thoroughfare. The starched stocks and faces under the double row of cocked hats stood out white and bold like a row of milestones. The slow creak of wheels came nearer and the king's equipage turned out of the rue St. Honoré and trundled round towards us, a black-garbed coachman perched uncomfortably on the box between two enormous gendarmes.

The horses were steaming, although they had proceeded at a walk all the way from the Temple, and the carriage crawled down towards the scaffold, which had been erected on the site of the demolished statue of Louis's predecessor. Surmounting the structure and, from where I stood, dominating the Place was the guillotine and, hardly a stone's throw away, the statue of Liberty, robbed now of the impressiveness that its size and novelty had until recently imparted to it.

I was in the second rank but I got a good glimpse of the interior of the carriage as it passed, for the window was down and the curtain drawn back. Louis was sitting facing the horses, with a gendarme on one side and his confessor, the Abbé Edgeworth, on the side nearer to me. The ex-king was wearing the same puce coat I had seen him wear in the Temple and appeared to be reading. The abbé was talking and gesticulating with the back of his peruke turned towards me.

The king did not appear to be agitated; indeed, he was far less perturbed than the man beside me, whose cognac I had shared. This fellow was straining forward, his lips parted and his eyes staring as though they would burst from their sockets. It was so quiet after the carriage had gone by that I could hear his quick breathing. As soon as the head of the procession had reached the Place the stiff ranks higher up the street billowed forward, the men staring after the carriage and its horsed escort led by General Santerre, the ex-brewer, whom I had seen ordering the attack on the Tuileries. Commands rang out, compelling a re-dressing of ranks, and the stir subsided as the horsemen deployed and formed up in front of the scaffold. I took a quick glance at the escort hoping to see André, but he wasn't there, and I also failed to identify him in the foot battalion that marched immediately behind. I soon forgot him in the drama that commenced some two hundred yards away. I was sufficiently near to the scaffold to get a general impression of what was happening without being able to differentiate between the principal actors, or do more than guess at what they were doing.

I saw a small group of men mount the steps of the platform, which was a very tall one rising several feet above the roof of the carriage. Then I heard a single, high-pitched voice addressing the huge crowd, but the words were indistinguishable and hardly a dozen had been said before a plumed horseman—Santerre, I suppose—pranced forward from the spot where the carriage had stopped and shouted an order, presumably an instruction to the drummers, for a moment later the silence was shattered by the steady rolling of drums which soon swelled into an immense volume of sound as it was taken up by every drummer on parade.

On all sides now guardsmen had broken their dressing and turned their faces to the Place. The rolling of the drums seemed to give them confidence and they began to shout to one another at the top of their voices, the parade soon losing all semblance of military precision. The excited little man beside me began to comment on what he thought was happening on the scaffold.

"It's done," he shouted, and then, correcting himself, "no it isn't. There's Capet, he's resisting! Look, he's fighting them!" He fumbled for his flask again but his excitement was so great that he dribbled the liquor over his tunic.

There was indeed some sort of scuffle going on at the foot of the guillotine but we were too far away to see whether it was caused by the fumbling efforts of the executioners to assist their victim to disrobe, or by Louis's reluctance, at this late stage, to submit to the inevitable.

My head began to spin. I had seen men hanged before when I took cattle into Exeter market. The executions at Heavitree Gibbet were always reserved for market days and I once witnessed, unmoved, the topping of a whole batch of my father's associates, but this spectacle was different. One could sense a dreadful tension in the breast of every man in that vast throng and the suspense went on mounting until the strain of it became almost unbearable.

I put my musket stock on the *pavé* and leaned heavily on the barrel, fixing my eye on the glistening edge of the roof immediately opposite and trying to stop my ears to the babel of sound that vied with the long, rolling note of the drums. I kept repeating to myself: 'We'll be out of this tonight, we'll be on our way tonight!' Then a sharp, unmistakable sound cut through the monotone of the drums and silenced the crowd as effectually as the slamming of a heavy door on the uproar. It was the harsh, metallic clang of the falling knife.

The next thing I was conscious of was the middle-aged guardsman's attempt to force his cognac flask between my teeth and the scalding taste of the liquor on my tongue. I don't think I had fainted, but I certainly didn't hear the shout that acknowledge Executioner Sanson's exhibition of Louis's head to the people. The formal lines of the National Guard had now dissolved into groups of semi-hysterical men, who embraced one another and capered about the pavements like circus animals lately escaped from their cages. Glee showed in every face and with it a sort of ecstatic relief, as though each of them had just been plucked from the jaws of death. I have only seen such expressions on the faces of men on one other occasion, when a barque ran on the rocks off Straight Point one night and lay there, cut off from human aid until morning, when it was swept by a freakish wave up to highwater mark, enabling the terrified crew to get to the beach unharmed. As a boy I had myself joined in the gleeful capers that followed this episode, but now the hysteria of the crowd sickened me, including much the same sort of revulsion as that I had experienced in the Abbaye courtyard on the first night of the September massacres. I was impatient to get back to Charlotte and to escape from my grotesque companion, who persisted in his good-natured efforts to stupefy me with raw spirit. Notwithstanding his good intentions, he disgusted me, for he kept repeating between his chuckles: "It's done, citizen, it's done!"

At last I was able to break away from this section of the crowd and shoulder my way towards the junction of the rue St. Honoré. Shopkeepers were out and about now and beginning to take their shutters down in anticipation of a good day's business. By the time I had recrossed the bridge and climbed to the top of the hill life in the streets had returned to normal, although even here a relaxation of the general tension was noticeable and everyone appeared to be in exceptionally high spirits.

I was just about to turn into our court when I saw André hurrying up the hill from the direction of the river, his cloak bellying in the east wind that had sprung up during our long stand in arms in the rue Royale. He caught sight of me and called, urgently.

"David! Wait!"

As he came nearer I saw that he was very much out of breath and looked very worried. He must have pounded along at that pace all the way from the Temple.

"Where were you?" I began. "I didn't see you in the

escort. . . ." I broke off in response to his impatient gesture, and asked: "Has anything gone wrong?"

They've moved her," he gasped out. "More than
half of the prisoners were redistributed the moment they
took Capet away. I don't even know where she is; I only
hope to God it isn't the Conciergerie!" Before I could
exclaim he went on: "You see, David, this thing'll start
them all dancing to the Jacobin tune. They'll get rid of a
hundred prisoners a day now that they've set the seal of
respectability on murder!"

I almost cried out with disappointment and chagrin.
All our carefully laid plans had been ruined by a single
stroke of bad luck. I knew that André woudn't leave Paris
without the girl and Charlotte wouldn't leave without
André, so here we were, the three of us, boxed up in a
city of lunatics, with very little prospect of getting out of
it in time to take up our passages at the port.

I cursed the Revolution then and everyone connected
with it, and I cursed myself for accepting Saxeby's advice
and not adhering to my own decision to make for America
in the first instance. In the wretchedness of that moment, I
overlooked the fact that my presence in Paris was due
largely to my own curiosity and even contemplated, for an
instant, washing my hands of the entire family and taking
my own chances at the barriers, but by that time we had
reached the green door of Rouzet's *salon* and Charlotte
came out of the powder-room to greet us, insisting that
we swallowed a glass of steaming coffee she had just prepared.

I knew then, as I warmed my numbed hands on the
tumbler and watched her quiet smile through the steam of
the brew, that my future was tied to hers and to André's,
and that whatever occurred now we should sink or swim
together.

Chapter Thirteen

As soon as we had an opportunity we got together in my room, which was the only place in which we could be sure of privacy.

Charlotte received the news with her customary calm and asked André if it meant postponement or cancellation of our flight. André said he would have to cancel our passages and try to reclaim the money, although he had grave doubts about getting it or, for that matter, of being able to book berths in the future.

"Now they've disposed of Louis," he prophesied, "every bourgeois in the country will run for it, and some of them have a good deal more money than we have. How much have you got left, David?"

I told him round about fifty guineas, some of which we had to keep by unless we wanted to land penniless.

"You and Charlotte had better go," he said, "there's no sense in throwing money away."

Charlotte shook her head. "We won't go without you, André, David wouldn't wish it."

This wasn't strictly true and I began to wish that everybody in the house would stop playing heroics, but I didn't care to admit as much in front of Charlotte. André must have guessed my feelings in the matter for he grinned and said: "Maybe you'd better let David speak for himself, Lottë. What do you say, David?"

I changed the subject. "Let's try and find out where Lucille's been sent," I proposed.

"It's either the Conciergerie or the Luxembourg," he said. "If it's the latter we stand some sort of chance, they still allow visitors. Getting her out isn't the most difficult part of the business."

"Then what is?"

"Passports," said André, and threw an oilskin packet

containing the four movement permits he had procured on
to the bed. "These are no use after tomorrow, they're
made out for the American brig and they're dated. You
can't monkey with passports nowadays, they're getting far
too spry at the barriers. Barère had a man shot at the St.
Denis gate three days ago for letting a market cart through
without an inspection! Liberty's getting the cramp, David!"

Charlotte had the one useful idea emerging from the
conference.

"Why don't you ask Paine to help you?" she suggested.
It wasn't a bad notion. Paine had a number of American
connections among the trading fraternity in Paris and I
wondered I hadn't thought of him before. Perhaps it was a
reluctance on my part to admit that I had long since despaired of his revolution. I hadn't set eyes on him for
nearly a month.

"All right," I said, "I'll go and ask him and you see
if you can get our money back while I'm gone."

André chuckled. "Trust an Englishman to worry more
over his guineas than over his head," he bantered as he
swung his long legs over the packing-cases that still served
me for a bed.

He would have gone out right away but Charlotte called
to him sharply.

"André!"

He turned in the doorway. "Well, Lottë?"

"You're not in love with this girl Lucille, are you?"

"No," he answered smoothly, "did I ever say I was?"

"Then why don't we make off, the three of us?" I
growled.

André came back to us and looked me squarely in the
face.

"I've advised you to go alone, haven't I? There are
your passports, all you've got to do is to pack up and
leave as soon as it's dark. You won't have any trouble
with those papers and you'll get to the coast in three days
if you don't mind spending a few more guineas on the
fast diligence!"

"You haven't answered David's question," said Char-

lotte quietly. "He's got a right to know why you decided
to take Lucille in the first place."

"You might understand, but I doubt if David would,"
he countered.

"Why not give him the chance?" replied Charlotte
evenly.

He thrust his hands into his breeches pockets and
wrinkled his forehead.

"When all this is over and half a hundred historians are
sharpening their quills to put an account of it on paper,
you'll read how the wicked Jacobins sent this one and
that one to the scaffold," he said. "They'll devote whole
pages to Louis and his family, even to describing what he
wore and which way he sat when they put him in the
carriage for his final coach ride. The final moments of all
the dukes and the vicomtes will be written down and no
one will bother to add that most of them earned their
fate, if not by cruelty or avarice then by sloth or ignorance.
But the real butcheries won't get into the records. Who
would bother to record the death of Lucille Souham, a
milliner, who might be stitching away in a basement at
this moment if she could have been persuaded to spit at
an employer who wouldn't have known her surname if she
had been asked!"

Charlotte nodded gravely and I saw that she understood
him but I didn't exactly, so I said:

"Whose side are you really on, André?"

"Whose?" He got up, yawning. "I'm on the side of the
Lucille Souhams," he said. "The way I look at it is this—
if their sacrifices don't count why should there be any
sacrifices?" He realized I didn't fully understand him and
laughed. "The trouble with me, David, is that I see things
as clearly as you do—that's something to thank your country upbringing for, but if you compel me to choose a
mistress to serve I won't pick Liberty, as the Jacobins
have done, or Dame Rhetoric, as have Biron and his fine-
feathered friends, or even Venus, to whom you seem to
have pledged yourself; I'd take Pity, then I can follow my
instincts without bothering to think things out."

He got up abruptly and left us. We heard him go whistling downstairs and out through the *salon* door.

Charlotte burst out laughing at my puzzled expression.

"That's what I love about you, David," she said gaily. "You're the only man in Paris who doesn't think in riddles!"

I called on Tom Paine the following morning. Owing to the extremely large number of visitors he was receiving, he had had to leave his hotel and take lodgings at No. 63 Fauborg St. Denis. Since the decline of his party in the Convention, Paine had spent most of his time writing and at that time was engaged on the first part of his *Age of Reason,* a survey of contemporary religion which subsequently gained him the reputation of an atheist, which he most certainly was not.

I was shown up to his study as soon as I announced myself. "Clio" Rickman, his London publisher, and Joel Barlow, his American friend, were with him and I was introduced to these two unusual characters who remained his champions when few of his French friends cared to be seen in his company.

I was reluctant to talk in front of strangers but Paine speedily reassured me and I told him the whole story of our attempt to leave Paris and our hope of settling in America. He was far less inclined to dissuade me from such a course than on the occasion when I had first broached the subject to him six months previously, for by this time Paine himself was beginning to despair, if not of the common man, then of that particular species of libertarian dominating the French capital. Most of his friends already went in daily fear of their lives, and were obliged to enter the hall of the Assembly to the accompaniment of the jeers and threats of a picked band of ruffians picqueting the door. Perhaps this was why, in his hour of political discouragement, Paine was turning his great mind to spiritual problems. Masses of manuscripts lay on the desk and I had interrupted a conference regarding the publication of the first part of the new book.

Notwithstanding this, Paine gave my problem his usual

close attention and expressed himself eager to help. He did this, not because he approved of running away, but because, on his own admission, he considered that America had urgent need of young couples intent upon founding families. Only by this means, he declared, could the former colonies be buttressed against the attempts of foreign powers to re-annex them.

As we had anticipated, the execution of Louis XVI had precipitated war with England, and although this made me an enemy alien, it also served to further a plan of escape, formulated in the lively imagination of "Clio" Rickman.

"This friend of yours, the surgeon, surely he will be without a practice now that the Temple has lost the greater part of its prisoners?" queried Rickman. "It should be a simple matter to arrange his transfer to the prison to which the young lady has been sent, eh, Tom?"

Paine looked troubled. "Whilst fully prepared to further Mr. Treloar's plans to emigrate," he said gravely, "I cannot, as a deputy of France, connive at the escape of a State prisoner."

This description of André's wretched little milliner was laughable, and I said so. "Lucille Souham is innocent of anything but an excess of loyalty towards her former employer, the Princesse de Lamballe," I told him. "If you had been in the prison as I have, Mr. Paine, you would soon discover that more than half the people now behind bars owed their position to chance and bad luck."

Paine nodded. "That's true," he sighed, "and unless I'm mistaken I shall soon be there myself. Why can't those ruffians realize that the immediate danger of Prussian invasion is past and that measures of severity must be relaxed if the Revolution is to gain breathing space."

In his agitation he got up and stumped to and fro across the low-ceilinged room, his massive head just missing the central beam as he passed back and forth.

"All the monstrous tyrannies that have sat upon the necks of mankind since the days of the Pharaohs have tried to break the spirit of the people by instituting sanguinary punishments," he declared vehemently. "Cannot we, as the first free republic in Europe, set a new example of mercy and forbearance? Would it not lift up the hearts of the people everywhere if one of our first public acts was to demolish the guillotine and the gallows?"

He broke off and smiled apologetically. "I am sorry, David; let me know the moment you have located this girl and I will persuade my good friend Danton to transfer the surgeon to her prison. Perhaps I might even be able to procure her release. Danton himself agrees with me that there has been too much bloodshed already, but his position, like ours, is entirely dependent upon the goodwill of Jacobin extremists."

The matter of the transfer of André was easy enough to arrange. Even before declarations of war had been exchanged English people of both sexes were being rounded up by the hundred and carted to the teeming jails all over the city. It was for this reason that the Temple had been cleared of suspects in order to accommodate large numbers of English seamen, arrested in the various ports the moment war with England became imminent. It transpired that Lucille had gone to the Luxembourg, where a number of private citizens of British nationality were confined. Paine, as the only Englishman in the Convention, was deputed to interrogate some of these people and it proved a simple matter for him to request the services of an English-speaking surgeon.

While I was with Paine, however, and seeing that the American Barlow was present, I thought I might as well sound the latter on the prospects of getting travel premits and passages. Joel Barlow entered into the conspiracy with the zest of a mischievous boy and promised to contact his Biscayan agents within the week, holding out good prospects of getting the four of us a passage on one of the trading schooners owned by the firm he represented. He also thought it likely that he could procure American papers of less dubious origin than those supplied by André's friend.

I left Paine's house in a very cheerful frame of mind and returned home snug in the belief that our unexpected delay would be instrumental in making our escape a safer venture than it migh otherwise have proved.

André awaited me impatiently and told me of the whereabouts of Lucille. I proposed going to the Luxembourg immediately and, if possible, acquainting her with our plans, but first insisted that this time André should acquaint both Charlotte and myself with his plans for freeing her. I pointed out that if it involved any great risk we would do better to rely upon Paine's efforts to procure a *bona fide* order of release.

Charlotte thought this reasoning sound, but André, who in such matters often displayed the vanity of a precious child, held out against us for some time but finally consented to outline the plan that had occurred to him. He said he had already studied the routine prevailing at the Luxembourg regarding the admission and exit of visitors. When the bell clanged in the late afternoon all visitors were required to assemble in the inner court preparatory to being let out and were counted by a tallyman as they passed out through the main gate to the terrace steps. Once installed on the prison staff, he thought it would be a simple matter to distract the tallyman's attention for a couple of seconds whilst Charlotte and myself, with Lucille between us, passed through the gate with the other visitors. We considered the plan a good one but we made André promise to wait a fortnight in order to see whether the release could be obtained. He agreed to this reluctantly. André always preferred the long way round.

The following day, a Thursday, André and I set out for the Luxembourg, but we had timed our visit very badly, for our journey up to the palace gates happened to coincide with the funeral procession of the murdered Deputy Lepelletier. This man, an extremist who had voted for the king's execution, had been singled out by a fanatical royalist and assassinated as he snatched a meal between sessions at Fevrier's Restaurant in the Palais Royale. He was now being interred in the Panthéon with full civic honours.

Had we been in a less serious mood this ridiculous public funeral would have provided a highly amusing spectacle. The patriots, determined to make a martyr out of the first of the number to suffer a violent death for his principles, had gone to extraordinary lengths to impress the Parisians. Lepelletier had been laid on a funeral carriage wrapped in an open winding sheet and the death wound he had received in the side was exposed to the public gaze. Immediately behind the cortège marched his fellow deputies, Girondin and Jacobin, arm-in-arm for the last time, and mingling torrents of crocodile tears. In front of the car marched the St. Antoine band, playing suitably mournful music, and as this strange procession wound its way up the hill towards the Panthéon the easily moved street rabble raised loud cries of lamentation.

Caught in the crowds, André and I watched it pass the Club des Cordeliers and turn into the rue de l'Observatoire. Among the shuffling deputies I caught sight of Marcelle's husband, Biron, and a number of his friends whom I had encountered from time to time at No. 12. There were strange bedfellows among the mourners, handsome Barbaroux, immaculately attired in black velvet; his friend Louvet, trying, and hardly succeeding, to keep his lips from twitching at the pantomime; Danton, looking very solemn; and his handsome shadow, Desmoulins, shaking his black locks and looking arrogantly from side to side as though searching out more assassins in the crowd. Robespierre was there, also faultlessly dressed and preserving that cold mask of detachment soon to become famous throughout Europe. Even Marat and the loathsome cripple Couthon had turned out, the latter carried on the shoulders of a couple of grenadiers. Some of the deputies looked the worse for drink. Those that did were the better for being the least hypocritical.

It was the first time I had ever seen Robespierre, and I can understand why his colleagues underestimated him for so long. He did not stand out, as did his rival Danton, and the murmur that he was accorded was a whisper compared with that accorded the wild-eyed Marat, who had risen from his sickbed to take part in his colleague's obsequies.

As soon as the tail of the procession had passed we pushed our way through the crowd and entered the Luxembourg gardens by the postern, where a surly sentry made a great to-do pretending to examine our passes, a facetious act on his part, for he was quite unable to read.

The Luxembourg presented a very different aspect from when I was there the previous Sunday with Charlotte. Its forecourt and terrace now bristled with cannon and there were picquets of troops all over the grounds.

Regarding this, André said: "We should make more progress against the counter-revolution in the field if we were less hysterical about it at home."

He was right. There were, at that time, no fewer than nineteen prisons in Paris and each had the garrison of a small fortress, which meant work for at least a dozen trained battalions.

The Luxembourg, however, if one of the most over-crowded jails, was among the best administered from the prisoners' viewpoint. The inmates were allowed to associate freely with one another and as many visitors as they cared to entertain from early morning until sundown, providing each visitor had documentary right of entry. I soon realized that if André's plan was used it would be comparatively simple to operate.

We met several prisoners with whom we had brief acquaintance. One or two loose-tongued deputies, or rather ex-deputies, were already there, amusing themselves by compiling memoirs and other tracts. If a Brissotin couldn't talk he was almost always just as ready to write. If the members of the party had shown as much energy inside the convention as they did outside it, they might have ruled France with time to spare.

Most of the new prisoners were English people and it was strange to hear English voices again after close on eight months in France. The only English voices I had heard since I arrived in Paris were Paine's and Rickman's.

The English families were not taking very kindly to their detention. In the main hall I heard a squat little merchant captain damn France and the Revolution at the top of his voice and call some of the jailers every abusive name he could lay tongue to; not far away was an exquisitely dressed buck, whose sightseeing tour of the capital had been cut short by the gendarmes. This prisoner went one better than the sea-captain, abusing the French nation in its own language and remaining quite indifferent to the threats and protests of the exasperated officer of the guard to whom he addressed his remarks. Having used all the French expletives he knew, he resorted once more to his mother-tongue.

"Demned insolence!" he kept repeating, in a high-pitched, lisping accent. "Demned insolence, sir, and liable to cost you a pretty penny before you've heard the last of this! I come over here to see for myself what a demned mess you're making, spending demned good English guineas to keep you and your demned country out of the hands of the Jews, and what do you do, sir? Do you flatter? Do you court me? Do you lick my boots for exchanging minted gold for your filthy paper currency? No, sir, gash my belly if you do, you thrust me into a demned flea-pit and won't even send to my sty of a hotel for a vinegar bottle to plug my tortured nostrils against the demned stench of your sweating hides, demn you! Slit my wind-pipe, sir, it's an outrage, a demned and shameless outrage!"

André was highly amused by this diatribe and would have stayed listening to hear the end of it if I hadn't hustled him into the guardroom and demanded to see the prison register in order the check the names of the transfers from the Temple. Lucille Souham's name was indeed there all right, and we crossed into the wing of the palace reserved for women prisoners, of which there were already several hundred and others arriving every hour as the gendarmes rounded up more and more aliens from the environs.

I experienced a shock when we ultimately came upon her, sitting a little apart from the other Frenchwomen and looking as though she expected a summons to the guillotine at any moment. She started violently when she saw André, but unless I was much mistaken even the unexpected appearance of her Prince Charming failed to kindle any hope in her listless, red-rimmed eyes, and the sudden flush his presence occasioned soon died away and left her cheeks as pale as new parchment.

The wing was so crowded that we were able to talk
without danger of being overheard, and André put on a
good show of playful assurance.

"We'll have you out of here in a week," he told her, and
outlined the essentials of our plan.

She listened apathetically, and when he had finished,
and laid a hand on her shoulder, her own hand shot up
and seized his with an intensity that made him wince.

"I don't want you to do it, André," she protested. "I
don't want you to wait for me any longer. You and this
gentleman must go away at once or I shall ruin everything
for you all, I know I shall; I've had dreams. . . ."

André snorted with contempt.

"I don't give a fig for your dreams; you'll do exactly as
I say!" he thundered. "Haven't we enough problems without you trying to ape the heroine?"

She calmed herself a little and withdrew her hand.

"I mean it, André," she said more quietly. "I'm nothing
but a hindrance to you and you ought to stop trying to
help me. I'm all right here; the people are kind and
friendly, and if I could only lay my hands on some clean
smallclothes I could manage without bringing trouble on
you and your friends. If you meddle with me any more
you'll be in here yourself, and your friends and family
along with you. I couldn't bear being to blame for that;
I should kill myself!"

She wasn't being heroic, not consciously at all events,
and I found my heart warming towards her for her hon-
esty and unusual courage, but André was extremely irritated by her attitude and, seizing her by the shoulders,
shook her until her dark hair broke loose from its pins
and fell across her white face.

"You listen to me," he shouted, ignoring the sudden
subsidence of the conversation around us. "I'm sick to
death of attitudes in this crazy city. What I want is action
—plain, planned, intelligent action, instead of third-rate
theatricals! For two straws I'd take you at your word and
leave you here to wait your turn. Then we'd see how
much your pose of martyrdom was worth!"

She began to cry then, not loudly and complainingly at

his roughness, but silently, like a child terrified of revealing its misery to a harsh parent. I saw that the ordeal of the last few weeks had used up what little fortitude the girl possessed, and I was angry with André for not realizing as much.

I didn't pause to think that he might have been suffering from strain himself. He strode away scowling and we hardly exchanged a word on the way home. When we arrived there we found Charlotte in the *salon,* sharpening razors and generally helping Papa Rouzet. She hardly ever came out of the perfumery during business hours, so I asked the reason.

"Vizet's left us," she said. "He's been elected a member of the Commune!"

"That'll be of assistance to us in a variety of ways," grunted André. "Has he left here for good?"

Rouzet said he didn't think so, but Vizet had told him he would have to spend a week or two at the Hotel de Ville in order to get accustomed to his new responsibilities. I was glad the fellow had gone and I'm sure that Charlotte was. Neither of us had cared to have him about the place but Rouzet was likely to miss him during his busy periods, for he was a good enough barber, despite his sullen manners and the embarrassment he caused ogling Charlotte when he had had a glass of wine too many.

André was in an unusually bad temper. The interview with Lucille had obviously upset him.

"You warn Marcelle to keep her lapdogs out of here," he told Rouzet shortly. "With Master Vizet sporting a Jacobin cockade we shall have a cross chalked on this door if they continue to use this place as their debating chamber!"

Rouzet spread his hands and puffed out his pink cheeks.

"Why isn't everybody civil to one another?" he complained. "This used to be a pleasant place to live, now it seems we have trouble with everyone."

"There's going to be enough trouble for everyone from now on," said André, and went upstairs to change his linen, coming down again shortly afterwards and going off to his surgery at the Temple. After that I only saw him once a week, when he came in to ask for news of his transfer and the permits Barlow was trying to get us.

They were a long time coming. All through the spring the tempo of life in the city continued to increase until the strain began to show in the faces and tempers of almost everyone afoot in the streets.

I went over to Paine's lodging every day and spent some time with him translating journals and discussing the situation in the Convention. Paine said that the Jacobins were not so strong as they imagined and that it only required a show of force on the part of the Girondins to swing the populace over to the side of the moderates. The Brissotin leaders, however, continued to show little or no statesmanship and blundered from compromise to compromise, emerging a shade weaker from each of them. Vergiaud and Condorcet arraigned Marat and actually brought him to trial, but they were too pusillanimous, or too divided in their counsels, to pursue their advantage, and Marat was acquitted of his bullies. It needed somebody less muddle-headed than a provincial deputy to silence Marat's ceaseless howl for blood.

News from the frontiers was not good in the weeks following the king's execution. The early victories of the republican armies had been more than counterbalanced by serious reverses such as Dumouriez's at Neerwinden on March 10th. Dumouriez's prestige was declining as rapidly as Lafayette's had done the previous year, and the general's insolent attitude towards the Convention was used as a weapon against the moderates, with whom he was supposed to sympathize.

When the news Dumouriez's final defection became known the Jacobins attempted a coup, but it was mistimed and a few hundred Brest Federals scattered the mob before it had properly assembled. The Brissotins might have been encouraged by this, but nothing short of the guillotine could stop them talking and most of them, including Biron and Marcelle, who visited us occasionally, seemed quite blind to the increasing menace of the Mountain.

April dragged by and most of May. In a city of this

size the approach of summer could always be noted by intensification of garbage stink from the choked drains and gutters. About midday it became insufferably hot in the streets and, as always, the public unrest rose with the heat. It was not necessary to scan the more popular of the revolutionary journals to know that every faubourg was a powder magazine and that any incident touching public imagination was liable to supply a spark to fire it at a moment's notice.

When I was not making a précis of articles for Paine I lent a hand in the *salon* and became reasonably expert with Rouzet's ivory-handled razors, scent-sprays and complicated powder sprinklers, but as spring advanced into summer, and the big elm in our court began to spread its leaves, I longed more and more to walk over the crest of Westdown uplands and sniff again the salt tang of the west wind blowing inshore from Torbay.

In the evening Charlotte and I often took a stroll in the Jardin des Plantes or the Tuileries gardens, and on Sundays we sometimes hired a trap from a local saddler and once went as far afield as the Trianon woods, where the wretched Antoinette had spent so many pastoral hours. This park was now flung open to the public and a sorry mess they had made of it, uprooting shrubs and plants, and strewing the deep glades with a townsman's litter. There were no gardeners now to trim the long privet hedges or cut the clumps into fantastic shapes and likenesses, and the network of paths encircling the Temple of Love were weedgrown and bedraggled with four years' neglect. Where the queen had once played at being a shepherdess, and entertained ambassadors to open-air banquets providing twenty-four courses from her portable field kitchens tended by innumerable flunkeys, were drab, canvas booths, displaying sherbet, lemonade and cheap confectionery. Tatterdemalion gamins of the streets performed acrobatic feats for coppers, and raw recruits of the Versailles volunteers shouldered their dummy muskets up and down the forest rides. We only went there on one occasion and I'm glad Paine wasn't with us, it might have

cost him what remained of his dwindling faith in the in-
herent decency of the ordinary man.

During these weeks I stayed on our side of the river
whenever I could, particularly when I was accompanied
by Charlotte, for the St. Antoine quarter had become
very dangerous and its population thronged the route
from the Pont Neuf to Place de Révolution every evening to witness the processions from the Conciergerie, and
other metropolitan jails, to the scaffold. These processions,
which occurred about six o'clock each evening, had become a regular feature of the city's life since the formation of Danton's Committee of Public Safety. Danton
wasn't a monster and I don't think that the giant republican had ever intended that his Committee should be
used as an instrument of terror, but that is what it became
once Fouquier-Tinville had been installed as President.

The daily tally of executions rose steadily during the
spring, and by midsummer they average two score a day.
Two guillotines were in constant operation and victims
seemed to be selected haphazard, at the whim of the concierges, or the representatives of the Paris districts in
which the jails were situated.

I feared for Lucille in the Luxembourg, but the fact
that she was there and not in the Conciergerie, or the
Palace of the Grand Prior adjoining the Temple, was
something in her favour, for by this time more than half
the prisoners in the Luxembourg were foreign internees,
not charged with any specific offense against the republic.

The St. Antoine mob delighted in these dismal spec-
tacles. It was as though a surgical blood-letting operation
had to be performed each evening to ward off an outbreak
of serious dimensions and perhaps this was partly why
the Convention countenanced such barbarity. The alley-
dwellers on the east bank were not wholly to blame for
the depravity they showed. Most of them had been born
and reared in conditions of revolting squalor and life was
cheap in slums where hardly one child in three attained
the age of ten years.

There was another aspect, too; the Bourbons as a family, if not poor Louis, had long accustomed the Parisians

to the spectacle of bloody executions. The illiterate pike-
man of the sections could hardly be expected to share
Paine's lofty principles regarding the desirability of dis-
pensing with capital punishment save in the most aggravated cases of murder and robbery. I only blamed
wretches like Philippe Egalité, the renegade Prince of the
Blood, who now sat in the Convention and could always
be relied upon to support the worse excesses of the Jacobins. I had seen him once, when he skimmed by in his
cabriolet at Louis's execution. He was a handsome man,
with fine hands and delicate features, and I could never
understand the astonishing enthusiasm with which he embraced the Jacobin cause. Paine said it was ambition, and
Biron the instinct of self-preservation. André accepted
neither of these explanations but put it down to the jeal-
ousy and vindictiveness of a highly educated failure.

In the last week of May, almost on the anniversary of
my flight from England, Joel Barlow summoned me to his
lodging and handed me our permits, each complete with
an official stamp. He wouldn't accept any money for
them but said we could reimburse the company for the
food we ate during our voyage. The papers were undated
but he had arranged for us to travel on the schooner
Pennsylvania, due out of Bordeaux on June 10th.

The rest of our plans were carefully laid. Paine's attempts to obtain a release had apparently failed, but
André had been assistant surgeon and accoucheur at the
Luxembourg for nearly a month, and although his duties
were so exacting that he saw little of Lucille, now segre-
gated in a wing reserved for French prisoners, he felt
confident that, when the time came, we could easily smuggle the girl out of the prison. In order to reduce the risk
of recapture to a minimum we decided to leave her where
she was until the last moment, and I bought seats on the
Orleans coach for the night of the 4th, which gave us
ample time to make Bordeaux in time for the sailing on
the 10th.

On the last night of May I went up to the Luxembourg
to confer with André and to study the tallyman's routine
for myself, since Charlotte and I were both to play a part

in the pantomime André had planned at the outer gate. I
had seen André the previous night and he was in high
spirits. He had found means of communicating our plan
to Lucille and drilling her in her part of the business,
brushing aside her renewed protests that we should abandon her and go to America ourselves without further delay. She did not seem to have shaken off the apathy she
displayed during our first visit to the prison, but André,
whose moods were always unpredictable, in this instance
made light of her reluctance to escape and dismissed her
weakness as the result of depression caused by lengthy
confinement.

"She's really a merry little rascal," he assured me.
"You should have seen her when they first brought her in,
before Lamballe was taken from her. Once out of jail
you'll see a change in her, and the voyage will do her all
the good in the world."

I wanted to ask him if he intended marrying her when
we got to Philadelphia, but I didn't, for one never knew
how André would receive a question of that sort, and I
couldn't risk getting him in a huff at this stage.

I arrived at the Palace about sundown and presented
my National Guard pass at the entrance to the wing where
I knew Lucille was detained. André had promised to meet
me here, but as he didn't appear after a quarter of an
hour's wait I went down the corridor to the grille at the
far end, which opened on to the women's hall.

There was some sort of stir going on beyond the steel
wicket and the concierge who usually stood there had left
his post, so that I had to wait on the outside and peer
through the grating into the badly-lit hall beyond.

A crowd of nearly fifteen women and half a dozen children had clustered round the iron door and some steps at
the far end leading to the smaller apartments now used as
cells. Their backs were towards me and I saw the concierge shoulder his way through them and clear a space
between the foremost women at the door.

At that moment the door opened and a little procession
began to descend the short flight of steps into the hall.
First came the women's concierge, jangling a huge bunch

of keys at his belt, then a couple of soldiers from the garrison carrying something between them, and finally André, looking dazed and stupid as he paused at the foot of the steps and stood blinking in the half-light.

The two concierges cleared a way through the assembled prisoners and motioned the soldiers towards the wicket where I was standing. As the bolts were shot back and the grille swung open, I saw what the men were carrying. It was the body of Lucille Souham. Her face passed within a couple of feet of mine and I saw at a glance that she was dead. The frayed end of a stoutish piece of cord protruded from her heavy black tresses, which almost swept the ground as the soldiers squeezed through the wicket and into the corridor. Her large brown eyes were open and staring and her legs dangled pitifully behind the second bearer. She must have weighed the merest trifle, for the two men marched down the corridor at a rapid pace, the principal jailer leading the way with his guttering flambeau.

I stared after the procession in such a state of bewilderment that I hardly noticed André pass to my side of the wicket as the concierge slammed and locked the grille.

Although we were within a yard or two of one another he didn't appear to see me but stumbled forward into the corridor after the body. I pulled myself together and hurried after him, but he took no notice of me until I caught him by the arm. He saw me then and turned a blank face towards me.

"She hanged herself a few minutes after I'd left her," he said hoarsely. "What do you think could have made her do a thing like that?"

He looked as if he was going to faint, so I got him out of the corridors and into a little alcove where a window had been blocked up and the builders had left a pile of rubble. My first thought was that he had been involved in the tragedy and I had to discover how much the concierge or anyone else knew about his connection with the girl.

I needn't have bothered. Bit by bit I coaxed the story out of him, and a pitiful story it was. Lucille had hanged herself as the only means at her disposal of preventing André from exposing himself to the risk of arrest in event of our plan failing. She had begged him to abandon it every time he had discussed it with her, and having failed to win him over to her point of view had hanged herself from a grating over her cell door. It was a salutary lesson on the folly of judging people by appearances. Lucille Souham had always appeared to me a dilatory, febrile little creature, without the resolution to kill a cockroach, much less herself, yet, having failed to convince André, she had calmly set about procuring for herself a piece of cord (a difficult task inside a prison), had awaited an opportunity of being alone in her cell at the hour when nearly all her fellow prisoners were gathered for supper in the hall, and had somehow contrived to climb to a grating twelve feet from the floor level and launch herself into space.

I managed to buy André a stiff glass of rum in the jailers' canteen, and he went into the guardroom to make his official report on Lucille's death. When he came out he was much calmer and we walked home together, taking the long way round and saying little. We had four days to make up our minds what to do, and I didn't care to reshuffle our plans without consulting Charlotte.

We got home about one in the morning and let ourselves in by the back door.

Charlotte met us on the first landing, coming out of her room with a candlestick in her right hand and a finger to her lips.

"Go in with David for the night, André," she whispered. "Marcelle's here and she's started her baby. I had to put her in your room!"

We stood there on the landing. I don't know about André but I felt about as helpless as a lost child. I didn't know whether to tell Charlotte about Lucille or wait until morning. Before I could make up my mind Charlotte had glided along the passage towards André's room and disappeared. I took André by the arm and pushed him into my storeroom, fumbling in my pockets for a tinder-box to light the stump of candle I kept on the packing-case that I used for a dressing-chest.

The first shower of sparks revealed Deputy Biron, sound asleep in my bed.

I lit the candle and was relieved to see a rueful grin crinkle Andre's mouth. With events crowding in on us in this fashion it was good to feel that André's sense of humour was bobbing up again.

He said: "If we keep quiet, he's sure to quote Livy in his sleep."

Chapter Fourteen

"Bon *Dieu*!" exclaimed André as we moved towards the bed, "the fellow uses a nightcap!"

It was not a nightcap, however, but a bandage, wound tightly round the temples.

I was dog-tired and disinclined to be more hospitable than I could help, so I shook Biron and jumped back when he jerked upright and produced a pistol from under the pillow. He had evidently been sleeping with his right hand on the butt.

His look of alarm faded when he saw that it was us and he climbed slowly out of bed, looking very comical in his frilled shirt and the bandage headdress.

"I'm sorry, Treloar," he mumbled, glancing at the rumpled sheets. "I was exhausted and just meant to rest for a while. I can't stay here, they'll come searching at first light."

"Who will?" demanded André. "The police?"

Biron looked at him wildly.

"Do you mean you haven't heard?" he asked incredulously.

"We've been up at the Luxembourg all evening, it's quiet enough there," I told him.

He sat down and began to pull on his elegant calfskin boots.

"Half the deputies will be in jail by midday tomorrow," he said, "all those of us who haven't escaped already. Barbaroux, Buzot and some of the others have made a run for it. I would have gone after them but Marcelle couldn't have travelled three leagues. It's the very devil her having a child at a time like this."

"You should have worked that out when you got married," grunted André, "it's too late to belly-ache now."

André never had much patience with Biron or any of

his friends, except perhaps the dramatist Louvet, who saw
life in terms of a similar drollery and evinced a like zest
for living on the edge of danger. I suppose Biron was a
feeble sort of creature in a crisis but that wasn't really
his fault. They had gorged him with power before his
intellect had had time to mature. Here in Paris his
ingenuous provincial instincts and training led him to
trust everyone able to throw a handful of égalitarian dust
in his eyes. Faced with the violent realism of men like
Danton, he reverted to what he really was, a rather vain
youth, quite unable to find adequate answers to Jacobin
questions, even in the classics on which he had been
educated.

He was in a sorry state of nerves now and kept crossing to and from the window and strewing garments hap-
hazardly all over the room as he attempted to restore
his disarranged toilette.

"Well sit down and tell us what's happened, man," demanded André brutally.

Biron obeyed him as promptly as a frightened schoolboy.

"There's a decree out for twenty-two of the party," he
said. "The Jacobins are going to storm the Convention
and make the arrests. We had a private session yesterday
to decide what to do but we couldn't agree on any one
course, that's why Barbaroux and the others took it into
their heads to make for Caen!"

"What in God's name do they think they can do in
Caen?" asked André.

"Raise the departments and come back here with an
army!"

"But that's civil war! You won't get anybody but
royalists to support a crazy scheme like that," argued
André. "You'll only unite everyone in Paris against you."

"That's what Valazé said," went on Biron, distractedly.
"He was for standing trial and committing suicide if the
verdict goes against us!"

"What good will that do?" I ventured, reflecting that
this proposal was altogether typical of Brissotin sentiment.

"Valazé thought it might inspire the waverers to overthrow the Mountain."

André chuckled and sat down. Facing the bewildered deputy, he said: "How do you suppose you'll strengthen the cause by sticking a knife into your throat? Why don't you arm yourselves and challenge the Jacobins to a street fight? You'd have every shopkeeper and decent-class artisan in Paris behind you in twenty-four hours. Do you think they want to be ruled by a mob? How many men can you rely on, now that half of you have lost your heads and scattered?"

"Not more than a hundred," admitted Biron dolefully. "And the Jacobins are moving cannon into the Assembly Court. That's how I came by this sabre-cut. I tried to order that drunken sot Hanriot out of the precincts and he just stood up in his stirrups and let fly. I went off to tell Barbaroux then and found he'd already gone. After I'd tried Buzot's and Salles's lodgings I found Valazé and he told me that some of them have decided to go to the Convention tomorrow and defy them."

"And how does that appeal to you?" asked André grimly.

Biron wrung his hands.

"I don't know," he groaned. "I'm not afraid to die but there's Marcelle and the child. She says. . . ."

"Precisely," interrupted André, "and she's sane, take it from me. What right have you got to throw away your life on tomfool heroics? We've just come from the Luxembourg where a girl I knew, who couldn't even read or write, showed more resolution in five minutes than you and your damned chatterbox party have shown all the time you've been in office!"

"What do you advise me to do?" asked Biron thoroughly chastened by André's plain speaking.

"There's only one thing you can do," replied André, "lie low and wait for better times, if they ever come! Is there anywhere you can hide for the next four days?"

"All my friends are in the same plight," said Biron, despairingly.

André held out his hand in my direction.

"Where's the coach booking you had for me?" he demanded.

I began to protest, but he cut me short.

"I'm not asking for yours or Charlotte's, you can do what you damned well please, but I shan't use mine now and he may as well have it. He can have the movement permit, too, and please himself whether he uses it or not when he gets into his own district."

Reluctantly I passed over the oilskin package I carried. André opened it, extracted his own papers and handed the document and the ticket to Biron.

He accepted them listlessly. "What can I do about Marcelle?" he said.

"There's a passport and ticket here for Marcelle when she's ready to travel," said André, and put Lucille's papers in his shirt pocket. "Make necessary alterations on your papers, they won't be extensive as we're somewhat alike —physically!"

He stressed the word "physically" and I thought Biron winced, but he only said:

"Where can I go between now and the fourth?"

I interposed before André could say "To the devil!" and suggested that Biron took refuge at Clio Rickman's lodgings. André thought this as good a plan as any and I made Biron memorize the address. Charlotte came in then and addressed André.

You'd better come and look at Marcelle," she said, "the child wasn't due for a fortnight but all this upset might have brought it on; she's complaining now!"

"Have I got to be midwife as well?" exclaimed André brusquely, but I could see the prospect of a professional job pleased him. He washed his hands in my camp toilette and told Charlotte of the plans he had made for Biron and Marcelle. He said that he and Lucille would not be leaving Paris after all, but he didn't say why. He left that for me and went out of the room, cursing the fact that his instruments were up at the prison and wondering how he was going to get them in time if Marcelle's labour began before morning.

I told Biron that he'd better think about dodging over

to Rickman's before it got light. We had been talking the better part of two hours and there was already a streak of light filtering through the shutters. He hesitated a moment and then, looking at Charlotte, said:

"I shall have to give Marcelle directions of where to go when she gets to Bordeaux. Do you think I could see her for a moment?"

Charlotte smiled. "You can give me the directions," she said, "but go in and say goodbye to her, she'll be a lot happier if she knows you're leaving the city."

His face lit up and he kissed her heartily.

They went out of the room together, leaving me to remake my bed and get into it. I put off thinking about our own future and was sound asleep in less than a minute.

Chapter Fifteen

I SLEPT until after midday. Despite a farmer's habit of early rising, whilst living in a city I could always sleep on until someone roused me. The street cries, with which Paris rang from early morning until three in the afternoon, the hour at which most Parisians took their dinner, never disturbed me as the sounds of restless cattle and barnyard fowls had done when I was at Westdown. Perhaps it was because the criers, unlike the animals, expected nothing of me.

When I opened my eyes the noon sun was streaming in through the shutters and the house seemed unnaturally quiet. I lay pondering the events of the previous evening, beginning with the death of Lucille Souham and ending with Biron's tale of disaster and André's abrupt exit to deliver Marcelle's child. I wanted to get up and find out what had happened, but before I stirred I tried to make up my mind what to do about our escape, now that Lucille's death, and André's impulsive generosity, had reduced our party to two. I was sorry for Biron, and sorrier still for his wife, faced as she was with bringing her first child into the world under the present circumstances, but I wished all the same that Biron hadn't accepted the passports, for I felt sure that I could have persuaded André to come with us. In addition, I couldn't help feeling that the use of these papers, which could easily be traced if Biron was recognized and arrested during the next few days, might easily cause Charlotte and myself a good deal of trouble. As I thought of this I felt a surge of irritation for all people unable to mind their own business and impelled to meddle in politics, and perhaps it was this that determined me to adhere to the original plan as far as Charlotte and myself were concerned and to let all the others, including André, go hang. I had a conviction that if we didn't get out of this infernal city now we should never escape from it and, sooner or later, both Charlotte and I would get fatally caught up in the whirligig.

With this resolution I got up, re-tied my cravat, plunged my face into the canvas trough and went out on to the landing to look for someone.

Immediately outside the door of my room I ran headlong into a stack of cartons, the sort used by Rouzet for storing customers' wigs. The cartons were piled in such a way as completely to screen the door and I had to push them back against the stair-rail in order to get out of the room. I could imagine no reason for their presence there, for nearly all Rouzet's stock was stored in my room or the powder-room downstairs, and why anyone should have virtually blocked the staircase with an eight-foot tower of wig cartons was beyond my powers of guessing. They were easy enough to shift, however, and I climbed through the barrier and up the short flight of stairs to the principal landing.

I had opened my mouth to call for Charlotte or André when I heard something outside that checked me, a grating, indeterminate sound, that seemed to come from the court outside, immediately below the little landing window that lit the first turn in the stairs. The window was open and I crept across to it in my stockinged feet and peeped out. I don't know why I should have been so cautious except that, after twelve months in Paris, a man tended to become suspicious of everything. It was as well that I made no sound for immediately beneath the window, and obviously acting as sentinels at the door of No. 12, were two National Guardsmen, their fixed bayonets leaning against the ground floor window-boxes that sprouted Rouzet's giant geraniums.

I withdrew my head as if I had been shot at and padded back across the landing to the entrance of the corridor, leading to André's room where Charlotte had recently installed Marcelle.

I was thoroughly frightened by this time and kept asking myself what could have happened and where Charlotte,

André and Rouzet could have gone, for although the hour before dinner was usually our busiest period the *salon* was obviously closed and the house was quieter than I ever remembered.

I tiptoed down the corridor and softly opened the door of André's room. Inside, in semi-darkness, for shutters and curtains were still drawn, was Marcelle, sound asleep. Beside her bed, and within easy reach of her hand, which was extended protectively, was an improvised cot made of a small packing-case and filled with cushions taken from Rouzet's armchair in the living-room. Fast asleep in the cot was Marcelle's baby, a brick-red morsel with screwed-up eyes and a mouth that looked smaller than a ladybird.

I looked carefully round the room in search of some sort of clue as to the whereabouts of the others. Even if I woke Marcelle I doubted if she would be able to give me any clear account of what had happened. I had never felt so wretched and helpless in my life and cursed myself for being such a sound sleeper. Marcelle stirred but she did not wake. She looked very beautiful, I thought, with her clear, white skin and tumbled black tresses.

Suddenly I felt very hungry and crept out of the room and along to the kitchen at the extreme end of the corridor. The remnants of a meal littered the table, which proved to me conclusively that Charlotte was nowhere on the premises, for she never left dirty platters about. I spooned out some honey from a pot that had been left uncovered and was attracting a horde of flies, and looked round for some bread to spread it on. There was one of Charlotte's long, home-baked loaves on the dresser and I picked it up, breaking off a length and cramming it into my mouth. As I crunched, my teeth bit into something hard and I spat out a curling-paper, folded, not lengthways, but into a compact pellet about an inch square. I dropped the roll and picked up the curling-paper, smoothing it out on the kitchen table. It was a note from Charlotte, hurriedly scrawled in charcoal eyebrow pencil. It read:

"Biron gone Papa self André taken. Trust Joseph look after Marcelle. Keep screen on your room Charlotte."

I read the note over and over again and began to sweat. It took me the better part of ten minutes to absorb its message. Then I concluded that Charlotte must have scrawled it shortly before they took her away and she had been shrewd enough to stuff it into the roll, guessing that I would be likely to go in search of food immediately I woke up and knowing how much I favoured her home-baked bread. Without much difficulty I pieced together what had occurred. A squad must have called to arrest Biron soon after he left the house and, finding him gone, had taken in Charlotte, André and Rouzet as suspects. The fact that they overlooked me had been due to the hurriedly erected screen of wig cartons piled in front of the door, either by André or Charlotte immediately before the Commune guardsmen had tramped upstairs. Joseph, the mute, had also been left behind, either because the sergeant-in-charge considered him a harmless idiot, or because his orders did not include the arrest of the boy.

I was puzzled at first by the fact that Marcelle had been left behind. Then I realized that she was being used as a bait for Biron, which explained the sentries on the door outside. Sooner or later, it had been expected, Biron would return to succour his wife and newborn child and could then be taken on the spot.

I reflected that the person behind all this must have knowledge of the family's connection with the fugitive deputy and it could only be Vizet, Rouzet's ex-assistant, in which case I would do well to keep out of sight.

It was difficult to decide what to do next. When Marcelle woke she and the baby would need some sort of attention, and while I knew a good deal about this sort of thing in the byre, my past experience did not extend to nursing a human mother and child. I would have to get help of some sort but I could not even leave the house. My only hope of locating Charlotte was through the boy Joseph, who was presumably present when the family had been arrested, but as Joseph was a deaf mute I couldn't expect much assistance from him, and even if I discovered the whereabouts of the prisoners I failed to see how I could help them, so long as Vizet was in the offing ready to swear a deposition against them as Brissotin sympathizers.

I crept back to my room and turned over a dozen plans without getting the slightest comfort out of the most practical of them. Then, about four o'clock, the most immediate part of the problem was solved for me by the arrival of Madame Gauzet, the wife of the saddler next door, whom I heard arguing with the sentries outside the *salon*. Madame Gauzet was an aggressive, mountainous woman and was loudly demanding to know what the sentries were doing there, and what had happened to her neighbours.

They told her to mind her own business or she might find herself in trouble, but this sort of threat could not frighten a woman like Madame Gauzet, who was known in the neighborhood as a termagant. Her outcry soon collected a small crowd, who, emboldened by their own numbers, began to abuse the sentinels as thieves and scoundrels with nothing better to do than pester good patriots. Rouzet's unfailing good temper and Charlotte's disposition had made the family popular in the neighbourhood and as soon as one or two tradesmen joined the crowd the attitude of the sentinels grew considerably less truculent and one of them explained that Rouzet and his family had been arrested about three hours ago by order of the Commune. The soldier had no idea where they had been taken, having only come on duty as a relief after the suspects had been taken away.

"Rouzet, a suspect!" jeered Madame Gauzet. "What's he suspected of, having lice in his combs?"

"I'm only obeying orders," protested the sentry, and the altercation continued, Madame Gauzet declaring at the top of her voice that the National Guard was rapidly becoming a training body for daylight thieves and vagabonds and nothing needed a purge so much as the Commune itself.

I took advantage of the quarrel to slip downstairs and

try the back door, which I found nailed up from the outside.

I went back into the *salon* and, taking care to keep a curtain between myself and the sentries, laid a finger to my lips and tapped softly on the window, close to where madame's husband was standing in the shadow cast by his wife. Old Gauzet saw me instantly and plucked at his wife's apron. She brushed him off a time or two but presently he made her aware of my presence and I was able to write on a piece of card: "Get inside. Marcelle's had a baby and is alone!" holding the message close to the window.

Madame responded very sensibly. She said to the most talkative guard: "Are you a father, m'sieur?"

"I've got seven at home," replied the fellow. "What are my brats to do with it?"

"There's a woman in there alone with her day-old child," declared Madame Gauzet.

The sentries conferred one with another. Obviously the challenge dismayed them, given as it was in front of a hostile crowd.

"We know there's a woman there all right," mumbled one. "She's the wife of one of the Brissotins we're after, but Citizen Vizet didn't say anything about a child."

Through the open *salon* door I could hear everything said, so I hastily crawled "Born last night" on another card and held it to the window.

"Born last night," prompted Gauzet, and his wife echoed him.

"All right," said the guard, "you can go in alone, but don't try any monkey tricks or you'll soon be behind bars."

The saddler's wife crossed the threshold and I hurried across the *salon* and up the stairs at fast as I could move. Madame Gauzet mounted to the landing, breathing heavily and cursing the steepness of the climb. At that moment the baby began to cry and without waiting to find me the genial old soul puffed down the corridor to Marcelle's room.

I waited a few moments to make sure that a sentry

didn't follow her, and then went in to join them. After witnessing her tussle with the guards I felt that I could trust her and most of the other neighbours. Somehow their attitude had cheered me and I began to see some prospects of usefully employing the liberty Rouzet's wig boxes had afforded me.

Marcelle, as I suspected, knew little or nothing of the circumstances in which the family were arrested. Biron had said goodbye to her in the small hours, after her labour had commenced, and she knew his plans about going south. Two hours later André had delivered her of the child, a girl they intended calling Lucille at André's request. She made light of the birth-pangs and, indeed, she did not seem to be worse for the event, but I could see that she was desperately worried about Biron, far more so than she seemed regarding the fate of Rouzet or her brother.

"Nobody's got anything against either one of them," she said lightly, and her unconcern was characteristic of the woman. Her precocious good looks had caused her to be thoroughly spoiled since childhood and she had grown up selfish and thoughtless regarding everything outside her own immediate interests. All she could think of, and talk about, was her baby and her fugitive husband's chances of getting out of Paris on his American passport. She never expressed a word of gratitude towards André, who had made Biron's flight possible, and when I pressed her to try and recall what happened when the gendarmes arrived she dismissed the matter with a shrug.

"I was fully occupied at the time," she said, and turned anew to her child.

I had never liked her very much and at that moment I couldn't have cared if she and her feeble husband had been slammed into the Conciergerie. I restrained my ill-temper, however, and sought the advice of Madame Gauzet, who was busying herself in the kitchen preparing some food for Marcelle.

I told the old woman as much of our circumstances as I thought she ought to know and asked her if she could get hold of the boy Joseph and send him in via the kitchen window as soon as it grew dark. She said she would do her best and strongly advised me to keep out of sight in the meantime as she thought it more than likely that by this time I had been proscribed as an English spy, despite my year's service with the National Guard. She also confirmed Biron's fears of the previous night regarding the Jacobin coup. There had been great excitement across the river that morning, she affirmed. A tanner, who had lodgings on her top floor, had described to her the Commune's demand for the arrest of twenty-two leading Brissotins, including Brissot himself, and most of the principal deputies of his persuasion. Biron's friends, or those that were left of them, had tried to defy the mob and had attempted to march out of the Assembly Hall in a compact body, but had been dispersed by threat of the cannon Biron had seen brought into the forecourt. It sounded as though all pretence at rule by the ordinary processes of law had been thrown aside and that henceforth the entire power of the State would be vested in the fanatics of the Mountain and Danton's Committee of Public Safety. The thought was a sombre one. It meant that, once inside a prison, people could count themselves fortunate if they stayed there and were not carted off to the guillotine.

I went back to my room and tried once again to formulate a plan but I found reasoned thought impossible in my agitated frame of mind and soon gave up the attempt and resigned myself to watching the court through the little grating under my window. Here I waited until dusk stole into the cul-de-sac and the only events that broke the tedium of my vigil were the changing of the sentries of the *salon* door and the determined waddling to and fro of Madame Gauzet, who, it seemed, had managed to bully the sergeant of the picquet into giving her some sort of official pass into the house.

For myself, I never remember having felt so lonely, helpless and afraid, not even during the time I spent in the badger's earth up on the Landslip waiting for news of the family. It wasn't too bad during the long afternoon, when I could watch people moving about the court, and listen to the conversation of the sentries under the window, but as it grew dusk, and a violet twilight settled over the cul-de-sac, these diversions ceased. The guards went into the *salon* and everyone else went indoors for supper and I was a prey to black depression brought on by gnawing anxiety over Charlotte and the sheer boredom of sitting there with my eye to the grating without being able to do the slightest thing to help her.

I began to see the life we had promised ourselves receding beyond the limits of possibility and being replaced by the gaunt spectre of the guillotine. I told myself over and over again that the most bloodthirsty of the Jacobins had nothing whatever against harmless people like Charlotte or Papa Rouzet, even if interrogation at the prison had uncovered André's pranks at the Abbaye in September, or his part in the projected escape of the little milliner, but such attempts at self-assurance failed to abate my fears. I thought it unlikely that André would be able to talk himself out of trouble for much longer and, much as I liked and admired him, the prospect of his death failed to fill me with horror. The mere thought of Charlotte passing between those lines of spectators, however, and mounting the scaffold where I had seen Louis die four months previously, almost choked me with fury as wild as it was impotent.

I think I might have succumbed to the urge to try and slip out, or at any rate to do something, anything, rather than sit on the floor of my room letting the minutes tick by, if my attention had not been attracted by a squeaking sound that seemed to originate from somewhere above my head. It was like the sharp squeak of a graphite pencil on a child's slate and for some moments I speculated vaguely on its cause. Then I happened to look up and see something that brought me abruptly to my feet. The sound came from the steady scratching on the window-pane by a twig from the huge elm tree which reached out from the massive trunk in the centre of the court and spread one of its branches as far as the joist supporting Rouzet's signboard below my window. There was absolutely no wind that evening and I knew, instantly, that the movement of the twig was caused by someone up the tree, obviously trying to attract my attention.

I flattened myself against the plaster and took a furtive peep through one of the diamond panes of the lattice. There, within a few feet of me, was the young mute, Joseph, his grimy face pressed down on the outlying bough and his shrunken little body interlocked with the sprouting foliage. He was holding a switch extended full-length in his right hand and was steadily passing its tip to and fro across the leaden window-frame of my room.

I knew that the sentries were in the *salon* and at supper, so I gently prised open the window and laid a finger to my lips. He grinned, happily, when he saw me and began to wriggle backwards towards the trunk, dropping the switch and beckoning urgently.

It didn't take me long to understand his directions and I cursed myself for not thinking of the tree before. In a couple of seconds I had forced myself through the narrow aperture, crawled on to the sign-joist and dived into the foliage of the branch, which sagged dangerously under our joint weight until Joseph, as agile as a Devon squirrel, clambered on to the trunk and dropped down on the side opposite the house, with me less than five seconds behind him.

We did not exchange a word or a sign as we moved out of the court into the rue l'Ecole de Médecine and I let him go on ahead until we had moved down the hill towards the river and had been swallowed up in the crowd of idlers promenading near the bridge. The thought came to me then that the boy was leading me towards the prison to which his employer had been taken and I had a horrid fear that it might be the Conciergerie, at that time the principal antechamber to the scaffolds in Place de Grève and Place de Révolution. We passed the Conciergerie, however, without stopping and went on down to the river bank, turning sharp left into the warren of one-storey hovels that surrounded the fish-quays.

I don't know how far we penetrated this region but it must have been above a half-mile, until we at last turned into a crumbling stone building that was used as the market.

Inside was a labyrinth of corridors running between hundreds of booths separated by worm-eaten partitions. The stench was sufficient to make a stranger vomit, for the filth of years had been strewn on the stone-flagged floor and a foetid mash of fish-heads squelched underfoot as we made our way to the far corner of the sprawling building and entered a little tarpaulin tent, slung gipsy-fashion, between one of the massive pillars and the last wooden partition.

The tarpaulin shut off any light that might have struggled through the filthy windows of the market but Joseph struck a flint and lit a saucer dip, revealing the wretched tent as his home. There were two bundles of fairly clean straw on the flags and a battered fish-box or two to serve as table and chairs. I realized then why Joseph preferred sleeping beneath Rouzet's counter on these stifling summer nights for even the combined reek of pomade, powder and singed hair must have been infinitely preferable to the stench of the fish market.

There was no point in talking to Joseph so I sat down on an upended box between the pallets and began to communicate with him by sign language. This was by no means as difficult as it sounds, for Joseph had been about Rouzet's premises ever since I had gone to live in them and we had certain accepted gestures which identified the people we wished to discuss. I made the usual sign for Charlotte, a stirring motion with both hands, symbolic of her work in the powder-room, and then went through the motions of shaving, indicating Rouzet, after which I spread my hands and shrugged my shoulders, implying that I did not know where either of them had gone.

I think Joseph enjoyed this sign conversation and I was reminded of Crusoe's first conversation with Man Friday, illustrated by a woodcut in Saxeby's fine edition of the book. The boy pondered for a moment and then slouched across the tent with a hang-dog look and his fingers held pinched to his nose, which immediately informed me that the arrest had been carried out on the information of Vizet, the police spy, who had a furtive gait and unsavoury breath.

Joseph then pointed deliberately at me, back to himself and finally out of the tarpaulin flap, indicating that we would go to see the family together, but when I jumped up and made a step in the right direction he pulled me down again and executed a succession of gestures, waving his hands towards the sky, pointing to the feeble dip and shaking his head. I gathered from this that we could not go until the morning and my interpretation was confirmed when he pointed to the cleanest bundle of straw and pillowed his head on his clasped hands.

There was nothing to do but to obey him and I shook his hand, felt in my pocket and offered him a guinea. His reaction was immediate. He shook his head violently and retreated to his pallet, holding up his hands as though I had offered him a live reptile instead of a gold piece. I guessed by this that he would gladly have died for Rouzet, or for any of Rouzet's family, and I suddenly felt shamed by his action and thrust the guinea back in my pocket. On my doing that he grinned again and quickly blew out the light, letting me grope my way to the pallet and lie down. I heard him begin to snore in a moment or two but I was by no means as satisfied with the lodging as he appeared to be, and the stench and the abounding fleas kept me awake for hours. When I awakened it was early morning and the market outside was in full swing. Joseph's corner was empty.

I lay there for a few minutes listening to the shrill outcry on the other side of the tarpaulin. To be there, in that place at that hour was an instruction in the causes of the Revolution, and I could not help reflecting on the hundreds of thousands of children, like Joseph, who had been born and reared in this disgusting squalor, and had grown up, without any responsible parent, to live by their wits in a harsh and indifferent society. When I first came to Paris I saw immediately that it was a city of appalling contrasts, of degradation and semi-starvation on one side and luxury and gluttony on the other; of filthy hovels like this market tent existing almost in the shadows

of the tall, elegant houses of the St. Honoré merchants'
quarter; of undernourished urchins like Joseph who, but
for the casual generosity of an eccentric tradesman like
Rouzet, would have gone barefoot all winter, splashed by
gilded cabriolets and velvet-lined barouches as they
begged in the gutters. I had no means of knowing whether
it was the same in any big city, probably it was, for
Saxeby had a poor opinion of London, which he had visited
once or twice, but here the legacies of the old régime stared
the most casual observer in the face and seemed almost to
justify, in my mind at any rate, the worst excesses of the
Jacobin-inspired rabble.

I shall never think of the Revolution as almost everyone in England seems to think of it, as a bloodthirsty
demonstration by an irresponsible mob of slum-dwellers,
but rather as the logical outcome of centuries of injustice
and stupidity on the part of a single class of society, the
majority of whom richly deserve the scaffold. The French
peasant, and his counterpart in the city, is not the stupid
beast his superiors tried for so long to make him believe
he was, but an ordinary, easy-going fellow very much on
the level of the hired hands of East Devon. A boy like
Joseph, deaf and dumb from birth and living under conditions that hardly anyone in this country would offer a
mangy dog, yet possessed the qualities of loyalty and
personal courage that would not disgrace a nobleman.
Joseph was not that much of an exception, there must
have been many like him in the various grades of Paris
society. Is it any wonder that in the majority of cases
such qualities withered under the onslaught of oppression
and neglect and were replaced by the bloodlust exhibited
by the crowds that flocked to witness the executions in the
Place de Révolution?

Eventually Joseph came in, carrying one of the immensely long rolls that were such a feature of Paris diet,
and an open can of lukewarm coffee. I don't know how
or where he procured this refreshment but I was very
grateful for it. He waited for me to complete my breakfast
before leading me through the crowded market and along
the banks of the river into a section of Paris with which I

was not familiar. We walked on together for the better
part of an hour, and climbed out of the crowded streets
towards the better-class district of St. Cloud where he
finally stopped and pointed to an isolated three-storey
building that stood well back from the highway in its own
well-kept grounds.

I looked at him in bewilderment for I could not imagine
that this stately residence was a prison, but from his repeated gesticulations I gathered that here were the people
I sought, and my bewilderment increased when I approached the wrought-iron gates and read the gilded letter-
ing of a plaque fastened to the summit of the archway,
which proclaimed: "Dr. Gemaine, Maison de Santé." I
then saw that Joseph was beckoning to me and I followed
him up a narrow carriageway than ran alongside the high
brick wall that surrounded the building. The drive ended
in a postern and, because I was tall, I was able to reach
up and peep through the gap between the top of the
spiked door and the lintel. I was by no means prepared
for the spectacle the glimpse afforded.

Inside was a well-kept garden, laid out in flower beds
and flowering shrubs. Across the garden was a high iron
railing which divided the enclosure into two equal parts.

On the section nearer the house was a broad promenade,
crowded with fashionably dressed men and women enjoying the morning sunshine and engaging one another in
amiable conversation as they moved among the shrubs.
There must have been close on two hundred people on
the promenade, or on adjoining lawns, and their de-
meanour contrasted strangely with that of the smaller
group on the far side of the railings. I only had to glance
twice at this latter gathering to satisfy myself that it was
composed of a batch of lunatics. A few of them were
clinging to the railings like apes, grimacing and gesticulating at the sober folks beyond the barrier. Others were
disporting themselves grotesquely on an overgrown patch
near a tumbledown summer-house, presumably their living
quarters, for two or three old men, dressed in rags and
with long, unkempt beards, were engaged in cooking something on a small stove near the porch.

I jumped down and turned, inquiringly, to Joseph but he was no longer in sight. I went back to the highway and looked in each direction but he was nowhere to be seen. There was nothing to do but to go back up the carriage-way and take a second peep at the peculiar inmates of Doctor Gemaine's establishment.

This time I took a good grip of the jutting stonework of the door frame and held my eyes level with the slit for a long minute. At the expiration of that time I had my reward.

Pacing slowly in my direction, swinging a cane and looking as spruce and dandified as on the occasion we first met, was André, engaged in an earnest discussion with a short, distinguished-looking man about fifty, wearing an old-fashioned full-buttoned wig and well-cut suit of black velvet. I was so surprised to see André that I called his name aloud. He heard me and said something to his companion, who ran after him as he strode towards the postern.

"My dear fellow," exclaimed André, when I had greeted him through the aperture, "we were only this moment discussing you. Why don't you ring the bell and ask to come in? This isn't the Abbaye or the Temple, one can always get out again!"

He turned to the man behind him. "Open up and admit my friend to your sanctuary, Doctor. He's an Englishman and I swear he'll be worth a hundred gold guineas to you if you give him an attic all to himself!"

The doctor chuckled and, selecting a large key from a bunch attached by a silver chain to his waist, he opened the door. In a few seconds I was inside the garden, with the door locked behind me and not at all sure that I liked the alacrity with which he cut off my retreat to the street.

"Where's Charlotte?" I demanded, but André only burst out laughing at my agitated tone and laid a reassuring arm along my shoulder.

"Why, bless you, she's here, and Papa along with her," he replied; "but don't look so distraught, David, the doctor doesn't care to have his patients distress themselves, it's bad for business, eh, Doctor?" and he poked his deferential jailer in the ribs. "Let me have a word alone with our friend, I'll soon iron the anxiety from his brow."

All this time the doctor was eyeing me speculatively. A winning, good-humoured expression never left his face, but I could see his eyes were unsmiling and it seemed to me that he was already assessing my possibilities as a profitable inmate of his peculiar establishment.

"As you like," he agreed, "but I must say he doesn't look as prosperous as you led me to believe."

"You can't judge by appearances these days," said André, himself running a critical eye over my soiled clothes, which were still decorated with pieces of straw from my makeshift couch and doubtless savoured strongly of the fish market. "He has more English guineas in his pocket than you have names on your waiting list!"

The doctor whistled through his teeth and, still smiling, shrugged and strode away toward the terrace, exchanging polite greetings with several of the better-dressed people on the promenade.

"There goes the shrewdest speculator in Paris," said André, taking my arm and leading me down the sloping lawn towards the railings. "There's the man Capet ought to have called in to set our finances in order! He'd have made Necker look like a market huckster. If he doesn't overreach himself he'll make twenty fortunes within the next twelve months and he'll deserve it, every sou of it!"

"Where's Charlotte and what is this place?" I demanded again. "I had the devil's own job getting out of the house and I spent the night in a fish market. Don't waste any more time, André, I've been half-crazy with anxiety for you all since I woke up and found sentries posted at the door."

"There's no need for any further anxiety," he said soothingly, "not whilst we can raise two thousand livres a month. We ought to get one month's keep out of the business, providing you can make a quick sale. Now let's begin to calculate. . . ."

He broke off, laughing, for I had swung him round and was shaking him by the shoulders.

"Let be, David, sit down here . . . don't heed these poor

devils, they're only permanent guests, displaced by the influx of visitors."

We sat down on a rustic seat, a stone's throw from the tall railing, to which more than one elderly lunatic was clinging, gibbering incoherent abuse in our direction.

"We're in the safest lock-up in Paris," said André, "and we can stay here, safe from transfer, for just as long as we can pay our host's board and lodging!"

"But what was that you said about selling the business?" I queried.

"The business will have to be sold first," he went on. "After that the charming doctor will set himself to bleed you white, David. Maybe you had better send to England now for the rest of your guineas. This place is already famous, I'm surprised you haven't heard of it. Doctor Gemaine used to run a private asylum here but when the Commune asked him to convert his premises into a *maison d'arret de luxe* he not only complied, he obligingly enlarged his establishment and packed it with men and women for whom there were warrants out. There are two or three counts here, half a dozen financiers and at any moment he's expecting a duchess. The average 'patient' pays something like a thousand livres a month for a square yard of an unfurnished room, in addition to a door-tribute on every meal that comes in from outside. This place used to house a score of patients, now there are ten score and more arriving every day. The trouble is, they come in a great deal faster than they go out!"

"But you said you were safe here," I protested.

"As long as you can pay, or somebody doesn't outbid you for your floor space," corrected André. "A charming fellow gave a farewell party last night. It was quite touching—it cost him four hundred livres, the last of his fortune. This morning he moved on to the Conciegerie and from there, I don't doubt, will proceed to the scaffold, though I must say from all I hear the doctor has got a certain sense of decorum about the business, for those who leave his care on account of poverty never go direct to the guillotine, there is always an interval of four or five days!"

"How did you get into the place?" I asked him.

"I had friends," said André, "and when Vizet ordered the cab driver to go to the Abbaye, I made the cabby stop at the Hotel de Ville and got our warrants altered. Vizet was furious and he went off swearing to prise us out of here in twenty-four hours, but not even Danton could do that, for the doctor has a private arrangement with the Public Prosecutor, Fouquier-Tinville." He chuckled softly at my open incredulity. "I know what goes on, I haven't been a jail surgeon for nothing."

He got up, stretched himself and abruptly changed the subject. "So the Brissotins have quoted their final tag?"

"There isn't a moderate left in the Assembly," I told him, and recounted some of the sentries' conversation I heard whilst crouching over the grating in my room.

"And dear Marcelle?" he asked languidly. "Wasn't that a fine piece of work on my part? Her baby was all of eight pounds and not so much as a dent in her. Did you see the child?"

I told him what had happened to me since he left me to attend Marcelle.

"Here's a devil of a fix," he muttered. "Charlotte says we have to get her to Biron so that they can both use the passports and leave the country together. Knowing Charlotte I doubt whether you'll budge her until she hears Marcelle's out of Paris. Come, you'd better see her yourself," and he led the way up the slope towards the terrace and in through the tall windows into the crowded withdrawing room.

We steered our way between several tables of whist and people overlooking the players and up the stairs to a small uncarpeted landing leading to a low-ceiling attic situated close under the tiles.

Under the begrimed window, placidly darning a stocking, was Charlotte, looking as cool and unruffled as I had seen her look when she sat at the head of Rouzet's table and poured coffee for Marcelle's garrulous guests.

If I had not already been in love with Charlotte I think that I should have fallen in love with her at that moment. Charlotte always took immense pride in her personal appearance and did so without the fussiness and ostentation characteristic of her sex in this respect. Here, after the ordeal of arrest, transportation across Paris, and twenty-four hours in a crowded prison, she displayed the same neatness of person and untroubled exterior that had been among her most striking characteristics at home. Not a ringlet of her chestnut hair was out of place and her dress and fichu were newly laundered, though how she managed to wash and iron them in these cramped quarters I could not imagine. Through the low doorway that led to the adjoining attic I glimpsed Papa Rouzet who, it appeared, had lost no time in returning to his calling, for he was engaged in powdering the hair of an elegant young man sitting on a backless kitchen chair in front of a steel mirror.

On seeing me Charlotte stood up and an anxious look showed in her eyes but André hastily reassured her.

"It's all right, Lottë, David's here as a visitor. I've told him he is liable to find the privilege an expensive one!"

"How's Marcelle?" enquired Charlotte anxiously.

"How should she be?" joked André. "Women of her type always produce children with the utmost facility. You haven't the hips, Lottë; you'll have a bad time, mark my words."

I embraced Charlotte and told her the gist of my adventures, not omitting to thank her for her prompt action in screening my room immediately before the house search.

"It was the only thing we could think of," said Charlotte, "there wasn't much time; it is fortunate Vizet didn't come personally, for the gendarmes had a warrant for you. What are you going to do? You can't go back there."

"There's always Joseph's tent in the fish market," remarked André drily, and, elevating his thin nostrils, made an exaggerated move in the direction of the window.

Rouzet completed his task and came in, dusting the powder from his pudgy hands. He greeted me cheerfully and I observed that he did not appear to be much put out by the circumstances in which he found himself. I began to suspect that André, doubtless determined to spare him anxiety, had been overoptimistic in the information he had imparted regarding the doctor's arrangements with the Jacobins.

At this juncture a harsh handbell began to ring in the entrance hall below and its first note sent the majority of the attic dwellers stampeding down the stairs like school-children released from lessons.

"That's the office bell," said André, with one of his slow grins. "Madame Tarbon dispenses it from a churn at eleven o'clock each morning. It not only earns her an apron-full of small change, it prevents the guests from feeling too hungry and causing an uproar when dinner is late."

We took advantage of the comparative privacy to hold an impromptu conference on the latest turn of events.

The family's position might have been worse. André felt certain that they were all safe for the time being, but that sooner or later the malice of Vizet might effect their trans-fer to one or other of the prisons to which the Jacobins repaired for their evening sacrifices to Liberty, and mean-time their personal safety was merely a matter of money. André estimated that it would cost about 2,000 livres a month to remain where they were but, providing the money could be found, they would be absolutely safe from trans-fer. The sale of the business should produce the equivalent of a month's keep and in that month I did not doubt but that I would find a way of getting both Charlotte and Rouzet out of Paris and down to the coast where we could embark for America.

André had by this time begun to regret the readiness with which he had handed his American papers to Biron. He had few doubts but that he could shift for himself and he was sorry he was now unable to give Papa Rouzet the same chance as Biron had of getting clear of Paris. I don't think the old fellow fully comprehended the danger in which he now stood, but regarded his arrest as due to an error on the part of some stupid gendarme or clerk at the Hotel de Ville. He kept saying: "Don't distress yourself, my son, I've got friends, good friends, and they'll make somebody pay for this!" He did not realize that now that the Jacobins had full control of the city and were in the ascendant throughout France, friendship would be ousted by fear of the guillotine and that almost everybody would be far too concerned preserving their own skins to worry about the plight of neighbours upon whom the hand of the Committee of Public Safety had fallen.

Charlotte had no illusions in this respect, pressed my hand as Rouzet reassured me, and I saw that she wished to keep her uncle in ignorance as long as possible.

The upshot of our talk was a decision that André, using Doctor Gemaine as his agent, should negotiate the sale of the business, that I should pay Dr. Gemaine a month's keep in advance on behalf of Rouzet and Charlotte, and then seek out Paine or "Clio" Rickman with the object of obtaining papers on Rouzet's behalf.

It is true that I myself was liable to arrest at any moment, but as long as I paid Gemaine in gold it was extremely unlikely that he would inform the authorities that I was still in Paris, and unless I had the misfortune to run into the police spy, Vizet, it was very doubtful that I should be recognized if I stayed away from the area of the Rouzet home. I knew where to find Joseph and had no doubt that he would succeed in fetching me a change of linen and various personal effects that I had been unable to bring when I left via the window.

As regards the major problem, that of getting Rouzet and Charlotte out of the doctor's clutches and on the road to the coast, neither myself nor André could provide an immediate solution, but I did possess the means of buying Gemaine's co-operation in the interval of obtaining the additional travel permit.

The doctor proved easier than even André had led me to believe. I managed to get a word with him on the terrace and paid him an advance fee of twenty guineas from the leather bag I wore day and night round my waist. At the sight of the gold he became extremely affable and assured me that, during their stay with him, the young lady for whom I entertained such an admiration (he missed very little did Gemaine) and her uncle would receive his personal attention in all matters pertaining to their comfort and security. I believed him. In revolutionary

Paris nothing greased the wheels so effectively as English guineas, for by this time the Convention's paper currency was almost worthless.

The doctor let me out by the front door and I made my way by a roundabout route to Paine's lodging in the Faubourg St. Denis.

I approached the house cautiously, and it was as well that I did for the Jacobins had already placed the alien deputy under some sort of house arrest and two or three ruffians were playing cards on his doorsteps. There was an air of feverish activity in the streets. Mounted patrols of gendarmes were galloping to and fro and in one of the main thoroughfares I saw a small mob breaking into a baker's shop and helping themselves from his ovens. I turned back from Paine's lodging and retraced my steps to White's Hotel, where I loudly demanded of the porter to be shown to Mr. Rickman's suite. Rickman was out but Joel Barlow, the American, was there and received me cordially. When I made my request, however, he told me flatly that he would have the greatest difficulty in procuring an American travelling permit for Rouzet. Only the previous day the deputies had been to his business premises in the Ile de Saint-Louis and had closely examined his books.

"Since Tom came under suspicion," he declared, "all his associates are suspect, and now that the Jacobins are in power all foreigners in Paris have been plagued by fugitives."

I asked him if he intended leaving Paris himself but he shook his head vigorously. "I shall stay as long as I can be of any service to Tom," he replied, adding, with a chuckle, "if it hadn't been for men like him my country would still be the milch-cow of the English excisemen. One good turn deserves another!"

Although he could not promise to produce the papers, however, Barlow proved of great service in advising me how to evade the horde of police spys turned loose on the city since the Jacobins' *coup d'état* of June 1st, and he provided me with a porter's pass with which I could masquerade as one of his Paris employees. He also gave me a suit of his firm's livery and advised me to let my beard

grow in order to heighten the disguise. Being dark, the
bristles on my chin show very rapidly, and as I had not
shaved since the evening we visited the Luxembourg, I
had no doubt that I could provide myself with an adequate
screen of whiskers within a week.

Having donned my porter's uniform, I ventured into
the street once more. At first I imagined that every gendarme and every civic guardsman I passed looked at me
with suspicion, but I soon persuaded myself that, short of
running into Vizet, or any of the members of my own file
of the St. Germaine section of the National Guard, I was
reasonably safe from recognition, and I thanked my stars
that my disposition had prevented me from turning bar-
rack-room acquaintances into intimate cronies whilst serving with the civic body. Apart from Rouzet's family I
knew hardly anyone in the city and my fluent French had
saved me from being singled out as an alien volunteer.

I made my way back to the fish market and waited for
Joseph. He came into the tent in the early evening and
brought me some goat's-milk cheese and some very stale
bread, which we washed down with a couple of bottles of
cheap wine, purchased at one of the market taverns. It
was with the greatest difficulty that I prevailed upon the
lad to accept token payment for my board and lodging;
I only succeeded after a long and tedious sign conversation.

I also managed to convey to him some of the information I had picked up at the jail. Our efforts to converse,
wearisome as they were, helped me to pass the time and
at last night came to the foul interior of the tent and for
the second time I stretched myself on the straw. The constant stir in the market and the general racket and noise-
someness of the place disturbed me less than on the previous night and I was soon asleep, remaining so until
Joseph roused me soon after dawn and gave me my breakfast, a roll, honey and lukewarm coffee.

After the meal I took stock of the situation. I had with
me approximately thirty guineas, the remainder being concealed in my palliasse at No. 12, where I judged they
would be safe enough until Joseph could slip in and fetch

them. I knew that Charlotte and Rouzet would want daily news of Marcelle and her baby, and that Joseph could come and go freely as messenger between myself and the kindly saddler's wife, so I wrote a note to Madame Gauzet, telling her where the family were held and begging her to attend to Marcelle until such time as the girl was strong enough to get up and fend for herself.

I had no idea how long the Commune would maintain guard on the house but I did not care to go near the court myself and determined to stay this side of the city, where the danger of recognition and arrest was negligible. I still had travel permits for Charlotte and myself and they were valid enough to get us past the barriers, notwithstanding the additional vigilance maintained by the piquets since the Jacobins had ousted their rivals, but I knew that it would be a waste of breath trying to persuade Charlotte to join any plan for slipping out of the doctor's profitable jail until I also possessed a pass for Rouzet, and that, I knew, would take me at least ten days to procure.

Meantime I thought I might go to the *maison de santé* every day, not only to give the family news of Marcelle and to keep in close contact with events, but also to give myself the pleasure of being near Charlotte, even though I could be of little immediate help to her.

Joseph went off at a run with my note and was back within two hours, an interval I spent in the difficult task of making myself presentable. I not only had to venture into the market to buy a ewer (for Joseph did not wash from one end of the year to the other) but to walk as far as the quays in order to buy some fresh water, for I wouldn't have cared to have washed myself in the Seine at any period of my stay in Paris.

I also managed to get a brush and a lump of yellow harness soap from one of the hundreds of tray-salesmen who had stands in this district, and with these articles I returned to the tent and scrubbed myself from head to foot, not forgetting to remove the accumulated filth from my shoes and breeches.

When I had finished, my garments looked reasonably clean and I laid the livery suit under the straw, ready for future occasions. It was too easily recognizable to wear on visits to the *maison de santé*.

Marcelle gave Joseph a cheerful note for Charlotte, assuring her that she was in good hands, and this alone made me feel less burdened with responsibility, for Marcelle was not the sort of person to spare another's anxieties by putting an artificially brave face on things. Judging from the tone of her message I felt sure that kindly Madame Gauzet was proving an efficient lying-in-nurse.

I walked boldly up to the front door of the doctor's house and rang the bell. Gemaine's extortionate door-keeper admitted me and demanded fifty sous visiting fee. I paid her double, thus hoping to create a favourable impression on the harpy.

Doctor Gemaine greeted me warmly and I realized that my guess of the previous day was an accurate one, and that he placed a man willing to pay in gold on his list of privileged visitors. My first visit had also done a good deal to improve the prisoners' condition, for they now had the attic to themselves, a privilege which, I later ascertained, increased their rent by another five hundred livres a month.

When we were alone I told André and the others what I had done, and André pulled a wry face when I mentioned the interval that must elapse before I could hope to get Rouzet's pass.

"Vizet was here again last night," he said, "demanding that we be transferred to a real jail. He got short shrift from the dear doctor, who now includes us among his favourite guests, but Vizet could cause a peck of trouble in fourteen days. The doctor is giving me a twelve-hour parole out of here tomorrow and I can arrange to dispose of the business within twenty-four hours. I had hoped to wait for a good offer, now it'll have to go for what I can get."

We talked about other things then, chiefly Marcelle's baby, which had entranced Papa, who now considered himself a virtual grandfather. I soon sensed, however, that Charlotte wanted to speak to me alone and André took the hint and persuaded the old fellow to take a turn on the terrace.

As soon as they had gone downstairs I took Charlotte in my arms and we exchanged a hundred kisses. I didn't have any doubts then but that I'd get her out of jail and the country somehow, even if I had to cut my way single-handed to the coast, but presently a troubled look came into her face and she said:

"I can't help wondering what Marcelle is going to do about her baby."

I wasn't over-worried about Marcelle and said so, but Charlotte went on: "You'll have to get her down south to her husband, David."

I gaped at her. "That would take me the best part of a month," I protested, "and how do you think I'd feel leaving Paris with you and Papa stuck here?"

"You've heard from André and Doctor Gemaine," she replied quietly. "We're perfectly safe so long as we keep our payments up. By the time you get back here we'll have Papa's permit and then we can arrange something!"

It occurred to me that Charlotte's estimate of the danger they were in was about as accurate as her uncle's. Even the people one loves can be maddeningly stupid at times and the vague, unsatisfying term "arrange something," to-gether with the cool proposal that I should make a leisurely journey to and from Bordeaux before I set about getting her and Rouzet out of the doctor's clutches, was uncharacteristic of Charlotte's practical self. Then I per-ceived that her sangfroid was assumed and that she was deliberately placing Marcelle's welfare before her own and had doubtless discussed the whole thing with Rouzet, if not André.

"Let Marcelle look after herself," I said. "She and that damned husband of hers are partly responsible for all the trouble we're in. If Biron had——"

"She's got a child," Charlotte interposed, and for a moment her eyes were hard. Warned by her expression I blustered for moment or two but it was only a token re-sistance. I knew that I'd go south docilely enough if Char-lotte had asked me to and would have gone to St. Petersburg barefoot if it had been of any service to her. When she saw that she would get her way she smiled and slipped her arm through mine.

"Do you think we should deserve any happiness, David, if we got out and left them here? I was willing to go anywhere with you as long as Biron was with her, but he's a fugitive now and has all he can do to look after himself."

I wasn't giving in without a struggle. "We're all fugitives, aren't we?" I growled, "and if positions were reversed Marcelle wouldn't lose an hour's sleep over you or Papa!"

"Oh, she's made that way," said Charlotte lightly. "I only know how I'd feel if we left her alone with the baby and she and Biron never saw each other again."

"What makes you think they will if I take her south?" I asked. "He'll be on the run, even in his own department. There are Jacobin clubs down there, I'm told."

"They'll get together again," she said quietly, "I saw them in my dreams."

"You didn't see us?" I ventured gloomily.

Charlotte smiled and sat clasping her knees on the single backless chair, apart from the two truckle beds, the only item of furniture in that wretched lodging.

"I did see us, David, and that's why I'm not afraid any more. It was the night before they brought us here, when Biron roused us with his knocking. I came down to let him in and couldn't imagine why he was so nervous and despairing; then I remembered he hadn't been dreaming."

"What did you dream, Charlotte?" I asked, not so much out of curiosity but because I knew that she was eager to tell me.

"I dreamed you and I were walking down a winding path to a beach, David. We passed through a little orchard, our orchard, and across a wide cornfield, our cornfield, with our cattle, red and mud-splashed, browsing on a green slope crowned by a big red cliff."

"Yes? What more?"

"Well, we walked slowly because the sky and the trees were so beautiful, forming a pattern of green, rose-pink and blue over the deeper blue of the sea and the gold of sandbanks away off the shore and on each side were splashes of yellow gorse and green bracken, and one side of the orchard was shut in by a little pinewood that went marching down to the water like a row of soldiers."

"Did we get as far as the cove?"

"Oh yes, in time to see Marcelle and Biron and the baby sail away in a barge, but we didn't go because we were already at home."

I remembered then that Charlotte had never seen the sea, and that her dream was composed of half-remembered fragments of my conversations about Westdown, for I had described the place to her during one of my particularly intense periods of homesickness for Devon. It made her appear so much like a little girl that I almost choked with tenderness and I held her close and said:

"I'll get you there somehow, Lottë, you believe that, don't you?"

She laid her cheek against mine. My face was stiff with half-grown bristles but she didn't appear to notice them. She only said:

"It's because I believe so much that I can fight against the impulse to let Marcelle shift for herself, David."

I gave in then. I knew that even if I succeeded in getting her and Rouzet out of the country she would never cease to reproach herself for abandoning Marcelle and the baby.

"I'll take her as far as Bordeaux and try to find Biron," I promised. "After that they must look after themselves; they've got valid permits, which is more than most of the Brissotins have got."

She was silent for a moment, looking down at the bare, dirty floor.

"There's one other thing I should like, David," she said, without raising her eyes. "I should like one of the non-juring priests here to marry us!"

Chapter Sixteen

IT WAS the strangest and quietest of weddings. Dr. Gemaine, who saw in this little ceremony an excellent advertisement for the *maison de santé's* claims to be the most secure retreat in Paris, showed a great personal interest in the preliminaries. He it was who engaged one of his prisoners, the Abbé Legarde, a sunburned little priest from an obscure living in the south, to officiate, and he insisted that the ceremony be performed in his own study, where the luxurious furnishings were in striking contrast to the drabness of the other apartments in the building.

Gemaine, indeed, would have gone a great deal further and would have invited the majority of his charges to a wedding breakfast on the terrace, but on this point both Charlotte and I stood firm. We were getting married because we were in love and not for the purpose of providing Dr. Gemaine and his customers with gratuitous entertainment.

The ceremony took place exactly a week after Charlotte had first arrived at the establishment. Rouzet, who loved a wedding ceremony above everything, was in high spirits, and long before I arrived at the house he became very mellow on Gemaine's brandy. His red face shone like the sun sinking into Torbay on a summer's evening, and his carefully powdered wig had fallen into disarray and kept sliding over one ear to reveal a crescent of polished pate. André, faultlessly dressed, was the principal witness, and Gemaine's disagreeable assistant, the woman who collected the revenue on incoming meals at the front door, was also engaged in this capacity.

I took an instinctive dislike to the priest, who was an ill-favoured fellow. His clothes were greasy and he smelled strongly of garlic. It seemed that he did not intend to take the affair very seriously, but he accepted my guinea fee

with alacrity, and André told me that his payments were
falling behind and he was terrified of receiving one of
Gemaine's sadly presented eviction notices. My guinea
represented his lodging at the *maison de santé* for at least
another week.

I had never seen Charlotte sweeter or more desirable.
Joseph had been able to smuggle out some clothes for her
and when Rouzet ushered her into Gemaine's plush-lined
study a few minutes after eight o'clock on the morning of
the wedding she looked even prettier than Marcelle had
looked on her wedding day.

Beyond the fact that she invariably appeared fresh and
cool in the gowns I had seen her wear at home, I had
never previously paid any particular attention to her style
and mode of attire, but I can remember every detail of her
apparel on this occasion.

She had on a tight-waisted, full-skirted gown of pale
blue, with close-fitting sleeves, ending in broad lace ruffles
and a row of tiny pearl buttons. Over her shoulders was a
spotless fichu, its starched folds crossed over her breast
and passing under the arms to a large bow at the back.
Her dark hair, twisted by Rouzet's expert fingers into a
thick cluster of ringlets, and cut in the new fashion to
shoulder length, fell from under a small lace cap finished
with a ribbon matching her gown. Her high-heeled satin
slippers drew attention to the unusual smallness of her
feet, and the vivid blue cameo, worn round her neck on a
thin golden chain, emphasized the cool whiteness of her
neck. The only jewellery she wore apart from the
cameo was a small turquoise ring that had formerly belonged to her mother. Gemaine had cut her wedding
bouquet from his garden and the cluster of vivid red
carnations, wreathed in tendrils of maidenhair fern, was
the gayest thing ever seen in that dismal house. She also
had an ivory-bound prayer book with—strange insignia in
a republican jail—the fleur-de-lis of the Bourbons, picked
out in silver on its cover. I suppose that she borrowed this
from Gemaine, it was just such an article that an equivoca-
tor of his disposition might possess.

As she moved alongside me the abbé began to mumble

the service, but I do not remember hearing anything he said and was hardly conscious of my responses, for the scent of Charlotte's hair came to me above the stuffy smell of leather upholstery and an occasional whiff of the priest's garlic, or Rouzet's brandy-laden breath, as the old fellow stood on her left, swaying slightly and breathing like a whale.

Apart from Rouzet's snorts and the drone of the priest, there was heavy silence in the room, and I remembered thinking how cool and firm Charlotte's fingers felt when, at the priest's muttered direction, I slipped on the plain ring Joseph had purchased for me for a few sous from a market huckster that morning.

When the ceremony was over, and they had all kissed the bride (the gallant Gemaine taking rather longer over this formality than conventional gallantry prescribes), the seven of us adjourned to the attic for the wedding breakfast, which had been provided by Gemaine out of his own pocket. It was the only tribute-free meal that ever ascended those carpetless stairs, and Rouzet and André, who had been on half-rations to save money for the past week, did it full justice, but I was so miserable at the prospect of leaving Charlotte that evening that each mouthful almost choked me.

We would have liked to have spent our last few hours in the limited privacy of the top floor, but Gemaine's two hundred and odd guests were determined to celebrate the unique occasion with a concert, staged on the lawn. Among the prisoners was an actor, a certain Albert de Lambour, who constituted himself master of ceremonies, and the bridal party was obliged to sit through a three-hour programme organized by this fellow from among a batch of volunteer artists. The quality of the items was good and I have no doubt that de Lambour had arranged the concert with the best intentions in the world, but I know that I wished him far enough that sultry afternoon. It must have been André who eventually won for us an hour's longed-for privacy down in the little rose walk that bordered the railing separating the paying guests from the *bona fide* inmates.

The moment we were alone Charlotte said: "I'm sorry it had to be like this, David, I planned it so differently."

"How did you plan it to be, Lottë?" I asked her.

We sat down on one of the doctor's elaborate rustic seats, putting a stunted laurel between us and the bearded idiots, several of whom were scratching round the tufted patch outside their ramshackle quarters.

Charlotte smiled and squeezed my hand. "I planned an ordinary wedding, David, because it would have suited us both. We're probably the most ordinary couple in France!"

"What happens to us isn't ordinary," I grumbled.

She laughed at my crestfallen expression and kissed me lightly on the cheek.

"I'm getting very fond of your whiskers, David," she bantered. "When you come back from Bordeaux you'll look like a patriarch."

I had a sudden doubt that I would ever return and held her so close that she gasped a laughing protest. I wished then with all my heart that I could share her serenity, but all I could feel was the horrid certainty that this was the last time I should ever press my lips to the rounded softness of her shoulder, or breathe in the sweetness of her hair.

I said: "Whatever you do, Lottë, you must promise never to leave here until I return. No matter what happens, stay here. Promise that damned doctor anything, only stay here, where I can find you."

"I promise," she said, "and now try and look more like a groom and less like an anguished widower, David. I tell you we're lucky as things are; think how different it might have been if André hadn't managed to get our warrants altered. Even a friend and confidante of the great Paine couldn't have got us out of the Conciergerie."

It was true; in a way we had been lucky so far, but I silently cursed Marcelle for giving herself the airs of a Madame Roland and for having her baby at such an inconsiderate moment. Love is supposed to make one less selfish and more thoughtful of others, but it didn't affect me that way. At that moment Marcelle, her baby, Rouzet, André and the entire population of France could have been swallowed up in a Dartmoor bog for all I cared. I was solely concerned with our own immediate future and our chances of leading sane, normal lives once again out of reach of the Jacobins and their bloodthirsty attempts to make society safe for the unprivileged.

We sat huddled together on the seat until dusk fell over the garden and Dr. Gemaine's porter arrived to shepherd the lunatics into the summer-house for the night.

A distant clanging from the terrace warned us that it was time to go in and that our honeymoon was over. It was only as we rose to go back through the shrubbery, and I felt the pressure of Charlotte's fingers tighten on my arm, that I knew she had been wiser than I about our wedding and that, poor, shabby, unsatisfactory thing that it was, it had somehow brought us closer than we could have been if we had waited for her problematical release. It was just that much better than nothing.

I said goodbye to André and left Charlotte at the foot of the stairs, pretending not to hear one or two sniggering jests made at our expense by the ex-courtiers, whose glee-singing had entertained us that afternoon. She went up slowly, holding her blue wedding gown clear of the dirty boards and just as she reached the first landing she turned and smiled down at me, pouting her lips as an earnest of a final kiss.

The little priest came snuffling towards me and I stepped aside to let him pass. As he put his foot on the first stair he said: "I'll do what I can, M'sieur Treloar, but hurry, hurry. . . ."

It was all that was needed to aggravate the gnawing anxiety of our parting and I went swiftly out of the house and down the hill towards the market. When I crawled into the tarpaulin Joseph thrust a grubby note into my hand. It was in Marcelle's highly stylized handwriting and informed me that she would be ready to travel on the morrow and would meet me at the Invalides coach stage in time for the evening mail to Rambouillet.

I do not recall much of the outward journey to Bordeaux for I suffered excessively from coach-drowsiness

and must have slept over the greater part of the seemingly
interminable stages. The roads were in very poor condition and I do not suppose the coach averaged more than
twenty miles a day, but after the first day's journey I became accustomed to the violent jolting and, greatly
fatigued by the uncomfortable sojourn in Joseph's tent
during the past week, I was able to sleep soundly and
hardly exchanged more than a word or two with my fellow passengers. I travelled on the outside and Marcelle
on the inside.

I recall being amazed at the girl's hardiness and her
general high spirits which the robust baby seemed to share.
Although Marcelle had only quitted her child-bed eight
days previously, she seemed to arrive at each posting
house as fresh as when she climbed into the coach at the
commencement of the journey. Maybe her natural youth
and vigour, and the prospect of being united with her
husband, sustained her during the journey, or perhaps it
was just that Marcelle had a knack of making other people take care of her in the way Charlotte had slaved for
her at home. She was not above indulging in coquetries
with any fellow passenger whose services would prove
useful to her, and both she and the baby were thoroughly
spoiled by the inside travellers over the whole length of
the wretched journey.

Usually we travelled by day and rested the night at one
of the posting houses along the route, but occasionally, if
the day's journey had been a short one, we pushed on
over a night stage and waited after breakfast for the midday coach heading south.

After Rambouillet, we travelled by Chartres, Tours
and Poitiers, over long stretches of flat countryside and
along dusty, rutted roads lined with soldierly poplars,
passing through poverty-stricken hamlets that clustered
round turreted chateaux, whose owners had long since fled
overseas or were waiting their summons to the guillotine.
Most of the fields had a sadly neglected appearance and
some of the smaller towns looked as if they had been
pillaged by the hungry republican battalions marching due
west to finish the civil war now ravaging La Vendée. We

overtook one or two of these ragged columns, marching to
the tuck of drum and the rousing choruses of the revolutionary songs. Despite the songs, the rank and file seemed
to lack the ardour of similar volunteer battalions that had
moved out to the north-eastern frontiers earlier in the year.
Doubtless this decline in égalitarian enthusiasm was due
to the fact that the divisions, composed chiefly of city-
dwellers, were bewildered at being asked to face the volleys
of Frenchmen instead of the cannon of foreign mercenaries. Even at this time, when the war in La Vendée had
not long begun, the campaigns in the west were extremely
unpopular among the volunteers, for there were many hard
knocks and little enough glory to be won in savage forays
and ambuscades with an enraged peasantry. Many of the
men who had responded so readily to the Convention's
appeal for volunteers must have wondered how the new
Government could hope to survive the combined onslaught of foreigners from the east and northeast and
royalists from the west, to say nothing of the eternal dis-
sensions among themselves, such as the recent quarrel
between the fanatics of the Mountain and the deputies
of the Plain.

We saw nothing of the war itself, however, which was
still centring in the wild country to the west, but an ostler
in Tours informed me that all the coach services between
the upper Loire and the coast had been cancelled on account of the aggravated brigandage of the peasants, the
majority of whom had risen to resist the Convention's
decree ordering all able-bodied Frenchmen to muster in
the republican armies. This was a final exacerbation to
provincials, already bitterly resentful of the Convention's
attitude towards their religion, and the indiscriminate
manner in which all members of the upper class, good and
bad, benevolent and rapacious, had been proscribed enemies of the State.

I didn't have much to say to Marcelle, or she to me,
until we reached the Gironde. I think she knew that I was
sorely troubled about Charlotte and her uncle, but all she
could think of was her wretched husband and how he
might be faring in the department he had represented for

the past two years. She had his mother's address in Bordeaux and during one of our brief conversations on the subject she expressed the belief that Biron would not only be found in that city but would be prominent in its administration.

A rude shock awaited her when at last the coach lumbered down from Angoulême and across the Cere into the Gironde proper. An innkeeper at Libourne laconically informed us that the agents of the Convention had arrived in the chief city of the south-west a month ago, and the guillotine was already doing brisk service in the principal market-place.

The Jacobins' arrival had created a chaotic state of affairs among the inhabitants in the area and, as is usual in such circumstances, everybody's first thought was for his own skin. We gathered from the innkeeper, himself a moderate in politics and none too favourably disposed towards the Jacobins, that some of the fugitive deputies had arrived in Bordeaux by boat, but that the local Jacobin Club had given them no opportunity whatever to plan a coup, such as the one that placed Lyons in the hands of counter-revolutionaries, and they had been obliged to flee the city and go into hiding.

The news prostrated Marcelle, who hysterically demanded advice on her next move, and after some thought I took a chance and confided our problem to the innkeeper. He advised us to remain where we were in Libourne and offered to send one of his stable boys as a messenger to Biron's mother. I followed this advice and did my best to calm Marcelle until the boy came back with the news that Biron had been last heard of in the company of two deputies, Gaudet and Salles, both of whom had homes and families in the district, and that he was probably hiding with them.

This was more than enough for Marcelle. Far more exhausted by the journey than she realized, she fainted and had to be carried to bed, leaving the baby, who had inherited the leather lungs of her father, in the care of a wet-nurse procured by the resourceful innkeeper.

By this time I was at my wits' end, not having the least

idea what to do with mother and child, or where to begin looking for Biron. Finally I did what I always did when faced with a problem in republican France, I jingled a few guineas in front of the nearest tradesman, who happened to be Bonnet, the innkeeper. The same night he came to my room and undertook, for a not unreasonable sum, to guide me to the house of ex-Deputy Gaudet's father, which was within a few hours' journey of where we lay.

I set off on horseback with Bonnet the following afternoon, riding south-west into the heart of the Gironde. Soon after dusk we reached the Dordogne and stabled our horses in the hamlet of Saint Pardon. From thence, moving stealthily through the vineyards that covered the slopes beside the river, we pushed on to the outskirts of a little town called Saint Emilion, on the outskirts of which Bonnet said Gaudet's father occupied a largish house.

We stumbled on the place about an hour before midnight and Bonnet, who seemed to know the ground very thoroughly, left me in a copse beside the road and went forward to reconnoitre.

He was gone the better part of two hours and I felt desperately lonely sitting there under the trees, with nothing but the owls for company. Down the road I could see one or two lights twinkling in the dusk but Gaudet senior's house was in darkness and I began to wonder if the Bordeaux Jacobins had already called there in the hope of arresting the runagate deputy or any of his associates.

At last I saw a figure dart across the highway and then another, bent double and moving very swiftly.

The two men entered the wood and came to a halt, one of them calling in a hoarse whisper: "Is that you, René?"

I remembered then that I hadn't given Bonnet my own name but had simply asked after the whereabouts of Deputy Biron.

I called softly: "Biron isn't here, it's Treloar—I've got Biron's wife with me."

"Oh God!" moaned a voice from the shadow. "More trouble!"

A young man moved uneasily into the starlight and I

saw that it was Gaudet, whom I had met on several occasions at the parties at Rouzet's house. With him was
Salles, another young deputy, and both of them looked
a good deal more like gypsies than representatives of the
sovereign people.

We shuffled farther away from the road and sat down
on a moss-grown bank.

"Why did you have to bring a woman down here?"
asked Salles. "Haven't we enough to do keeping our own
heads on our shoulders?"

I told them, as briefly as possible, how and why I had
conducted Marcelle to the south and they listened gloomily. Gaudet said: "Biron's at Madame Bouquey's in the
town. If you've got American papers for his wife and can
bring them together, there's just a chance that the three of
you may get off unchallenged, but you'll have to be quick
about it, the district is swarming with spies and thief-
takers. They didn't take this much trouble to catch poachers when Capet was alive and thriving!"

Gaudet told me what had happened to the batch of
Brissotins who had decided to run for their own country
before the storm broke in Paris. A dozen or so of them
had succeeded in raising a few half-hearted troops in Caen
but had been speedily defeated and had then made a bolt
for the coast, where they managed to get aboard a ship
for Bordeaux. Here, however, they had been forestalled
by the Jacobins and found every door closed against them.
Even Gaudet's father had to be threatened with his son's
suicide before he would take two of them in. Gaudet and
Salles were now concealed in a tiny attic under the roof
and only came out to stretch their legs at night. The rest
of the party, which included Barbaroux, Louvet, Pétion
the former Paris mayor, Buzot, lover of the doomed
Manon Roland, and Biron, who had joined them during
their first visit to Gaudet senior's, were still on the run
and had only found a temporary asylum in Saint Emilion
a few nights previous to my journey south.

The plight of the fugitives was desperate. Even those of
their former friends and associates who were willing to
assist them were unable to do much on their behalf for

they were closely watched. To make things worse, every one of those gay young men who had hurried to Paris to make a new world two years ago was a distinguished-looking fellow, not readily disguised, and not one, save perhaps Louvet, possessed a temperament calculated to sustain them in an ordeal such as this.

They might well have been under lock and key in Bordeaux a week since, had it not been for the gallantry and ingenuity of Gaudet's sister-in-law, the wife of a man called Bouquey, who, on hearing of her brother-in-law's plight, had found a refuge for nearly a dozen of them in Saint Emilion, where she owned a large, rambling house in the centre of the town. In the garden of her home, overlooked by a dozen neighbouring houses, Gaudet told me, was a deep well and twenty feet below the surface a recess leading to a subterranean chamber about the same size as the garden above. The cave could only be reached by climbing down the projecting stones of the well-shaft.

In this retreat the brave woman had not only housed the fugitives but had undertaken to feed them.* Gaudet and Salles had conducted their friends to the refuge and had returned later in the week for blankets and writing materials, and I had been lucky to catch them at Gaudet senior's before they returned, which they intended doing within a few hours.

Having told me this, Gaudet asked for the latest news from Paris. I told him all I knew of the Jacobins' coup in the Convention and the arrest of Brissot and the other deputies in the Salle de Manège.

"We might as well have stayed and made a fight for it," said Salles.

"What happened to those who did stay?" said his companion. "They'll all go to the guillotine within a month!"

---

* The gallant Madame Bouquey ultimately paid with her life for her generosity. She was guillotined in Bordeaux, 1794. Almost all the men she sheltered were ultimately hunted down and executed, although some of them eluded capture until within a few weeks of the fall of Robespierre. The dramatist, Louvet, made good his boast and escaped to Paris, where he lay hidden until the overthrow of the Terrorists.

"They've got a guillotine in Bordeaux," Salles reminded him. "We'll all be caught sooner or later!"

Gaudet groaned. "Why don't we all get over the Pyrénées?" he complained.

"Because the Jacobins have got agents at every pass, you fool," snapped Salles.

As always when in the presence of these people, I felt a spurt of irritation, for even here, when they were hunted like wild beasts and might be taken or betrayed at any moment, the Brissotins lacked self-discipline. They were still ready to bicker and argue among themselves and their chief characteristic, indecision, continued to wrestle with a theatrical fatalism that had been one of the principal causes of their overthrow. I cut short the argument that threatened to develop by demanding, point-blank, to be conducted to Biron's hiding place that night.

They looked at one another and Salles jerked his head nervously in the direction of Bonnet, who was sitting on a log placidly smoking his pipe in a clearing between us and the road. "What about him?" he queried.

I made a gesture of impatience. "He would hardly have guided me this far if he was not to be trusted," I said. "In any case he needn't come with us, I can send him back to the inn."

"Very well," said Gaudet reluctantly, "we'll go into the house, get our luggage and meet you here in two hours. It is no good trying to get into the town until everybody's in bed."

They rose and crept out of the wood. I rejoined Bonnet and told him that I had located the man I sought and would bring him to the inn the following night. I asked if he would convey this information to Marcelle and warn her to be ready to leave as soon as possible. I was satisfied that once I had brought the two together and handed Marcelle her American papers, I would be freed from all further obligations and I was impatient to get back to Charlotte again and set about unravelling my own complicated affairs.

I bought Bonnet's willing co-operation with another of

my precious guineas and he not only promised to do what
I asked but also undertook to make discreet inquiries regarding the sailing dates of certain American vessels then
anchored in the Gironde, a voluntary piece of service that
ultimately saved me at least another forty-eight hours.

He went off towards Saint Pardon and I sat on in the
wood until Gaudet and Salles, both carrying bulky portmanteaux, joined me and we set out along the road for
Saint Emilion. Both deputies were as nervous as cats as
we made our way over the ruins of the old town hall and
through the silent streets, towards a large church which
dominated a huddle of houses from the summit of the hill
upon which the town stands. We were unchallenged,
which was just as well, for there was no fight left in my
companions and they would have dropped their luggage
and run at the first shout of a watchman.

We entered the Bouquey house by the garden gate.
Salles laced the two portmanteaux together on a length
of cord he had brought with him and Gaudet slipped over
the low wall of the well and began to descend, whispering
to me to follow and exercise the greatest care in securing
footholds upon the slimy surface of the stones. Salles
waited at the top to lower the portmanteaux.

We reached the recess in safety and pushed into the
cave that served as the refuge for all who remained at
liberty of the once proud party of the Gironde.

I was quite unprepared for the spectacle that greeted
me once my eyes had become accustomed to the half-
light of the cavern. The cave was slightly bigger than the
entrance hall of a moderate-sized country house, and, at
first glance, it appeared to be chock full of men, some of
whom were stretched on blankets on the uneven floor,
others sitting cross-legged over rush lights, scratching
away at their interminable memoirs and epic poems; still
more were pacing up and down the confines of the chamber engaged in the favourite Brissotin pastime of political
discussion.

I recognized plump Barbaroux, vivacious Louvet and
the handsome Buzot, who was one of the deputies engaged in writing.

Among the men pacing to and fro I noticed Pétion, friend of Paine and, until a short time since, the darling of the Paris mob. He didn't look much like a mayor now. His clothes bore unmistakable evidence of a long and painful sojourn in hedges, ditches and quarries, and his beard, like those of his colleagues, was as thick and matted as his disordered hair.

I reintroduced myself as the Englishman who had been employed by Paine, and he smiled, wanly, at the mention of the famous republican.

"I'm glad Tom can't see us in our warren," he said. "It might destroy what little faith remains in him for bringing sound government to a nation of wild beasts. If you ever see him again tell him to write a treatise on the folly of overthrowing one régime before you have something more solid than a few folios of theory to replace it!"

Pétion had learnt wisdom and so, probably, had some of the others, but too late for it to be of any service either to France or to themselves. I have never seen a more dejected crew in my life.

Of all the men there only the dramatist Louvet exhibited any lightness of heart, and his ringing laugh, when he pointed out the sleeping Biron to me, sounded as incongruous as a joke at a funeral tea.

"What do you think of us, Treloar?" he joked. "The party of the Plain gone to earth, with the hounds baying at the well-head and only a friendly mole to keep them from tearing us to pieces and hanging the brushes on the statue of Liberty! *Ma foi,* but we're a precious assortment, I must say, millions of quotations and not a constructive plan to share among us, and with hardly enough energy to kiss the hand of the goddess who brings us our supper each night."

"What are you going to do?" I asked him, as he stirred Biron with his foot. "You can't stay here indefinitely."

"Personally, I have no intention of staying," replied Louvet, "but when I do cut I'm cutting alone and heading straight back to Paris where the Mountain is least likely to ferret for me. I might get there if left to myself, but I should be taken inside two leagues if I stayed to argue at every crossroad with these chickens! Look alive, my hearty!" he shouted at Biron, who had sat up and was staring about him in a daze. "Here's a good friend of yours come to unload more trouble on you!"

He strolled off, chuckling, and Biron, seeing me, scrambled to his feet and poured out a flood of hysterical questions.

I told him why I had come and what I proposed to do. He bit his lip in perplexity and of all the deputies he seemed to me the most unnerved and indecisive.

"I can't go away from here," he cried. "I might as well blow my brains out!"

"That isn't going to help your wife and child," I told him. "You've got a good passport and you stand a better chance than any of them."

He thrust his hand into his jacket and took out the folder of documents André had given him in my room the night Lucille died.

Pétion strolled over and Biron put the question to him. "What shall I do, Pétion?" he implored.

Pétion shrugged contemptuously.

"I should run for it. Why not? They aren't looking for a man with a wife and child."

Biron turned to Barbaroux and asked the same question, getting an identical answer.

I knew that he'd never be able to make up his own mind, so I took out my watch and held it in the palm of my hand.

"Look here, Biron," I said, "I'm leaving here in five minutes, with or without you. If you come I'll take you as far as Libourne and hand you over to Marcelle, but if you prefer to rot in this hole I'm heading straight back to Paris for Charlotte, and Marcelle can take her chance alone. Which is it to be?"

"But we can't start now," he protested, "it'll be light in less than an hour."

"We've got American papers and can travel openly," I said. "You've got four minutes to make a decision."

I didn't like treating him like that in front of his friends, but I knew Biron too well and it was the only thing to do.

He hesitated a few seconds longer and then, with a gesture of resignation, rolled up his blanket and followed me across the cave to the well-shaft.

Biron went up the shaft first, trailing the cord with which he could pull his pack after him, and just as I was about to step off the rock platform Buzot took my arm and thrust a letter into my hand.

"If you get to Paris, smuggle this into the Abbaye and you will be doing me an inestimable service," he whispered.

I glanced at the sealed folder and saw that it had no name and address written on it but everyone associated with the Brissotins was aware of Buzot's passionate attachment for Madame Roland.

I pocket the letter and promised to do what I could to deliver it. Buzot thanked me warmly and said, with a sad smile: "We shall never see one another again."

When I got to the top I found Biron crouching under the garden wall. It was quite light by this time and down in the town a few people were already astir. We walked openly into the street and down the hill towards the Bordeaux road, Biron saying nothing and keeping close to my side.

I showed Joel Barlow's porter's pass to the yawning sergeant at the town gate and we got through without any trouble and branched off into the vineyards towards Saint Pardon.

The ease with which we had got clear of Saint Emilion gave Biron more confidence and his spirits mounted as we made rapid progress towards Libourne. By midday, when we were resting beside the path, he was cock-a-hoop. I think it had done him good to breathe pure air again and he had the good grace to thank me for the pains I had taken to get him this far. He seemed both amused and delighted when I told him that Charlotte and I had been married in the doctor's jail. He didn't make any suggestions, however, on how I was to get her out, but confined himself to vague speculations on what he and Marcelle would engage in when they arrived in Philadelphia.

"I think I might keep a shop," he mused, "it's a pleasant enough life once you get used to it."

I was glad he didn't propose to start farming over there. Six months on a wilderness clearing would have broken Biron's back and driven Marcelle crazy with boredom.

We got back to the inn about suppertime and Biron rushed madly upstairs to his wife's room, while I took a bite of supper in the kitchen with Bonnet. The innkeeper didn't ask any questions but, true to his promise, he produced a list of foreign shipping and probable departures from the port. There was a Boston brig due to leave in two days' time and I marked it with a cross and told Bonnet to give the paper to Marcelle. I also gave him two more guineas to guide the pair to the coast and see them aboard, and this the honest fellow undertook to do at all costs.

When that was settled I decided to go. If I went up to say farewell to Marcelle I knew that Biron would try and prevail upon me to see them to their ship, and this I was not prepared to do, having lost too much time already.

I slipped up to my room, packed my small bag of luggage and ran downstairs and out into the dark, putting four English miles between myself and Libourne in the next hour. About midnight, tired to the point of exhaustion, I lay up in the woods and waited for the rattle of the northbound coach.

Chapter Seventeen

My return journey was along a more inland route, through Bergerac and Limoges, and, feeling reasonably secure with a passport and a commercial pass in my pocket, I took an inside ticket and travelled in comfort.

The passengers who joined or left the mail at various stages were mostly businessmen ready to discuss everything except politics. Nobody cared to broach this subject until the general climbed aboard at Vierzon, a stage where the coach road to Lyons formed a junction with the Paris road.

The general was an impressive-looking scoundrel, tall and generously proportioned, with a huge head, a port-wine complexion and a fluent gutter vocabulary. His thick, greasy hair was tied in the military queue and the five-inch lapels of his braided coat, flanked by a pair of enormous woollen epaulettes, were generously decorated with tricolour cockades and various other patriotic emblems.

His name was Fournayville and he was so markedly the embodiment of active, aggressively vindictive republicanism that he soon reduced the two other inside passengers to a state of terrified silence and they were glad to leave the coach at the first stop, doubtless preferring to lose a day or two on the road than face the general's stern inquiries into the political health of their families and friends. I would have preferred to do the same but I dared not risk further delay.

Fournayville seemed to take a brusque liking to me, particularly after he had scrutinized my papers, which he loudly demanded as soon as he had settled himself in the most comfortable seat. He had a Jacobin's theoretical admiration for the American Revolution which, at this distance, appeared to have been accomplished smoothly and permanently, and he asked me a hundred questions

regarding the affairs of the colonists and the system of
government they had established since breaking with
Britain. It was fortunate for me that I was familiar with
the American background. I had learned a good deal
about America during my long conversations with Paine
and Barlow and was thus able to supply satisfactory answers to most of his queries.

When he had done questioning me, and had forced me
to help myself liberally to his snuff (which he took in
such prodigious quantities that his white waistcoat was
soon as brown as an autumn leaf), he volunteered some
information about himself and told me that he was a native
of Chateaudun and had been apprenticed to the leather
trade in that district, before breaking his indentures and
running away to join the 1st Regiment of King's Foot
Guards. He had subsequently seen active service in Flan-
ders and must have given his officers a good deal of trouble,
for he told me jovially that on several occasions he had
been tied to the triangle and flogged and had once drawn
lots for his life, the loser of the lottery being shot for in-
citement to mutiny at Courtrai.

Like most of his kind, he saw in the Revolution a glorious opportunity to advance himself and, soon after the
fall of the Bastille, he had welded the malcontents of his
regiment into a compact force of mutineers, stormed the
officers' quarters at Lille barracks and butchered all his
superiors from the colonel downwards. He described, with
considerable relish, how he personally had flung three
sixteen-year-old lieutenants from the dormitory windows
and left them to die in the yard.

Long before he had finished the account of his youth I
had come to regard him with a loathing disgust that I
found difficult to hide, but by this time a vague plan had
begun to form in my mind and I encouraged him to tell
me more of his present circumstances and his reasons for
leaving Lyons and going north into La Vendée.

He did not need much encouragement, particularly
when I plied him with cognac. At the first stop I invested
in a bottle of the best liquor the inn could supply and we
drank deeply all through the next stage. By the time we

were nearing Orleans we were on affectionate terms with one another and I was calling him "old comrade" instead of "citizen general."

He had come, it appeared, fresh from the most frightful scenes of butchery in Lyons, where the Convention's army, twenty thousand strong, had hemmed in the insurgent Lyonese, stormed the town and put hundreds to the sword. According to Fournayville, Lyons, the second city in France, no longer existed and those among its population who were spared the extreme wrath of the Jacobins had been reduced to the status of homeless beggars. Between bellows of laughter he described how the loathsome cripple, Couthon, whom I had seen among the distinguished mourners at Lepelletier's enshrinement in the Panthéon last January, had had himself carried from door to door in one quarter of the town, striking each entrance with a silver hammer and exclaiming: "I condemn thee as the house of a rebel!" whereupon demolition squads of republicans rushed at the building and proceeded to level it to the ground.

The guillotine, which the republican armies now carried with them as part of their armament, broke down under the strain during the first few days and the executioners had to resort to more novel methods of extermination, such as the herding of scores of prisoners into a square where cannon discharged grapeshot into them at point-blank range. The shores of the River Rhone, said Fournayville, had been piled with bloated corpses which the occupying troops were obliged to bury, much against their will, in order to forestall an outbreak of pestilence.

When the work was done the army had been split and part of it, under Fournayville's command, was now moving into La Vendée, where the general promised himself some campaigning that would make the Lyons affair look like a schoolboy prank.

He continued in this vein over a number of leagues and finally shot a totally unexpected question at me.

"You read and write, I presume, citizen?"

I admitted that this was so. He took another huge pinch

of snuff, smothered the sneeze in the cognac flask, and cocked a rheumy eye at me.

"I will appoint you general's secretary at the next stop!" he announced.

I was about to voice a mild protest against this arbitrary enlistment when something prompted me to choke back the words and smile at the wretch, for the hazy plan, conceived an hour or so after Fournayville had entered the coach, suddenly assumed a practical form.

"That would be a very great honour, citizen general," I said respectfully.

He was so accustomed to terrified obedience on the part of civilans that my ready acceptance of his offer did not surprise him in any way, and as we drew into the Orleans posting-house yard he swung out of the coach and called loudly for paper, pens and ink, which were instantly procured by a badly frightened ostler. Whereupon he sat down at a table, pushed the materials in my direction and began to dictate my terms of enlistment.

"They sent me an usher from Arras as my secretary when I took over command of the division," he told me, whilst we were waiting for the ink to dry. "He was a scholarly fellow, I daresay, but he lacked stomach and I overheard him promising to do what he could to persuade the Commissioners to spare the wife of a Brissotin whom we had hanged. I gave the old rascal the death of his dreams. The wench who appealed to him was buxom enough to make a younger man's mouth water, so we stripped the pair of them, tied them face to face, and threw them into the Rhone. It was a waste of the wench no doubt but it made Citizen Couthon clap his hands for glee and he pronounced me just the man for the pacification of La Vendée!"

I gave what I hoped was a passable imitation of an appreciative chuckle and handed the general my enlistment papers, which he scrutinized as we went inside for our dinner, the personnel of the inn falling over each other in their efforts to avoid serving our table.

After the meal we still had an hour or so to wait, so Fournayville suggested that we should call at the military depot and collect my uniform. This fitted in admirably with my plan. We found the depot, signed for tunic, breeches, shako, underclothes, sabre and pistols, and returned to the inn just in time for the Chartres coach, which set off about sunset. I was lucky again. There were four outside passengers and the general and I had the inside to ourselves.

The general had suggested that I should complete the journey as a soldier and dispose of my civilian clothes in the Orleans market, but as we had no time to spare when we arrived back at the inn I assured him that I would change at the first halt and sell my clothes in Chartres, where I knew of a reliable dealer. It was lucky for me that he did not press the point, for the clothes I had drawn were several sizes too small. I had no intention of wearing them myself.

About halfway between Orleans and Chartres the main coach road runs over an escarpment, the slopes of which are covered by a birch forest. As we descended the incline and passed through the little town of Artenay, the general began to nod, and I suggested that he should take the opportunity to get some sleep during the remainder of the journey. Like most tyrants of humble origin, he revelled in the ministration of a bodyservant and by the time I had unwound his voluminous stock, and tucked him up in his greatcoat, he was purring like an old cat and congratulating himself on having found such an admirable valet. He was a long time dropping off, however, and drowsily speculated on the glorious times we would have together in La Vendée, where, he declared, he had personal knowledge of the districts famous for their wines and wenches, of which he promised himself, and me, a conqueror's share.

Whilst he was going to sleep I was in a fever of impatience, but once his snores had joined the concert of the rattling hooves, jingling harness and the regular creak of the heavy equipage, I was in no hurry to settle upon a means of disposing of him, for my plan involved cold-blooded murder, and, although I had witnessed many scenes of violence since that eventful summer night at

Westdown, I had yet to kill anything larger than a badger. All the killing at the farm had been done by my father or my brother Noah.

It is one thing to ponder upon murder in the abstract, particularly when one's position is perilous, and the plight of those one loves is desperate, but quite another to sit facing a total stranger and tell yourself that within the next half hour he must die by your hand.

Had the general been less of a monster I should have abandoned my design there and then, but his jovial descriptions of the appalling scenes in Lyons, in which he had confessedly played such a willing part, helped me to steel myself for the business and I began to consider the best means of accomplishing it before we trotted into Chartres.

I had my pistols, but using them was out of the question, for the passengers immediately above, to say nothing of the coachman and guard on the boxes fore and aft, would certainly have inquired into the report of a firearm from the inside of the coach. I also had my knife and two sabres, my own and the general's, but I shrank from the thought of plunging a weapon into the sleeping man and decided that, whatever means I eventually employed to kill him, there must be no bloodshed.

I considered clubbing him with a pistol butt and throwing him from the coach as we passed over favourable ground, but I knew that I dare not risk his recovery and an alarm might deprive me of a good start on the Paris road. I finally decided upon strangulation and I picked up Fournayville's stock and twisted it into a rope, making a strong slipknot at one end.

I then transferred my small amount of luggage into the general's half-filled portmanteau and stripped down to my small clothes, rolling the discarded garments into a compact bundle.

Even then I would probably have dodged this issue and jumped out, leaving the general to his dreams, had not the coach, at that moment, bumped over a deep pot-hole and jolted him half-awake.

He opened his eyes and glared at me, unable to com-

prehend what I was doing sitting facing him in my small
clothes, with his cravat on my knees. I gave way to panic
and hurled myself across the coach, slipping the noose
over his lolling head, pulling the knot tight and holding
on with every ounce of strength in my arms.

I might have broken his neck with the first violent tug
for he was sprawling at an angle which added the weight
of his body to my pull. He was such a powerfully built
rascal, however, that I doubted whether I was strong
enough to do the hangman's work so mercifully and so I
held on, pulling with all my might until his eyes bulged
and a thin rim of froth showed on the underside of his
enormous moustache.

The coach, meantime, was ascending a slight rise at a
trot and I heard nothing from coachman, guard or passengers. All the time I knelt on the twitching body I forced
myself to picture incidents he had related to me of the
sack of Lyons, of terrified civilians herded up to the muz-
zles of belching cannon, of the timid usher, his former
secretary, drowning in the Rhone tied to the naked body
of a woman whose pleas had touched his pity, and as
these pictures passed through my mind my grip became
even stronger until his twitching finally ceased and the
corpse of General Fournayville, sometime of His Late
Majesty's Footguards, butcher of Lyons, and potential
pacifier of La Vendée, lay sprawled in grotesque posture
under the yellow glow of the single lamp.

Succeeding in some measure in controlling the violent
trembling that seized me, I then began to strip off my
victim's tunic, breeches and boots and don the flambouyant
uniform. This done I turned down the lamp, raised the
blind and tossed my own clothes out of the window. I
did this more as a test to discover whether the outside
passengers were awake than from any desire to dispose
of them. I stuck my head out of the window and listened
for any comments from above but heard nothing but the
metallic beat of the horses' hooves and the accompanying
rattle of coach and harness, so I judged that I might now
attempt to put into execution the second part of my plan,

which was to dispose of Fournayville and follow him off
the coach at the most suitable moment.

The chance came sooner than I expected, when the
road ran level through two stretches of tall woods, whose
branches interlaced above us, cutting off the glimmer of
starlight. I opened the door, held it ajar by the window
strap and with my free hand dragged the body of Fournayville from the seat, and pushed it through the open
door into a ditch that ran alongside the road. It rolled
over once or twice and disappeared, almost soundlessly,
into a deep patch of shadow. I waited a moment or two
before I threw out the portmanteau and followed it in a
matter of seconds, leaping clear of the coach and rolling
over a low bank into the woods. I grazed my right knee
on a tree stump, but otherwise landed unhurt. I lay quiet,
until the sounds of the coach had died away in the distance and then walked back along the road until I stumbled on the baggage. I then crossed the road and struck
out through the woods in the direction I judged the most
likely one to enable me to pick up the Chartres–Paris road
in the vicinity of Rambouillet.

The general's boots were not meant for walking and
I had a hard job getting through the tangle of briars and
close-set pines in the dark, particularly as I was laden
with the portmanteau, containing my spare uniform, the
general's small kit and the two heavy sabres and sword
belts, which I had strapped round the bag. Eventually,
however, I struck a charcoal-burner's track and passing
through a silent hamlet found a side road that I followed
for the remainder of the night. I struck the main highway shortly before dawn, and pushed on eastward as fast
as I could hobble.

Just as the sun got up I came in sight of a small town,
which I subsequently discovered to be Eperon, the stage
before Rambouillet, and here I walked boldly into the inn
and demanded breakfast, my uniform ensuring that I was
not questioned by the startled innkeeper, who, none the
less, favoured me with a somewhat curious glance.

He might well have been puzzled for I was limping
badly and was scratched all over with briars, and when

he brought food I attacked it like a famished wolf. I thought it best, however, to offer no explanation but to rely upon the terror tactics of the man I was impersonating. I must have succeeded rather better than I supposed for I remember the innkeeper's look of intense astonishment when I paid my bill and gave him a gratuity in addition. Apparently he was quite unprepared to find a libertarian of my rank ready to settle his score.

The Paris coach was due from Chartres about nine a.m., but I judged I had better not wait for that and ordered a two-horse chaise at a livery stables, farther up the road, paying in gold in order to avoid a lengthy argument with the proprietor. The equipage, which I drove myself, was a fast one and I bowled into Versailles in the early afternoon, handing over the chaise at an address given me by the livery stable and catching the public coach into Paris.

I flourished the general's papers and consequently had very little trouble at the barriers, the officer on duty recommending a good hotel within easy walking distance of Gemaine's *maison de santé*. I had intended to call at Gemaine's the same night, but when I saw the bed in my room the temptation to rest was too strong for me and I drew off my boots and stretched myself, fully dressed, on the counterpane. In less than a minute I was asleep.

Chapter Eighteen

It was just as well I fell asleep when I did for the time lapse prevented me from committing an act of supreme folly.

I had been in such a fever to get back to Charlotte that I had not considered the means at my disposal to get her out of Gemaine's clutches or even how I could do anything more than contribute to the maintenance of Charlotte, André and Rouzet until the scoundrelly doctor had squeezed me dry. I had no illusions regarding what he would do with us when he had pocketed the last of my guineas, he would simply turn the four of us over to the Committee of Public Safety, and even if I eluded him the case of the others would be hopeless.

If I had not fallen into an exhausted sleep at my hotel it is probable that I should have hurried off to Gemaine's within the hour. I still believed that the man who held the guineas held the key of Gemaine's jail. I was not aware that during the period I had been away from Paris a number of drastic changes had taken place and, in the current situation, none of them favoured persons under arrest or under suspicion.

Feeling thoroughly rested on awakening I sipped a coffee and took stock of my position. One of the first things I learned, from an out-of-date journal I found in the bedroom, was that the demagogue Marat had been murdered by an enterprising young woman of Caen, a girl called Corday, who seemed to have gone about the business with the deliberation of a professional assassin.

Most of the Jacobin deputies were haunted by the fear of assassination and it was clear that the slaying of a person as prominent as Jean Paul Marat would result in the application of even sterner measures of repression than those that had already been enforced against the Brissotins and other moderates. I had no means of knowing how this would affect Gemaine's power to sell his prisoners, even if he was willing to do so, and after sending out for a dozen journals and spending an hour or so studying their contents, I came to the conclusion that it would be the action of a lunatic to march up to Gemaine's establishment as plain Mr. Treloar, the Englishman interested in the Rouzet trio and a man for whom a warrant had already been issued. Money could not solve the problem, for a nervous Jacobin valued blood above gold.

I lingered over my coffee for a long time, turning over this plan and that, but not arriving at any satisfactory conclusion until I happened to glance at my face in a fly-blown mirror I found among the general's kit. The reflection I saw gave me a spurt of confidence for I hardly recognized the bearded ruffian I saw in the mirror.

More than five weeks had passed since Charlotte's arrest and I had not stropped a razor since the evening of Lucille's suicide in the Luxembourg. Lack of sleep had inflamed my eyes and in the general's plumed, tricorn shako and uniform I looked more like a successful brigand than a fugitive civilian. I had passed successfully as Fournayville thus far, why not present myself in the same disguise to people like Gemaine and his doorkeeper?

The idea took hold of my imagination and I set about mixing a solution of dye from wine dregs, water and a pot of blacking that I found in the portmanteau. Ten minutes later my whiskers had passed from dark brown to coal black and I finished off the transformation by blacking out a tooth or two on the left side of my face.

I then packed my bag, throwing out some of the general's luggage to make room for the spare uniform, and passed down the backstairs into the street. It was midday and the traffic was heavy. I got out of the hotel without so much as a glimpse of patron or chambermaid.

I soon noticed that my uniform was the best defence I could have selected, for I now represented the military arm of the all-powerful Committee of Public Safety, and almost every person I encountered skipped out of my path as though I was a wild beast. After a while I began to enjoy myself and went out of my way to glare at home-going linkmen, street porters, National Guardsmen and other pedestrians I passed on my way up to the *maison de santé*. It was not until the door of the establishment had been opened to me by the rapacious drab who collected the meal tribute, however, that I congratulated myself on the excellence of my disguise, for the woman's face turned the colour of a cod's underbelly when I brusquely demanded to examine her prison register.

She tried to slip off and get Gemaine, but I knew that the key of the hall cupboard hung from her belt and made a grab at it, standing over her threateningly whilst she fumbled in the cupboard and handed me the book.

I thumbed through the pages until I came to the original entry relating to Rouzet, Charlotte and André. Against the names of Papa and his nephew were two notations, but the doctor's handwriting was so bad that I had to ask his jailer to interpret them.

"What does this mean?" I demanded, pointing to the scrawl.

The woman hesitated. Sweat began to show on her forehead and she fidgeted with her key-chain.

"The girl is still here but the two men have gone," she said reluctantly.

"Gone where?"

"Don't distress yourself, General," she went on hurriedly. "The old man went to the Conciergerie and is probably buried by now, and the younger one was transferred to the Bicêtre at his own request."

"The Bicêtre! That's a hospital, you liar," I growled.

Her face began to twitch and she looked despairingly into the back of the hall, hoping desperately that Gemaine would appear.

Nobody came out of the cardroom, however, and it occurred to me that the place was far less crowded than when I had left it on my wedding day. Possibly the Committee, maddened by Marat's death, had made a clean sweep of the majority of Gemaine's paying guests.

Seeing no help for it, the woman told me all she knew.

"The young doctor was offered a chance to go to the

Bicêtre as resident surgeon," she explained. "They couldn't get a man there and they withdrew his warrant when he agreed to accept the post. Doctor Gemaine received orders to transfer the old wigmaker a week ago and he went, owing a week's score. The movement order for the girl was cancelled."

"By whose command?" I bellowed.

"By order of Citizen Fouquier-Tinville, the public prosecutor," she muttered, and I knew then that she had told me the truth.

I had to have time to think for I was bewildered. I had hoped that once André and I had an opportunity to talk in private he would soon have hit upon a safe ruse for getting all three of them out of Gemaine's hands and to a place of comparative safety, but with André at the Bicêtre and poor old Rouzet dead, or as good as dead, I didn't know how to act. André was so much better than I was at this sort of thing.

My first impulse was to growl my way out of the building and hurry over to the Bicêtre to seek his advice, but I soon abandoned this idea for it would have meant that Gemaine and his assistant would have a chance to put their heads together and when I returned the chances were that Charlotte would have gone, too, and, most likely, the doctor along with her.

Finally, I said: "Stay by the main door and don't move from it until I've had a word with your employer. These people I seek are dangerous counter-revolutionaries and you and the doctor are answerable for them!"

She muttered a dutiful "Yes, General!" and scuttled back to her customs bench. I knew that I wouldn't have any more trouble from her, she was far too badly scared by the interview.

At that moment the seedy little priest who had married us crossed the hall on his way to the terrace window and as he shuffled by he gave me a curious glance. I suspected that he had recognized me and I went after him, catching him by the arm and propelling him down the terrace steps on to the deserted lawn.

I did not like the idea of trusting him but I had to get

some more information before I took the risk of confronting Gemaine, whose eyes were a good deal sharper
than those of his porteress.

The priest had recognized me and the first thing he
said when we were out of earshot of the house was:
"Take off your ring, a disguise doesn't end at the wrist,
my friend!"

I whipped the signet ring from my finger and handed
it to him. It had belonged to my mother's father and was
one of the few personal possessions I brought out of England.

"What happened to my friends?" I demanded.

He looked troubled, pocketed the ring and said, without looking at me:

"Don't blame your wife, Treloar, she couldn't help
it. She came to me for advice and I absolved her. What
else could I do, or she either? She wasn't to know Gemaine hadn't the power to carry out his part of the bargain."

I took him by his narrow shoulders and shook him
violently.

"Bargain? What bargain?"

"Your wife has moved into Gemaine's suite," he muttered. "The doctor promised to cancel her transfer and
her uncle's, too. He got her name off somehow, but
Rouzet went the day after she made the bargain."

"But what about her brother?" I shouted.

He took my hand gently. I had sadly misjudged him;
he was a kindly, courageous little soul and, unlike most of
the prisoners at Gemaine's, genuinely interested in other
people's troubles.

"Her brother had already gone," he informed me. "It
was a wise decision as well as a humane one. Do you
happen to know the Bicêtre?"

Everyone in Paris knew of the Bicêtre. It was a filthy,
pestilential lazar-house full of poor wretches dying of
loathsome diseases. Anyone but André would have preferred to take his chance at the Conciergerie.

"Where is my wife?" I asked hoarsely. The thought
that Charlotte had sold herself to Gemaine for Rouzet's

life, and had done so in vain, made me sick with rage.
If it had not been for the restraining hand of the priest
I think I should have rushed up to the house with drawn
sabre.

The abbé shrugged and look critically at my disguise.
"It's a chance you'll have to take," he said. "Come,
they're in there at dinner now. As your wife will certainly
recognize you, perhaps I had better try and get her alone
first."

I rejected this offer. For all my blind rage and misery
I had a clear enough head to wish him out of the business,
so I thanked him and slipped into Gemaine's study
through the terrace window.

The room was empty but I could hear the chink of
cutlery from the dining-room adjoining and I guessed that
Gemaine was at table. I took another look at myself in
the oval mirror over the fireplace and then quietly un-
fastened the portmanteau and rummaged among the general's papers, extracting a blank sheet of official note-
paper, surmounted by the republican device and the usual
jargon surrounding it. Using Gemaine's gold-tipped quill
I wrote: *"The bearer has authority to convey the suspects
named below to any house of arrest he deems fit, for the
purpose of questioning them regarding activities on behalf of the Brissotins."* I dated it a week ago, wrote in the
names of Rouzet, Charlotte, André and the little priest,
and signed it in the name of Deputy Couthon, whom I
knew to be safely out of the way in Lyons. It was a very
amateur forgery but it was the best thing I could think
of on the spur of the moment. When the ink was dry I
opened the dining-room door and strode confidently into
the room.

Gemaine was sitting with his back to me finishing off a
cold chicken. Opposite him, at the other end of the elegant walnut table, sat Charlotte, ladling out the sweet.

I was profoundly shocked at the change in her. It
seemed to me that she had aged five years since we
parted. Her generous mouth, usually so ready with a quiet,
welcoming smile, was now set in a sour line, and her
large eyes had a blankness beyond that of misery.

She recognized me instantly and stared as though I had walked in from the tomb; for an instant her lips parted to scream but she choked back the sound as it rushed from her throat. Then her expression of incredulity faded and was replaced by a look of bewildered terror.

I did not know how Germaine had treated her during those weeks I had been absent but he appeared to have broken her spirit to a degree I should never have thought possible. She never afterwards referred to that period and, as is easily imagined, I didn't care to press the subject; I never even told her of my talk with the priest.

Gemaine must have read my entry in her expression but the dissembling rogue suppressed whatever curiosity he felt, reaching for his dessert and swallowing a spoonful of compote before turning languidly and greeting me with one of his charming smiles, at the same waving me to a seat.

"Good morning, General," he said cordially, "and to what do I owe this honour?"

He dabbed his lips with a napkin and motioned to Charlotte to pour me some wine.

I could have killed him for that alone, for his gesture implied that she was there to dispense routine hospitality to callers and it maddened me to see the prompt manner in which she complied. Neither of us, however, failed to note the nervous rattle of the decanter on the rim of the glass.

I told Gemaine gruffly that I had been sent to him from the Hotel de Ville and that my purpose was to interrogate certain of his prisoners who were suspected of Brissotin sympathies, and I handed him my warrants. He ran a cursory eye over the scrawl, cocking an eyebrow when he saw Charlotte's name in my handwriting. My nervousness subsided for it was clear that he took me for the man I posed to be. I glanced at Charlotte once or twice but she kept her gaze lowered.

"Really, General, this is a matter of some surprise to me," he said at last, sifting the pages with his long, be-ringed fingers. "I had no notion that I was custodian to

Brissotins sufficiently important to interest Citizen Couthon."

Feeling some further explanation might be necessary, I said: "They caught a fugitive down there, a deputy by the name of Biron. He gave the tribunal certain names in the hope of escaping justice."

Gemaine yawned and stood up.

"And they sent a general all the way from Lyons to make these arrests?" he queried.

"Not specifically," I told him. "I was instructed by Citizen Couthon to see that these suspects were brought before the Committee prior to joining my division and setting out for the west."

He turned to Charlotte, who had not uttered a word.

"I'm afraid I shall have to cut short our idyll, my dear," he lisped, "for it seems that you and your family are trout, not minnows. But perhaps it is better that way, your English husband might not understand our relationship if he succeeded in getting back to Paris. What do you think?"

He smiled, and his cool contempt pricked the bubble of my conceit and I knew in the instant that my clumsy disguise had not fooled him for one moment but merely encouraged him to enjoy a few moments' cat-and-mouse sport with the pair of us.

As he finished speaking he strolled casually across the room to his bureau and I, idot that I was, felt secure as long as his back was to me.

The next moment I was looking into the muzzle of two pocket pistols which he had whipped from a half-open drawer.

"I can't imagine what I'm going to do with a dead general in my dining-room, Mr. Treloar," he said with a smile, "but we must deal with one thing at a time, don't you think?"

"You won't kill me here, Gemaine," I told him, trying to put a bold face on things. "I haven't so much as an assignat on me and you'll want your bill settled before you squeeze those triggers. I know she is the only one here so take a hundred guineas and let us go; you can easily say I used force!"

"Why shouldn't I collect my account plus credit from the public prosecutor for handing over an English spy?" he asked quietly.

Although the smile never left his face I could see that his brain was busy with several queries, and it was only his uncertainty regarding them that had prevented him from pulling both triggers the instant he had his hands on the pistols. He was trying to decide whether I had left men in the street, how I had come by warrants that were beyond question official and, above all, whether I carried my gold on my person or had deposited it elsewhere before calling on him. I think it was his avarice that saved me, for he could easily have killed me and denounced my corpse to the first sergeant he met in the street, and when my true identity had been established he would have further ingratiated himself with his partners for so readily accounting for an English spy.

He backed towards the far end of the room, where the bell-tassel hung, moving carefully round the furniture and never taking his eyes off me for a fraction of a second.

"One hundred?" he mused. "Come now, Mr. Treloar, that was good enough for the third-storey apartments, but since then your wife has indulged her tastes rather more extravagantly. I couldn't have done more as a host; I'm sharing my apartment with her."

I ground my teeth with rage but I was helpless with those two little barrels directed at me. Even when he laid one pistol down and reached for the tassel, he advanced his right hand across the table and kept an unblinking eye on my chest. I could almost feel the ball tearing into me and I'm not ashamed to admit that I kept as still as Notre Dame, my brain all the time casting round for a means of bluffing him into a bargain far in excess of my actual means.

I heard the bell jangle in the hall and saw his left hand let go the tassel and grope for the other pistol which he had laid aside on an occasional table close by.

It was then, while his attention was fixed wholly on

me, that Charlotte acted. One moment we formed a tableau, Gemaine and myself facing each other, with the table between us, and Charlotte sitting perfectly still at his end, the next we were in a thrashing heap on the floor, with the table and its contents overturned and Charlotte lying half across the prostrate doctor plunging away at his exposed side with a fruit knife she had somehow contrived to slip in her lap whilst he approached the bureau for his pistols.

She seemed to extract a fiendish delight out of killing him and, during the brief instant it took me to join them after I had overturned the table, she must have stabbed him half a dozen times, for when I turned him over blood was gushing from his mouth and he was all but dead.

I had to drag her back from his twitching body and strike the knife from her hand, and I think her exultation was the ugliest thing I had ever seen, for notwithstanding the fact that her spring had saved our lives, her behaviour momentarily placed her on a level with the murderers of the Swiss Guardsmen in the Tuileries and the inhuman monsters who had perpetrated the massacre at the Abbaye.

"Have done, for God's sake, Lottë!" I begged, but she flung herself on her knees beside him again and began fumbling in the bloodstained folds of his cravat.

"He keeps his key here," she exclaimed breathlessly. "We can get some of our money back. I know where he—"

I took her by the hair then and dragged her to the door by main force. All I wanted at that moment was to be out of that evil house and I didn't care what risks we took in leaving.

As we got to the door Gemaine's woman came in answer to his bell and when she saw the shambles in the dining-room she let out a shriek that could have been heard on the Versailles turnpike. Prisoners began calling over the banisters to know what had happened and I let go of Charlotte for a moment and clapped a hand over the terrified woman's mouth. At my touch she obligingly fainted, so I pushed her in with her employer's corpse

and quickly slammed and locked the door from the outside.

I saw that Charlotte was holding Gemaine's key by its
broken cord and I heard her saying over and over again
that we must find the doctor's strongbox and get our
money back, but by this time the little abbé had run in
from the garden and, after one glance at Charlotte's blood-
soaked apron, he pushed us both into the study, shouting
to the people on the stairs to keep out of the way unless
they wanted to be mixed up in a murder.

Once inside the study I realized that Charlotte was hysterical. She began pulling out all the drawers and tearing
down the doctor's pictures in the hope of discovering
where he had secreted his money. It was the priest who
succeeded in calming her, taking hold of her shoulders
and shaking her until her hairpins cascaded to the floor.

"You've got your life and your future," he shouted.
"What good did the money do him, eh? He's in there lying
in his blood and you're wasting time grubbing for gold.
Take her out of her, m'sieur, before you have to take the
life of that wretched woman; she's got a voice that'll fetch
them in from the street in less than a minute."

Charlotte stopped bleating about the money and sat
down, staring before her, as though she had suddenly
realized all that happened in the last ten minutes and was
horrified by her act.

I turned out the small portmanteau and gave her the
clothes I had drawn from the Orleans depot, telling her to
put them on as quickly as she could. When she didn't respond, but only stared stupidly at me, I began pulling off
her dress and petticoats and the priest helped me until we
had got her into the breeches and tunic of the general's
secretary. She didn't resist but she didn't help us; it was
like undressing and dressing a drunkard.

When she was nearly ready I poured her a stiff glass of
cognac from the doctor's flask, but although the spirits
brought a dark flush to her cheeks it didn't seem to bring
her out of her trance and she reeled so much when she
stood up that I had to support her under the armpits.

"You'd better take a cab from the corner," advised the

abbé, and until then I had supposed he would accompany
us and told him so.

"No, no, my son," he said, "I'll take my chance here;
you'll have enough trouble getting clear of Paris without
another passenger."

"What about the others?" I asked. "There's nothing to
stop any of them going if they go now."

"There isn't one of them who doesn't suppose he's safer
here than in his own home, but I'll explain what has happened and they can go or stay as they please. Get yourselves out and leave Paris as soon as possible; I'll attend
to the woman here; she won't make any further trouble, I
promise you."

I asked him how, short of murder, he proposed to
silence her.

"I'll take the key, just to make sure." The sly old
fellow chuckled and I guessed then that he would hand the
key Charlotte had found to the doorkeeper and urge her
to decamp with the money and keep her counsel about
what had occurred. If she did this we had a fair chance
of getting away without a hue and cry.

I didn't like leaving him like that but he would not be
persuaded to change his mind, so I sprinkled Charlotte's
tunic with cognac, helped her into the passage and let ourselves out, the abbé waving us farewell and closing the door
again immediately we had reached the street. I often wonder what happened to him and to all the rest of Gemaine's
lodgers. I hope that he at least succeeded in dodging the
guillotine and got across the frontier to await better times.
I don't suppose he was much of a success as a priest but
he was a good friend to me and I shall always recall him
with gratitude.

I signalled a cab and the driver took us across the river
and through our old section to a quiet hotel I knew behind
the Panthéon. I booked a room, telling the concierge that
my young friend had taken more wine than was good for
him and I would be obliged if he were left undisturbed
until I returned later in the evening. I carried Charlotte upstairs and laid her on the bed, but, when I told her I was
going to find out what had happened to Rouzet and André

she showed no interest and turned her face to the wall. I began to have serious doubts then as to whether recent events had unhinged her reason and I didn't like the prospect of leaving her, but I had to find out about the others and I realized that it was imperative to get out of Paris as soon as we could. I also had hopes of finding André and shifting the responsibility of our future plans on to his capable shoulders. I locked the door, put the key in my pocket and went out, telling the concierge on no account to disturb my aide-de-camp as he suffered from the effects of a wound in the head received at Jemappes and was liable to grow very violent when in liquor. Then I took another cab and asked the driver to take me to the Bicêtre. We crossed the city without incident, arriving outside that gloomy fortress about sundown. I showed my papers, gave André's name to a surly turnkey and was instantly admitted.

"You'll find the surgeon in his quarters in the west turret," he told me, indicating the general direction. I crossed the inner court and clanked my trailing sabre up a steep stone staircase to a low iron door at the summit. I hammered on it and was overjoyed to hear André's voice bidding me enter.

He was sitting on a camp bed in his shirt-sleeves, smoking a long clay pipe, and the fumes of tobacco did nothing to improve the foetid atmosphere of the wretched little chamber, which looked as though it hadn't been cleaned since the year the fortress was built. Cobwebs festooned the high ceiling and the rays of the setting sun hardly penetrated the narrow embrasure that had once served for window and archer's vantage point.

He looked tired to the point of exhaustion, but when he recognized me he gave one of his habitual grins and said: "My word, David, but that's rapid promotion for you. Private to full-blown general in—how many weeks is it—five, ten, fifty?"

Some of his old waggishness was there but it couldn't mask the tragic apathy of his voice or his tired eyes. I felt sure that had there been more light I should have been shocked by his appearance.

"Are you ill, André?" I asked him.

"I'm the healthiest man in the Bicêtre," he replied with a chuckle. "So you got back after all, David. You know about Charlotte, I suppose?"

"I've got Charlotte out of Gemaine's and he's up there with a fruit knife under his ribs," I told him shortly.

André whistled and showed more interest.

"Did you do it?" he asked laconically.

I told him what had happened and he looked down at the dirty floor for a moment. Then, without raising his head, he said slowly: "Don't luxuriate as an outraged husband, David, she did it for Rouzet, and for you, too, in a way. If she hadn't you wouldn't have found her there when you got back."

I had been so occupied getting out of Gemaine's that I had not had time to ponder this side of the business, neither did I care to now and deliberately pushed it into the back of my mind.

"I've got two passports and Joel Barlow's porter's pass, besides the two uniforms," I said. "What do you suppose we should do to get Papa over the wall?"

He sighed and slowly rubbed his palms together.

"You'd better forget Papa, David," he replied. "I received word from the Conciergerie this morning. He was numbered among last night's lambs at Place de Grève."

"Are you sure?"

"Quite sure," said André. "They have an honest executioner down there; he sent me his watch."

He pulled Rouzet's ponderous silver watch from his breeches pocket and swung it idly on its massive chain. I thought: This is all that was needed. How am I going to tell Charlotte?

André slipped the watch back into his pocket with a shrug of his narrow shoulders. "It'll double your chances of getting through the barriers," he commented.

"What about you?" I asked. "It ought to be easy enough for you to slip out of a place like this."

He shook his head and stood up.

"I'm staying here," he said shortly.

I gave a grunt of irritation.

"Who's playing heroics now?"

He grinned and moved over to the window.

"I learned them from Lucille," he said, "and not only heroics either; the child had more courage and more understanding of the real issues than any of us. I've thought about her a lot since I've been here."

He turned back and faced me and began to speak more seriously than I had ever heard him speak during the period of our acquaintance.

"Have you stopped to think why this revolution of ours is going sour, David?"

I replied shortly that I wasn't concerned with their damned revolution but only with the means of putting the Atlantic between myself and Paris.

"I don't blame you for that, David," he said. "You're a farmer first and last and, in any case, you English had done with your revolution a hundred and fifty years ago, but would you believe me if I told you I was once as starry-eyed about the new order of things as our mutual friend Biron?"

I didn't believe that but I let him run on.

"There was a time, about a year before you got here," he went on, "when things looked promising. The Revolution was in the hands of people like Lafayette, who had been brought up in a tradition of power with responsibility. Well, that didn't last, the windbags moved in and, behind them, knowing wind wouldn't sustain them very long, were the mean little men, half-starved advocates who mistook a classical education for administrative ability, planners who knew a little about legal phraseology but nothing whatever of human passions. They're all down at the Convention now, trying to reduce the needs of twenty million Frenchmen to a sheaf of sonorous edicts. Danton's seen his mistake already and admitted it, but they'll pull him down and when he's gone God help us all."

"All the more reason for getting out while we still have a chance," I told him. "America's big enough for us."

"It's right that you should go," said André, "if only because of Charlotte. She deserves a chance to live a decent, normal life and raise a family of farmers, but some of us ought to stay or we'll forfeit the right to complain. There's sure to be a reaction some time and I want to be here to see the Jacobins packed into the carts."

"If you live that long," I reminded him.

"They won't interfere with me if I keep quiet," he said. "No one else will take over my job here and someone has to do it."

"Where does Lucille come into this?" I asked him, thoroughly disgruntled at the prospect of getting to the coast without André's ready intelligence at my call.

"I thought for a long time that she killed herself in despair," said André thoughtfully, "but I realize now that it was an act of pure self-sacrifice. That set me thinking. What use are books and all the fine talk we drug ourselves with when it takes an illiterate child like Lucille to show us how to die?"

I didn't fully understand him at the time, but I think I do now. His pity had been touched by his wretched duties in the dungeons of the Bicêtre and the prospect of running away and leaving the sick to the care of a few ignorant ruffians seemed a monstrously cowardly act when measured against Lucille's behaviour at the Luxembourg.

The contrast stirred his manhood and the act of renunciation entailed in staying on at the Bicêtre appealed to his romantic vision; there was always something of the would-be martyr in André, and even more of Don Quixote. He affected to sneer at humanity and to wash his hands of its boundless capacity for wallowing in a sea of wretchedness, but all the time he had a deep, underlying love for his fellow-men, even the worst of them, and he never quite despaired of the millennium.

I shall always regret that I was never able to bring André and Tom Paine together; they would have understood one another after five minutes' conversation.

It was never any use arguing with him; so I accepted his decision and asked his advice on our situation.

"Travel as the general by private chaise as far as Le Mans," he said. "You won't be challenged among all the reinforcements going west."

"But suppose General Fournayville's staff have already joined the army?" I queried. "Someone is certain to denounce me."

"You'll get there first if you select good horses. It'll take Fournayville's cut-throats a fortnight to come up from Lyons. I'll wager they're so weighed down with loot that they don't make more than a dozen miles a day."

André's advice seemed reasonable. In a country at war it is always safer to travel in uniform. It was for something like this that I had killed Fournayville, but Gemaine's instant recognition of me had shaken my confidence in the disguise.

"How am I going to get away from army headquarters when I've once reported?"

"You'll have to chance that," said André, rising and slipping on his sweat-soiled jacket. "The west is rough country and if I were you I'd take to the woods by night, bury the uniforms, and make for the coast on your American passports. Don't show them until you're in royalist territory."

"Won't you see Charlotte before we leave, André?" I asked him.

He shook his head. "What good could that do? It's better this way, she'll have all she can do to stand the news of Papa."

He was right and I was grateful for his consideration. Charlotte and André had been very fond of each other and it must have cost him a good deal to let her go without a farewell.

"You'd better tell her I'm travelling after you alone," he added. "There will be time enough for the truth if you get to Philadelphia."

We embraced and he gave the last chuckle as his lips brushed my cheek.

"I'm sorry, David, I forgot," he said, finding and wringing my hand. "You English save your kisses for your women, don't you. Well, pass that one to Lottë from me. She'll make a good farmer's wife, I promise you!"

I went out and down the worn steps feeling lonely and wretched and the surly turnkey let me out into the stifling

street. There were no carriages about so I clanked away
down the hill and kept my back to the Bicêtre until its
towers were lost behind the huddle of chimney-stacks
and tumbling slate roofs.

The sun was going down as I entered the St. Germain
quarter. My thoughts had been so much occupied with
André, with Papa Rouzet's cruel fate, and with our own
immediate problem, that I had walked without any destina-
tion in mind. When finally I looked about me I discovered
that I was outside the Luxembourg Palace, not a stone's-
throw from the spot where I had first encountered André
the day of my arrival in the city, more than fifteen months
before.

There was a crowd collecting outside the big, wrought-
iron gates that gave access to the main approach to the
building, and as I was about to push through the press
and cross the road the gates creaked open and a pitiful
procession rolled through and swung right down the hill
towards the river. It was the Convention's evening offering
to the Goddess of Liberty.

There were three carts, with approximately half a dozen
occupants in each, both men and women but with a pre-
ponderance of the former. They were sitting three a side
with their arms bound behind their backs and on their
faces was a look of sullen resignation.

The hindmost cart passed quite close to me and I suddenly recognized one of the prisoners, a clerk named
Ronsin, who had been in the employ of Pétion at the
mairie when I had called for my introduction to Paine. I
guessed then that this batch was composed of the lesser
lights of the Brissotin party, clerks, muniment-keepers,
shorthand-writers and little printers whose crimes consisted
of copying and distributing Girondist speeches and who
had been swept into the net with their employers on
June 2nd.

Apparently the public prosecutor had decided to dispose of the small fry first, for as yet none of the principal
Girondists had been brought to trial.

I felt a good deal sorrier for these people than for
the Brissotins I had seen cowering in the St. Emilion

cavern, for few had acted with the hope of any reward beyond their weekly pittances and they were now dying for their trade rather than for their political convictions.

I took a good look at the crowd that surged round the carts and at the National Guards who marched stolidly on each side of the cavalcade carrying fixed bayonets.

One or two of the spectators raised a feeble shout of *"Vive la nation!"* and *"A bas les Fédéralistes!"* but the majority were silent, staring at the doomed scriveners with much the same morbid curiosity as the Devon drovers watch the hangman's cart trundling to Heavitree Gallows on market days.

I think almost everyone present was saying to himself: "There, but for the Grace of God . . ." but only a few of the onlookers had sufficient hatred for the group to applaud this useless piece of butchery. How can I criticize their apathy when I kept my own mouth tightly shut and waited impatiently for the procession to pass so that I could get back to Charlotte?

Then something happened which silenced the scattered parrot-cries of the malign bystanders and the low, anxious murmur of the others. Ronsin, the clerk whom I had recognized, began to sing a parody of the republican air, the "Marseillaise."*

---

* *"Allons, enfants de la patrie*
  Le jour de gloire est arrivé;
  Contre nous, de la tyrannie
  Le couteau sanglant est levé."

Chapter Nineteen

I WAS glad that I had seen Ronsin and his associates demonstrate their courage in such a striking manner, for the spectacle cleared my brain and hardened my resolution.

I found Charlotte lying on the bed in the same position as I had left her, her face to the wall and the expression of vague horror still in her eyes. I touched her shoulder and she shivered slightly but otherwise made no sign of recognition.

I locked the door, took a chair and sat down beside the bed. I realized then that before we could so much as plan our flight something would have to be done to restore her to a more normal frame of mind. At first I was half inclined to withhold from her the news of the judicial murder of Papa Rouzet, but instinct told me that this new shock might have the effect of breaking the ice which seemed to have frozen her faculties since the moment she had plunged the knife into the doctor's side. Speaking slowly and carefully, I said:

"I have been to see André, Charlotte; he's alive and well but Papa was guillotined yesterday."

I waited a moment for the intelligence to penetrate but for a few seconds she made no sign of having understood or even that she had heard me. Then a slight flush enlivened the pallor of her cheeks and her eyes slowly filled with tears. Encouraged, I put my arm under her head and drew her very close. "We've got to leave here, Charlotte," I whispered. "We've got the means and you must have confidence in me. I have talked it over with André and he thinks it is best we go at first light."

Suddenly a great sob convulsed her and the tears began to flow, steadily at first, working up into a storm of emotion under which her boyish figure rocked and shuddered.

I said nothing more but let her indulge her misery to the full. I knew how much she had loved old Rouzet, who had been better than a father to them all, and I knew also that the tears she shed for him, and perhaps for all of us, would do her more good than all the drugs in Paris.

When the sobs at last began to subside I laid her head back on the pillow and covered her limp body with General Fournayville's heavy travelling cloak. In five minutes more she was fast asleep and lay like a child, the tears still wet on her face which in slumber reassumed the expression of tranquillity it had always worn in the kitchen of No. 12. I felt much better then and faced the morrow with more confidence than I had known at any time since the night Biron came to us as a fugitive.

Too exhausted, both mentally and physically, to sleep myself, I set about making preparations for our journey. I packed our few necessities, which included a change of linen apiece, into my own small valise and then, for the first time since I had jumped the Orleans coach, I made a close examination of the contents of the general's portmanteau. I packed his handsome sandalwood toilet case, reflecting that it was probably looted from some wretched Lyons citizen, and a pair of silver-mounted pistols, together with the powder horn and a bag of bullets. I also kept some of his small-clothes and an oilskin packet of documents which included his commission, signed by the cripple, Couthon. I then sat down to consider the most promising means of getting to the coast.

At first glance the successful accomplishment of a long-distance flight across land and sea appeared a sheer impossibility. France was at war with most of Europe and I knew that the Channel was certain to be thickly patrolled by British naval craft and privateers, so that the northern ports were closed to me.

If I attempted to leave France by the south the chances of capture by the British were just as numerous as would be run on the coast of Normandy, particularly as the port of Toulon had just been surrendered to them and was at that time the principal venue of the Medierranean squadrons. If I turned east I would have to cross a frontier into hostile territory, and would almost certainly be arrested as a spy. Quite apart from these contingencies any move to the east would necessitate passing through the cordon of the republican armies where, even in the guise of General Fournayville, I would have no possible explanation of my presence, for the general's commission explicitly drafted him to the war in the west. My only chance then, and that a slim one, appeared to be a variation of my original plan, namely to push into the heart of the western provinces and flourish my commission under the noses of any military authorities who challenged me. This course also carried with it grave risks, particularly if any of Fournayville's personnel had arrived in the area and knew the general personally. I would probably get as far as army headquarters without much difficulty but after that our final bid for the coast would depend on luck. If I did get through the republican armies I thought I might count on being received as a royalist fugitive and getting a ship for Philadelphia or some other American port, but in any case I would have to run the gauntlet of the blockading British frigates even though they were far fewer on this coast than in the Channel or on the Mediterranean, owing to the difficulties of maintaining station in the face of the frequent Atlantic gales.

Before lying down beside Charlotte to try to get an hour or two's rest, however, I took one further precaution, I wrote a brief letter explaining my position and addressed it to Joel Barlow. I then summoned the concierge and promised him a reward if he delivered it immediately and brought me an answer before dawn. I was aware of the risk I took in thus putting myself at the mercy of a total stranger, but even that was less dangerous than calling personally upon Barlow or Rickman, whose associations with Tom Paine, now, according to the journals, under close house arrest, were widely known to the horde of Jacobin informers. Fortunately the concierge proved an honest fellow and the letter must have been delivered to Barlow unopened, for the latter wrote a reply giving me a piece of information which promised to prove invaluable to the success of the first stage of our flight. He told me that his firm had recently dispatched a consignment of uniforms, and other miltary stores, to Angers, on the Loire, and that the wagon-train, which had set out two days ago, would still be less than thirty miles from Paris.

He had no need to hint at the use to which I might put this piece of intelligence for once outside the Paris barriers Charlotte and I could travel a good deal more safely as members of a convoy escort than two individual soldiers lacking regiment or staff. Apparently Barlow did not trust the hotel concierge as readily as I did for his letter was cleverly couched in the terms of a communication from employer to employee and he urged me to pick up the wagon-train with all possible speed. I kept his letter, thinking it might be useful.

There was one other duty I should like to have fulfilled before leaving Paris, that of delivery Deputy Buzot's letter to his captive lady-love, Manon Roland, still in jail and earmarked for the guillotine. I decided that an attempt to deliver this letter personally might be fatal to us and I was not justified in exposing Charlotte to the risk, so I compromised by addressing the missive and leaving it propped up on the commode, together with some silver as payment for a possible postman. I then lay down and tried to sleep.

The next thing I remember was a voice repeating: "Your coffee, *mon* General; your coffee, *mon* General!" and when I opened my eyes it was broad daylight and Charlotte, attired in the aide-de-camp's uniform, was standing in a patch of sunlight smiling down at me, holding a mug of coffee in gauntleted hands.

I took the drink and I recall now the sweet sense of relief that swept over me as I recognized in her smile and manner the Charlotte I loved instead of the strange, hysterical woman I had half-carried into the hotel the previous afternoon. Apparently the long sleep had completely restored her and she had awakened and slipped downstairs for the coffee after cropping her hair and donning the military accoutrements I had laid on the chair beside her when I packed our valises.

I took a good look at her and decided that she would

pass all but a strict scrutiny. The clothes fitted her very well and with her dark hair cropped as close as a man's she was reasonably safe as long as she kept her gloves on.

Neither of us referred to Rouzet again, or even André; instead we concentrated on our own plan, which I unfolded to her in detail as I dressed and breakfasted on the hot rolls she had fetched up, together with a small pot of honey. God knows we had no right to feel lighthearted, with poor old Rouzet two days dead, and our own plight as hazardous as that of galley-slaves on the run, but somehow our circumstances failed altogether to depress us that sunny morning and we gaily paid our score and went out into the streets with the air of two young people about to commence a holiday instead of a two-hundred league journey fraught with fresh perils every step of the way.

We had incredibly good luck for the next few days, so good that when we finally ran into disaster it didn't catch us by surprise, for we both felt that since our escape from Paris we had enjoyed more good fortune than any two runaways deserved.

Looking back on the various stages of that final adventure I have come to believe that we almost enjoyed it, for we were travelling alone for the first time and faced every hazard together, which, seeing that we were people in love, converted danger shared into a privilege.

Our first piece of luck occurred at the St. Cloud barrier, where the picquets were fully occupied with a truculent market-gardener, whose wain had been over-turned by a furiously driven mail-coach. The highway was blocked for the better part of an hour and in the resultant confusion we slipped through almost unnoticed and made for the livery stables where I had left the chaise on my return journey to Paris.

The proprietor recognized me as a man prepared to pay in gold and, since his chaise was out on hire, he gave me the best saddle horse in his stables. Charlotte had never ridden on a horse in her life but we settled her in the pillion saddle and set off at a brisk pace down the road to the west, putting nearly a score of miles between ourselves and Paris on that first day.

There was a good deal of traffic, both military and civil, on the road to Rambouillet, but we didn't attract any attention until we got to Eperon, where a group of Evreux volunteers were drinking outside an inn. We trotted boldly up to them and the lieutenant in charge saluted and respectfully asked if we were making for Le Mans or for the Loire. I told him that I was not in the habit of divulging my orders to chance acquaintances on the road and that he had better get his men into some sort of soldierly formation and strike out for the combat area instead of guzzling wine by the roadside. I left him with his ears burning and pushed on into the dusk with a scowl that did no injustice to the memory of the late General Fournayville.

We camped out that night in a loft, full of sweet-smelling hay, and poor Charlotte was glad of a soft couch for she was suffering severely from saddle galls.

Despite this I am sure we both look back on that night as one of the happiest we ever spent in each other's company for we were flushed with confidence in the manner in which we had slipped out of the capital and fooled the volunteers at Eperon. Both of us, no doubt, were exhilarated by the adventure and the beauty of the September night was something to remember. The sky was bright with stars and a light shower, just before sunset, had laid the dust and made the countryside smell as sweet and inviting as a clover field at Westdown.

We didn't speak much but sat hand in hand at the open door of the loft, and the steady champ of our mare in the stable below, where she was enjoying a feed provided by our unknown host. We were staking our lives on a flight which we hoped would lead us to security, but the insecurity of our present position did nothing to spoil the idyll of the hour. We sat there a long time, treasuring every second; the following day we expected to catch up with Barlow's wagon-train and from then on we knew that we should not be truly alone again for months and in the joy we brought to one another on that still night we were able to blot out the memory of previous disappointments, of old Rouzet paying with his life for his love of good fellowship and good wine, of strange, chivalrous André sweating among the filth of the Bicêtre, and of the terrors of a city gone mad. I don't think either of us had a thought beyond the softness of the night air or the nearness of the other.

We learned from a carter next morning that Chartres was full of troops and we instantly decided, nothwithstanding the loss of time involved, to skirt the town by means of side roads and rejoin it nearer Chateaudun. It was probably a wise plan but it cost us dear, for we lost ourselves in the woods and had to spend the following night in a charcoal burner's cottage, where we were savagely attacked by battalions of fleas. We moved on before it was light and rejoined the main road beyond Vitray but it soon occurred to us that we must have passed the wagon-train in the detour and would have to continue our journey alone. We might have hung about waiting for the wagons to overtake us but our presence would have certainly excited suspicion and neither of us was equal to the strain of inactivity, so we pushed on at a walk towards the nearest inn in search of a hot meal and some sort of salve for our myriad fleabites.

At a hamlet some four leagues from Chateaudun we ran straight into a commissary-general engaged in conveying a string of remounts from the horse-fair at Chartres, to the La Vendée headquarters of the Republican Army.

He greeted us with open arms, for he had been provided with a totally inadequate escort, a mere trio of Norman bumpkins in uniform. I would not have trusted the best of them to defend the horses against a determined child.

The commissary-general, an enthusiastic young Jacobin called Houdier, was very much afraid of gypsy horse thieves, as well he might have been for they infested all routes between the supply depots and the army, and grew fat on profitable pickings. The Jacobins showed no mercy to failures and any shortages on the commissar's manifest would have cost Houdier his head when he reached Angers, so the young fellow insisted that we should travel in company over the remainder of the journey and divide the night into watches as a precaution against thieves.

I wished him in hell but I could see no way of refusing his request without arousing his suspicions, for I had already admitted that we were bound for Angers when he made his demand. I knew that, sooner or later during the journey, he would be certain to discover that Charlotte was the wrong sex for a general's aide, so I took him aside and, with a good deal of winking and nudging, gave him to understand that even a general needs a little relaxation now and again and that, as the Minister of War had forbidden camp followers to enter La Vendée, I had adopted this means to circumvent the puritanical edict of the Convention. The explanation was received well enough. He chuckled and called me a crafty fellow, but he was far too glad of my presence to raise any objections to travelling with such a promising young soldier (as he dubbed Charlotte), so we struck a bargain then and there and sealed it with a bottle of burgundy which the promising young soldier shared.

After that we got along very well. We left our hired mare at a post house outside the town and Charlotte rode in the two-horse wagon that followed the remounts with farrier's equipment. Houdier and I rode at the head of the string and the Norman ploughboys trotted along with a dozen horses apiece, shouting to one another in a strong Calvados dialect that made me think of my mother calling to the hens and geese in our poultry run at home.

Houdier was such a talkative fellow that he didn't expect much from me in the way of conversation. He had been a grocer's lad in rue de Vincennes until the restless times had persuaded him to exchange the cheese counter for a clerkship in an army depot near the frontier. It did not take me long to assess him. Being an astute young man he joined the local Jacobin Club and rapidly bettered himself by the simple expedient of expressing violent republican opinions whenever he was within hearing of his superiors. When the armies surged into the frontier areas he had earned a timely recommend from General Dumouriez by supplying a quantity of arms and ammunition to the general's light cavalry during a critical juncture of the Jemappes campaign, and by keeping a shrewd eye on the constantly changing political trends he had advanced from store clerk to his present rank in less than three years. Constitutionalist, Federalist, Brissotin and Jacobin, this ex-grocer's boy had sympathized and hobnobbed with them all, and as we jogged along I reflected that his was a disposition ideal for revolutionary present-day France, where reputations might be made and broken in the short space of a few days, or as a result of a single chance conversation.

Undoubtedly Houdier took me for what I appeared to be, an energetic young Jacobin intent upon carving a career out of the new army in La Vendée. I told him as much about my imaginary career in Lyons as I deemed it prudent for him to know, and by the end of the first day's stage we were boon companions of the road, safe at once from the depredations of prowling horse thieves and the blunt inquiries of Jacobin agents on the towns through which we passed en route for Angers.

We made rapid progress and lived in style on the strength of Houdier's requisition chits, for no landlord cared to risk the displeasure of two such important patriots as Citizen General Fournayville and Citizen Commissar-General Houdier. We never left the horses unguarded and Charlotte was able to get two good nights' rest at Vendome and La Fleche, a route I persuaded Houdier to take in order to avoid the risk of encountering units of Fournayville's division marching due west along the river road from Tours.

On the evening of the third day we watered the horses at Pellouaille, a short march from Angers, and I began to ponder on the steps we should take of getting rid of our accommodating friend and crossing over into royalist territory in our final dash for the coast.

The difficulties of reaching the coast now appeared less great than I had imagined them to be. Our chances were increased by the broken and wooded nature of the ground and the wide dispersal of the republican troops. The floodtide of the La Vandée rising was passing. Two months before, the rebels, under a nobleman called La Roche-Jaquelin and an ex-naval officer known as La Charette, had tried to storm the important town of Nantes but had been bloodily repulsed, largely owing to the resolution of the garrison commander, General Canclaux. They still held, however, a number of smaller towns in the Nantes area and were in strength south of the Loire. Republican troops had hurried up from Lyons and Paris and were in the process of forming a cordon round the provinces affected by the revolt, but the peasants had the advantage of fighting in familiar country, and with home-made arms and scanty ammunition, continued to harass the conscripts in the defiles and on the wooded slopes of La Vendée. Dozens of ambushes were prepared and usually the peasants had the best of the exchanges, for they fired from behind cover and fled the moment they were pursued, shedding their wooden *sabots* as they ran.

General after general tried his luck in La Vendée, but until the new republic adopted a policy of extermination it made no progress with the campaign and its officers were nearly always recalled and summarily guillotined.

We passed through a town which had recently been held by the rebels and found it a smoking ruin. Not a man was to be seen and the few women, picking about among the rubble for what remained of their wretched household goods, looked like spectres from the graveyard. Houdier, who had been out here during the June fighting, told me that at Pillau the republicans had roasted women and children in an oven. What little I saw of the campaign convinced me that the inhabitants had even worse in store for them and when La Vendée is finally pacified the survivors would be well advised to take their own lives and those of their children.

By the time we had reached Pellouaille I had learned a good deal regarding the situation and had made up my mind to avoid Nantes like the plague for the garrison here was an extremely vigilant one and exit by boat from the port sure to prove an impossibility. Houdier told me, however, that the island of Noirmoutier, a short way south of the mouth of the Loire, was still held by the royalists, and

I guessed that there was bound to be American shipping there. The problem was, how were we to get through the republican lines to Noirmoutier without a guide? In the meantime, here we were a few leagues from Angers, where I was virtually certain to be thrown into contact with officers and men who had served under the real Fournayville in the Lyons campaign, and among whom I had not the slenderest hope of shielding under my disguise.

I pondered this problem deeply but could find no solution until chance, which proved so kind to us during these anxious days, threw another opportunity our way.

Houdier and I had billeted ourselves in the only good-sized inn in the town and left the stabling of the remounts to Charlotte and the Normans.

We were halfway through our meal when Charlotte came in, and I could see from her expression that something was wrong. I excused myself and followed her out into the courtyard.

"The Convention's representative for Nantes is arriving here," she told me. "The blacksmith has been summoned to mend an axle two leagues outside the town."

This was alarming news. We had settled for the night and it would prove difficult to persuade Houdier to move on. To move was imperative, however, for the arrival of a Jacobin deputy in the town was sure to cause a minor upheaval and I knew that our papers would be severely scrutinized.

"Did you learn anything about the fellow?" I asked Charlotte.

She looked glum. "His name is Carrier and the blacksmith says he's a positive demon," she said. "The poor wretch came in here just now shaking life a leaf, having been threatened with a dozen violent deaths for taking an hour to finish the repair job." She jerked her head towards the stable. "The blacksmith is in there now, frightening everybody out of their wits with his story."

I crossed the yard and went into the stable buildings. The blacksmith was surrounded by a wide-eyed cluster of ostlers and stableboys, who were listening to him with expressions of horrified amazement. The smith might have been chastened by his interview with Deputy Carrier but he was nevertheless thoroughly enjoying the sensation he was creating by the recital.

"A sallow young fellow with a mouth like a gash," he was saying. "I was sweating underneath the springs and doing the job as fast as any man living could do it, but it wasn't fast enough for Carrier, I can tell you—he stood over me with a ferruled staff swearing and striking at me every time I shifted my position to get a good purchase on the damned axle-tree. 'I've got a watch here, my fine fellow,' he sings out, 'and there's a portable guillotine in the cart behind the coach, brought along for just such a neck as yours, thick as it is, you lumbering, clumsy rascal. If you keep me standing here another five minutes we won't wait to show you how the national razor will shave the traitors in Nantes, we can erect it here, on this very spot, and give you all a demonstration now. Have you a family, smith?' he goes on, as true as I am standing here. 'Have you a wife and a couple of sons learning the trade from their indolent father? No doubt we could find room in the basket for their heads as well as yours!' "

At this juncture one of the ostlers caught sight of me and I thought he was going to throw a fit. He gobbled a warning and ran up the ladder to the loft with the speed of a terrified monkey, while the rest of the group scattered like hens in every direction, led by the unfortunate smith, who must have considered himself as good as condemned out of his own mouth.

At that moment, however, there was a general outcry in the street and I ran into the yard, just in time to get back into the inn before Carrier's cavalcade swung into the approach. I caught a glimpse of the deputy staring moodily out of the carriage window, but I didn't wait for a longer scrutiny and seized Charlotte by the arm, bundling her upstairs and telling her to get our valises repacked as quickly as she could. Then I composed myself and strolled into the dining-room, where Houdier was calmly finishing his supper.

"What's all the noise about?" he asked, casually commencing to pick his teeth.

I told him the nature of the new arrival and I fancy he went a little pale.

"I heard Carrier was coming," he admitted. "Have you ever met him?"

I said I had not had that honour.

"He's the Devil personified," said Houdier. "They picked the most ruthless party man in the Convention for this job, in the hope of terrifying the district into giving up the struggle. He'll put the whole of Nantes in mourning before the month is out. They've got over three hundred prisoners awaiting him, but he'll want more by the time he's been at the Hotel de Ville twenty-four hours, mark my words!"

"Why don't we move on?" I suggested. "I've no notion to make the closer acquaintance of politicians."

Houdier sucked his teeth.

"Too late now," he grunted. "He'll have heard we're here and if we decamp he'll take it as an insult and lay for us in Nantes. Keep your little poppet out of the way, I've heard he's partial to young women. Watch out, here he comes."

As Houdier spoke, the landlord backed into the room, bowing as though he was an usher at a royal ball, and a second later Deputy Carrier strode through the door, pulling off his gloves and tossing them to a servant who trotted beside him. He was a young man, not above thirty, with a close-knit frame and dark, straight hair that framed a narrow, humourless face. The blacksmith's description was an accurate one, for Carrier's mouth was so thin and compressed as to be hardly more than a slit. I never saw cruelty and pride written more clearly on a man's features, and the eyes, brown and deep-sunken, were those of an eagle searching out prey. He was tolerably well-dressed, nervous and quick and decisive in all his movements. He glanced at the table the host had prepared for him but, his eager gaze resting on us, he turned aside and strode across to our corner, looking us up and down with a swift intensity that made my stomach turn over and did as much for Houdier's if the movement of his Adam's apple was anything to judge by.

"En route for Angers?" Carrier snapped. His voice was

as shrill as a child's and I noticed that his hands were white and slender, with neatly trimmed nails.

"We expect to get there tomorrow, Citizen Carrier!" said Houdier promptly.

The deputy cocked an eyebrow.

"You know me?"

Houdier bowed slightly. "Every true patriot knows you, Citizen. Welcome to La Vendée!"

I thought Houdier had misjudged his man, but I was wrong. The commissary-general had not spent three years among all the beggars on horseback at the frontier without learning the full value of flattery. Carrier's sallow face flushed with pleasure and he signed to the trembling host.

"I'll sup with the generals!" he announced shortly, and threw himself down on a chair that the host thrust behind him.

I wished then that Houdier had been less sycophantic for I felt certain that sooner or later Carrier's conversation would turn to Lyons and I didn't feel equal to the demands of lying into that flat, pitless countenance. Houdier, however, was in fine fettle and I soon realized how he had risen so rapidly. He talked deferentially, yet persuasively, of a variety of matters related to the war and current topics generally, giving me a much-needed interval to think.

From where I was sitting I could keep a furtive watch on the stairs, through the door behind the servery, and presently I saw Charlotte come down with our valises and go out into the yard. Dusk had been falling when we ordered supper and by now it was quite dark. I listened with half an ear to Houdier's chatter and Carrier's monosyllabic replies, turning over one plan or another for getting out of this wretched situation and putting as many leagues as possible between ourselves and this ice-hearted rascal, but all my schemes foundered on the same snag, namely how could I find my way across country to Noirmoutier in the dark without blundering into a dozen picquets and, if lucky enough to dodge them, how could I avoid the fire of rebel outposts? I did not even possess a compass and as yet there was hardly a glimmer of starlight.

Carrier himself solved my problem. Turning his fishy eyes on me for a moment he said:

"I shall have work for you before we retire tonight, General."

"At your service, Citizen Deputy," I replied, ignoring Houdier's swift wink.

Carrier's long, delicate fingers toyed with the stem of his wineglass and he smiled, if a faint twitch of his almost invisible lips could be called a smile.

"We picked up a prisoner in the woods between here and Lesigne," he said, "a truculent fellow, a charcoal burner he assures us, but I think he has neglected his occupation of late and taken to more aggressive enterprises. He was carrying concealed arms and I have a notion that he might provide both you and me with some useful information."

I knew what was coming but I tried, stupidly perhaps, to anticipate it.

"Most of the peasants in these parts are opposed to us, Citizen Carrier," I told him. "I doubt if your prisoner will talk."

Carrier spun the wineglass with such force that the dregs of the wine spurted on to the tablecloth.

"Come now, General," he said softly, "surely they know how to make prisoners talk in the Army of Lyons. Take a look at him, he's under guard in the coach-house, and I'll join you later."

He got up abruptly and both Houdier and I imitated him. "I have certain letters to write to Paris," he said, "shall we meet again in, say, one hour and ascertain whether or not our charcoal burner is inflammable?"

"In one hour, certainly, Citizen Carrier," I responded, and saluted stepping on one side to let him pass.

Houdier yawned. "For myself, I'm for bed," he informed me. "I don't envy you, Fournayville. I enjoy a good hanging and I've served a term as tallyman under the field guillotine in Arras, but I'm far too squeamish a man for an interrogation under our friend's tutelage. There'll be no need to watch the horses tonight with the deputy's escort on guard. I intend to get a good sleep for once. Good night to you."

He went off upstairs and I knew that he at least was safely out of the way. Slowly, and lighting my pipe as I walked, I strolled into the yard to find Charlotte impatiently awaiting me by the stable door. As I joined her I noted that on the other side of the yard gates stood a small stone building, probably the harness shed. Outside it were two soldiers, standing guard with fixed bayonets.

There was an ostler in the stable so we walked into the road and I told Charlotte briefly what I intended doing. It was a desperate plan, bold to the point of foolhardiness, but no more so than our situation warranted, for inside that harness shed was a local man as desperate as ourselves and if we could free him, and get but a brief start, we all three stood a good chance of threading the republican lines and getting unharmed into coastal territory.

We hadn't much time to waste for I judged Carrier to be a punctual man and once he descended from his room any attempt to leave the inn would be hopeless. I coaxed the ostler out of the stable on some trifling pretext and Charlotte took the valises into the road, leaving them behind some bushes a stone's throw away from the gates and returning with the general's pistols, bullet-bag and powder flask.

We loaded the weapons in the light of the stable lantern and I gave Charlotte one and showed her how to pull the hammer to full-cock. Then we went across the yard to the harness-room, and the sentries, seeing my epaulettes in the glow of the kitchen lamps, came to attention and presented arms.

One was a conscript, who looked as though he had never smelled powder, and the other was a hatchet-faced fellow whose weatherbeaten equipment indicated that its wearer had several campaigns behind him. Both men obviously belonged to Carrier's Paris escort and the deputy's truculent attitude towards his subordinates stood us in good stead, for it was clear that both these fellows were in a bad state of nerves.

"Is your prisoner safe?" I inquired, after a final glance over my shoulder towards the empty yard.

"Chained to the floor," replied the older sentry, and smacked his belt where a bunch of keys hung.

"The citizen deputy has directed me to question the man," I said carelessly.

The man hesitated, glancing helplessly at my epaulettes and then at his companion, who was no help whatever, for he stood stiffly to attention wearing that expression of idiot vacancy peculiar to untried soldiers.

"Come, unlock the door, you fool," I snarled, "the citizen deputy will be here in a moment!"

The mere mention of Carrier tipped the scales. The sentry stacked his musket against the shed and turned to fumble with the huge padlock and chain with which the door was festooned. The moment his back was turned I tipped off his cocked hat and struck him a violent blow with the pistol butt on the crown of his head, catching him as he fell and stepping aside for Charlotte to move up and thrust the barrel of her pistol into the stomach of the younger fellow.

If we had planned every movement the onslaught could not have been more successful. Over on the far side of the inn we could hear some other members of the escort carousing, but nobody came into the yard and the lamp in Carrier's room burned on, showing that the deputy was still safely engaged with his correspondence.

Charlotte's behaviour was superb. She grabbed the keys from the belt of the man I supported and thrust them into the trembling hand of the conscript.

"Throw open the door and don't attempt to move from where you stand," she said quietly, and the man obeyed promptly, although his fingers shook so much that I had myself to pull the chain from the hasp when he had sprung the lock.

"I'll stand outside with this one, he won't feel so terrified of the dark if he has company," said Charlotte, and I remember chuckling softly to myself at her coolness as I kicked open the door and dragged the unconscious sentry across the threshold, leaving Charlotte to stand guard over his companion, whose musket she appropriated after stowing the pistol in her belt.

The inside of the shed was as dark as a bag, so I dropped the man I was holding and groped for my tinder box, lighting a short length of tarred cord that I had about me and holding it up to light my way.

The shed was, as I had suspected, a harness-room, and was chock full of old saddles, horse blankets, tarnished bits, stirrup-irons and various cleaning materials, and smelt strongly of linseed oil and pungent yellow soap. There was one window, opposite the door, but it was so heavily cobwebbed and begrimed that not a glimmer of light penetrated the pane. On the floor, to which he was clamped by a short length of harness chain, was the prisoner, and at first glance it occurred to me that he would not be able to use his liberty even if I was able to set him free, for his captors had not only chained him in a position which prevented him from obtaining any ease, but had added to his discomfort by binding him hand and foot with rabbit snares which were cutting his wrists and drawing blood.

The poor wretch lay with his buttock humped and his head twisted on one side, looking more like a trussed fowl than a human being, and when I held my taper near his face he only blinked stupidly and gave one or two moans, twisting this way and that in a fruitless effort to relieve the agonies of cramp he was suffering.

I whipped out my knife and sawed through the bonds that held his wrists. The strands were so tight that I cut his flesh slightly, but he made no complaint when I rolled him on one side and thrust the guttering light into his numbed hand whilst I tried the various keys on the padlock of his chain.

None of them fitted and I guessed Carrier had these keys about him so I seized hold of the chain and pulled at the staple with all my strength. It came out, leaving the loose end of the chain still fastened round his middle.

He sat up with a gasp of relief but said nothing whilst I busied myself cutting the bonds round his ankles and rubbing his wrists to restore circulation. I saw him glance at the inert heap in the corner and back at me, and then suddenly he grinned, his bearded lips parting to reveal a row of white, even teeth. Speaking in a soft, cultured voice, he said:

"I don't know who you are, my friend, or what your business is, but I was never so glad to see a general in my whole life. I'm afraid you've done for poor Hervé there, he'll never sing 'Ca Ira' again!"

I glanced at the man I had bludgeoned and saw that the prisoner had sharper eyes than mine, for I had supposed the fellow no more than stunned, whereas I now saw that, without a doubt, he was practically dead, for his brains were bubbling out at the top of his head. Even as my piece of tow went out I saw his jaw drop and his legs give a final jerk. I hadn't meant to kill the poor devil but I didn't regret it now, reflecting that Carrier would have certainly sent him to the guillotine when he discovered that the prisoner had escaped.

"Don't light up again," said the supposed charcoal burner, "I can find my way to the woods blindfold. Are you alone?"

I told him that I was a fugitive and that my wife was outside, keeping watch on the other sentry.

"Your wife?" he whistled. "No matter, time to explain when we're on the march. Let's get out of here."

He rose stiffly to his feet and went through a series of violent physical jerks in the dark.

"Can you walk?" I asked incredulously. He gave a short laugh.

"I can run," he replied, "if it means putting a dozen leagues between me and that fiend in there. Merciful God, but Nantes has an ordeal before it when that monster settles at the Hotel de Ville. Are there many like him in the Convention? I'd as soon sell myself to the Moors in Algiers. Come now, we must run for it!"

Delighted to discover the prisoner with such unexpected qualities of courage and resource, I followed him out into the yard, where the conscript was still standing a foot away from Charlotte's determinedly advanced bayonet tip.

"Is this the only one?" demanded the Vendéan.

I replied in a low voice that the remainder of the escort

were over in the barn and wondered, with some misgivings, whether we should now be compelled to dispose of this terrified boy in cold blood.

The Vendéan, however, whose air of authority was remarkable seeing how recently he had been a trussed captive, now took charge of operations. Seizing the conscript by the shoulders, he said fiercely:

"Listen boy, the citizen deputy will have you flayed alive for this business. Take my advice and desert to the peasants now. Make for the woods, run as if the Devil was behind you."

He pulled the man away from the shed and propelled him roughly through the yard gates. I motioned Charlotte to follow, but before I could move a step the prisoner laid a hand on my arm.

"Give me your tinder box," he demanded, "we'll give the escort something to think about!"

I did as he requested, but I have no clear recollection of what happened in the next few minutes except that Charlotte cried out "Carrier's light!" and I glanced up to see that the deputy's window was now dark. A moment or two later there was a fierce glare of light from the interior of the shed and out dashed the Vendéan bellowing "Fire!" at the top of his voice. The next moment he was through the yard gates, with Charlotte and me at his heels.

As we turned aside to grab a valise apiece from the spot where Charlotte had dumped them I heard a rush of hobnailed boots on the wooden ladder of the loft and, looking over my shoulder, I caught a fleeting glimpse of naked flames shooting from the open door of the harness shed. After that we ran like hares, Charlotte and I hand in hand, the Vendéan just ahead and all we evoked in the way of immediate pursuit was a scattered volley that might have been fired in the opposite direction for all the inconvenience it caused us.

We kept on running, however, and the Vendéan, despite his stiffness and the chain about his waist, gained on us, for the valises we carried were heavy. When we were about two hundred metres from the inn I lost sight of him altogether and I thought that was the last we should see of him, but as we staggered up to the fringe of the woods he hailed us and, grabbing Charlotte's valise, turned and dived into the undergrowth, calling to us to follow and weaving a path this way and that with the unerring instinct of a fox.

The hounds were not far behind. After our initial start, due no doubt to the Vandéan's act of incendiarism, the escort came plunging down the road and thinned out on either side of us, but in their haste they had forgotten to bring torches and their task, notwithstanding the strident blasphemies of Carrier, whom we heard directing operations from the road, was quite hopeless. It was easy to see why the Vendéans had been able to play fast and loose with the republican levies when the insurgents were led by men like our guide, operating in a countryside in which they had been born and over which they had ridden and hunted since they were old enough to sit horses. It was like my father and brothers playing hide and seek with Portsmouth dragoons on our own slopes at Westdown.

Before long the scattered shouts of the conscripts died away to our right and we were able to slacken our pace somewhat and follow the guide through the shoulder-high bracken and birch coppices until we turned into a cart track that crossed the shoulder of a thickly wooded escarpment. Along this we trudged until we could look down on the winking lights of Perouaille, more than two leagues away, and we knew then that we were safe, at any rate until sunrise, and gratefully flung ourselves down to rest in a clearing scattered with freshly sawn timber.

The moon had risen and in its pale light I was able to take stock of our guide, whose features, until now, I had hardly observed. He was a shortish, barrel-chested young man, clad in the roughest of home-made clothes, breeches of untanned leather and a coat that would have disgraced a Devon beggar. His clothes, and his unkempt beard, however, could not disguise a bold and self-assertive manner, emphasized by the cultured tone of his voice, so unlike the harsh, rural burr of the peasants of this part of France, and obviously belonging to a man of breeding and education. His hands, too, were not those of a man who earned his bread in the fields but were small and white, with fingers as slender as Charlotte's. He seemed to regard our recent adventure as nothing more important than a boy's prank and he must have been in excellent physical condition, for although Charlotte and myself were sobbing for breath long before we reached the clearing, he seemed to have been more invigorated than distressed by the long uphill run and made nothing of a valise that must have weighed all of sixty pounds.

"When in doubt, start a fire!" he said gaily, seating himself on a felled tree. "I learned that under Captain Goulessé. We took the *Osprey* that way and six months later saved ourselves from one of your frigates by the same device. No captain afloat will grapple a burning vessel!"

He must have been as observant as he was active, for he was the first Frenchman in fifteen months to detect my English accent.

He chuckled and flung back the hanks of blue-black hair that tumbled across his face. "I was eight months in England less than a year ago," he laughed, "but if we stay there, teaching dancing and fencing, we deserve to forego our patrimony. Exile is well enough for the ladies and the dotards, but anyone capable of bearing arms is needed back here, keeping the lilies flying in La Vendée. I'm obliged to you for your prompt intervention, M'sieur . . . ?"

"Treloar," I told him, for he was not the sort of person one tried to deceive, "David Treloar, *en route* for Philadelphia, and mighty obliged to you for a route to Noirmoutier!"

"You are leaving us then?"

"As speedily as we can, with your assistance."

"But the fun is only beginning, m'sieur!"

"It began a long time ago for us," said Charlotte drily. "My husband is a farmer, not a soldier."

The Vendéan leaned back and clasped his hands behind his head. "My ancestors have been farmers since the Crusades," he said, "and I suppose the love of the soil should be in my bones, but it never has been, that is why I consider myself fortunate to have been born a younger son of a younger son, a circumstance that gave me an opportunity to try something else, privateering for instance, where a lucky venture will set a man up for life in less time than it takes my cousin to raise sufficient money for his annual tithe. I was at sea before I was fourteen and had pocketed my first officer's prize money a week after my fifteenth birthday. When we are driven out of here I shall go back to the sea and fly the ensign of Saint Louis until better times, for there are always better times beyond the woods, no matter what Cousin Henri complains to the contrary."

"Who is Cousin Henri?" asked Charlotte, upon whom this engaging fellow had made a strong impression.

"Henri is our commander-in-chief, Henri La Roche-Jacquelin, a good man in his way, but too chivalrous for war to my way of thinking, especially war against vultures like yon deputy. He had more than a hundred prisoners after the ambush at St. Hermité and turned them all loose after shaving their heads that we might recognize the rogues if we caught them breaking parole. Parole!" He laughed, musically. "What does a man like Carrier understand of such niceties? I would have flung the whole batch of them into the quarries after the way they behaved at Pillau!"

"Then why did you spare the conscript back at the inn?" asked Charlotte, smiling.

The ex-privateersman shrugged.

"He was a conscript, dragged from his plough by the Convention's decree; these fellows we took were zealots who will turn La Vendée into a desert before they go back to their slums."

"If you have no hope of successful resistance, why do you continue to fight the Convention?" I inquired, for the paradox had been puzzling me ever since I entered the west. Notwithstanding their matchless courage and ingenuity, a few thousand peasants could never hope to defy the organized might of revolutionary France for more than a few months at the most.

The squat Vendéan rose and stretched himself. "You ask an eternal question, M'sieur Treloar," he replied. "Why

did your Kentish peasants march against Feudalism under
Tyler and Cade? Why did the followers of Johan Huss
offer themselves up as martyrs for a page or two of dogma?
Why do the redskins of America continually sacrifice their
lives in a hopeless effort to confine the white colonist to
his coastal strip?"

"All of those people fought to maintain their own ideas
of personal freedom," I suggested.

The Vendéan shook his head and shouldered the largest
valise.

"Nonsense, m'sieur. That is what the books say. There
is no freedom for the man like yourself, who seeks security
and a hearth. Each system, however poetically conceived,
has its own limitations, which lead directly to new tyrannies. The only free man is he who holds life cheap, as I
do, and who fights for the joy of fighting, going off to
seek a fresh war as soon as the one he is engaged in ends
with a patched-up peace. Come now, keep close to me,
and I will guide you to a ship that will carry you to your
dreamland, where they tell me the colonists are already
fighting merrily among themselves over the ambiguities of
their holy Declaration."

He strode off at a brisk pace and we followed him along
a maze of forest tracks which he traversed as readily as
I could have threaded the leafy lanes between Ottery and
the Devon coast. At each junction of tracks he chose his
path without hesitation and at last, after we had been
stumbling in his wake for more than three hours, we
emerged on to a plateau of ploughed land where I smelt
the sea. There, immediately below us, was the shining
Loire, winding through the folds of the hills like a broad
ribbon, its surface broken by an occasional wooded islet.

Once over the river, and deep into royalist-held territory, we should be well on the road to safety and the
hearth and acres our guide so cheerfully despised.

Chapter Twenty

WE began to descend a steep declivity which ended in a strip of marsh that I should not have cared to traverse in broad daylight without a guide. Eventually, dog-tired and splashed from top to toe with mud, we arrived at a tiny bay cut in the steep river bank by the swirling current. Here the Vendéan paused and, putting two fingers in his mouth, emitted a shrill whistle which was immediately answered from an islet about two hundred yards from the bank.

A few minutes later a shadow glided across the path of moonlight and soon we saw a flat-bottomed skiff edge into the bay, propelled by a single oarsman operating his sweep, smuggler-fashion, from the stern.

As soon as the boat was close inshore the Vendéan called: "I've two passengers, Louis!"

"Prisoners?" queried the boatman.

"Fugitives," replied the guide, and the oarsman, reassured, grounded his little craft on the gravel and we dropped over the bank and climbed aboard, the boatman immediately pushing off into mid-stream.

We did not make for the islet from which he had come but for another, larger island, nearer the opposite bank. When we drew closer in I could see the glimmer of camp fires and guessed that we were now in an area held by the Vendéans.

My supposition proved correct, for on leaving the boat we walked up a shingly path into a forest glade, dotted with makeshift hutments and strung with fires over which coffee-tins were suspended. The island was obviously a peasant outpost and our guide was required to give the password before we could pass the picquet lines.

The cantonment was full of the most heterogeneous array of fighting men I had seen since I watched the faubrog rabble storm the Tuilieries. A few of the insurgents

wore the tatters of royal uniforms and some were evidently
fishermen who had exchanged their nets for the fowling-
piece and the locally forged pike. The majority, however,
were simple land-jacks, in sheepskin jackets and the
fragments of uniforms looted from their dead enemies,
with here and there a genuine charcoal burner easily recognizable by his sooty apron and red-rimmed eyes. They
were a hard-bitten, wolfish bunch and I trembled for the
wretched conscripts who entered the insurgents' wooded
valleys at the command of the amateur generals of the
Jacobin clubs. One did not have to be a professional soldier
to decide that these truculent rebels would give a good
account of themselves before they were finally driven into
the sea by weight of numbers and gun-metal.

Poor Charlotte was at the point of exhaustion. She had
kept up valiantly, and uttered no word of complaint during the eight-hour night march, but now I saw she was
swaying with utter weariness and I asked the Vendéan if
we might have a hot drink and some rest before we discussed with him the final stage of our flight.

He apologized profusely and conducted us to a largish
hut in the centre of the compound, where we found straw
palliasses and one or two homespun blankets. I made
Charlotte fairly comfortable under the only section of
roof that did not let in light and poured her a steaming
drink from a can the boatman Louis brought us, but when
I turned to give her the mug she was already fast asleep,
so I pulled off her sodden boots and lay down myself, the
Vendéan saying that he must report to the chief and give
an account of our presence and of his own mission. With
that he left us and I lay back on the damp straw, which
I found as comfortable as a feather-bed. I must have been
asleep in thirty seconds.

It was high noon when a peasant shook me awake and
told me that I was to follow him for my interview with the
outpost commander. I left Charlotte, still asleep. She
looked as young and fresh as a girl of sixteen to whom
the morrow is just another day of uneventful domesticity
instead of a continuation of a never-ending journey towards
freedom.

The peasant led me across the empty compound to a
camp-table set beside a smouldering fire on which a huge
can of soup was simmering. The soup was tended by an
aged crone, who looked as though her skinny body was
held together by rags.

Sitting at the table was a spare, heavy-jowled man of
about forty. This was La Charette, one of the most cele-
brated of the insurgents. He wore clothes vaguely resembling those of a French naval officer and the cocked hat
of a republican general with the tricolour cockade replaced
by a cluster of white ribbons, the insignia of the royalists.
He was studying a sadly creased chart, and giving it the
whole of his attention, for when the peasant presented me
he did not look up for several moments but pursed his lips
and traced a route across the soiled page with his fore-
finger.

Finally the peasant touched him on the shoulder.

"Here is the Englishman Captain de Rochambeau
brought us last night," he explained, without a trace of the
usual deference a subordinate usually shows his superior
officer.

The officer nodded and then, turning on me suddenly,
said: "Why can't your country realize that this is the place
to strike the enemy? Why do they send all their driblets to
Holland where they are obliged to campaign on open fields
against superior forces of cavalry? Is there nobody in the
British War Cabinet with the reasoning powers of a barnyard fowl?"

He crammed the chart back into his pocket and spread
his hands to the miserable fire. "Old Mother Picart could
plan a better campaign than your royal dukes, couldn't
you, mother?"

He touched the old crone playfully with his foot and
she grinned up at him toothlessly in acknowledgment of the
compliment, muttering something in a dialect I could not
understand.

La Charette chuckled. "Mother Picart says the soup
would be tastier for the liver and kidneys of a couple of
Blues. She has a reckoning with the Blues; they hung two
of her sons and four grandsons when they took Pillau in

June. Are you a volunteer or an observer from the British Government?"

I confessed, with some embarrassment, that I was neither, and briefly explained our presence in the camp.

La Charette scratched his head. "Here's a disappointment," he said. "I was hoping to send letters across the Channel and get you to speak up for us. The British are forever promising men and military stores, but they do nothing beyond blockade the coast with their damned frigates. No matter, you did us a good turn by cutting young Rochambeau loose last evening, though I haven't a doubt that the rascal would have given the Blues the slip somehow. He'll die in his bed when all the rest of us are dust and folksongs. I made sure of that when he was serving with me in *La Mouette*."

I guessed then that this La Charette was another former privateersman and discovered later that he was a person of great consequence with the rebels, sharing a command in this area with the nobleman La Roche-Jacquelin, of whom our guide Rochambeau had spoken as a kinsman. He was a capable, matter-of-fact individual and a ruthless partisan of the Bourbons, but our part in rescuing his friend Rochambeau made him extremely affable to Charlotte and myself during our brief sojourn, notwithstanding his disappointment on learning that I was hardly fitted to plead his cause with the Government in London.

He told me a good deal about the war as we drank a bowl of soup together and seemed pessimistic about the outcome of the revolt, prophesying that before long La Vendée would be reduced to a desert and such partisans as survived would be faced with the choice of submitting to the Paris Convention or crossing the Loire with wives and families to carry on guerrilla warfare in Brittany. With English help, he declared, it would have been possible to overthrow the republic and restore the Bourbons that summer, but now it was too late and Nantes could never be taken without siege artillery. The peasants were short of firearms and their crops had been wasted far and wide, so that it might prove impossible to sustain the bands during the coming winter. "We can take a convoy without powder but we can't live in the open with empty bellies," he added. "Soon enough we shall have our backs to the sea and a hundred thousand bayonets hemming us in from the south and the east."

He asked me a good deal about the state of affairs in Paris and I told him all I knew of the Jacobins' *coup d'état* during the summer, and the fate of such Brissotin deputies as they had been able to catch.

"Our only hope is that they quarrel among themselves," was his comment. And then, despondently, "To think that it should have come to this! A few discharges of grape into that rabble a year or two ago and we should have heard no more parrot-talk of equality!"

He shared the error of many educated Frenchmen who supposed that the Revolution, and all the sweeping changes that accompanied it, were a malady which had developed from some neglected social sore mysteriously poisoning the entire body of State and Church. He was incapable of understanding the immense forces that had been gathering strength through three long reigns of absolute despotism, namely the measure of desperation induced among the poor classes of city-dwellers by the crushing inequalities of taxation and the frustration caused by the rigid caste system that had stifled the ambition of talented young men and given them no chance, short of armed rebellion, of improving their lot. Reared in the atmosphere of medieval feudalism, which had endured right up to the present time in this remote part of France, he could see nothing wrong with the old order and was prepared to die rather than see it overturned. It was not fitting for me to champion the Revolution, seeing that I myself was a fugitive dust mote from the new brooms in Paris, but while I admired La Charette for being the brave man he undoubtedly was, I considered his political outlook as blind and stupid as that of the Jacobins and I was certain that thousands of ordinary Frenchmen would have to die before a balance could be struck between the pitiless zeal of fanatics like Robespierre and Couthon and the sour obstinacy of La Vendée reaction. The average Frenchman possesses a vitality and sparkle rarely found among men of the English shires, but his reasoning powers are those of a light-hearted savage.

That day arrangements were made for the final stage of our flight. Whilst Charlotte and I slept off the effects of our prodigious march from Perouaille, Rochambeau, who had the physical endurance of a packhorse, had obligingly crossed to the left bank of the Loire and had returned to the camp before sundown with news that two or three American sloops had been discharging mixed cargoes at the island of Noirmoutier recently. His informant had told him that the Yankee skippers would probably agree to take off two passengers if they were paid in advance.

Charlotte and I went through our valises again and disposed of some of our unwanted effects, including certain articles of spare clothing, which were readily snapped up by the partisans, some of whom were half-naked. I raked over what remained of my guineas and found I had less than twenty left in my pouch, but Rochambeau said that one English guinea was worth a satchelful of French assignats, and that the amount I possessed would be sufficient to pay for our passages even if it meant that we arrived in the New World with nothing but the clothes on our backs.

So we discarded our uniforms and disguises and set off as plain Mr. and Mrs. Treloar, sub-agents for Joel Barlow's firm, under our two more or less genuine American passports. Rochambeau escorted us as far as Beaupreau, after which he handed us over to a morose young fellow called Gidier, who had been a groom at our guide's chateau before the Revolution, and had followed his young master through all his wanderings on sea and land.

We parted from Rochambeau with genuine regret and I often wonder whether La Charette's prophecy regarding this spirited soldier-of-fortune remains to be fulfilled, or whether the energetic fellow has since met his end in some desperate skirmish in the woods of his unhappy province.

We followed the man Gidier along the banks of the Loire as far as Pellerin and, from a safe distance, saw the republican flag flying from the towers of Nantes. Later we turned south-west and headed for the open sea. We travelled in a light-hearted frame of mind, for it seemed as if at last our troubles were almost over and the prospect of starting afresh in America, with nothing but our bare hands to support us, caused me little concern, for Tom Paine had always spoken of the former colonies as a land of unlimited opportunity for a young man with good health and a practical knowledge of farming. I conjectured that I could work as a field hand or Negro overseer for a year or two and put by money to clear a patch of my own.

The early autumn weather was chilly but ideal for foot travel, and the three of us arrived in Beauvoir, the little port opposite Noirmoutier, in excellent spirits, having taken less than three days to complete the rough journey from the partisans' encampment.

I lost no time in inquiring for the captains of the sloops Rochambeau had mentioned, but found that two had already sailed. The vessel remaining, a hundred-ton schooner called *The Pennsylvanian,* was shipping a cargo of local wine and would be weighing anchor the following Sunday.

There had been a good deal of American shipping in the area since the troubles had begun. Some of the Yankee captains who owned or part-owned their vessels were making a good thing out of the war in Europe, shipping in various stores, either for speculation or under a commission of the British Government, and taking out cargoes that could be disposed of at a good profit anywhere along the American seaboard. Some of them were making as many as three trips a year and as far as they were concerned the war could last for ever. There were risks to be run, of course, privateer challenges for all, and frigate inspections for the independents, but most of the traders were fast enough to outsail most of the challengers and once out in the Atlantic they had little to fear beyond the press-gangs of the undermanned blockade ships. This was a risk that I, too, would have to run, but I felt reasonably safe with my American passport and the captain I engaged assured me that the danger from this source was negligible.

The captain of *The Pennsylvanian* was not typical of his class and calling, being a Levantine whose brother had a business in Boston. He was a shifty-eyed rascal who, I suspected, had served a long and profitable apprenticeship as a slaver and was not above picking up live cargo again if the chance presented itself, but sooner than hang about on the coast for another week or more, looking for a more savoury skipper, I paid over ten guineas in advance and took lodging at a filthy inn to await the sailing date. I gave Gidier the last of my underclothes and some loose silver for his services as guide and he went off immediately to rejoin his chief.

After that Charlotte and I kept out of sight as much as possible, for we heard rumours that British naval patrols were in the vicinity and I didn't want to practise a Yankee drawl unless it was strictly necessary.

Our enforced inactivity was very irksome after the hazards of the last few weeks, and I recall only one incident of that five days' wait at the inn.

It was on the afternoon before we sailed and I was lying on the thin straw mattress in our room overlooking the harbour watching Charlotte launder my sole remaining shirt. Suddenly she looked up, her hands still lathered with suds, and said:

"David, do you ever think of Lucille?"

My thoughts were far away, probably at Westdown, or probing our immediate future, and I had to ponder a moment before I recalled the wretched little milliner who had hanged herself rather than expose André to the risk of capture and the guillotine. I had to admit that I hadn't given the girl a thought since I left André alone in his dismal quarters at the Bicêtre.

"I think of her often," admitted Charlotte, "and wish she was here with André"

"André could have been with us if he hadn't enjoyed being equally heroic," I said shortly. I did not care to be reminded of André, for somehow, contrary to all the dictates of common sense, his steadfastness made my own retreat seem shabby. I thought perhaps that it might also appear thus to Charlotte, but I was wrong, for she smiled, jerking the tattered shirt from the tin bowl and wringing it out.

"I think that must be the reason I fell in love with you, David," she said, exercising the faculty she had of accurately reading my thoughts from the shades of expression that crossed my face.

She came across from the window and kneeled on the bare floor, taking my face in both hands and smiling down at me.

"Whatever happens to us now, Davy, I should like you to know that for me these last months have been worth all the time I lived before you came home that night with André. Up until then—although I hadn't quite realized it— I don't think I had ever set eyes on a real person."

"That isn't true," I argued, although her admission warmed my heart and filled that squalid little room with the radiance her presence always shed for me, "there was André and Papa Rouzet besides all those splendid young men Marcelle brought into the house."

"Pah! They were animated attitudes, every man among them, strutting, preaching and theorizing. That is what's wrong with our country and that's why I'm glad to leave it, Davy. Everybody talks too much about the unimportant things. I knew it even then and I kept waiting for you to start, but when you didn't, not even when they tried to make you, I fell in love with you on the spot and made up my mind then and there to marry you and make you take me away from it all!"

"I only held my tongue because I had nothing to say, Lottë," I told her, and that was the plain truth.

"You've got plenty to say about the things I care about!"

She sat back on her heels and a shimmer of late afternoon sunshine stole in through the dirty window-pane and set fire to one side of her face.

"What do you care about, Lottë?" I asked her.

"The things your father threw away," she answered, "good things, simple things, things that are always worth fighting for and waiting for, even if you never get them. A kitchen to keep clean, a man to cook for, a fire to mend, a roof that doesn't leak, children you can teach to value the things you value, a bed you can sleep in with your man's arms about you when the rain lashes the window-

pane outside. That's all women really want, Davy, even
women like Marcelle and poor Manon Roland and that
pretty thing who stabbed Marat, but all this talk they listen
to makes them ashamed of wanting ordinary things and
they teach themselves to despise people like me because
they know I'm right and don't mind owning I can't be
bothered with politics. If we ever get out of this, Davy,
don't let's aim for anything more than the farm, let the
money and the politics and the attitudes go, promise me,
promise me now, Davy!"

I promised her. I couldn't have expressed my yearnings
as simply as she did, but I had never wanted anything
more than the things she had mentioned and this was the
first time such things had ever seemed within our reach.

Chapter Twenty-one

IT must have been soon after dawn on our second day at sea that I was awakened to the deplorable discomfort of my bunk by the boom of a gun. I sat up and, as all landsmen do in such circumstances, struck my head a violent blow on the bunk above. Half dazed, I crawled out of the rat-hole and up on deck to see a frigate flying the British ensign lying-to some half mile off *The Pennsylvanian's* port bow.

The schooner was too small a craft to permit Charlotte and me to berth together and she had been accommodated in the mate's cabin, the mate having been bribed to move into a deck-house. The cabin was far too small for both of us, so I had gone into the cramped forecastle, sharing the tiny space with the remainder of the crew, mostly mulattoes.

I saw from the puff of smoke drifting low over the water between the vessels that the frigate had fired a shot across our bows, an order to heave-to and await a boarding party, and even as the Levantine captain bellowed orders to shorten sail a longboat jerked away from the naval vessel and began pulling through the choppy water towards us. It was bitterly cold up there in nothing but a shirt, so I hurried down into the forecastle and dressed as quickly as I could, tumbling on deck with my American passport and feeling a little sick with apprehension.

A young lieutenant in a well-worn uniform was just swinging himself aboard by a rope ladder the mate had tossed down.

The Levantine, looking resigned but sullen, marshalled his crew in the waist and a moment later Charlotte came on deck and joined me beside the mainmast, both of us trying to appear as though we were not at all put out by the business.

The lieutenant seemed a pleasant enough fellow and began by being studiously polite.

"I'll have to take a good look at you, skipper," he apologized, "we've orders to search everything that comes out of the Loire, even the fishing smacks. Can't have Johnny Frenchman sending rascals to plead his cause with the independent gentlemen over yonder."

I suppose the frigate's challenge had some semblance of legality, for although England and the American colonies were not at war it was recognized that the colonists had more sympathy with the republicans than with their late enemy King George. I guessed the object of this search was not a press-gang inspection but an attempt to stop persuasive Paris representatives from getting the ear of America. Having found them, a technical charge would be sufficient to transfer them to the British ship and from thence, no doubt, to a jail in Plymouth, Portsmouth or Chatham.

"We haven't a Frenchman aboard," protested the Levantine. "We brought sugar in and are taking wine out. Here are my manifests!"

The lieutenant examined the papers seriously and I held tight to Charlotte's hand. If she wasn't trembling I'm certain that I was and I had a queasiness in my stomach that wasn't due to the schooner's Biscay roll.

When he had finished scanning the manifest the lieutenant went below, taking his boatswain with him and they rummaged around for the better part of an hour during which time I didn't dare leave the deck. When, finally, they emerged the lieutenant expressed himself satisfied and asked to purchase a couple of hogshead of wine for the frigate.

Up to this moment I am certain that the officer had taken me for one of the crew and Charlotte's presence had not excited his curiosity, for most of these trading vessels had a woman aboard, usually the captain's wife or light-o'-love.

At the prospect of a private barter, the Levantine's sulkiness vanished and he and the lieutenant drank each other's health in brandy whilst the boatswain whistled up a couple of sailors from the longboat to bring up the hogshead.

I was about to take Charlotte back to her cabin when the first of these fellows dropped over the bulwarks and came face to face with me as I followed Charlotte across the deck. The moment he confronted me the tar let out a yell of surprise and clapped a hand on my shoulder, greeting me delightedly in a brogue I had not heard since the day I hid out in the badger's earth on the Landslip.

"Why Lor' bless us if it bain't Maister Davy!" he roared, wringing my hand and executing half a horn-pipe.

I looked at him closely then and realized, to my utter confusion, that he was Charlie Venn, the youngest son of old Jake, our carter at Westdown. It was Charlie's niece that had first come to me with her plovers' eggs as I lay out on the Landslip after the raid and Jake himself who gave me news of my mother's death.

Charlie must have known all about my circumstances but the Venns, although good enough workers, were not renowned for their thinking powers and the joy of coming upon a neighbour so unexpectedly quite outweighed the poor fellow's discretion. He didn't need me to respond to his enthusiastic greeting, having more than enough exuberance for the two of us, and before I could escape from his boisterous embrace the lieutenant had sauntered over and was regarding our reunion with considerable interest.

"Do you know this man?" he asked Venn.

"Know'n, zir? Why bless 'ee us've worked un since us was tackers, me'n grandfeyther, an' Marty too bevore 'ee was took an' transported be they Georgies! Dorn 'ee know me Maister Davy, dorn 'ee now?" and he stood back and spread his huge arms that I might get a better look at him.

"This is interesting," commented the lieutenant drily. "When and where did you work for him?"

"Why at Westdown, zir, where us lived, bevore it was burned out by the Georgies more'n a year since." The puzzled fellow ran his hands through his matted beard, suddenly quite upset that I had failed to recognize him. "P'raps it's these yer whiskers," he complained. "I didn' grow no whiskers 'till I 'listed."

The lieutenant turned to the Levantine.

"Who is this man, skipper?"

The Levantine shrugged.

"He and the woman are passengers, but he's no Johnny Frenchman, he was on the run when he came aboard. He paid for his passage and a man can't afford to ask too many questions."

"We'll ask the questions ourselves," said the lieutenant, and turning to me: "Be so good as to come below and show me your papers."

I cast one despairing look at Charlotte, who had stopped by the companion-ladder when Venn had first accosted me, and followed the naval officer down to the skipper's cabin, leaving Venn with his mouth wide open and the Levantine looking about as shifty as a monkey caught with his paw in a dish of cream.

I'm a very poor liar at the best of times and it would have required a professional politician to talk himself out of this fix. At first I relied on my passport and maintained that I was an American agent, acting on commission for Barlow, but having been given the clue as to my true locality, the lieutenant, himself a West Countryman, soon decided that I had never set eyes on America and told me so without preamble. Then I tried to pretend that I was refugee French, on my way to join my brother, a former agent of the Rochambeau estates, in his exile in Philadelphia, and as I spoke French very fluently I might have succeeded in convincing the lieutenant if he hadn't exposed my first lie, which naturally aroused his grave suspicions.

He asked about a hundred questions, some of them meant to be clever ones, but I had an answer for most of them and when the boatswain came in and reported a signal from the frigate ordering him to return he was clearly at a loss what to do next. Finally he said:

"Look here, Treloar, or whatever your real name is, I think you had better come aboard and see my captain. We've had orders to assist refugees but we've also been instructed to intercept all French-American emissaries and I'll be damned if I can determine just exactly which of 'em you are."

"Suppose I establish that to your captain's satisfaction? Who is going to compensate me for interrupting our passage?" I asked him.

"I'll get your passage money from the master," he said, "and if you satisfy the captain I've no doubt he'll put you aboard the first outgoing vessel we pass on our way back to Plymouth."

"And if you don't happen to meet one?" I queried.

"We're overdue for revictualling now and there is plenty of Yankee shipping in Dartmouth, Falmouth and half a dozen other ports. You'll get your passage all right, I'll pledge myself to that."

What else could I do but comply? It was no use resisting his demand, for, even if the Levantine refused to hand over his passengers, a schooner couldn't run from under the guns of a frigate. The prospect of having to talk my way out of the situation with the captain, and the naval authorities in Plymouth, was a disturbing one, but we had been in worse situations than this, and so far we couldn't complain of our luck. So I said that I'd consent to come aboard if my wife could come too. He agreed to that and we went up on deck with out valises and the lieutenant asked the Levantine to refund our ten guineas.

The wind was freshening somewhat and the frigate sent out another signal, "Return at once," which prompted the lieutenant to cut short the furious argument about our refund and threaten to throw the Levantine overboard if he failed to produce the money within ten seconds. The skipper ultimately parted with eight guineas, having deducted two as payment for the expended portion of the voyage, and with this we had to be content and were bundled into the longboat and rowed back to the frigate.

Poor Charlotte watched the schooner turn into the wind with the stricken expression of a child about to be punished for an offence she didn't comprehend, for she had not been able to understand a word of Charlie Venn's dialect and could only guess that something was sadly amiss with our plans. I didn't care to explain to her, for

the lieutenant understood French very well, and we sat
watching Charlie Venn tugging at his oar and looking, as
well he might, completely bemused by the turn of events.

When we got aboard the lieutenant put us in charge of
a sergeant of marines and I told Charlotte that we had
been transferred in order that our papers might be more
closely examined, but before I could explain the situation
more fully the lieutenant was back with an order to bring
me before the captain and conduct Charlotte below until
further notice. I kissed her and we parted at the top of
the companionway leading to the officers' accommodation
under the quarterdeck. She went for'ard, walking erectly
between two marines, and gave me a final despairing
glance as I turned to follow the lieutenant down the gilded
ladder.

Captain Narcott, R.N., in command of the frigate
Falcon, was a leathery, precise little man, more like a
justices' clerk than a man who had probably been at sea
since he was a child. I found him dry and inclined towards pedantry, but nevertheless scrupulously fair according to his own interpretation of the word "duty."

The lieutenant had outlined my case but we went over
it all once again, more slowly this time, for the captain's
secretary was scratching out a transcript of the questions
and answers.

I told more or less the same story. I denied being
David Treloar but admitted that my father, now dead,
had been a Devonian, which accounted for the element
of West Country brogue in my speech. I said that my
mother's family had been in the service of the Rochambeau family and that in the years preceding the Revolution my father had obtained a situation as chief forester
on the estate in the Beaupreau area. My recent sojourn
in La Vendée helped me to supply plenty of circumstan-
tial detail, and I ended by saying that I had taken part in
the recent insurrection against the Convention, but, convinced by now that it could not succeed, I had determined
to take my wife to Philadelphia, where the surviving
members of my mother's family were already domiciled.

I admitted that my American passports were forged,

but said that without these documents I should never have reached the coast.

I believe I told the story well, and I think I should have convinced even such a punctilious old ferret as Captain Narcott had it not been for the fatal introduction of my valise, which the boatswain brought in and dumped beside the captain halfway through the interview.

When I had satisfied my examiner, who said he would have to report my case to his superiors in Plymouth but doubted not that I would shortly be allowed to proceed to America without further hindrance, the lieutenant took a look through my luggage, which had shrunk very considerably since leaving Paris.

Nothing in the valise appeared to interest him but the sole remaining item of the late General Fournayville's kit, namely the boots which I had retained on account of my own being in such a wretched condition.

They were good boots, but the general had not looked after them as he might have done, and soon after I had acquired them a crack began to appear in the stiff leather where the spur-straps had rubbed the heel of the right boot. Finding that the crack let in a certain amount of water, I had, for want of handier materials, stuffed the lining with a small wad of paper which was still in place.

The sharp eyes of Captain Narcott soon detected the makeshift repair and he plucked the wad from its crevice and carefully unfolded it, spreading the paper out on the green baize table.

From where I stood, immediately before him, the paper was upside down but I saw that it was a piece taken from the general's papers and carried the usual noteheading of the republic, consisting of a scroll of oak leaves surmounted by the Phrygian cap of Liberty and the superscription: *"Force è la loi"* with the words *"Liberté"* and *'Egalité"* on either side. I remembered using the paper but, until I saw it a second time, I hadn't noticed that the sheet had some writting on it, and this writing attracted the attention of the lieutenant, who was standing behind the captain's chair.

"Translate, Lieutenant Barker," said the captain crisply.

Barker read: "On arrival at Le Mans, and on the information of Citizen-Deputy Lebas, you will cause to be arrested the family Gaudet, relatives of the traitor Gaudet (since prescribed out of law) and send the same under escort to Paris. Signed— I can't read the signature, sir."

"Couthon," I volunteered, "Deputy Couthon, who doubtless issued that order to General Fournayville after the fall of Lyons."

"Indeed?" said the little captain, thoughtfully scratching a sprouting mole on his chin, "and how did you come by the general's correspondence?"

"I stole his kit after I had strangled him in a coach en route for the north," I admitted. "Those are his boots and that is his valise."

"And are we to suppose that the late general used his superior's instructions to stuff a leak in his boot?" pursued the captain.

"He didn't, I did," I said, "whilst I was travelling to Paris in the stolen uniform."

"But why should you do that when you were in possession of an American passport?"

"Because I had to get my wife out of a *maison de santé*," I protested and it occurred to me that the truth often sounds more improbable than a pack of lies.

The captain and the lieutenant exchanged a glance, the latter grinning broadly, the former compressing his lips, as though fearful of betraying a trace of amusement.

"M'sieur is remarkably glib," was Narcott's sole comment as he folded the paper carefully and dispatched the perspiring secretary for the armourer.

That was all. The captain was satisfied that he had completed his duty and I never saw him again during the remainder of the three days' voyage, which I spent in a partitioned-off section of the cordage room, with light manacles on my wrists and ankles. I was not allowed to communicate with Charlotte or anyone else and my meals were served by a sailor obviously forbidden, on pain of the cat, to answer any of my questions.

The rest of my story can be found at far greater length

than I care to record it, in the mountain of depositions and statements that must have accumulated from my various examinations before the Naval Commissioners and the City Magistrates, prior to my transfer to Exeter.

In all that time I have received only one message from my wife, a note passed to me by a rueful Charlie Venn as I stood shackled on deck soon after we had docked. I managed to read (and subsequently swallow) the message in my first place of detention. All Charlotte said was: "I have a card. Please let me play it. I will never be far away, Davy. Think of our farm."

And with that I have had to be content, although, in the days preceding my identification, and before I was able to occupy myself with compiling my "confession," I was often near despair and might have destroyed myself had I possessed the means.

I am calmer now, however, for the Assizes open in less than a week and they are taking this prodigiously wordy confession to the chief magistrate's office this afternoon. I don't think it will do me much good at the trial, but it has served its purpose in passing a tedious ten weeks. The effort of writing it has been immense and I can well understand why Tom Paine used to look so wretchedly tired when I called on him during his labours on *The Age of Reason*.

I've thought about Old Tom a good deal since I've been in here and wondered if he is weathering the storm in Paris or if he has already followed all the other dreamers up the ladder to "sneeze into the sack," as the Jacobin Barère so picturesquely describes decapitation.

Poor Tom, it would be a comfort to have you here, expounding so enthusiastically your dreams of a millennium. I need, so much, a hope and a faith such as yours.

Charlotte and I had a dream once, not a big one, like yours, but just the modest dream that most men, and the women they choose as their mates, have had since Adam and Eve were turned out of Eden. It seems that even little dreams, insignificant when matched against yours, are equally difficult to realize.

Chapter Twenty-Two

I HAD handed in my laboriously composed account of my life since leaving Westdown on Monday night, and, exhausted by sustained concentration, slept through to the following daybreak.

It was about an hour before his usual breakfast visit when Jenner called with the news. I was lying on my mattress with my eyes fixed on the ingenious construction of the stone vaulting above, trying to exclude despair by musing on the quality of the masons' craftsmanship that had gone into the building of a mere jail. I called out:

"Come in, Mr. Jenner," and raised up on my elbow.

I noticed immediately that something unusual had happened, for his wrinkled old face, that always seemed to me to be the sort of visage that goes with a jail, sad, flat and doom-stamped, wore an air of uncertainty about it, as though its customary expression had been disturbed by a sharp dislocation of routine and was undecided how to register the change. His manner, too, lacked its characteristic deliberation. Instead of leisurely swinging back the heavy door and shambling over the threshold, slamming it to behind him, he hung back, irresolute, his enormous bunch of keys swinging listlessly from his left hand. A man in jail notices these things.

I swung myself into a sitting posture.

"What's the matter, Mr. Jenner?" I asked him bluntly. He came in slowly but left the door wide open behind him. He had not done that during all the months I had been in his charge.

"Us'll be partin', Number Four," he announced briefly.

Jenner had always referred to me as "Number Four," not solely because my identity had remained a mystery for so long, but because I occupied the fourth chamber

of the corridor set aside for prisoners in solitary confinement.

I gaped at him. "You mean I'm to leave here?"

He nodded. "Right now," he confirmed.

I recalled then that the postponed Assizes opened on
Monday and I was very puzzled for I could imagine no
purpose whatever in removing me elsewhere, when my
case headed the calendar.

"Where are they sending me?"

"They'm zending 'ee nowhere, Number Four," he replied, with a note of truculence. "Orders come down yer
not an hour zince to turn 'ee loose. You'm free, so sheriff
says. They never tell me nothing not with all their comings
and goings about the place."

I saw a folded paper protruding from the frayed lip of
his jacket pocket, so I reached over and plucked it out.
It didn't tell me much, being a simple order of release,
dated the previous day and bearing my correct name,
written in bold, clerkly handwriting on a blank space some
halfway through the jargon.

I suddenly began to sweat and tremble.

"I don't understand," I stuttered.

"No more do I," said Jenner, his features slowly assuming their habitual expression, "but sheriff's chit is
sheriff's whim and yer tiz, in black an' white, so you'll
'ave to go, whether you'm minded or not, an' me wagerin'
a shillin' with Mark Manaton that you was for topping,
not transporting."

I knew all about Jenner's bet on the outcome of my
trial. It was a regular practice between him and his deputy
warder to lay wagers on all the trials and Jenner, a
natural pessimist, always put his money on the gallows.

We went down to the turnkey's quarters together and
he gave me a long pull of brandy before solemnly shaking my hand.

"If you'm this way again, look in and pass the time
o' day, Number Four," he urged. "You bin nice an' quiet-
like, 'specially since you took to that scribbling. Us dorn
want it clutterin' up our place, do us?' and he gave me

my manuscript, which I had given him less than twenty hours previously.

"Didn't you even send this to the sheriff?" I demanded.

"Not me," said Jenner, "it bain't my business to run round to Cathedral Yard wi' confessions, it's the parson's dooty to call yer Wednesdays and collect 'em. Don't 'old with 'em anyhow, I sin many a likely lad get 'imself topped that way. If you got anything to put in writin' save it 'till the cart begins to move, that's my advice; if you does it bevore they on'y 'olds it up against you when you'm facing the beak!"

I took the bulky parcel and went out through the grille into the courtyard. It was a dismal morning, with thin Devon rain quickening the pools between the uneven paving-stones and a punishing east wind blowing in from the Mendips.

I didn't know where to go or what to do and stood there in the rain feeling more bewildered than ever in my life.

Suddenly, a voice behind me said:

"Put this on, Davy lad, before you catch cold!"

I spun round to face a bulky figure in a huge coach-man's cape. Two ponderous arms embraced me and I looked into the beaming face of Saxeby.

I was so surprised to see him there that I could not speak. At length I began to stutter but he cut me short and threw a cape he carried over my shoulders.

"I've got a trap at the bottom of Castle Street," he said, looping the cords of the cape, "I couldn't get it this far up, there was a dray blocking the road. Come now, before you get really wet," and he dragged me by the hand across the miry courtyard, under the portcullis and down the steep gradient of Castle Street.

I stumbled in his wake like a sleepwalker. After four months' close confinement the fresh air, the rain beating in my face and the bustle and noise of the thoroughfare stupefied me. I kept my eyes fixed on his beaver hat and followed it down the hill to the High Street, where a neat, canopied trap stood waiting outside St. Sidwell's Church, the bridle held by a pinched-faced boy. Saxeby gave the boy a coin and we climbed in. With a flick of his whip we turned and trotted off across the city to the Honiton Road.

We were branching off the turnpike into a lane that led us to the fringe of the common when Saxeby spoke again.

Pointing to the Heavitree Gibbet, he said: "You shouldn't be so careless with dead men's papers. If you hadn't married a careful woman you'd as like as not been scaring the crows up there on this day week."

"Where are we going?" I asked him. It was one of a thousand questions that had been jostling each other through the corridors of my brain since Jenner had interrupted my musing in the cell.

"Where should we be going but Westdown?" he said, and although the old fellow tried to sound jovial there was a noticeable tremor in his voice. I knew why well enough. Of all the people in the world, Charlotte excluded, Saxeby was the only one who knew what those red acres meant to me.

We were trotting through Woodbury before I could trust myself to speak again. At length I said:

"How did you do it, Mr. Saxeby?"

"I didn't do anything but give an opinion," he replied. "She did it all, Davy, and by God, she'll make ye a grand farmer's wife. With her at your side I'll wager my gold hunter to an old shoe that you'll squeeze a crop out of the Goyle meadows yet, and if you'll take my advice, let her drive in here on Fridays to market your beef and your poultry, she'll haggle the top price out of a Crediton middleman in a glut year!"

"What was that you mentioned about a dead man's papers?" I asked.

Saxeby settled himself under the dripping canopy and lit up his churchwarden. In that confined space the pungency of his tobacco was so great that it was a wonder that the smoker himself could tolerate it, but he puffed on notwithstanding and told his story slowly with relish.

"They held Charlotte until they found out who you were," he said. "After that, seeing there was no charge against the girl, they turned her loose with her valise and one guinea, holding the other seven back against her board since she landed. Well, now, what would most women in her shoes do, with one guinea in a strange country and her not so much as speaking the language? Mope around as like as not, snivelling at the mayor's secretary and wasting time in scratching up a petition that the janitor would light his stove with."

"What did Charlotte do?"

"She posted down to Plymouth as an outside passenger and took a firm grip on the Admiralty's queue and she went on twisting it until it hollered 'nuff,' and undertook to turn you out in the rain. That's what she did, and after that she walked from Plymouth to see me and size up the farm!"

"She walked from Plymouth to Littleham?"

"Every step o' the way, but what was that compared with holding the Navy to ransom and starting a rumpus between the Admiralty and the Excise thieves that won't be over until you and I are holding up turf in Littleham churchyard?"

Finally, I coaxed the incredible story from him and it was a story that made our joint flight from Paris to the coast seem like a trifling adventure, for Charlotte, unaided, had bartered my pardon and farm against a packet of papers that I had tossed aside in Paris as useless freight, and the Admiralty, and through them the War Cabinet, had ultimately been very glad to strike the bargain.

The conception of her plan was worthy of a skilled diplomat, but its execution had the dash and resolution of an Elizabethan seadog.

Charlotte, once aware of my critical situation, had taken careful stock of her resources and in her valise was all that remained of General Fournayville's papers after the captain of the frigate had extracted the inconveniently placed letter that had landed me in jail. All the way across France, Charlotte had nursed that oilskin packet without examining the contents, and when she did so, aboard the frigate, she had the good sense to realize the full value of her find, for the papers included a detailed summary of the republic's military strength in the west, together

with its current facilities for establishing depots for re-
mounting and revictualling its divisions along the vital
stretch of river road between Nantes and Saumur. It did
not need a professional soldier to assess the full value of
such information to a government engaged in a war with
the republicans, and Charlotte, correctly assuming that
her baggage would be searched at Plymouth, destroyed the
oilskin wrapping and concealed the papers about her person.

As soon as she was alone in the Plymouth roundhouse,
she set about finding a safe hiding place for the packet and
eventually selected a cavity under the floor of an outhouse
used by the debtors for laundering. The papers lay there
during her brief detention at Plymouth and whilst she was
held in the Exeter sponging-house. As soon as she was released, she applied for an interview at the Plymouth Navy
Office.

This, of course, was refused, but Charlotte had lived in
Paris, the home of intrigue, and after picqueting the lobby
for a week she attracted the attention of a naval secretary
and soon succeeded in winning his interest in the matter.

Saxeby chuckled when he came to this part of the story.
He said he liked to imagine the feelings of the spry young
secretary who, under the impression that he was establishing gallant relations with an attractive female, suddenly
found himself used as go-between in a matter of high
policy involving the Lords of the Admiralty and the War
Cabinet.

All this took time, of course, but Charlotte persisted
and at length, going before the Commissioner, she calmly
explained the nature of her bargain. At first the Admiralty
representatives were dumbfounded and inclined to treat
the whole project as absurd. Then a captain, who had
served as liaison officer with an *émigré* battalion in La
Vendée, asked her one or two shrewd questions about
conditions in Western France and established once and
for all that Charlotte obviously possessed a good deal of
accurate information that the British Admiralty would like
to share.

The Lords of the Admiralty, meantime, successively

resorted to cajolery, bribery and threats, none of which
had any other effect than to confuse the issue and drive
the interpreter to despair, for all negotiations had to be
carried on inside the framework of three-cornered conversations. Charlotte, of course, understood a good deal
more of the discussion than she pretended, but never once
did she allow her opponents to suppose she knew any
word of English but "No!"

At last the Admiralty agreed to obtain king's clemency
for me, in exchange for the documents, but here the
Customs and excise had to be dragged in, for Charlotte's
cool request for an impounded farm and livestock (or
compensation in lieu of) was quite outside the Admiralty's
power to grant. By this time, however, the naval men had
crossed the floor and taken up the battle on Charlotte's
behalf, and after frequent exchanges between Plymouth,
London and Bristol a compromise was agreed upon, the
terms of which were that I was to go free under a Royal
Pardon, that the farm was to be restored to me as my
father's sole heir, and that the Admiralty was to pay over
the sum of £200 for the dispersed or slaughtered stock.

This having been agreed, and committed to writing, a
squad of marines then conducted Charlotte to the debtors'
laundry in Plymouth, where the papers were hurriedly ex-
humed in the presence of an astonished warden.

Only then did Charlotte set out for Littleham, accomplishing the journey in four days, finding Saxeby and
establishing herself in the ruined kitchen of Westdown.

I listened to the story in mute astonishment, but my
surprise was even more when Saxeby's tired cob rounded
the high banks of the lane leading from Littleham to the
plateau, for here, instead of desolation, I came upon a
scene of ordered activity.

The rain had ceased and a watery February sun lit the
familiar undulations of the meadows marching south to
Waterchute. Two thatchers were at work on the roof of
the large byre and tilers were closing the gaps between the
new rafters of the house. All over the yard, among the
heaps of charred débris, were sawn timber and builder's

stone, and through the open kitchen door, as the trap came to a halt, I glimpsed the cheerful wink of a log fire.

I expected Charlotte to come flying into the yard, but only a mongrel dog, that I did not recognize, sidled up to the trap and snuffled at Saxeby's legs.

The old fellow, glad of an excuse to hide his face, bent down and patted the wet fur. I hesitated a moment longer and then walked slowly over the pebbled approach into the large, half-familiar room. A whiff of smoke billowed from the vast chimney as I entered, and when it eddied away from the fireplace I saw her sitting in the inglenook, holding the handle of a large, shining frying-pan.

There was something uncannily familiar about the way she sat, her body bent forward, her eyes on the fire, and then I saw her almost as the reincarnation of my mother, who had occupied just that corner year after year as she cooked for her men assembling at the long table under the window.

The memory was the one thing needed to melt my heart, frozen hard since the moment Charlotte had walked away, back erect, between the two marines on the frigate more than four months previously.

I must have given a sob, for the next moment she had dropped the pan and was in my arms, covering my hands and heavily whiskered face with kisses.

"I didn't hear you, Davy—after all this time I didn't hear. I thought Mr. Saxeby was late and I began to cook —so much to do, Davy, so much for one. . . ."

I stroked her hair, inhaling its sweetness as a man inhales the damp west wind on an autumn morning when crossing our plateau to High Orcombe.

I didn't say anything, there was no need.

Over our heads the tiler's little hammer tat-tattered as he filled in the last of the chinks between the shining new rafters of the kitchen roof.

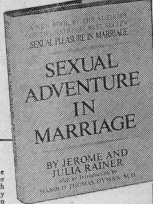